Love Drove ~~Them~~ *,*
Destroyed Them—
and Saved One. . . .

Surlina Defore—the "Silver Belle," a ravishing, headstrong brunette, she is torn by her love for two men—and the fortune she must regain.

Peter Defore—cunning and ruthless, father of Surlina; shipbuilding and silver were his life—and his death.

General Grant—a Union officer, dynamic and sensitive, beloved of Surlina but haunted by his loyalty to the North—and to his wife.

Julien Rainbeau—tall and lean, the mysterious "Mississippi Pirate"—a Southern gentleman whose love for Surlina threatens to destroy everything he lives for.

Thad Muller—an unsavory brigand, his lust would devour the Defore fortune—and Surlina herself.

About the Author

Lynn LeMon is a native of Dallas, Texas. When her husband was in the navy, she traveled extensively throughout the United States and the Orient. For the past fifteen years, she and her family, including three teenagers and a cat, have lived in Oklahoma City, Oklahoma.

When she is not writing, Lynn LeMon enjoys cooking Chinese food, listening to Hawaiian music, and cheering for the Oklahoma Sooners.

A graduate of the University of Oklahoma, she has written a college-level history text, a Hollywood biography, as well as numerous stories and articles. *This Rebel Hunger* is her first novel. She is currently an editor in the creative studies program at Central State University, Edmond, Oklahoma.

THIS REBEL HUNGER

Lynn LeMon

PUBLISHED BY POCKET BOOKS NEW YORK

To Pete
for love undivided

A POCKET BOOKS/RICHARD GALLEN *Original*
publication.

POCKET BOOKS, a Simon & Schuster division of
GULF & WESTERN CORPORATION
1230 Avenue of the Americas, New York, N.Y. 10020

ISBN: 0-671-83560-2

First Pocket Books printing April, 1980

10 9 8 7 6 5 4 3 2 1

POCKET and colophon are trademarks of Simon & Schuster.

Printed in the U.S.A.

1

Surlina had the dream often: a man's hand, strong but gentle, caressed the back of her neck. When she turned in her sleep, responding eagerly to his powerful touch, no one was there.

Her eyes fluttered open, searching her St. Louis bedroom for the lover whose face she'd never seen. Then she shut her eyes again, blotting out the first day of spring, 1862. She buried her brunette curls into the feather pillow, shaking away the dream which always left her breathless and excited . . . but alone. Twenty-six years old and a virgin! The idea of calling herself a spinster made her recoil. She was far from reconciled to a life as companion, nurse and dutiful daughter to her ailing father. Further, she refused to live out her days tagged as the Silver Belle, heiress to the largest fortune dug from the Sierras. She liked the ship-building firm she and her father ran, but surely there was more to the world than launching steamers onto the Mississippi River. She took a deep breath, letting the dream slip into her mind again.

She could feel the touch of his fingers lifting her curls, stroking the sensitive flesh of her earlobes and spine, his hands uniting to travel forward toward her throat, stroking in time to the beat of her veins. Suddenly, the hands tightened against her neck. Not the hands of an unknown lover, but the calloused tough hands of someone intent on choking her.

Instantly she was fully awake, fighting away the confusion of dream mingling with the real force which held her. She struggled upright, clawing at the hands cutting off her breath. Her scream emerged as a hoarse gasp, "Muller!" She pushed the old woman away, shock and fear compounding as she recognized the servant's gnarled face and fingers, "What are you doing?" Surlina scrambled to her feet, letting the eyelet quilt drop around her and the green gown that covered her body fall open at the ribbon ties across her full breasts. Grabbing the pillow, she beat at the frowning woman cowering at the side of the bed.

Muller, the maid, shielded herself with her bony hands, complaining, "For God's sake, Surlina! What are you doing, you crazy old maid? I only came to wake you early, like you told me to do."

Abruptly, Surlina quit flailing the pillow. "What? But you were choking me! I hardly call being strangled by a crone pleasant!"

"I barely tapped you on the shoulder!" protested Muller, shaking her sparse gray hair across her wrinkled forehead. "Stood outside and hollered nigh onto a dozen times afore I had to come in. You sleep like dead wood, Surlina!" She drew herself into a pose of injured dignity, arms folded and face defiant.

Surlina's hands touched the hot places on her throat, trying to confirm that Muller had attempted harm rather than help. There had never been trust between the servant and mistress of the Defore household. Surlina disliked servants; she preferred privacy and the privilege of looking after her ailing father alone. Yet Peter Defore, cantankerous even in the best of health, had insisted on employing Mrs. Muller, the widow of one of his old mining partners. Surlina thought it suspicious that Mrs. Muller had appeared seeking employment in their household only a few months ago when the rights and wrongs of the mining camps had taken place a full fifteen years earlier. Now Surlina saw a reason to end the maid's employment. Surlina stepped forward, brandishing the pillow like a shield. "Muller, you're fired! No one touches me!"

The elderly woman's eyes blazed with anger. "Firing me again? For an hour or so until your father wakes and makes things right, eh? No, no, I ain't that easy to be rid of!" She turned aside and handed Surlina a green silk dressing gown. "As for touching—you're a dried-up prune and still waiting to be touched by a man, I figure!"

2

Surlina grabbed the dressing gown and slung it around her shoulders. "My father will fire you himself," she threatened, knowing her boast was untrue. "I must not upset him today," she thought aloud. "He must come on the trial run of our new steamer. But tomorrow you'll find yourself packed and gone, Muller!"

"Such sass from the Silver Belle!"

"I hate that name!"

"But you ain't got much hope of changing it! No man I know of has asked you to share his name, or even his bed!"

"Get out!"

"Sure, sure, Muller's on her way now. But I ain't never intending to give you peace, Surlina. And when I die, my boy Thad knows what to do to take my place."

"Thad Muller? That ignorant bean-farmer son of yours can't make a crop in Indiana, much less make trouble for me!" Surlina flounced to the window and drew the damask drapes. She was sorry she had insulted Thad. Certainly he was not worth the irritation of getting upset. But Muller always mentioned Thad like a sticker-burr, a way of taunting Surlina, had even gone to the laughable length of bringing the uneducated unskilled rube for a visit in the obvious hopes of matchmaking. Surlina had found him to be a lecher and had rejected his advances. Despite his disgusting behavior, she offered a halfhearted apology. "I'm sorry, Muller! I'm sure Thad will make good as a bean farmer."

"Oh, no, not a chance of that," glared the servant, taking the drapery cord and lashing at the heavy material. "You couldn't see fit to give him the time of day when he paid you a courtesy call! Now he's been conscripted into the Union Army, thanks to the war you and your father refuse to acknowledge!"

"Don't worry. They'll probably send him home for insubordination if he's as undisciplined as you, Muller." She was amazed at her own haughty indifference. If it were a man she loved going away to war, the story

3

would be different. Staring at the shriveled woman before her, she shielded her thoughts with the sworn neutrality her father had decreed. "Come, Muller, let's have peace between us, even if the two parts of our country cannot agree." She smiled, trying to undo some of the damage of the morning. "Help me with father. He'll need a hearty breakfast if he's to make the journey aboard *Radiant*."

Muller was not appeased so easily. She muttered as she crossed the floral carpet, shaking her apron and head rhythmically, "I'll see to Mr. Peter as you wish, 'cause he's done me good turns. But mark my words, missy. War will come knocking at your door wherever you hide that silver fortune of yours. Wars and tides have a way of turning on them that discovers 'em. As for that steamboat *Radiant*, you may be in for more of a trip than you've bargained for!" With a laugh, she darted from the room.

Surlina was astonished, then intrigued by the maid's threat. What could one old woman do to endanger either the fortune of the Silver Belle or the glistening *Radiant*, pride of the Defore shipyards? Surlina, combing out her brunette curls and patting them into place with her long fingers, was ashamed that she'd wasted time arguing with a half-senile hag. Muller threatened grandly and often, but no more came of that than Surlina's frequent firings of her. 'I'll put her out of my mind,' thought Surlina, opening her closet to select an outfit for the two-hour trial run of the new steamship. Nothing will spoil this first day of spring and the launching of *Radiant!* She reached into the shadow of the closet and pulled a turquoise velvet two-piece suit toward her. Smoothing the material across her heated cheeks, she knew how wounded she'd been by Muller's taunts about being an old maid. Well, her cheeks could flame and her body burn in hell before she'd consider the likes of such men as Thad Muller! She shivered, remembering his foul breath as he'd attempted to fondle her during his "courtesy call." Yet what other choices had she been offered? Fortune-hunters from the gutters of St. Louis, financiers from

4

the competing shipyards hoping to collect her into their empires, dandies seeking refuge behind her silver from the encroaching demands of war.

She ran her hands over her body as if to assure herself that her ivory neck and soft breasts existed for more reason than to decorate velvet dresses. She pinched at her nipples and felt the stings of sensation travel through her, making her thighs flinch. Twenty-six and unmarried! 'Surlina, behave yourself—you have a father who needs your care. A steamship company which needs your business acumen. A trip downriver which needs your full attention. And, a servant who needs firing,' she added, again angered by Muller's comments. Once more the uneasy suspicions of the woman prickled her. Could a crone somehow make trouble for the maiden cruise of *Radiant*? Quickly, Surlina ran from the room, hurrying toward the cherished advice and calming aid only her father could offer.

Surlina stopped in the hallway outside his bedroom and plucked a daffodil from the flower arrangement she'd made the day before. Flowers were her favorite ornaments. She wore them in place of jewels, which she found heavy and unseemly. And flowers suited her —daffodils the color of her favorite silk petticoats, roses the color of the rouge she sometimes put on her cheeks when no one could see her, tulips with their velvet texture like the breasts she corseted tightly. Purple crocus, black-eyed susans, dahlias—she loved them all. Knocking lightly, the slender fingers of her left hand barely touching the wooden door, she entered her father's sickroom.

How she dreaded to admit it was a sickroom inhabited by an old man ravaged by disease. Each day she was aware how his touch faltered, his eyes dimmed, his gaze turned distant. More and more, she knew her decisions were the ones respected in the shipyards and that those decisions were regarded as those of a full partner. *Radiant* had been her approved design, a fascinating and speedy new steamer for the river trade, the fastest thing on the Mississippi! Her father, Peter

Defore, had once been known as the silver king with the iron will. Now he was reduced to good days when he matched his wits and skill against her in chess games, in ship design and financial bargainings. When he'd finally given in about *Radiant,* he'd smiled and said, "As for the name, it suits both you and the ship, my daughter." It was a compliment she'd cherished; he dealt her far more business comments than personal ones. 'Yes,' she thought, 'on good days he's cantankerous, charming and clever.' On bad days he was quarrelsome, demanding and contradictory.

Pray God this would be a good day! She entered his room, extending the daffodil as an offering. How ambivalent she felt toward this man who ruled her as a tyrant, loved her as a father. Good days or bad, she cherished him, yet felt trapped in a life not of her choosing by his poor health and competitive ways. Why, for instance, did he beg Surlina to nurse him and then hire that rebellious Muller?

She crossed the room to the huge oak bed where he lay rounded beneath the patchwork comforter. Imagine her father, who had once been six feet tall and broad as a lumberjack, now reduced to the shrunken size of a twelve-year-old child. Asleep, his white hair and ruddy face benign against the white linen, she thought him handsome despite his age. Awake, she knew they'd begin another battle.

Rubbing his shoulder with a gentle hand, she whispered, "Father? Wake up. It's the great day for *Radiant*'s debut." She put the daffodil into his bedside drinking cup. Yesterday's *St. Louis Post* lay open alongside the cup and medicine bottle. She glanced at the picture of their pride, *Radiant,* held at the pier by ropes decorated with bunting. The *Post* reporter must have been impressed to have spent the money on a newfangled daguerreotype reproduction! Then she read the caption and her face twitched with displeasure: "Surlina's silver steamer to debut with the spring season!" Always the silver! Always she was Surlina the Silver Belle—never simply a woman of intelligence and

6

charm! The story which followed predicted that Peter Defore would not be aboard for the trial run.

"Get up, old man! The *Post* has given you up for dead again. Come, come, rise and shine!" She rubbed his back and smoothed back his white hair as he yawned sleepily, his gray-green eyes catnapping as he tried to sit up straight. Surlina felt her heart flutter as she again realized exactly how frail he was. But she covered her sadness by speaking in a chipper, teasing way. "Hurry, Father. A quick breakfast and then off we go! If you don't come on *Radiant* and don't pass away into eternal damnation, then the reporters will have nothing to write about today!"

Peter Defore stirred like a wiry animal, inhaling sharply, twitching his jowls. "I'll be on *Radiant* if I have to crawl up the gunwale!" He pulled his knees upward and clasped his thin arms around them. "Hell no, the silver king ain't turned to stone!" His coughing, deep in his chest, cut off his protestations of strength.

Surlina reached for his medicine. He brushed aside her hand as she tried to pick up the spoon. "Don't succor me, girlie! None of that blasted cough syrup. Fetch the brandy if you want to aid me!" He laughed between coughs, his pale eyes brightening.

'Good,' thought Surlina as she turned aside to pour the cough syrup into the spoon without his notice. 'He's alert today, frisky enough to want his brandy, strong enough to argue.' She watched him in the dresser mirror, noticing how alike their features were—the large hands with the long fingers, the gray-green eyes, the extra-thick hair, his once as curly and dark as hers, and the lithe, elegant stature. In temperament, too, they were alike. Logical. Skillful negotiators. Competitive. Too much alike in many ways. Contesting each other's skills in shipbuilding, battling each other in games like chess and monte, outwitting each other in endless verbal sparring just for the sake of argument. But when it came to their views on love, they differed like night and day. Peter had little use for marriage, had valued Surlina's mother, a Sierra dance-hall girl, little more than the rocks he'd dug from the ground.

7

When Julia had died, he'd grieved only that she was no longer able to care for the two daughters she'd borne—Surlina and the younger, frailer Tandy. As a child, raised in the bitter warfare of the placer mines of California, Surlina had seen how marriage was nothing but confinement. Then, sent to the care of the convent, she'd revised her thoughts to view marriage as a form of escape. Now, as a grown woman of twenty-six, she held radically different ideas. Marriage! Love! Children! The words touched her heart like live coals. But her father turned away all would-be suitors, just as he'd disinherited Tandy before she'd had time to cut her wedding cake. Surlina despaired; she couldn't leave him. But neither could she make him understand that beneath her prim and businesslike formality lay a soul yearning for passion, fulfillment and adventure. Her hand trembled as she attempted to pour the cough syrup into the spoon.

She turned back to her father and offered the medicine. "Take it and don't give me any nonsense!"

"Now, daughter, where would we be without arguing? Why, the moon wouldn't set and the sun wouldn't rise without us arguing 'em to their rightful places!" He steadied himself against the oak post of the bedstead, then made his way haltingly to the armoire. To Surlina's surprise, he pulled out a bottle of brandy. "A nip of this will cure more morning shakes than that bitter brew concocted by Muller."

"Muller! I almost forgot! Father, that vile woman infuriates me! Can't we get rid of her?"

"No."

"Why not?"

"She's the widow of my old partner from the Sierras. I'll never turn away the widows and orphans of them that helped me when the times were rough."

"Not even Thad Muller, that ignoramus who fawned over me and wheedled money from you?"

"He's no more than a panhandler . . . and if I know you, your sarcasm curdled any amorous intent on his part."

"I still believe Muller means to make trouble for

8

us. She even blames us for Thad's being conscripted to serve with the Union."

Peter Defore snorted and recapped the brandy. "War's no concern of ours. Side with the group that has hard cash. That's how we'll continue to prosper."

"But Muller threatened something about war and *Radiant.*" She hadn't meant to worry him unduly, yet she needed his counsel. Her father's long experience had made him suspicious. Now it might come in handy. "Do you think we should hire guards for the afternoon cruise? Half of St. Louis will be aboard."

"Trouble's not likely, Surlina. As long as Missouri is contested territory, no one can touch us. *Radiant* can tote cargo to Cairo and passengers to Fort Madison while Billy Yank and Johnny Reb twiddle their thumbs."

She was pleased at his confidence. "And we thumb our noses at *both* sides!"

"And keep our silver safe in Erlanger's International Bank in New Orleans! And our own tough hides safe in St. Louis's finest mansion! And our ships safe in the channel under the flag of neutrality." He patted her cheek and held her gaze for a moment. "Ah, Surlina, how I wish I believed our safety would last, but the overtures are getting more brazen. First the North tries to buy *Radiant* while she's still a-building."

Surlina ndded, remembering. "We turned them down flat. Have there been more communications from that obnoxious Commander Halleck?"

"No, only that he would pass the matter on to one of his subordinates—Sam Grant, a backwoods general who apparently has nothing better to do than purchase riverboats. Never read of him in the papers, so he must be sitting out this war on his backside."

Surlina was impatient. Her father had an annoying way of digressing. "I don't think the Union will try buying us out on our maiden cruise." She tried to hurry Peter toward the breakfast room. "But perhaps a Pinkerton man or two would be in order—"

"And the South! Those damned fools without a navy had in mind to make a ram of *Radiant!* Jesus and

Holy Mary help them if they ever threaten to steal a ship from under my sheds again!"

"Steal *Radiant?*" Surlina was indignant at the idea and surprised that she had not been told of the threat. She bristled with impatience as she suspected her father of livening up her morning with fabricated stories.

He edged around her as she stood with cough syrup and spoon, then darted toward the bath, locking the door with a quick flip of his hand.

Foiled again! Surlina threw back her curls and laughed heartily, pleased to see him so lively. "Are you taking a liking to soap and cold water for baths?"

"No more than you're taking a liking to bean farmers and cough syrup!"

She dumped the spoonful of cough syrup into the water which held the daffodil. "I'm confiscating your brandy," she taunted through the closed door. "If you're coming on *Radiant*'s debut, you're coming sober!"

"Afraid the old man might cut loose and embarrass you, girl? Ah, you should have seen me in my dancing days when I was courting your mother."

Surlina smiled at the stories she'd heard of her mother—the tallest dance-hall girl in the Sierras, the girl who could kick the highest and catch the silver dollars in her slim fingers like picking apples. Surlina flexed her own slim hands and admitted that she, too, had a passion for dancing. Flowers and dancing, her big indulgences, would be appropriate during this afternoon's festivities. She made another decision without consulting her father. Detectives. A few plainclothesmen could circulate through the crowd and damned be toady Muller, her foul son Thad, the Union's trader Sam Grant or any evildoer the South had to offer. When Surlina Defore gave a party, the city sat up and took note. Today, there'd be longstemmed roses in the grand salon, champagne on the afterdeck, and she and her father reigning in the pilothouse.

She lost herself for a moment in the grandeur of the coming cruise, letting ideas of war and responsibility

10

slip away like the last of the snows from Missouri's hillsides. She felt radiant as her ship, ready to wield the power that went with being the Silver Belle. Then she remembered her recurring dream. What was power when it only brought her the attentions of men like Thad Muller and the financial chicanery of army generals like this Grant? What was treasure to her? Nothing, compared to her desire to see the face of the lover she dreamed about and never knew. Would she really give up everything for love? At the moment, she thought it possible. But where would she find a man who didn't judge her desirability by the number of shipyard sheds she shared with her father and the size of her silver account in the bank in New Orleans? Did such a lover exist? Or was it only in her dreams that he took her in his arms, sought her lips with his, laid his body alongside her and whispered ardently that their love was all that mattered.

2

At one o'clock on the chilly March afternoon, Peter Defore was carried aboard the *Radiant*. He was wrapped in a shawl and seated in his silver-armed rocking chair. The cream of St. Louis society, already standing impatiently at the *Radiant*'s railing, twittered and nodded, "Oh, he definitely looks ill."

Surlina patted his arm and held her own head high, as if to make up for his illness. "Don't droop, Father! It only adds fuel to their gossipy fires."

Peter Defore responded by launching a spirited argument about where he would like to sit. Surlina hissed at him under her breath. "And don't argue with me this afternoon either!"

"What? No fun for an old man? I want competition, not an accomplice."

"Not now," she begged, stroking his arm as if to

11

calm him down by her motions. Why did he take such pride in their public discussions? Was he showing her off? Was he perversely proud that she 'thought like a man'? Would he truly be shocked to know of her inner desires as a woman? Or was he merely hoping against hope of keeping her as a dutiful daughter? Arguments. Chess. Ship designs. High finance. Yes, he'd taught her well. Also taught her to read men's minds by what they said with their eyes. At the moment, the thing she saw in *his* eyes was that he was desperately pleading, 'Don't leave me! Stay! Be my eyes, ears, mouthpiece and brain.'

All right. She was here of her own accord, because she loved him, was of his flesh, blood and spirit. Competition? She thrived on it! Long ago in the mine fields she'd learned to play poker with a straight face and bake sourdough biscuits that could win county-fair ribbons. Courage? She wasn't sure. Yes, she had no fear of plunging a horse into a flooded mountain stream. But to break away to make a life of her own? She'd seen the awful consequences her younger sister Tandy had faced as a result of marrying against their father's will. Tandy—dear foolish, frivolous sweetest Tandy! Surlina longed to see her sister. But with this foolish war disrupting the Mississippi River, it might be years before they met again in New Orleans.

She was jolted back to the moment by the sounds of the cooing matrons lined up against the rail, all bending their heads for a glimpse of Peter and herself. Let them look! She smiled defiantly at the bobbing heads, the feathered hats waving in the March breeze. Sometimes she imagined what they said about her. "Ah, yes, that Surlina is a recluse, a reigning heiress without a sign of a suitor. Did you hear she snubbed the winter ball? Well, I say it's more than mere pride that's stiffened her corset these twenty-six years!"

She left her father in the pilothouse long enough to parade past the society-matrons. I can pass muster, she told herself confidently as she walked the length of the ship, smiling and returning curtsies, shaking hands and exchanging pleasantries. She was well groomed, she

12

knew. At the last moment, she'd decided against the two-piece turquoise velvet suit. Instead, she had chosen a taffeta gown that accentuated her narrow waist, laced her full breasts high and displayed the full length of her ivory throat. Atop her curls she wore a tiny beaded hat, held securely with long pins. She was a tall woman, nearly equal to many men at five feet, seven inches. Most of her height was in her legs, which tapered long and slender to trim ankles and feet which fit perfectly into dancing slippers. For the deck, however, she'd chosen sturdy boots. No jewelry, of course. A single bunch of lilacs, smuggled by the florist from farther south, was pinned to her bodice.

At the end of her promenade, a young man stepped to her side, offering his arm as an escort down the steps to the grand salon. "At your service, Miss Defore." He swaggered as he introduced himself. "May I present my credentials? Reporter for the *St. Louis Post,* correspondent for the weekly *Journal* and liaison for the monthly *News.*"

Surlina shook away his possessive hold on her gloved hand. "May I suggest that you do not pester me or my father for interviews until we return? I have business to attend to at the moment. No help needed!" She swung away from his surprised grasp and left him standing speechless on the quarterdeck. Immediately, she took herself to task. The poor man was doing his job, attempting to talk to her. She turned back and smiled at the reporter. "See me after we are underway. I'll be happy to grant you an interview." Again he looked surprised, but Surlina had learned to cope with the fact that she intimidated most men she met.

Now she hurried to the pilothouse. "Here, Father," she said quietly as she handed him the cord to the polished steam whistle. "You be the one to let the world know that the *Radiant* is the fastest ship on the river!"

Peter Defore's strength failed him. His first tug at the cord yielded only a flimsy toot. Surlina deftly put her hand over her father's frail fingers and helped him tug. Her long, tapered nails dug into his bony hand as

13

if to infuse him with new muscle and sinew. "Hurrah!" she cried as the earsplitting whistle resounded through the clear spring air.

"Hurrah!" came the answering cry from the guests. She saw her father smack his lips in satisfaction, but his hand trembled and fell away to his lap. She glanced around the cabin, trying to identify the plainclothes detectives she'd hired. They were conducting themselves with decorum, blending perfectly with the fine ladies and stalwart gentlemen of St. Louis. "Watch for anything out of the ordinary," she'd told the detectives before they'd come aboard. "You are to guard my father and my ship," she had instructed, and would tell them nothing more. As she again spotted the young *Post* reporter eyeing her quizzically, she wished she had told the detectives to save her from annoying inquiries. What did this young man want from her, watching her so intently? He seemed to check his pocket watch every minute, as if waiting expectantly for her to make some false move. She shifted sideways to avoid his stare.

"Father, I must play hostess in the grand salon. Will you be comfortable here in the pilothouse?"

He nodded, the distant look of fatigue dimming his eyes. Two hours would seem terribly long to him, she feared. For a moment she thought of having the cruise cut short. But no; she'd promised St. Louis society this spring outing, and she'd not deprive them of their occasion to see the Missouri hillsides abloom with Queen Anne's lace and the Mississippi River spilling its banks while the *Radiant*'s reciprocating engines whirred like quiet, powerful lions.

As she entered the main French double doors to the spacious salon, the *Post* reporter moved to her side again. "Don't touch me," she warned, as he lifted his hand to guide her through the entry.

"So, it's true the Silver Belle who loves flowers is a touch-me-not?" His question was accompanied by a smirk. "I'd heard you favored roses. But perhaps you'd best trade in those succulent lilacs at your bosom for something less fragrant . . . something more in keeping

14

with your icy manner." He bent his head as if to smell the flowers, but she prevented him from coming nearer by turning swiftly toward the ship's orchestra. What an aggravating man!

She caught his thin smile as she tried to conduct business matters to cover her confusion. Yes, the waiters were attired in the morning suits she'd selected from the Philadelphia tailors. The magnums of champagne were at the proper temperature. The cigars. Had the Nicaraguan shipment arrived in time? As she flitted back and forth across the ballroom, greeting and nodding and scrutinizing, she wished she'd worn her dancing slippers. For a moment she thought of stripping off her boots and going barefoot. That would certainly give the *Post* reporter something to write about! She saw him taking notes on her every movement.

Finally she confronted him. "What have you written?"

"Censorship, Miss Defore?"

"Curiosity," she admitted. "Why are you studying me as if I were an anatomy skeleton?"

He consulted his watch. "I could tell you it's because of your beauty, or your wit, or your relentless need for perfection in this perfect ship." He moved toward the folding doors and peered across the river toward two barren sand spits which extended a half mile into the yellow river. "The truth is I am watching you for your reactions to history."

"History?"

He twitched his mustache while executing a dapper bow but kept his gaze on the far side of the river. Politely he said, "Yes, Miss Defore. You are about to be today's news and tomorrow's history."

"What? I don't understand your silly—" Her statement was cut off by the sound of gunfire. Alarmed, she rushed out the doors to the railing, straining to see the shoreline. "What's going on?" Another volley shredded the afternoon. Then the nose of a tug appeared from behind the nearest sandbar. She spotted a cannon mounted in the bow. "My God! We're being attacked!" For a moment she was seized with anger at the re-

15

porter. He'd known! She fled toward the pilothouse as the cannon's roar turned the women of St. Louis into screaming, frightened females. A few men rushed to the railings in an attempt to see what was happening. By the time Surlina had climbed the stairs, the pilothouse was in chaos. The captain shouted orders; the river pilot paled and overrode the directions; her father ranted his fury. "Who is it?" she demanded, grabbing for spyglasses. "River pirates?"

She focused the lenses on a second armed tug blockading the *Radiant*'s path. "Defenseless," she cried, aghast at the sudden attack and the obvious plight of the ship. Warning shots echoed across the bow. She ran to her father, steadying his shoulder against the assault of noise. Quickly she read the message in his eyes: 'Bargain with the attackers, no matter who they are.' Furious, but revealing only a composed coldness to the river pilot, she gave the signal to turn the ship in the channel.

In the next five minutes, as Surlina and her father stood helpless, the *Radiant* was held motionless in the current by the tugs. Boarding ladders were strung, and suddenly the decks swarmed with men in dark blue. "Union troops!" she gasped. "An act of war! How dare they set foot on a merchant ship in neutral waters?"

She demanded that her Pinkerton agents "do something" but they merely shrugged their shoulders and stood aside. "Out of our hands, ma'am, when the government steps in! The army's in command now."

"Oh, is it? Find me the army commander who dares come aboard without my personal permission!" She spoke loudly, enunciating every syllable, while inside she shook with fear for her beautiful new ship's fate. The facts screamed betrayal; Muller and her threats, the acquiescence of the Pinkerton guards, the smug knowledge of the *Post* reporter. Surlina made a mental list of scores to even. Again she ordered, "Bring the army commander here immediately!"

Amid a flurry of scurrying feet and whimpering women, Surlina barged to the pilothouse ladder. Standing at the bottom, looking directly up at her was an unassuming army man in a homemade uniform and dusty boots. He tipped his hat to her, then saluted. "Madam, I hereby commandeer this ship in the name of the Federal Army."

Overwhelmed with fury, Surlina could think of only one thing to do. With spontaneous violence, she threw herself down the rungs and across his chest, lashing at his neck with her long nails. He staggered forward under her assault, then bucked like a stallion, tossing her to the deck. She hit on her side, slamming her elbow into his dusty boots and whacking her head against his legs. Planning to renew the attack, she grabbed for her hatpin. Suddenly she felt her arms pinned behind her as she was lifted to her feet. Twisting, she sought to break free. Instead Surlina found herself against the man's chest, their mutual exertions causing them to crash against each other.

"Turn me loose!" she demanded, jerking back from his hold without success.

The harder she fought, the tighter he held her to him, crushing the delicate lilacs. She tried to scratch but could only flex her long fingers without moving her wrists. How could a man no taller than she be so strong?

When he spoke, it was with softness, steadiness, sureness of his power. Smiling at her, he said, "A tigress must be kept in chains. Do you wish to remain a lady, or shall I send you below decks to a makeshift brig?"

She saw the *Post* reporter edging closer, making notes furiously. She cast a curse in his direction, then straightened and relaxed against the army commander. "You may tend to your business. I'll see to my father!" With her eyes, she struck a bargain with the Union officer: 'Leave me alone and I'll not interfere—for now.' He stepped back, releasing his grasp.

What a strange and compelling man, Surlina thought, so small in stature, so large in confidence. Fascinated, she saw him execute his plan. The fine ladies of St. Louis were loaded aboard the tugboats and sent home upriver. The elegant gentlemen were herded

17

onto the barren sandpits like jostling, bellowing cattle. The *Post* reporter managed a last conversation as he was escorted from the deck. "Miss Defore! Have you been conscripted? Are you not returning to St. Louis with the other women?"

"I'll fight my battles from the bridge!" she shouted back.

"Go down with the ship like a captain? General Grant will grind you under his boot heel like a used cigar!" He was shoved onto the rowboat taking the men to the sandbar, but he waved his hat in departure.

"Grant!" She blurted the name without thinking. "So that's who that bastard is!" No backwoods army man—brigadier general or not—would take the *Radiant* without Surlina to reckon with. It was time to regroup. She rushed to find her father. Together they'd outwitted the thieves of the mine fields, the pirates of the shipyards and the financial robbers of partisan banks. Surely one unknown general with a homemade uniform would not be much of a threat.

To her shock and dismay, Surlina found her father asleep! He was dozing placidly in the silver-armed rocking chair, his shawl tight across his knees. Her first instinct was to shout at him, grab him roughly by the shoulder and shake him awake. How could he sleep through the capture of their ship? She cradled his head against her breasts, fearing for his health, knowing that whatever challenges lay ahead, she'd have to meet—and conquer—them alone.

Surlina was planning to outshout the two men opposite her. From experience she knew she could easily outyell her sickly father. However, Grant might be another matter! He stood before her with folded arms and a stern expression. Surlina shifted her weight and rearranged the folds of her skirt.

It had been two hours since General Grant had cleared the decks of passengers, another hour since he'd ordered the *Radiant* to proceed downstream. Now he'd ordered Surlina and Peter Defore to meet him in the grand salon. Surlina looked at the littered dance floor, the musicians' instruments turned topsy-turvy, the empty champagne bottles rolling about the deck. She took a deep breath and fired the first verbal shot. "As far as my father and I are concerned, no war exists. This is our ship and we refuse to be prisoners of war aboard it!"

Grant smiled briefly. "Do you always speak for your father?"

At that moment, Peter Defore broke into a spasm of coughing. Surlina immediately moved to his side. Surprisingly, she saw Grant glance at her father with obvious concern. She turned the conversation back to the raid on the *Radiant*. "You have no authority to keep us here, General. Return this ship to St. Louis immediately! I speak as my own authority."

"I, too, am my own authority." He stepped closer to her and extended his hand in a gesture of peace. "I fear I already owe you a corsage of lilacs and a steamship. Please don't make me harm you any further." His pale blue eyes softened as he spoke, a slight tinge of pink coloring his fair skin. "Please consider yourself my guest aboard my new command."

Her cheeks flushed red and her eyes sparkled with anger. "*You* are the uninvited—and unwelcome—intruder! The *Radiant* is our property." She stooped and patted Peter's shoulder. In support, he managed a nod and fitful cough.

Grant's broad shoulders twitched, as though amused by her antics. "Perhaps your dignity will suffer less if you consider yourself a pawn." An impatient glance at the baroque trappings of the grand salon said plainly that he felt out of place. He concluded quietly, "A pawn on the chessboard of war."

"The war does not exist for us," she insisted.

"The fact is, Miss Defore, a war does exist. I have been ordered to fight it. You have been enlisted to help me. You, your father and your silver."

At the mention of the silver, Peter Defore betrayed how alert he really was. "No, by damn!" His hands flailed at the arms of the rocking chair, a rasp of coughing tumbled his white hair across his forehead and he shook violently. "No silver for war! You'll never finance bloodshed with the Surlina silver!"

Grant stepped forward, about to answer, when Surlina blurted, "My father is extremely ill. He needs nursing care and medical attention around the clock. Unless you are prepared to have a surgeon's jacket made for you as well as an officer's coat, you had best return us to St. Louis! And at once!" She flounced aside, dismissing the subject as finished. Then with a slight, mocking smile, she added, brightly, "Keep the ship. My gift."

A flickering grin broke Sam Grant's placid features. "Indeed, I accept! Especially since at this moment we are making twelve knots. This ship is headed for Cairo, a naval captain and fourteen Dahlgren guns."

Peter Defore haltingly asked, "Then we . . . my dear daughter and myself . . . we're free to go home?" Surlina noticed his conciliatory tone.

"No. I have further orders for both of you."

Surlina, now quite interested, turned back fully to face her adversary. "Kidnapping and ransom?" On one level, she was enjoying baiting this general who seemed alternately shy and superior.

Grant explained succinctly, ignoring her smirk. "I am ordered to convey you to New Orleans."

Surlina gasped.

"New Orleans," confirmed Grant. "I am to take you there by boat. Or oxcart, or on foot, if necessary. We shall be enjoying each other's company for some time, so I suggest a truce." He smiled at Surlina, adding, "Especially between us."

"New Orleans!" she stammered again. "That's nearly a thousand miles! And for you, at least, that's enemy territory!"

Grant shrugged, quite calm at the prospect of such an outlandish journey. "By the time we arrive, Farragut will have the city open. New Orleans will once again fly the Union flag. I am to escort you to Erlanger's—"

"Oh, no!" Surlina flinched at the mention of the bank, knowing their fortune was at issue, not merely the steamer or her honor.

Suddenly Grant's blue eyes darkened with storm warnings, his voice changing from polite to adamant. "You will withdraw your silver and deposit it with the United States government. A course of action which, as a loyal citizen, I'm sure you prefer!"

"The hell you say!" she answered forthrightly. She felt the heat of temper in her throbbing veins. How dare he suggest robbery! She stared at him—they were precisely the same height. She wondered how old he was and where he'd gotten such willful ideas about her fortune. She guessed his age at thirty-eight, perhaps forty. Despite his military bearing, he looked tired, as if he had worked long and hard at a demanding physical occupation. His posture was excellent except for his rounded shoulders. The creases around his eyes and the firm lipline indicated a hard, determined man. 'Hard and handsome,' she thought. 'And bent on carrying out his orders!'

For a moment she wondered about those orders. Had he thought up this plan entirely? Or had he been tipped off by Muller, who knew precisely when the *Radiant* would be finished? Had Sam Grant mocked the Defores by inviting the *Post* reporter to see the spectacle? It occurred to Surlina that she must not play all her cards if she wanted answers to such questions. She must charm this man, seek out his weaknesses, play his game as if it were a battle of wits, not guns. She tensed as she remembered the feel of strength in his chest and his arms as he'd held her against him. Shocking herself, she wondered how she would feel clasped naked against his broad shoulders, her lips at first soft against the fair cheeks and coppery beard, then seeking out his determined mouth. A sensation of heat startled her back to the moment. What had they been talking about? The silver! "I wouldn't trust you with a copperhead cent!" she declared.

"Yet you trust me with your father's safety, your ship and your own honor—"

"You compliment yourself too much, General! I take full responsibility for my own honor! As to our safety, it lies in continued neutrality. No silver for

21

either side! Surely you know we've been approached by both the North and the South in this war. We're firmly neutral."

"Not anymore. Neutrality is not possible."

She wondered if he were in the position to make her believe that remark. Perhaps her best attack was a bold retreat. She gathered her skirts, turned and marched to the salon door. When she grabbed the handle and pulled, intending to make a dramatic exit, the door would not open. Startled, she tugged again, then stepped back. "Locked?" Receiving a nod of assent, she replied with a gaze of scorn. "Please be assured, General, that neither my father nor I will jump overboard from our own ship."

"You have my permission to move about in the grand salon. No further."

"This is my steamship!"

"But my command." He bowed. "And your memory is poor, Miss Defore. I distinctly remember you gave me the *Radiant* as a gift. Are you a woman who offers and then rescinds her favors at the last moment?"

She caught her father's eye and saw him nod slightly, as if warning her to opt for subtlety instead of head-on confrontation. She decided she would tease Grant, a glib act she disliked and accomplished poorly. "Didn't you say I was only a pawn? Pawns are able to move."

Grant chuckled at her ironic reasoning. "My goal is to keep you in check." He produced a gold watch on a chain from his pocket, ducked his head and looked past her. After clearing his throat, hesitating, he mumbled, "Would you *like* to play chess with me?"

What a frivolous idea. Suddenly she felt unbalanced. Was this shy invitation her opportunity to meet with him privately? Were there deals to be made with the quiet Yankee general? "Yes, yes, of course, I like chess," she replied, her mind racing ahead to wrench every possibility from his suggestion. "Certainly I'd trade you a game in return for a stateroom for my father."

"I'll see to his quarters immediately." The conversation halted as general and lady stared at each other, then quickly looked away. Something more was in the air than a game, Surlina realized, but she was unsure what. It was as if she and Sam Grant had touched opposite ends of a branding iron, then dropped the hot metal simultaneously. She felt her heart race as he spun his keys, nodded toward the door and murmured, "After you, Miss Defore."

3

Surlina busied herself in her father's new stateroom, settling him into the bunk, adjusting his shawl, offering him a sip of water. Grant stood decorously in the passageway, leaving the door slightly ajar as if to be handy if needed.

Peter Defore lifted his trembling arm from the shawl and clung to Surlina. "Don't leave me! Don't leave!" His voice was a whisper which rattled with waning strength.

"Of course I won't abandon you, Father!" Why would he question her allegiance? Had he caught the way she and Sam looked at each other? "We'll work this problem out. I have a feeling that General Grant may help us—"

"Help us? He'll help us out of our silver—that's what he has a mind to do! Just like he's helped us out of our steamer!" He managed to push himself onto one elbow, still shakily holding to Surlina's arm. "Don't have anything to do with him, daughter!"

"But I want—" She stopped short. Even to herself, she did not want to fully admit how strong her instincts were about this quiet, handsome man. "It would do us more good to have him as a temporary friend than a permanent enemy! Besides, a chess game is hardly a sign of giving up our neutrality."

Peter lay back, eyes closing, but his words still sharp. "I saw the way your eyes moved over him. You saw more than a uniform, more than a soldier. It was the man you were gazing at. I warn you, there'll be no sending of the Surlina Silver to war—not even if I have to cut you off from your own inheritance!"

Surlina dismissed the threat she'd heard before. "How silly you are when you're tired." She closed the door firmly, hoping that Grant had not overheard the conversation. Her father could be a man of his angry word where the fortune was concerned. Hadn't he disinherited Tandy for marrying against his wishes? But Lord God in heaven, a game of chess was not the same as walking down the aisle and pledging holy wedlock! Surlina laughed aloud at how the whole conversation had gotten out of hand. Fortunately, she could expect her father to have forgotten it by the time he awoke.

Grant had moved a few steps down the passageway, and Surlina hurried toward him. As she approached, she studied him anew, trying to temper her strange liking of his determination with an assessment of his ordinary physical appearance. The cut of his pants indicated he was lean, with the build that made excellent cavalry officers. There was no denying she felt drawn to both the strength he'd exhibited in holding her and the power he exuded in taking command of the *Radiant*.

She fell into step alongside him, taking a shy glance sideways to see him in profile and liking his firm jawline and softly curling beard. Her attention was so focused on him that she jumped slightly when he asked, "Is he comfortable?"

"Who? Oh, father. Yes, thank you. I appreciate your concern for him." She sensed Grant's sincere interest, his kindness for those weaker than himself. "He is aging rapidly. You've seen how illness makes him drop off to sleep. At first I thought to fool you by boasting of his strength, but his condition is apparent, I fear."

"He is a strong man in many ways—still capable of brilliant ideas," Grant noted quietly, his voice emphasizing that he'd assessed Peter Defore minutely and

24

rated him a worthy opponent. "You must surely be aware that this taking of your ship was not a matter of blind blundering. We've watched your father for many months. I know you are not boasting when you say that his mind remains capable."

"You've spied on us for months?"

"Not I personally. But armies must have eyes and ears, and we often find—"

"Muller! That vile, disgusting old woman! I'll have her strung up by the neck when I get home!"

He smiled slightly. "I think you will find she has left your employ . . . without making claim for wages due."

"Oh, I'll find her all right! She has a son in Indiana. That's where she'll go—" Surlina curbed her angry outburst, seeing beyond the maid's duplicity to still greater evil. "Thad Muller! *He* was behind this! Now he's part of your army, and good enough for you! With the likes of Thad Muller, you'll never win a battle, much less a war!"

Grant seized her wrist with his hand. "Hold your tongue, young lady! I have only one intention in this world, and that is the unconditional surrender of those who oppose me!"

"Does that include me?" she flung at him, yanking away her hand. She was torn between defending her rash temper and further enjoying riling this man. "I think I might well force *your* unconditional surrender, Sam Grant!"

He looked shocked as he caught the bright tone of her voice. She saw the muscles of his lips tighten, the vivid blue eyes blaze with astonishment, the delicate skin beneath the copper beard redden. 'The idea shocks him,' she thought, 'yet he likes it.' "I am not a little girl playing at war," she said primly. "I am a woman who finds herself unexpectedly on this battlefield. I should not hesitate to use all my resources." She experienced a wave of tingling through her body as she made the boast. Let him think her a brazen camp follower if it would gain her access to his strategies. And access to his bedroom? She refused to let her

25

imagination roam past their actual situation in the passageway. But she did touch his hand lightly, unsure how to caress him beyond softening her gaze and slightly parting her lips to smile at him.

"Despite your own admissions and against my better judgment, I think you are not the harlot you pretend. Although you are under my command, you have nothing to fear as to personal abuse. There is a matter of honor here, Miss Defore, as well as matters of silver and steamships."

She was taken aback by his frank understanding of her, impressed by his honesty and again lured by his modesty. Here was a man with standards, with the ability to command, with the power to take, yet he would not force himself on her. She felt fierce pride in him . . . and a bit of disappointment for herself.

A slight roll of the ship caused him to shift his weight. She reached out her hand to steady herself, and this time he caught it without harshness. Guiding her lightly, he tucked her hand around his proffered arm, stroking her fingertips as they came to rest on the blue jacket. She felt the ripple in his forearm as she squeezed his arm gently. A flickering deep within her set her senses on edge. Suddenly the damp spring air was beautifully fragrant. The lapping sounds of the river seemed to resound through her ears and blend with the sounds of her fast-beating heart. Then she felt weak and pliable, as she had never felt with any man. She gave herself over to the languorous warmth spreading through her. A slight shiver passed through her as she thought of Thad Muller. God! She still felt his fumblings at her bodice as he had bent his foul breath near her. Was it only men whom she could control that she disliked touching her? It seemed now the tables had turned. A man with great power was touching her, and she found it most pleasant indeed.

"You are traveling without much more organization than I!" Surlina laughed, as they reached Grant's disheveled cabin. Obviously he'd had no time to properly stow his gear. Maps were dumped atop the desk. A pair of clean boots rested on a chair. He reached to pull out the chair for her. She reached for the boots, then could find no place to put them. Papers, books, a lantern, a sidearm in a holster, a battered felt hat and two army cots took up all the space. For a moment, Surlina held the boots, then she handed them to him.

He, too, attempted to stow the boots without success. After rummaging the duffel bag on the bunk and pushing aside charts, he finally let the boots drop to the deck. "I apologize for the condition of things," Grant said, pushing aside the boots with his foot. "I've not had time to stow my gear, having come aboard—"

"So preemptorily!" she interrupted. How could she feel drawn to this man one moment and repulsed by his actions the next? Was this the way wars were waged? Between brothers and countrymen who could love and hate at the same time? Surlina inhaled deeply, trying to settle her emotions on a more even course. The tightness through her breasts made her nipples ticklish against the lace chemise. 'I will concentrate my energies on my father,' Surlina told herself. "I'm glad you recognize the strength my father still possesses. Often he borders on arrogance, but we have been a team for years, ever since he took me and my sister to live in the Sierra placer mines."

"You have a sister?" Grant seemed concerned. "Is she aboard? Why have I not been told of her?"

"Ah, I see you are not privy to *all* the Defore secrets! Yes, I have a sister in New Orleans, but Tandy is disowned! She had the gall to marry against Father's wishes. Tandy acquired a husband, but lost her share of the silver. Sometimes I think my father's threats are fair enough. Thayer Cabell was a bad choice for a husband if there ever was one."

"Thayer Cabell! That notorious Southern fire eater? That rebel whose chief aim is to bring England and France into this war? My God, your sister is married to the Confederacy's chief hothead, and yet you proclaim neutrality!"

She did not see why he was so upset. "Tandy made

27

her choice and got disinherited in the process. I still love my sister, but not her politics."

Grant turned aside for several moments, apparently thinking over the situation and sensing the truth of Surlina's statements. When he turned back, he asked her directly, "Why have *you* not married?"

"I've had no choice." She held up a hand to cut him off from asking further questions. "I don't care for any sorry-for-the-spinster smiles from you, either!"

He smiled despite her orders. "This war will bring you choices aplenty. War is nothing but choices." He pushed his equipment out of the way in order to perch on the bunk. "Let me tell you a story concerning choices."

She settled back, pleased with this turn of topics. She looked deeply into his blue eyes, fathoming their intelligence and guilelessness.

"Surlina, suppose you became lost in the desert."

She shut her eyes, remembering the hard dry rocks and grit of the Sierra lowlands.

"Now, after many days, when you are near death from thirst, you suddenly stumble upon a well. It's a miracle—a well in the desert. And just as miraculously, there is a cool dipper of water drawn! But wait! Don't seize the dipper and drink yet."

"Why not? I am dying of thirst, am I not?"

"There is danger in the quick choice! By the well is a sign that states: 'Pour the water in the dipper down the well to prime the flow, assuring all the water you may need, now or future.' "

Surlina opened her eyes and stared at him as if he'd tortured her. "Why, I might die either way! Prime the pump? Pour out the water in the dipper? What kind of story is this, Sam?" She was aware she'd used his first name effortlessly and that it sounded natural to her.

"The choice is yours, Surlina. Do you grab the first thing available, or are you able to steady your nerves and ambitions long enough to gamble on the future?"

She understood that he was talking about warfare. But she applied the lesson to herself. Would she throw

28

herself into a marriage as Tandy had done simply to be married? Or was she strong enough to hold out for whatever the future might bring? She tapped her shoes against the plank flooring of the stateroom.

"Your choice?" he asked again.

She dipped her head coquettishly. "Surely you would not pressure a woman for a quick answer."

"Indeed not! I am not used to having a beautiful woman flirt with me and bat her long eyelashes in my direction. You confuse *my* sense of choice, Surlina, far beyond the choices of the chessboard."

She was delighted with his acknowledgment. She had completely forgotten their planned game. Surlina made an excuse to postpone the confrontation—and her choice concerning the dipper and the well. "You need time to stow your gear properly. I need to scavenge for some clothing and toilet articles if I am to be a passenger downriver for many days," she reminded him pointedly. "I brought no toothbrush nor nightgowns, thinking I would be going home tonight!" She moved toward the doorway.

In a decisive movement Sam followed her, pulling her against him and laying a finger across her lips. "Say no more! I require no choice of you. For now I will make the decisions for both of us."

Was he sending her away? She seemed about to raise her arms around his neck, to press herself against his muscled thighs and broad chest. Instead, she turned the brass door handle with a quick flip of her wrist and darted from the room. Her sense of expectation was heightened, but her choice was far from clear.

'Sam Grant is supposed to be my enemy! He's chosen to steal *Radiant,* consorted with Thad Muller, spied on the shipyards.' What was Sam Grant to her? A quick moment to be seized? Or could this man with the shy, firm command be something deeper and more lasting?

Surlina was jailed in the grand salon by a dour young sentry. Once, when the ship stopped at a woodyard near the Illinois shore, she thought she heard the clatter of horses' hooves against the gravelly loading area. "What are they doing? Why are we stopped far longer than necessary to load wood?"

"Loading the cavalry detachment, miss," replied the boy, polishing his Colt.

"Cavalry! Horses on this elegant steamer? General Grant must be out of his mind!" She heard splashing and whinnying and discovered the horses swimming into the cargo hold while the carved mahogany and teakwood gaming tables of the lower salon were thrown overboard. Horses and hay! Muddy boots and sabers! Surlina sat down with her head across her arm, weary and wretched. Soldiers' boots scuffing the *Radiant!* Lice and bedbugs in the passenger staterooms, and her father too ill to make the overland journey back to St. Louis.

She barely moved when she heard the French salon louvers creak open, heard voices, then the rattle of the Colt being sheathed. She heard heavy boots moving toward her and peeked through her hand to see who was coming. Sam Grant. No, she wasn't surprised to see him, but was shocked to see he held in one hand a chessboard and in the other a tiny bouquet of fresh lilacs. She sprang to her feet, the tiredness evaporating. "Where did you find them?"

He gestured toward the shoreline. "I cannot give back your steamship, but I am more than happy to replace the flowers I destroyed." He presented them to her, cupping his hands around the purple blossoms and letting the stems slide into her palms.

What a thoughtful gesture! Surlina pressed the lilacs to her heart, overcome with a tightness in her throat which prevented her from thanking him. Oh, surely she wasn't going to cry! Not over a handful of wild lilacs stolen from a riverbank and given to her by a sworn enemy! When she finally felt in control, she said, "I love flowers. And music! I love flowers and music. I had neither of those things when I was a child. Do you like music, Sam? Do you like to dance and sing and listen to the orchestra?"

"Music?" He tilted his head to the left, perplexed.

"I have to admit I know only two songs. One is 'Yankee Doodle.'" He paused. "And the other isn't."

They laughed together. So he had a sense of humor! And he seemed genuinely interested in her. He pulled a chair close to where she sat and watched her intently, asking questions and urging her to talk of her youth.

"The Sierra mine fields were no place for little children," she assured him. "Rattlesnakes, freezing winters, Indians, broiling summers, and nothing but rocks, rocks, rocks—which my father wanted to crush for ore."

"I spent my early army career in California," Grant said, assuring her with a grin that they shared a common bond of experience.

"I imagine the hardships of a military life are comparable to the misfortunes of the mining camps."

"But the rewards seem to have singled us out differently. I left the army with a cloud over my head and a blot on my record. You seem to have found a silver lining."

How honest and clear his eyes were, even as he admitted to trouble in his past. 'This is the kind of man I would trust with my life,' Surlina thought unexpectedly.

Unaware of what was going through her mind, Sam continued speaking. "My army days in California taught me to subsist on biscuits and beans. What did you learn?"

"Actually, despite the physical hardships, I learned my days in the mining camps were a time of freedom. After we finally found the silver deposit, my father immediately dispatched Tandy and me to a convent. How I hated those high adobe walls. I vowed then I'd never live behind barriers again."

"Yet now the gates of war are swinging shut, closing our countrymen into separate camps. Closing you away from your sister."

"Don't let them hold *us* apart, Sam!" She was instantly drained of courage to say more and rushed to the porthole to hide her face from him. Why had she been so bold? Why would she speak out to a man she

31

hardly knew? Because he brought her lilacs? How foolish!

"Surlina?" She heard his caressing voice behind her. She put her hands to her flaming cheeks, bracing herself against whatever he might say. "Surlina, do not hide from me . . . or yourself. We all have hard choices to make in this war." He laughed good-naturedly. "Oh, excuse me! I did not mean to imply that the choices for a brigadier with a threadbare coat are the same as those for the Silver Belle."

She whirled, striking her palms together with a loud clap. "Never call me that name! I detest it!"

"Silver Belle? I meant no discourtesy—"

"I'm no empty-headed chit!"

He reached out gently and took her face in his hands. "Indeed not, my dear. You are every inch the tigress I suspected when you attacked me this morning. Tell me, have you thought again of my dipper-and-well story? What choice would you make?"

She leaned against him, the exciting events of the day leaving her stimulated yet exhausted. "No decision. Not yet, Sam. I'm too weary."

"No decision is itself a choice, Surlina. Often choices are bad—the classic lesser of evils. Nevertheless you always choose; even if it's letting circumstances or someone else take it out of your hands." He motioned her to a table. "Let me order you some supper. A glass of brandy, perhaps." He smiled indulgently, then admitted, "Your steamer seems well stocked with amenities." He glanced at the instruments on the orchestra stage. "You like music? Perhaps we can find the musicians to play while we have our chess game. I considered them part of the crew and didn't let them leave the ship."

Surlina was grateful for the food and the tactful way he had indicated he'd stay and sit with her. She lapsed into thought while the linen cloth monogrammed with the ship's crest was spread. Choices! For all her wealth and travel, for all her power and intellect, she lived a life of few choices. She bit her lip, thinking how the choice of a husband had almost passed from

32

her because she couldn't make a decision. Part of her reluctance was due to her sister's example. Surely there was more to married life than being the wife of a man seventeen years her senior. Poor Tandy! Always a frail and delicate girl, now as a wife she seemed incapable of doing anything more than drinking herbal tea and fanning herself in her courtyard in New Orleans.

Surlina realized Sam Grant was speaking to her again. He held up a small bottle of brandy. "It's from your private stock." He poured a small amount into her glass and indicated she should sip it if she wished, though he drank none himself.

She toyed with the stem of the glass, still thinking of her limited choices for a husband during the past years. Braggarts, politicians and fortune hunters—that's all they'd been. Then, with the coming of war, the choices had narrowed further. At the opening of the St. Louis cotillion two weeks ago, she'd wondered aloud, "Where are all the men?" Her father had known precisely. "On the battlefields, which will be a hard place for you to go a-hunting, Surlina."

Now, in a strange way, the war had placed her on the battlefield. She looked directly at her host. "You're very young for a general."

"And ten months ago, I was quite old for an ex-captain of infantry, an ex-quartermaster and an ex-farmer."

She didn't believe in mincing words. "Are you married?"

"Indeed! One wife. Four children, two dogs and a passel of cats."

She was struck by the genuine enthusiasm apparent in his voice concerning his familial relationships. A wife and children! Oh, double damn! First she felt distress, then guilt. "Then war is difficult for you."

"No. It's a godsend."

She stared at him, searching his face for a clue to such a surprising statement. He shrugged, then blushed. Perhaps he felt an explanation was in order, for he continued, "This war is a good thing for a man whose

33

farm was named Hardscrabble, who failed as a real estate agent in St. Louis and who spent last year working in his father's leather store for a total yearly wage of eight hundred dollars."

The facts amused her and at the same time made her uncomfortable. "Last year I was in Paris buying gowns that cost eight hundred dollars apiece!"

"Why did you return, if you wished to hold yourself above the war?"

How concise his mind was, always twisting things to bear on the war. "It was mostly my father's decision. He saw a chance for a new fortune to be made in shipbuilding."

"Constructing vessels for both sides?"

"Of course." She smiled. "How often must I wave the flag of neutrality before you finally acknowledge it?"

"You cannot sit on both sides of this war any longer."

"Missouri manages to send complements of soldiers to both Union and Confederacy. I manage to live in the Union and do my banking in the South."

He reared back in obvious disapproval, clenching a fist and cursing softly. "You appall me!"

She toasted him with the small glass of brandy. "Do I not please you in *any* way?"

He scrambled from his chair, bowing and stepping away hurriedly as if he did not trust himself in her presence. "All I bring to this war is my haversack, sidearm, four shirts, a razor strap and writing pad. I must take advice from incompetents above me and give refuge to civilians below me. But I do not have to match my code of conduct against your money!"

She rose, facing him with her hands on her hips. "Sam, Sam, how have I managed to offend you? I don't understand half of what you're hinting. You want money? Fine. My father believes in moneylending. Talk to him. But don't let money barricade us before we have even become friends." It was surprising that she wanted his friendship. A few hours earlier, she would have preferred his expulsion. She touched

34

her forehead, feeling fevered. "I find the events of the day overwhelming. The *Radiant* has been sacrificed—"

"And you feel like a lamb on the altar as well?"

The brandy had done its work, making her silly in lieu of the wrenching weariness. She tossed her brunette curls, proud of inheriting both the glossy hair and the long, supple legs from her mother. "Oh, come, Sam! Dance with me! Find those lazy musicians and put them to work!" She raised her hands to the dancing position and waited.

He blushed crimson, apparently undone by her giddiness and joking. "Please . . . no."

She curtsied, refusing to listen to his denial of interest. "Come now, surely you can dance!"

"Honest, I do not know how!"

"The square dance? The French Four? The Pigeon Wing? None of those?"

"Not one." He stuck his hands in his pockets, looked glum, then admitted, "I've spent my time on horses, not dance floors."

"Are you too old to learn?" She tugged at his elbow. "Call the orchestra immediately or I shall do it myself!"

He appeared uncertain and she smiled at him. "The Virginia Reel. It's very simple."

"Very simple, very simple," he muttered, crossing the room. "I must be the one who's very simple!" He put his head out the louvered doors and spoke to the yeoman.

To Surlina's delight and Sam's continued embarrassment, shouts soon rang through the ship. "Musicians to the grand salon! On the double!" One by one the members of the orchestra arrived, taking their places and tuning their instruments while whispering among themselves about the Silver Belle and Yankee general.

"You will have to teach me," insisted Sam, his arms hanging stiffly at his sides.

"It won't hurt, so you needn't look so grim! Dancing is wonderful. Why have you neglected such a social grace for so long?"

"The regimen of West Point is conducive to pro-

35

ducing engineers, not dancers. I should be happy to engineer a battle plan or oversee an expedition involving dynamite for you. But have mercy on me, Surlina! Don't make me dance!" He blinked alarmingly till she feared he might faint.

She signaled the orchestra, which began "Abide with Me." She gestured them to stop. "This is not a church service—play something lively! Can't you see the general wishes to dance?"

The musicians tried "My Old Kentucky Home," but Grant objected. "Something more neutral. Kentucky is still disputed ground."

A compromise was reached with "Jingle Bells." Surlina led him through a frisky rendition of the basic steps. She halted abruptly. He looked at her with alarm. "Am I too much of a challenge?"

"Nonsense! I cannot dance in these heavy shoes." She plopped down on the low stage platform and began unlacing the leather boots. "They slow me down. I'd much rather be barefoot!" She tugged off the right shoe, flexed her toes in the thin wool stocking and peeled it away like shucking an ear of corn. "I never wear shoes when I can avoid them," she admitted. The utter silence caused her to look up. Sam Grant stood pale as a ghost, fascinated and scandalized by the saucy show of her ankles. "Oh, my! Oh, my poor Sam! You'd have fallen over dead if you'd seen me in acres of lacy petticoats trying to learn the high kicks my mother did in the dance halls." She dropped the left shoe and stocking and admonished him, "Now, if you'll pull yourself together, we'll try again!"

"But I might step on your toes," he protested solemnly.

"I shall take my chances." She giggled, then pirouetted, extending her fingers to him as the orchestra attempted "Beautiful Dreamer."

"I feel capable with men," he said humbly, "but with you, I cannot get my bearings. I enjoy your beauty, and your wit—"

"And my steamship," she prompted, guiding him gently into the turns.

"I fear I shall miscalculate more than dance steps if I stay in your presence."

Despite his complaints, he did not attempt to break away. They moved slowly, more to their own rhythm than to the music, she humming softly, he gradually forgetting his surroundings until he only had eyes for her.

He moved her slightly closer. She liked the feel of his wool jacket. The buttons were polished and the lingering scent of the brass wax blended with the masculine smell of shaving soap. The fit of their bodies was fine, too; his slightly stooped shoulders forming a shelter for her thinner shoulders.

At that moment the yeoman burst through the louvered doors. "Quick, sir! Fighting below decks!"

Sam flinched and did not hesitate even long enough to say good-bye. In a motion of abrupt withdrawal, he was gone from her arms and out the doors, issuing orders. The orchestra looked confused. "Dismissed," she concluded. "We are both dismissed."

4

Surlina spooned the cornbread into the glass. "Father, please try this. General Grant instructed the kitchen to fix anything you want. I'm sure he'd even send ashore if there's anything you're hungry for—"

"Surlina, how you babble!" He sat in the rocking chair, tapping on the deck with his cane and poking the tartan shawl around his chest. "Give me that damned pap!" He took the glass of mush and drained it, wiping his mouth with the back of his hand. "Now that dinner's over, let's get on to more important things!"

"What's more important than keeping you strong and healthy?" Why was her father so cantankerous this afternoon? He must be up to something! When she'd checked on him during the morning, he'd been engrossed in writing letters, a task he normally hated. He'd refused breakfast, then gobbled dinner. She'd never understand his changes of mood. She repeated, "What's more important?"

"Getting us off this riverboat."

She gave him a look of indulgence. "Easier said than done. Even if the steamer does bear our name we are prisoners!"

"Then let us remove ourselves."

"Perhaps at Cairo. Sam said we'd put in there—"

"Oh, it's 'Sam' now, is it? Only a day, and you've taken to calling him intimate names and letting him fawn over you on the dance floor!" His eyes blazed anger and the white hair fell in waves as he nodded vehemently.

"How did you know we danced? Oh, Father, you've got things all wrong. I asked *him* to dance! Were you spying on us last night?"

"Spying? Surely you'll credit me beyond that game! Surlina, you underestimate my vigor and overestimate my infirmities. While you were reconnoitering the dance floor, I was tending to business." He looked her up and down, appraising her figure. "Unless, of course, you consider it a business seducing Yankee generals!"

She tried to tolerate his ravings. He was ill. He was old. He was probably a bit jealous of her attentions to Sam Grant. She stood behind the rocker and smoothed back his hair. "You're first among my affections, Father. I'll not desert you for any cool-eyed federal in a blue coat and britches!" As she said the words, she meant them, but then a stab of underlying tension caught her. 'I'm lying,' she thought, amazed. 'At some point in my life, I shall have to desert my father if I'm ever to know love of more than the familial kind.' She tossed back her dark curls as if to fling away the notion of hot passions, but her mind lingered on the fantasy of smothering kisses, silky nipples rising hard against a man's furry chest, muscles tightening and pulling until she could hold back no longer.

When she realized Peter had turned his head and was watching her, she blushed crimson. She hid behind a faked cough, covering her cheeks, then sought to throw the accusations back at him. "So you spied on me last night! And what did you find? Only that I was left standing on the dance floor all alone when fighting broke out below decks."

Peter Defore laughed heartily. "How little you know of the ways of skulduggery! That was no fight, my dear daughter! That little mutiny was camouflage."

"For what? How do you know these things? What was going on?"

He pointed to the bunk with his cane as if prompting a recalcitrant pupil to a school desk. She sat with her back straight, ready to be instructed. Her father involved in below decks scuffling with common foot soldiers? God help her, she did underestimate him!

"Last night I found a man willing to help us escape."

"Did he ask for thirty pieces of silver?"

Peter ignored her. "We are lucky he's aboard—a man we know and can trust to help us."

"Someone we know? One of the crew? Who is it?"

He drew back in his chair with a faint smile of satisfaction on his lips. "Thad Muller."

"Thad Muller! Oh, Jesus Christ damn!" She leaped up.

"Surlina! Didn't the convent nuns teach you not to swear? Never mind. Thad Muller is aboard—a most unhappy and unwilling Union soldier—and he will be delighted to help us escape."

She was frantic with hatred. "He won't help us! He'd more likely kill us! Can't you understand, Father? Thad Muller and his mother are the ones who set up this kidnapping! That ugly hag spied on us in our own home! Passed information on to the army. She's a vicious woman and that oaf Thad is worse."

"Sit down and stop that infernal pacing. You act like a caged cat!"

She could not sit back down. She must find a way to reason with her father. Any deal made with Thad

Muller would be worse than slitting their own throats. She shivered with revulsion, remembering the raised tattoos on the back of Thad's neck. She'd seen the ugly fish-face when he'd bent over her, attempting to suck at her breasts. She'd cuffed him, repelled by the smell of beans which clung to him, his unshaven face, his red eyes and dirty hands. Now he was here, and her father wished to deal with Thad!

It was best to be careful, to make her father think she'd go along so that he'd include her in his plans. "How did you manage to find him?"

"I saw him come aboard with the cavalry troops in the afternoon."

"I thought you were sleeping then."

"That's not all I saw. I saw your fine general out picking flowers in the woods!"

"Lilacs," she corrected. "Oh, Father, you are one hundred percent wrong about Sam Grant and Thad Muller! Thad is our enemy and Sam, if we'd only let him, could be our friend!"

"Money buys my friends. I paid a few troopers to cause enough commotion to keep Grant and his officers busy. That gave me time to contact Muller." He leaned back, obviously proud of himself. "Yep, while the Silver Belle was sashaying around the dance floor with her general, old Peter Defore was right in the thick of the things that needed doing!"

She appealed to him directly. "Father, promise me you won't see Muller again! We don't need him! There must be other ways to return to St. Louis—"

"Who wants to go back there? Lord, Lord, Surlina! Didn't you understand that our fortune is at stake now? The Union won't stop with a steamship. Our only hope is to get to New Orleans and withdraw the silver from Erlanger's."

His words made sense, but his sense of logistics was poor. He'd never stand the journey to New Orleans. And, presuming he made it there, presuming he withdrew the treasure from the safety of Erlanger's, where would he hide it? "Have you forgotten you're not talking about burying a few silver teapots? We'd be fools

40

to take possession of it—be robbed of it before the day was out! No one can touch it as long as it remains in a neutral foreign bank. Not North, not South—"

"*I* can touch it and I intend to! I've already set the wheels in motion, written the letters, sealed the signature, studied the route, arranged with Muller to gather the supplies we'll need."

"No! We're not going off on a wild-goose chase with Thad Muller in tow! You're not talking about escape from the *Radiant,* you're talking about escape from your senses!" Her mind raced with details of the damage she must undo. First, get Sam to find Muller and have him tossed in the brig. Second, read the correspondence her father had written to see exactly what his plans were. Think of a way to get her father back to St. Louis where he belonged. She hated to work behind his back but it would be necessary for his own safety. Usually she thrived on such tugs-of-war. But this was the wrong place and the wrong time to play games!

Suddenly she was aware that Peter had moved from his chair toward the bed. She hastened to help him. In moments his eyes had dimmed and he was resting quietly as a babe. She berated herself for getting so riled at him. Why, he hadn't the strength to attempt an overland trip to New Orleans. She understood him better; it was the challenge he wanted. Yes, she must let him play the role of master planner; but she need not fear; nature would keep him in check.

She covered him with the shawl, then tiptoed from the room. She half wished she could lock him inside and put an end to his chicanery. That wasn't practical, but she'd keep a better eye on him. She shivered with fear. She'd have to keep an eye out for Thad Muller, too. Suddenly she remembered the silver dagger with the emerald in the handle her father always carried. It was a small folding type which passed as a pocketknife. Silently she reentered the room and took it from his jacket. On second thought, she took his wallet, too.

Surlina justified her actions on the grounds that she

wasn't really stealing. She simply wanted to make sure Peter couldn't buy any more disturbances. The folding dagger would come in handy if she had to do battle with Muller. She had never believed the dogma taught by the nuns at the convent, but now she made a quick sign of the cross and breathed, "Holy Mother, protect us."

When she went into the passageway it was as a warrior on the prowl. The feat excited her, the danger stimulated her until her heart beat loudly. A musky scent of sweat mingled with the perfume of the day-old lilacs in her hair. She advanced a few steps, then waited, listening. The heat of her hand warmed the inlaid silver of the knife. Was this the way man and woman met, smoothing and warming their flesh, the soft lips encompassing the harder needs within them? She must not get off guard thinking of gentle submission and rising passion. Yet before she went to see Sam Grant, she would go to her cabin and dress with care!

An hour later, Surlina was hurrying toward Sam's cabin, pausing in the passageway only long enough to smooth her hair and safely secrete the knife and wallet beneath her waistband. For her outfit, she had discarded her taffeta skirts in favor of the less elegant uniform of one of the *Radiant*'s chambermaids. The white tucked blouse was too small and tugged at her shoulders while the mother-of-pearl buttons fit between her breasts like a row of ornaments bound to her skin. The black linen skirt flowed over her hips and fell in gores to her ankles. She had not bothered with stockings at all and had appropriated her father's soft slippers for shoes, filling the toes with stuffing from her pillow in order to make them fit. Now she patted her curls and knocked briskly on Sam's closed door.

"Enter."

She darted inside, planning to cry out her woes. But she stopped short as she saw another person in the room. Sam was seated at the desk, a soldier at attention in front of him, the man's back to Surlina. Suddenly her hands covered her mouth in a silent gasp of horror. Thad Muller! That tattoo on the back of his neck was the shape of a fish with ink beneath the flesh combining with the wrinkles of his neck to make the tattoo appear scaly. She tried to back away before he was aware of her presence.

"Surlina!" Grant pronounced her name with concern, obviously wondering why she would enter in haste, then immediately exit. At the sound of her name, Muller whirled, and she was face-to-face with him.

An army uniform had not improved his appearance. He still had red eyerims, a dark complexion offset by tufts of blond, scraggly beard, unruly hair which smelled of grease and the odor of beans clinging to his clothing. Confronting him, she had the urge to pull her dagger and do battle. Instead, she lowered her eyes and ignored him, imploring Sam quickly, "This man has tried to bother my father. Have him sent away."

She saw Muller's eyebrows jerk upward and heard him laugh. What was going on? There was an exchange of glances between the two men. My God, were they in cahoots? Indignant, she cried, "Sam, don't you understand who this is? Muller's the son of the woman who spied on us! He's the no-good bean farmer I told you about!"

Both men guffawed. She backed away, fumbling for the knife in her waistband. Sam came to her side, apologizing. "I'm sorry you're shocked, Surlina. Perhaps you'd better hear his story. It seems your father is planning to escape. Muller has brought forth this intelligence of his own accord. I can hardly have him bound, gagged and tossed in the brig for doing his duty."

She snarled at Muller, "You dirty double-dealing dog! You treacherous bastard!"

Sam took her arm firmly. "So! It is true! Your father, and you, perhaps, were intending treachery?" His blue eyes were cold this morning, alert to her slightest bit of trickery. Muller had obviously planted seeds of distrust with him, and now she saw enmity blossoming between them. Oh, Muller was cleverer

43

than she'd given him credit for, double-crossing her father with promises of help while scurrying to Grant with the details. Lying, sneaking son-of-a-bitch! And Sam Grant was no better, currying the favor of spies, laughing at her discomfort, accusing her of duplicity. No, her father was right. She must trust nobody but herself!

"Excuse me," she said icily. "I have no further business here." She whirled to leave the room, but Sam caught her wrist.

"Wait!" He motioned Thad Muller to leave. "Back to your post, Muller, and see to those recommendations I gave you."

"Yes, sir!" Muller saluted. Then, as he passed Surlina, he opened his mouth in a leer. His dirty beard jiggled and she caught a whiff of his offensive breath. How stupid could Sam Grant be! Taken in by this villain's lies and scavenging. As soon as the man was gone, she gave Sam a vivid description of the way Thad Muller had once come to pay a "courtesy call" and ended by attempting to abuse her. "He'd rob me of virtue and silver both if he could!"

Grant listened quietly, returning to his desk after closing the stateroom door. He lit a cigar, puffed on it several times, stubbed it out and leaned back, arms behind his head. "Have you finished blowing off steam, Surlina? I do not think Muller will make trouble for you."

"How little you know!" She remembered again Muller's attempts to force his tongue into her mouth, his knee between her thighs, his rampant fingers down her bodice.

Sam leaned forward, folded his hands on the desk top, then spoke again, more forcefully. "Let me phrase it differently. I do not intend for Muller or *any* man in my command to cause you or your father harm or humiliation."

"How kind of you! Yet you detain *me* and let Muller run free!"

He did not answer her angry outburst but reached for a stack of yellow papers. Shuffling through the communiques, he pulled out one brittle sheet. "Yes, here it is. Surlina, please calm yourself enough to at least listen. I am no more taken in by Muller than you. He was transferred to my command only yesterday, and without much to recommend him." He tapped the sheet and read, "Deserted enlistment center, recaptured, escaped jail at Belmont, chicken and horse stealing in countryside before being captured by Confederates. Returned to our lines in prisoner exchange. Transferred from Halleck's command to cavalry brigade." He grinned. "Impressive record for a man who's served in army blue for only two weeks!"

"But . . . but . . . you were laughing with him! Bargaining with him!" Surlina sank into the chair beside his desk. Confused, she bit at her knuckles.

He chuckled, "Now, tigress, no need to sheathe your claws. If you wish to tongue-lash me further, that is your privilege. Or did you come to report your father's escape plans?"

"No," she admitted. "I wasn't going to tell you."

He smiled. "Your loyalty to those you love is admirable. For the moment I will neither question nor tamper with it."

"My father is not strong enough to escape. His great plans and involved arrangements are simply—"

"His nature." As Sam finished spreading a river chart and anchored the curling corners with heavy books, he reached for her slender hand. "I would not deny an old man his dreams, Surlina. I feel as you do. His schemes cause no trouble. Indeed, they also keep Muller busy and out of worse mischief! So, let your father devise ingenious methods of escape. He'll confide in you and Muller. Both of you will report to me."

"You'll not make me a spy in your service!" She yanked her hand from his grasp.

"You have no choice."

"Choices! That's your favorite word! Well, it will be a cold day in damnation before I'll betray my father to you or anyone else!" She held her head high, feeling ridiculous in the chambermaid costume. If she was going to fight in this man's war, she'd best start dress-

45

ing in trousers! She ran her hands over her sides, tucking the blouse into the waistband.

"You look fetching," he assured her, perhaps thinking she was concerned with her appearance. "You look lovely on the dance floor, too . . . even when you are stranded without a partner. I am sorry about last night. Perhaps you will teach me again tonight?"

She was startled from indignation and confusion into lightheartedness. "You have taught me a lesson in strategy today. I should be happy to teach you waltzing tonight." She could not resist one last jibe at Muller. "But, Sam, let us both be careful. Perhaps my father is not a threat, but Muller is very much so, at least to me."

Grant's good humor was apparent. "I should think it the other way around. Surlina, you are a threat to any man!"

The teasing pleased her, soothed away her fears and reminded her of how warm and pliable she'd felt in his arms. "Am I a threat to *you*, General?"

"More so than I care to admit." Sam busied himself with the charts, rolling and unrolling the pages until he'd restored the impenetrability to his blue eyes and the even color to his cheeks.

'He's not a man for words of sweetness and bantering,' she thought. 'I will not force him.' She pointed to the maps, leaning across the desk top, seeing the course of the Mississippi from Minnesota to the Gulf of Mexico. "I see you are already studying your choices."

Sam traced the river route with his finger, measuring distance between thumb and little finger, calculating rapidly. "Every inch must be open!"

Surlina looked at him, sensing an aura of destiny for him. "A river seems an unlikely landscape for a soldier to find greatness."

He flared at her. "*No* landscape of war is glorious! Shall I romanticize this business for you? This carnage? The sound of sabers through flesh is enough to turn any man sick. The sight of oaks and maples in a forest shining with blood instead of sap is sufficient to

46

curdle any man's honor. No, this war on the western waters will be long, deadly and primitive."

Without warning he grabbed Surlina's shoulders between his hands, shaking her gently. "Don't confuse river warfare with the stories you've read of naval glory. We are in danger at this very moment from raiders and rammers. Below Cairo, we shall have to fight for every bend in the river. The Confederates hold Island Number Ten like a Gibraltar. They have engineers like Beauregard and pirates like Julien Rainbeau who can maneuver in these currents with the skill of alligators! I shall be glad to be off this steamer and back to dry-land soldiering! But the fight for our lifeline is the fight for the river."

She marveled at how his mind traveled. Already he could see the future—brutal, bloody, extending over a horizon of endless battles. A spiral of excitement looped through her, tingling her fingertips and making her hands go cold. She wanted to be part of this history! She wanted to be by his side, hearing the discussions of strategies, planning the advances, basking in the success of the surrenders he'd force. She closed her eyes, dizzy with the desire to share the power he held. Swaying against him, she realized her intent to seduce him. Not because of any commitment to the North, but only as a means to remain with Sam! The idea was shocking at the same time that it made her blood run hot. She felt a persistent quickening between her thighs and a pain of longing within her breasts. Her own heavy breathing jarred her back to the reality of the moment.

Sam was holding her lightly, his own breathing ragged, his shoulders slightly atremble. She whispered, "I would make the kind of woman a warrior needs."

"How you satisfy me just by standing close, Surlina! Last night, when I held you in my arms, I forgot all the world but you! Your eyes burn into me; your face shines with innocence; your hands touch me with tenderness. I believe that could I but have you, I would forgive the world its cruelty!"

She was on the verge of crying out to him, "Take

47

me, love! Yes, take me as your own!" But as he bent to kiss her and her need for his touch bubbled like a spring, they were interrupted by a heavy knocking at the door. Instantly they sprang apart, guilt shifting their eyes, the knowledge of mutual desire making them turn away from each other.

"Who is it?" Grant demanded brusquely.

"McIntyre, sir! Of the Missouri Volunteers. There's been a stabbing, sir! Two soldiers gambling and drinking. Private Oaks and Private Muller were—"

"Thad Muller!" roared Grant, crossing the cabin in two steps. Go to your quarters, Surlina. You're not safe if Muller's gone to knifing people!"

She was afraid of Muller, but she was more afraid of losing Sam. "I'll wait for you," she said under her breath. But he was already gone. Tears came to her eyes as she thought how quickly his interest in her had vanished. The demands she felt in her body were of long making and would be long in being satisfied. She was determined to someday know the sweetness of Sam Grant! Only then, would she consider her private skirmish won.

She leaned against the desk, letting her hands travel over her long throat, across her throbbing breasts. This waiting was agony, but his flesh would be relief. She imagined him standing over her as she leaned against the wooden desk. His long fingers would be sensitive as he undressed her. His coppery beard would rub her cheeks, his firm lips would seek hers in short kisses that would give way to lingering pleasure. She blinked at the pressure of her cascading emotions, then smiled and composed herself. When the time came, her body would be abundantly ready, her senses kindled to flame like a torch, and her soul fervently abandoned to the joys of love.

5

Muller had disappeared. "Why can't they find him?" Surlina grumbled to her father. "That damned Thad Muller! First he stabs another soldier in the foot, then manages to hide somewhere on this ship and the whole brigade can't find him! He's been hiding a day and a half and no trace of him! Oh, they're all imbeciles!"

"That include Grant?" Peter Defore yawned and pushed away the breakfast tray she'd brought to his cabin. "Surlina, I think you're just ranting and raving because you didn't get to go dancing last night as you'd planned."

"No," she lied. Again she felt bitter disappointment. She'd seen nothing of Sam all evening, had slept poorly while still hoping he might come to her.

"Here, eat some of this hardtack that passes for toast," Peter said, offering her an unbuttered, dry piece of unleavened bread. "You'll need your strength when we make our dash tonight."

"Oh, stop joking! We're not going anywhere, and you know it!" She was out of patience and showed it by stamping her foot and crossing her arms.

"If you'll help me into my jacket, we'll take a turn about the deck. Fresh air might do us both good."

"All right. But no more talk about escape. I suppose the only good thing to come of Muller's escapade is that he is no longer available to abet your wild plans." When her father didn't answer, she was struck with terror. "Holy Mother of God, no! Oh, surely you don't know his whereabouts, do you, Father? Do you have him hidden?" They moved onto the sundeck.

"Fine morning for a stroll. Lovely morning. See the shoreline there—yes, there on the Illinois side—reminds me of the marshes where you and Tandy used to play when—"

"Answer me! Do you know where Thad Muller is hiding?"

"Tandy was always such a frail girl. Used to worry me sick. You, though . . . never worried about you. Always strong. Headstrong, too." He flashed her a toothy smile. "But it won't buy you the secrets of my brain."

Now Surlina was convinced that her father had helped Thad Muller disappear. But where could he be? Sam Grant had all but turned *Radiant* upside down looking for him and to no avail. She narrowed her eyes. "Where is Muller?"

Peter countered with a question of his own. "Where's my wallet and folding knife?"

Ah, he didn't miss a thing! "I have them."

"So I surmised. You also have Muller."

"What? Father, I don't understand these riddles. Where is the man hiding? We must turn him over to Sam at once!"

"Not to my way of thinking." He hobbled toward a deck chair on the starboard side, leaving Surlina standing incredulous before him. "Sit down, daughter. The spring breeze is good for what ails a body." He tamped his cane against the deck, rapping for order. "This war is a bickering amongst fools. I've fought fools all my life. Don't aim to stop now. There are ways to deny our silver to every last cross-eyed dirty dog North or South of the Mason-Dixon line!"

"Even if it means jeopardizing your life?"

"Even if it means cutting the throats of those nearest and dearest to me."

"Are you angry with *me,* Father? Is your real complaint in all this with me?"

"Partly. You've gone starry-eyed and limp-legged over a Yankee. Next you'll be handing Grant your maidenhead and your fortune on the same silver platter!"

"You make it sound as if I should have an apple stuffed in my mouth as well! Leave my maidenhead, as you so delicately call it, out of this. Your true interest is in the silver. And if you have any brains left in that senile body of yours, you'll leave the treasure in Erlanger's!" She had not been so angry with him since the day he'd disinherited Tandy.

Peter did not bother matching her insults. Instead, he grew quiet, trembling slightly with a gust of cool breeze. "Don't forget that silver floats well on the tides of war."

"You've said that over and over." She spoke her next words cautiously. "Perhaps—only perhaps, mind you —neutrality is no longer possible for us."

"It is the *only* possibility." The old man's dim eyes watered as he squinted at the bright sun. "Surlina, the silver is your only hope. Take it—and Tandy—to Europe."

What an impossible plan! More impractical than his previous schemes of escaping downriver, removing the fortune from Erlanger's and cutting her off from her share.

He pulled a letter sealed with wax from his jacket. "This is how I ouwit the brigand who steals my flagship and my daughter."

Surlina put out her hand, thinking he meant her to have the letter. She controlled her voice. "To whom are you writing?"

He yanked back the parcel, hiding it in his coat. With melancholy in his deep voice, he said softly, "I'll not live to see this war finished, no matter who wins. Promise me you'll take your sister to the safety of the Continent."

"How . . . how can I promise such a thing?" She must talk her father out of such dreary nonsense. "Take Tandy to Europe? Thayer Cabell is not likely to approve of my spiriting his wife away to the Continent —and don't forget their allegiance to the South." She put her hands over Peter's, stopping the tapping of his cane against the deck. "Besides, I've no mind to sit out the next God-knows-how-many years away from . . ." Her voice faltered as she almost uttered, "Sam." Quickly, she covered by saying, "Away from you!" She could

51

see she hadn't fooled him. "I love Tandy, just as you do! But I simply cannot deal with that cloying pig of a husband she chose!"

"You are right for once this morning. Still, Tandy is your sister, and you're the one to see to her."

Surlina felt the burden placed on her as heavily as if it had been a sack of rocks. Of course she was the one—who else? This had always been her father's way. "Surlina, you're to see to the sluice boxes. You're the one to oversee the household. You're the one to learn the shipbuilding trade." She had done all the things he'd asked, done them out of love and family duty. Would the day never dawn when someone would say to her, "Surlina find your own life. Fight for your right to love and be fulfilled!"

She could not refuse to answer her father, but her heart was weighed with indecision. "Of course I'm the one to see to Tandy . . . if there is anything to see to! But you've cut your ties to her completely. She's a grown and married woman who may not take kindly to my suddenly appearing and proposing Europe."

"You've never understood, daughter. It was never frail, frivolous darling Tandy I sought to alienate . . . only her conniving tyrant of a husband!"

"You've been suspicious of every man who ever came near us!" Perhaps he'd succeeded too well, for she, too, had never found a man to please her. Until Sam Grant. Her mind ran in a maze of confusion. Was this "take Tandy plan" another of her father's covert ways of keeping her from falling in love? Perhaps it was not Tandy he wanted out of the country, but herself. Too many questions were unanswered. Where was Thad Muller hiding? What was in the parcel? She shook her head. "I cannot promise anything when you have not trusted me to know everything."

"I'll tell you nothing more—you'll only go babbling to Grant. Sail with your sister to Europe."

"No."

"I order you to take the treasure and Tandy to Europe."

"Please . . . please, oh I beg you, Father! Please

52

. . . I can sit in the garden for an hour and push needles sewing with her. I can sit in the drawing room for an evening listening to that rebellious Thayer Cabell. But I cannot sit out an entire war with her. I'd be ready for Bedlam!" She had saved the highest card until last and she played it now. "Besides, as frail as Tandy is, I doubt she could make the voyage without endangering her life!"

He played a higher trump. "Then stay in New Orleans with her."

She was aghast at the very idea. "Seek refuge in New Orleans? In the central jewel of the Confederacy's crown? I'm no daughter of the South!"

"While I commend you for that, the fact remains that you are my daughter, and I hereby charge you with your sister's care."

He had spoken plainly, with calm anger in his eyes that turned them gray. She could easily understand how he'd acquired the title, "silver king with the iron will." There was iron in his voice and cold steel in his heart. And no telling what mayhem was contained in that letter sealed in his jacket! She could not trust his games. "Give me that packet with the wax seals!"

"Sh . . . quiet! I hear someone!" He let his head droop against his chest and his eyes close as if slumbering. What a sly old fox he was! Surlina felt pride in his ability to disguise himself, yet warned herself not to fall for his wily camouflage.

She saw Sam approaching with a worried look on his face. A straggly growth of new whiskers filled in the flesh above his lips, indicating he'd had little sleep and no time to shave. Although she smiled at him in greeting, she felt panicky. She must finish the conversation with her father!

Grant greeted her casually, then turned directly to Peter Defore, touching his knee gently, asking sympathetically, "Feeling better today, sir? Do you think you might feel up to dining with us tonight in the grand salon?" His manner was courteous, certainly not military commander-to-prisoner.

To Surlina's disgust, her father hid behind his sick-

and-senile act. "I doubt I'll be able to come, but thank ye kindly, young man. You see my daughter eats hearty, will you?" Peter smiled as if grateful to be included in the invitation. "Perhaps you could send a toddy to my stateroom?"

"I'll bring it myself," vowed Sam, sounding like a devoted son. Surlina was miffed that Sam should be taken in by what she knew was a performance. Or was she misjudging Sam once more? Oh, who was spying on whom in this crazy war!

Surlina stood naked in front of the stateroom mirror. She'd been trying on and discarding various articles of clothing. Tonight, for certain, there'd be dancing and she intended to dress for the occasion . . . and for the opportunity the night might bring.

She started with her feet. Not boot-shoes with their buckles and laces. She'd feel silly in her father's slippers packed with feathers. Barefoot dancing had scandalized Sam. How was she to be demure and uninhibited at the same time? She lifted her feet, one at a time, moving the trim ankles in a circle, extending the muscles of her calves and feeling the tension travel up through her knees and thighs.

She turned sideways to look at her figure in profile. Her breasts were full, but had no hint of falling. Lifting them with her hands, the nipples stood out prominently, pink against the rosier brown surrounding them. Her slender waist pleased her. She'd never had to worry about gaining unwanted fat. She ate hungrily without restraint. Suddenly she heard a noise. Alarmed, she glanced around the cabin. Door locked. Porthole covered. She listened with her ears straining while her eyes held her image in the mirror. Perhaps only the scuffling of someone walking by in the passageway.

She held her hands intertwined across her taut stomach, measuring to make sure she'd added no pounds. Her rounded buttocks felt cool as she touched them, smooth and downy as a baby's. She spread her legs apart slightly, aware of the rubbing sensation beneath the triangle of dark curls. The soft mound of hair glistened like the shiny ringlets atop her head.

Another tiny sound, like wind nipping at loose shutters, caused her to lose the delicious feel of the moment. She had seen her body and admired it, but it did not impress her as needing pampering. She enjoyed the strength of her limbs, liked swimming with powerful strokes, liked horseback riding with thighs clutched tight against the heated flanks of a stallion, and, most of all, loved the exertion of dancing. Her body had served her well in mastering these activities. She did not doubt its ability to serve her well in love.

Surlina checked the cover on the porthole to make sure it wasn't emitting the wheezing sounds. Secure. The built-in drawers had internal latches, and all were tightly closed. These little noises must simply be the creaking and settling of the understructure of the new ship.

It was time to dress. In place of a chemise and undergarments, she slid two aprons over her head and tied them, front to back. The cotton molded nicely to her breasts and waist, allowing her to move freely. She'd borrowed her father's tartan shawl, and now she draped and pinned the plaid wool into a sculptured blouse with scooped neckline. The bright red and green of the tartan blended with the high color displayed in her cheekbones and emerald eyes.

She'd have to make the plain black chambermaid's skirt do for dancing. Her original taffeta was soiled from when she'd leaped on Sam's back and been summarily tossed to the dirty deck. She threw back her head and laughed softly, remembering how he'd called her "tigress." Was that how he thought of her? As sleek, fierce, beautiful and catlike? God, she hoped so!

She completed dressing quickly, skipped around the room as if dancing the polka, and laughed again. She confided to the mirror, "Tonight nothing but Sam Grant shall occupy my thoughts," she winked brazenly, "and my arms!"

A tiny muffled chirp put her instantly on guard. It seemed to be in this very room with her! She flung open the closet door, the chamberpot station, the extra blankets on the top bunk. Nothing! She shuddered at the idea of a rat trapped in the cabin with her. A cricket, maybe; yes, she could stand the idea of a friendly cricket and immediately assured herself the noise had been very cricketlike. Nevertheless, she pocketed her father's wallet within the folds of the black skirt band and secured the silver dagger to the ties of the aprons turned lingerie.

Now she was back to where she'd begun—with nothing on her feet. Sighing, she reached for her wool stockings. She wouldn't attempt to shock Sam by bare feet tonight. What a quaint and bashful man he was in little matters! She piled her hair high on her head, straining the shining, amber tresses to their full length, leaving long saucy curls to drape her forehead.

On her way to the grand salon, she stopped at her father's cabin. He was asleep . . . or pretending to be. "I love you, Father. I've thought hard about the things you asked of me concerning Tandy and the treasure, but I cannot—"

"Buy me time, Surlina." The words were mumbled, as if he were talking in his sleep.

She leaned close. "What? Are you talking to me, Father?"

"Buy me time tonight. You can fool him if you try. When a man falls in love, he thinks the clocks, guns and chapel bells all stop when his lover is in his embrace."

"Are you awake? Do you know what you're asking?"

There was no answer except a rippling of a snore.

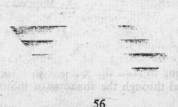

56

6

Surlina entered the louvered doors and breathed the fragrant smell of lilacs and beeswax candles, French champagne and the damp river breeze. Running across the dance floor in her stocking feet, making modestly sure to keep her skirt low, she felt coltish. How glad she was to have long legs made for dancing, full lips made for kissing, and a heart made for love! As if on cue, her heart fluttered as she saw Sam enter from the far corridor. How handsome he was tonight in a well-cut jacket, the stripes of his wool breeches tucked smartly into the glossy leather boots. She did not trust her voice to speak his name, so she simply glided toward him with the shimmery candlelight shadows tossing silhouettes on the wall panels and her smile tossing impudent kisses toward his mouth.

He did not speak either. Looking deeply into her eyes, he touched her hand to his lips. She felt the warmth of his breath across her fingertips and let the sensation of heat travel up her arm. With a twinkle of mischief in his blue eyes, he bowed formally. "Your pleasure, Miss Defore?"

She moved into his proffered arms, leaning close to his ear. "You, Sam. You are my pleasure."

"Shall we dance?"

"Without the musicians? Aren't we rushing things?" She felt giddy with laughter and longing, delighted they were alone. "Of course! How useless musicians are to us when we can make our own music!" She moved to him joyously, feeling the throb within her hand as it rested on his shoulder. Restraining herself, she did not press against him. Rather, she held back slightly, wanting to read the message in his eyes.

They moved through the shadows of the candlelight

as rhythmically as if a symphony had been providing the tones. She saw in his eyes the delicate shading of blue which spoke of tenderness and loyalty. His lashes, reddish-brown like his beard, seemed dark and were flattering to his pale eyes. She liked the way he always watched her. He did not use his eyes seductively, undressing her by letting them move over her figure. Rather, he used his eyes to command, to direct her which way to move, to bend her responses to match his own. She was certain his gaze spoke of the same desires she felt, of a night of expectation and the first of many kisses. She placed her arms around his neck, clasping her hands behind his head as if to cradle him, then moved against him with a sigh of delight.

Sam ran his fingertips along her forehead, pushing back the dark curls. As his fingers stroked her earlobes, traveled across her throat and pressed at her spine, she trembled until she could hardly breathe. This afternoon, in her daydreams, she'd given herself to him. Now the night held promise of reality, of sharing clean sheets as he entered her with the same commanding presence which set her vibrating under his touch at the moment.

Suddenly he stopped. "I must go on deck to supervise the loading of wood."

"Will you come back shortly?" Her rising voice betrayed how desperately she hated to part from him for even a few minutes. "Please say you'll come back!"

He consulted his gold pocket watch. "It is early yet. We must take on sufficient wood to carry us to Cairo. Also . . ." He ducked his head closer, obviously divulging confidential plans, "also, I think stopping may lure that rascal Muller from hiding—and back to the brig where he belongs!"

"I think my father knows where he is," she blurted.

Cries of "Woodyard! Downstream and to port!" interrupted her from revealing more. "Woodyard! Thirty minutes to docking!"

Again Grant checked his watch! She shied back from him, wondering if her admission of her father's possible knowledge would alienate him. "I'm not sure,"

58

Surlina added hastily. "My father sometimes invents little strategies for his own amusement."

"He gave you no hint of where Muller might be?" Sam's voice was controlled as if interrogating a prisoner.

"He said *I* had him hidden! That's nonsense, of course! There's no man I'd rather see behind bars . . . or dead!"

Unexpectedly, Sam swept her toward the doors with one hand on her elbow and the other behind her waist. "We must search your cabin at once! That's one stateroom we have not torn apart inch by inch!" He dragged her along the passageway roughly, pushing aside a group of lounging soldiers who snickered crudely at the sight of the general pulling a woman through the darkened hall.

Surlina was too overcome with fright to protest. How humiliating if Muller had been in her stateroom. Oh, Jesus, no. Surely he could not have been lurking and watching her pass judgment on her naked body, prancing in front of the mirror, caressing her breasts! She thought of the funny noises, the unidentified soft whirrings. Could they have been a man's labored breathing? But there was nowhere to hide in that stateroom! Nowhere! She relaxed a bit as they turned down the starboard deck.

She stood outside as Sam thrust open the door, surveying her room. He opened the closet, slammed it shut with a curt nod, inspected the bedding and the halfroom which held the chamberpot, pitcher and basin. He shrugged as if to say their suspicions had been mistaken. Then, in an instant of furious action, he flung away the chenille coverlet on the bunk, upended the feather mattress and cried, "Aha! So here's where the dirty dog made his bed!"

She rushed inside to see, startled to see the anger on Sam's face which plainly indicated that he suspected her of knowing Muller's whereabouts all along. "I didn't!" she defended herself, only now realizing the drawers beneath the bunk had been cut apart, leaving a space large enough for a man to squirm into. Once secreted, he could pull down the mattress and coverlet and no seam, bulge or ripple would betray him. While half the Union Army had been ransacking the recesses of the ship, Thad Muller had been living cozily beneath her mattress! Surlina went hot with the idea that she'd probably slept atop him last night as well as paraded for him this afternoon. "But where is he now?"

"You tell me," Sam said coldly.

"Surely you don't think I know!"

"All I know is that whatever information you reveal to me always seems to be too little too late!"

"You can't accuse me of anything! You're the general who looked high and low without finding him! He's outwitted you again—maybe you should look in your own stateroom!" Furious tears welled up in her eyes despite her attempts to hide them.

Then he was suddenly against her, kissing her tear-stained cheeks, letting his tongue taste the salty drops, burrowing his beard against her ivory throat. "Oh, Surlina, Surlina, I could not accuse you of anything, my darling!"

He sought her lips with compelling force, drawing a response from her whole being. Her mouth parted, taking him into her lips playfully, diving and wrestling new sensations from her. She responded to the honey-salt taste of their mouths, to the soap-scent perfume of their bodies, to the overwhelming motions of desire which pitched them against each other. When he ran his hands down her back and over her hips, she tilted her head back for another kiss.

She waited for the whispered words of endearment which she expected. Instead, Surlina heard the sound of running feet, a muffled noise, then shouting. "Man overboard! Man overboard! This is not a drill!" Bells began to clang. A shrill whistle sounded. Instantly Sam was off and running. Instinctively she followed him, racing down the port passageway, through the narrow amidships opening. There, against the dark railing, a cluster of soldiers were shouting excitedly and pointing.

Grant lost no time speculating. "Who was it?" he

60

demanded. He grabbed a lantern and shone it across the empty expanse of river.

"We don't know, sir!" answered a lieutenant. "Apparently a man and a woman—"

"There are no women aboard this ship! All right, soldier, when did they fall? How long ago?"

"We're not sure, sir. But a dinghy is missing, too."

"Broke loose from the davits?"

"No, sir. Lowered. Removed."

"Then this is no accident! That was no woman!"

Surlina saw his jaw tense as he spun toward her. Already she could feel his mind reaching out, grabbing new conclusions from the meager facts. "Where is your father?"

She took off running for his stateroom. Could he have made good on his threats to escape?

Grant's voice followed her, "Did you lend those ladies' garments to Muller? Or did you sell them to him?"

Panic kept her from replying, panic that her father might have deserted her, panic that Thad Muller might have used her taffeta skirt as a disguise. As she reached her father's cabin, she prayed Peter was inside, asleep. Surlina shoved against the door. "Locked!"

Grant reared back, ran at the door and kicked it in with one well-aimed thrust of his boot. Empty! She sucked in a hot breath of utter dismay. He would die in the cold dark river! He'd die at the treacherous hands of Muller! She cried out, "How could he do this?"

"With help from you," Sam stated. He was now a military presence and not a man who only minutes before had kissed her with ardor. He spat the words at her, "Your doing?"

Appalled that he would accuse her, she replied, "How dare you even think that of me!"

"Where will he go? St. Louis? New Orleans?"

She lied quickly, "I have no idea!" Her mind surged with the many hints he'd given. My God, how she needed to know the contents of that sealed letter! How dangerous it was for him to attempt a long journey!

"Oh, I have no idea where he's gone," she wailed. "He has simply left—"

"Left you with quite a problem!" retorted Grant. "Left you with a silver fortune and a political risk!"

Another lieutenant rushed up with further news. "All crew and contingent accounted for, sir—except that man who was in hiding, of course."

"You can safely assume he's deserted! An old man and a deserter! They'll not get far. When we put in at the woodyard, dispatch a cavalry detachment to scour the riverbanks. Send a rider to the telegraph at Cairo." He turned to Surlina. "I assure you that your father and Muller shall both be returned—in good health and in handcuffs! As for you, you have forfeited your claim to neutrality. Guard! Put this woman in the brig below decks!"

She stared at him. "In the brig? Ten minutes ago, you wanted me in your bed!"

He slapped her cheek with the back of his hand. It stung lightly, but the wound to her spirit was deep. Crushed, she bit her tongue to keep from raging at him, but it was no use. "It's *your* fault my father is gone! You should have kept a guard on him!" Despite her worries for her father's health, Surlina was proud that he'd made his escape. He might have outwitted her, but he had also outplayed the Union Army.

Impetuously, she cried, "I daresay it will be a goddamned long time before you recapture him! He's plainly too smart for the likes of you, Sam Grant!"

"Guard! Get this woman out of my sight!"

The dour young man with the Colt pistol who had stood sentry with her in the grand salon now pushed forward and grabbed her arm. She fought him away. "Don't touch me!" The boy seemed unsure what to do and looked to Grant. The general nodded that Miss Defore should be allowed to proceed on her own. Surlina gave him no thanks for the small favor. Instead, she picked up her skirts and headed out of his sight without a backward glance. Perhaps when both their tempers had cooled, she'd consider an apology . . . from him!

62

"I want my things," she told the guard.

"I suppose that'd be all right," he drawled, slapping his hand against his holster.

She hurried to the stateroom, only to have her suspicions confirmed. Her taffeta skirt was missing.

As they headed along the outer deckway she again heard the cries, "Woodyard! Woodyard!" The eerie yellow light of burning fires smeared the dark sky. Flames reached twenty feet in the chill air, making the night air seem to hover. Around the fires she could see busy farmers, pointing at the cords of wood, motioning the steamer to stop and assure them of a season's wages. They shouted, waved and threw caps in the air, beckoning excitedly as the steamer neared shore.

Surlina felt the *Radiant*'s engines slow, the steamer drift sideways, the bow pointed toward the dock. She shivered in the cold night air, for the fires on shore sent only the smell of acrid pine smoke and a dull yellow light into the night. The smoke clung to the river, thick as fog in places, blotting out sections of the shore.

Suddenly she heard muffled shouting. "Ho there! Cast off!" At that moment a brilliant green flare went up from the shore. Shots rang out and then she heard a terrible high-pitched yell. More shouting, closer and louder. "No woodyard. It's a trap! Attack! Full back. Get underway! Quick!"

Her first fears were for the *Radiant,* then for her father somewhere on the river, then for herself. The sentry behind her faltered in confusion, unsure of whether guarding a woman took precedence over guarding his post. As he cursed and fumbled for his pistol, she whirled back, shoving him sideways against the deck stanchions. He staggered, bumped his head against the metal post and moaned with pain. Before he could regain his balance, she was gone, darting into the amidships opening, half-climbing, half-leaping down the forward ladder, racing to starboard.

There was chaos everywhere, men running, explosions, shooting, and those bloodcurdling yells. The *Radiant* had no chance to escape into the channel before hordes of guerrillas swarmed aboard and torched her decks. Already fire bombs were hitting the stern and ropes were swirling around the railings, holding the ship to the shore. Raiders were attacking by rowboat while sharpshooter fire peppered the ship.

Surlina took everything in as she ran along the starboard deck. She must not stand idly by—not to see the *Radiant* fired by the torch, captured by rebels or even successfully defended by Sam's disorganized troops.

To leave Sam when she had only found him, never known the full measure of his passion. To leave her ship to the mercy of attackers! But her father's orders had been clear; get to New Orleans and see to the safety of her sister and the silver. Now there was an even more compelling reason to journey down the hostile river and into the forest full of gunfire. Her father! In the company of Muller, plus the dangers of the battlefield and the peril of his health, he'd not last long. Her only chance was to find him soon! She hid for a moment in the shadow of the pilothouse, checking to see that the wallet and knife were secure.

The sentry's curses pursued her. Go now or not at all! Yes, go!

Surlina ran faster, gathering her skirts above her knees. She scrambled back through the midships opening, racing for the dark of the port side. There the river stood out black and wide in contrast to the bright, savage fighting going on against the shore.

She climbed the liferails, scampering over the cables, clawing a hold by reaching backward with one hand, curling her toes around the polished metal rim of the *Radiant*'s decking. She let loose of the cable, balanced for a second, then flinging her courage away, she dived.

7

The exhilaration of being airborne gave way to the sharp wet slap of the river as she hit. Surfacing, the pain in her lungs caused her to gasp for air. She lay back in the water, trying to catch her breath and make certain her hasty departure had not been noticed.

In a moment, the tug of the current caught her. She must swim downstream or drown. The whirling coldness pulled at her legs, wrapping the black skirt in a tangle. The wool clothing would have to go! She fumbled beneath the water, disposing of stockings and skirt. Next she bit the wallet securely between her teeth, then struggled out of the shawl, flinging it away. Now Surlina wondered how she'd survive attired only in two aprons.

How long could she stay in the river without cramping or numbing with cold? To come ashore too soon would be to risk recapture by Sam!

She plotted a course diagonally ahead of the burning ship, aiming for a clump of cottonwood trees which stood out from the shoreline fifty yards downstream. Her teeth began to chatter and her arms ached each time she forced them to pull against the current.

After twenty minutes her toes were numb, her shoulders twitching in spasms of exhaustion, and Surlina felt dizzy as she neared her goal. A large cottonwood stood deep in the stream, its roots exposed and overhanging limbs beckoning like life rings.

Her eyes were beginning to go hazy, the focus marred by too much water and exertion. She could hear her heart protesting. It was necessary to fight her body as well as the river. Thrashing for shore, Surlina paddled furiously in a last burst of energy. She flailed for the safety of the cottonwood, went under, struggled up again, thrashed for the tree and fell back short of the roots. She hurled herself forward again, both hands straining for the tree. Catching a precarious handhold Surlina dragged herself up the steep incline. Inch by inch, shivering and breathing like a hunted animal, she dragged herself onto the shore. Face down, clutching the earth so tightly she smelled the dirt in her nose, she let out a heartfelt gasp, "Safe!"

At that instant, Surlina heard a noise. Thinking only of her thankfulness of being on land, she dismissed the sound. Then it came again and she froze.

She started to change her position but the moment she moved, a heavy blow fell across her back. She was crushed to the earth with a force that expelled the breath from her. Struggling to inhale, struggling to find what had hit her, Surlina threw out her arms and attempted to sit up.

Twisting against the pressure still in her back, she turned her head enough to see the rim of a man's pant leg and a boot. Her first astonished instinct was to dive back into the river. However, the man's other boot, firmly planted in her back, prevented her from moving.

A voice came out of the darkness above her. A beautiful voice—resonant, clear, musically pitched, with the syllables rising and falling as if in song. "So, by the ever-loving saints and sinners, it's true! Rats do desert sinking ships!"

Surlina squirmed in the mud, arching her back in an attempt to lift the man's foot. A sharp click caused her to stop bucking—the unmistakable sound of a pistol's safety catch locking into position. The voice chimed again, "Now, fellow, set up slow and easy, 'cause in this particular war, we shoot deserters on both sides of the Mason and Dixon parallel."

He lifted the boot slightly, causing Surlina to fear she might slide back down the incline. She reached forward to secure a better handhold on the tall grasses. Instantly the man's boot smacked down across her extended fingers, the pain in her hand forcing her to cry out, "Get off! Get off my fingers!"

"Saints preserve me! What kind of drowned female baggage have I here?"

She sat up, covering her soggy apron with both hands across her chest. Her teeth chattered, her shoulders shivered and she heard her voice as desperately shaky. "Leave me alone! I'm on my way to New Orleans!"

Surlina sensed the man reaching for her and shied away, scooting backward on the grass. Then she realized that his exertions were his struggle to remove his jacket. In the darkness she could make out only that he was tall, lean and able to move with the precision of a panther. As he threw the poplin jacket around her shoulders, he laughed. "New Orleans? I applaud your choice of destination. A lovely, lovely city, indeed!" He dropped to his knees, pulling the jacket closer across her chest, then laughed again, not so merrily. "What kind of traveler traipses about the countryside without a coat? Indeed, without much lady-like apparel at all, if my eyes serve me right!" He moved both hands downward from the jacket, grasping her naked legs. "Aha! As I thought—a young whorefish from the river! It's not every night one comes flopping at my feet!"

She twisted away from his grasp, pulling at the jacket and bunching her knees upward. "Who are you? Keep away from me!" She fumbled for her dagger, tangled among the apron strings where she'd tied it.

Her threat seemed to amuse him. He reached for her again, resting one warm hand on her ankle to prevent her from resisting. "Let me think. I know of no brigades of fancy ladies camped near here. So, unless you are a soiled dove who has alighted from the trees, I suppose you must come from that tramp steamer upriver!"

"*Radiant* is no tramp steamer! She's the fastest thing on the Mississippi!" She had blurted her knowledge of the boat before she thought of its implications. Now he'd know she'd come from its decks.

The seductive, teasing tones of his voice rose and fell like wind through treetops. "Why, I should think a girl of your profession would consider herself, not a steamer, the fastest thing on the river!" He laughed heartily, stroking upward from her ankle until he

67

hastened his grip on her knee. "Come here! Let's see how well you ply your trade! Flop over on your back there and spread your wares!"

"Get away from me! I'm Surlina Defore on my way to New Orleans! Keep your distance!" She pulled her arms through the jacket sleeves to work at untying her knife.

"On your way to New Orleans? Your voice tells me that's not home. Here, here, give me a feel. Usually I can tell by the firmness of a girl whether she's one of those full-breasted Memphis tarts or a tight-assed St. Louis lady of the night." He caught her to him by grabbing the back of her neck and let his other hand rush deftly under the jacket. "Dressed for action, I see! Or were you caught in the act when that steamer caught fire?" He squeezed at her left breast as she twisted, shaking her head and hunching away from his teasing fingers.

She dared not tell him that the *Radiant* was once her property, but she'd be damned if she'd let him think her a whore. She repeated her name in a hoarse whisper, warning him with a hiss, "Surlina Defore's my name! I was a . . . a . . . chambermaid on that ship!"

"Oho! You're much too lovely to empty chamber-pots and tie up ladies' corsets!" She wished she could see him clearly. How much easier to fight a known enemy! "No, I believe you ply your trade flat on your back. So, a little demonstration, perhaps? You river-boat girls should have lots of experience adjusting to the rolls of the river. Let's have a feel of that saucy tail in action! On your knees, wench!"

Surlina determined to run, but though she lurched, she could not break his grasp. She managed to get to her feet with him still holding one wrist, but as she took a running step, he dragged her down. He scooped her upward from the earth by putting both hands around her waist and positioning himself directly behind her. "Hands and knees, that's the fashion!" he cried and pressed himself hard against her flimsy garments. She felt the soft chamois of his pants rubbing

68

up and down across her hips while she was caught on all fours like a dog. She ducked her head, hoping to bite at his hands, but he slid his fingers lower, rocking her hips against the tight organ straining his pants.

Surlina dug her feet into the ground as a springboard, then used her elbows to jam into him. She managed to spin him backward, but her own forward motion ended by falling on her face. She howled in rage, fearing humiliation and worse at the hands of this man with the aroused body and lilting voice.

He scrambled alongside her, helping her to a sitting position while planting his leg across her lap to prevent her from rising. "Why such resistance? Is it cash in advance you want?" He tossed a coin toward her. Aiming her hands in the dark, she batted it away. "Not enough? Oh, you girls are all alike—love a man only for the payday bulge in his pants instead of what's there naturally! By God, you ragtag army of bedhoppers are worse than a plight of grasshoppers!"

She protested her lie once more. "I'm a chambermaid!"

"Decided to take to the waters rather than go down with your craft?" He stood suddenly, watching the landscape upriver, leaning out toward the cottonwoods to check the glow in the sky. "About burned out, I'd say. I'd best see to my boys, so I must say adieu, miss." Despite his words, he did not release his grasp on her jacket.

Again she noticed the resonance of his voice, how it sounded like faraway church bells in its range and depth. He sounded civilized, not at all a local bushwhacker. But if he'd had a hand in torching the *Radiant,* she wanted nothing to do with him, cultured or not! When he released her jacket, she faced him defiantly. "I must get to New Orleans! Can you tell me if there's a ship downriver where I can book passage?"

"Indeed there is!"

Good. She'd board the ship, pay passage with the money from her father's wallet and, hopefully, make

69

her way to New Orleans to carry out his orders. It seemed now that this local bushwhacker had no further interest in her. She began to relax, thinking his voice the most charming—though his words were not— she'd ever heard. In return for his jacket, she owed him a warning. "Be careful," she said, touching his arm. "The woods are full of more than local folk. I think it's rebels who torched the ship. You'd best see to your crops and family!"

"Well, well, well," he roared, pulling his pistol from its sheath with a flourish. "Let's see exactly how many of those damned southerners we can attract!" He fired a single shot in the air, counted to four, then fired again.

'Christ in heaven!' she thought, slowly understanding the obvious. Surlina squinted through the dark night, making out the image of the man beside her. She could ascertain only his boots, tight pants, and shirt with flowing sleeves. Civilian clothing, yes, but hardly the attire of a Missouri farmer. "You're not a local," she said matter of factly, embarrassed at her own stupidity. "Not a farmer. Not a woodyard owner, not a—"

"Captain Julien Rainbeau, milady," he introduced himself, bowing low and sweeping his arm across his chest. "Confederate River Defense Force."

She laughed spontaneously. "Rainbeau of the Confederate *Navy?* Why, what a joke! They've no ships, no officers, no—" Surlina stopped, aghast at her gall in antagonizing a man who had the obvious power to either shoot or rape her. She tried to cover mistakes. "My father says the South has only a paper fleet—" She broke off again, sensing she was continuing to damage her own position. This man might be an animal, but he was obviously not unprincipled. A rogue when aroused, perhaps, but only his veneer was swashbuckling. His voice had already betrayed him to her as a man of vitality and excitement.

"Yes, paper fleet," he said. "And what do you think people will say about that paper and ash steamboat of General Grant's?"

She faced the horizon where the salmon glow of the *Radiant*'s remains lit up the sky. Her pride! Gone into smoke and water-soaked debris. Because of the man standing before her! Angrily she accused him, "You fool! Torching the *Radiant* is a crime!"

"Yes," he admitted. "And wishing to live to fight another day, it is now time to run away like a criminal."

"Where are we going?" she demanded, not holding back, but not aiding him in his flight.

"Aboard a ship . . . as you wished!" He lowered his voice. "And perhaps ultimately to New Orleans."

She struggled along behind him held securely by his left hand. Vines slapped Surlina's face and thorn bushes pricked at her unprotected ankles. She ignored the discomforts and coldness. "I need safe conduct to New Orleans, as a noncombatant," she said.

"There's no such thing as a safe conduct." He stopped for a moment as they crested the top of a hill. From the clearing she could see down the long slope around the bend to the south. There, protected by sentries, sat a strangely shaped boat. It was broad in the middle, pointed on both ends, had a snubnosed snout like a pig and two stacks forward like antelope horns!

Captain Rainbeau nodded at the contraption. "My command. The C.S.N. *Quail*."

"It looks like a coal barge!"

He ignored her unimpressed comment, dragging her forward. "Properly, my ship is called a Pook turtle, after the engineer who designed her. Built like a packet boat, as you can see. But there's a difference . . . as you can see, too!" He pulled his gun, gesturing toward the edge of the forest. As her eyes strained against the curtain of night, she made out the forms of men silently making their way downhill to *Quail*.

Captain Rainbeau pulled her down the slope. "I command thirteen guns and as motley a crew of Southern gentlemen as you'll ever have the pleasure of meeting. The *Quail*'s not a beauty, as *you* are, but she can float on a bayou mist and sail on the morning dew!"

Surlina was amazed at his poetic rendering of the

71

dumpy barge. Suddenly she was stabbed with fear. If she went aboard a rebel boat, she might never reach New Orleans! If she went aboard with this violently moody Captain Rainbeau, she might never see morning! As they rushed up to the rough plank used for boarding the unwieldy vessel, she pulled away.

He did not force her across the plank. Rather, he left her lifting her arms in indecision while the jacket whipped about her thighs in the cold night air. Rainbeau turned his attention to the groups of men approaching through the canebrakes. "Step lively there, boys!" When the last of the stragglers had run across the boarding log, he turned to her, taking her arm gently. "Well, miss? As you can plainly see, we are outnumbered on land and outgunned on the river. Our departure may seem hasty to you but I assure you it is imperative. Are you coming along?"

"Will you assure me safe conduct to New Orleans as a neutral?"

He seemed to be thinking of his choices. Throwing his hands up in mock dismay, he said, "I suppose it would be remiss to leave a naked belle shivering on the shore."

"Don't call me that!"

"Naked?"

"Belle!"

He gave a loud sigh of despair. "Do you plan to argue with me all the way down the Mississippi?"

Surlina looked at him in the glow of the lantern lights which shone discreetly from the quarterdeck. Her previous assessment of a tall man, graceful and lean, proved true. Now, by the yellow shine of the coal oil, he appeared huge and golden. His blond hair was thick and his neck muscles bulged ramrod stiff above his powerful shoulder girth. Without his poplin jacket, he seemed a silhouette of strength, shirt tucked taut across a flat belly, the sleeves flapping on gathered wristbands. While she was appraising his figure, he was watching her with what seemed to be a smile of indecision.

"Ready aboard?" he called to the deck, while gesturing her aboard but not insisting.

"Aye, aye, sir!"

"Very well!" Without warning, Rainbeau suddenly moved toward her, scooping her up like a wet puppy. "Ahoy! Lieutenant Donlevy! Look alive there!" He stepped across the gangway as a dark shape approached from on deck. In an instant of jostling, he tossed her across to the young man.

She could not distinguish her own shriek of surprise from the startled curse of the man in whose arms she found herself. "Put me down! Don't touch me!" she fumed.

"Yes, ma'am!" agreed the young man, dropping her unceremoniously onto the deck.

Julien Rainbeau sprang across the boarding plank with elegant grace. He helped Surlina from her seated position, then directed her to move toward the bow. "Come along, little dove, and I shall acquaint you with the *Quail*. She's not as elegant as the steamer you so recently abandoned, I fear." His voice took on the sarcastic tone he'd used when questioning her sexual experience on shore. "This is *our* main salon, liberated not from teak and mahogany forests of the Philippines, but from the Yankee strongholds along the Tennessee shoreline! And our decks, not shimmery with the *Radiant*'s varnish, but more useful in this distressing time of warfare. Note the scrollwork on our pilothouse, made from the finest tin Missouri's chickenhouses have to offer."

Sometimes Surlina wished her mind were not so logical. "What makes you think this godawful contraption can outrun Sam Grant's cavalry brigade? He's bound to send horses and riders ashore after your treacherous ambush at the woodyard!"

"Oho! He has horses aboard, has he? What an observant young chambermaid you are!"

"Enough men and horses to pursue you through hell and high water, Julien Rainbeau!"

"My, my, what disdain you show toward me. Well, I hold General Grant in equal disdain. Fool Sam Grant

73

—booted out of the old army, barely let into the new! Faith, he'll do well to find his horse in the dark. If I know him, he'll be sitting in some corner swigging on his bottle!"

"That's not true! He's a fine—" Surlina clamped down on her tongue with her teeth, attempting to stifle her outbursts.

"If you're afraid of Grant, miss, you can rest easy. He had orders to steal that steamer, it's true. But that's the extent of it. He'll have no choice but to sit still . . . and sit, and sit, and sit till he gets boils! Halleck's the Yank's boss, and he'll not take kindly to Grant's losing that steamer. Grant may have made a name for himself at Fort Donelson up the Tennessee, but this fiasco rates like his earliest debacle at Belmont. Why, half of Missouri laughed when he lost the battle *and* his stallion! For damned sure, I don't fear Sam Grant!"

It took all Surlina's strength not to shout her praise of Sam Grant, but she checked her wild tongue, though she felt her cheeks flame in the darkness. Neutrality! Wasn't that her shield? She moved apart from Captain Rainbeau, trying to focus her attention on her immediate needs—something more than a loose jacket to cover her, a plan to find her father, a way to New Orleans.

She huddled in the shadows as Rainbeau quietly, efficiently, maneuvered the *Quail* into the stream. Some of the men helped paddle with wide oars until the ship was around the cottonwood bend. "Light off the engines," called the captain, and a mild cheer went up from the crew.

Suddenly the gangly youth who had caught Surlina when she'd been thrown aboard returned to her side. Now he had a lantern and appeared composed of all lengthy arms and legs. Surlina guessed his age at about seventeen. "Uh, miss . . . miss . . . if you'll follow, uh, I mean Cap'n Rainbeau said you should—" He paused, obviously uncertain of what to say next. Finally, holding his lantern low so his face was hidden, he finished, "you should sleep in his quarters. This way." He took off at a trot.

74

Surlina followed him to a stateroom which was cramped and spartan—an iron bunk, river charts piled on a file cabinet and a cat asleep atop a hard pillow on the mattress.

Practically beyond words at the idea of directing a lady through his captain's quarters, Donlevy managed to say only, "I guess you can find what you need. Cat's named Squeebob." He stammered good night backing away hastily.

Surlina lost no time in shedding her wet garments, letting them drop to the deck, making a brown puddle on the wooden floor of the stateroom. Then, in a rush of practical necessity, Surlina pushed aside the cat and dived into the bunk. She rolled up in both blankets, noting only in passing that one was marked in large letters "U.S. Naval Academy, Annapolis." On second thought, she felt for the cat. It was a large, fluffy animal, gray-and-white spotted on the rump like a miniature paint horse. She patted him soothingly and drew him under the blanket, anxious to borrow some of his bodily heat.

Although she was tired, she found the strength to wonder if Sam Grant had missed her yet. Would he think her drowned? Or treacherous? How quickly she had come to want him, and how quickly she had run away. What of this man Julien Rainbeau? Was he a man of courage and vision, of daring and resourcefulness, or merely a river scoundrel intent on his own greed and glory? She shook her head, trying to clear it of the image of a Confederate river captain. To her surprise, Surlina felt a sudden warmth when she remembered how the rubbing of his chamois pants had felt against her hips. She attempted a thankful prayer for her deliverance from the river, but the last words on her lips were "Julien . . . Julien Rainbeau."

8

Surlina awoke as the rising sun cast golden threads of light through the porthole. For a moment she was startled by the unfamiliar, bumpy motion of the flatboat skimming the river. The *Radiant* had been so lordly smooth! Why, this frisky little *Quail* was like riding a bucking pony! Comparing the ships renewed her sorrow for her former vessel and tortured her mind with the memory of how she and Sam had parted under circumstances of anger and deceit. Dismissing him from her mind to avoid the feeling of loss she tried to sit up. Her bones ached with every motion and she discovered fat Squeebob perched atop her stomach.

From far off she smelled a marvelous aroma—coffee! "If I can find something to wear, my nose will surely lead me to the source of that wonderful smell," she announced, pushing the cat aside and casting back the blanket.

Her muscles protested each move she made, and the humping, thumping motions of the packet boat kept her off balance. Surlina felt drunk as she dipped and swayed, reached for handholds on the metal chest and missed, grabbed for the blanket and only half-succeeded in wrapping it around her. "My God, I look soggy!" she complained, addressing herself in the tiny shaving mirror nailed to the bulkhead. She squinted at her puffy face, the cascade of brown curls matted in the texture of dried seaweed, the lips chapped by exposure to the wind and water. "Captain Rainbeau will toss me overboard when he sees me in broad daylight," she assured the cat.

Something to wear! Assuredly she had no use for that pile of muddy aprons. Surlina forced her knees to bend while she retrieved her knife, then bundled the

76

soiled garments together and deftly opened the port-hole. Out they went, flapping in the morning breeze, over the flat deck and into the wide yellow river. The wallet! Surely she hadn't tossed that out, too! Then she remembered she'd put it in Captain Rainbeau's jacket pocket the night before. Quickly she retrieved the leather folder, thinking she must find a place to spread the greenbacks and let them dry. Someplace private, *not* atop a Confederate captain's personal bunk! She laid the wallet face down on the cabinet beside the cat, while turning her search for clothing toward the built-in drawers.

In the top drawer she pulled out men's long cotton stockings, two pairs of pantaloons, and a white mono-grammed shirt. Her next rummaging brought linen slacks with a webbed belt and brass buckle, a formal planter's shirt with gathered wristbands and mismatched buttons. "Ah, a full set of long underwear. Just the thing for a fashionable St. Louis heiress stranded in the middle of a rebel barge!" She pulled on the under-garment, belted the linen pants and planter's shirt into place, and tied up the sleeves with elastic bands she found in the desk drawer.

Unexpectedly, there was a rap at the door. Squeebob mewed, picking up his ears and leaping from the cabinet. Surlina ran her hands through her curls, trying to comb their tangled mess. She licked her lips, hoping to hide the chapped cracks, then called, "Come in."

Julien Rainbeau strode in, two cups of steaming liquid in his hands. "Good morning, here's your chicory," he said, managing to use a full octave of tones in his voice. The liquid was so hot that moisture rose in a vapor, condensing on his clean-shaven face.

Surlina stood back, taking her first clear look at him. 'My God, what a handsome man!' His golden hair waved softly, curling in an unruly manner at his long sideburns. Eyes: gray, with flecks in them that shone like opals. Age? She guessed slightly past thirty, with years spent in the sun and wind which had left him tanned, with creases near his eyes and a complexion clear as springwater. Last night in the darkness she'd detected a hint of scandal in his voice. Now, shocked at the handsome face and elegantly trim body before her, she immediately sensed the lilting speech accompanied the personality of a rogue. If he'd chosen river piracy as his trade, he fit it perfectly. He was exactly the type to wield a saber or sit a stallion with the ease of an adventurer.

Nevertheless she'd not fall for any golden-haired giant who'd mishandled her dignity so rudely. She must keep her mind on business. Oh, surely her father wouldn't attempt to take the money from Erlanger's. But she wasn't convinced; he'd outwitted her more often than she wished to admit. So, when Captain Rainbeau smiled, causing a boyish dimple to appear in his chin, then extended a coffee cup toward her, she merely asked, "How many days to New Orleans?"

Long intervals between snatches of conversation apparently didn't bother him. "Memphis to New Orleans . . . Hmmmm, the record is six days, but it will take us ten. Or more. Once we finally start."

"Start at once! You don't understand! My father is traveling overland. I must arrive in New Orleans before him!"

"A race?" His eyes were curious as he slowly sipped the hot chicory.

In truth it was a race—a race to outmaneuver Thad Muller, a race to keep her father from chicanery that might endanger the fortune, and now, a race to protect him. It would be foolish to divulge the nature of her plans—or her full identity—to Julien Rainbeau. She liked his appearance, but she hadn't the faintest knowledge of his sense of honor.

Before she'd phrased an answer to his question, he put down his cup, picked up his cat and changed the subject. "How did you find my cat as a bed partner?" His gray eyes traveled to the rumpled bunk, the muddy spot on the deck, the wadded naval blanket and then back to her. "Or do chambermaids prefer to sleep alone?" That tease was back in his voice!

"Set sail immediately! For New Orleans!"

His musical laughter taunted her beyond reason.

"Regrettably, the age of sail has drawn to a close. Besides, we're headed for sentry duty downstream at Island Number Ten, not a racing derby to New Orleans. Oh, we shall arrive in the Crescent City eventually, but it will be a matter of weeks, not days." He tossed the cat on the bunk. "I hope I shall have the pleasure of your company, my lady of mystery."

The cat jumped back to its place atop the cabinet, knocking the wallet to the deck. Surlina jumped, then gasped as she realized her mistake in leaving it in the open. Julien caught her surprise, immediately moving his eyes from her to the splattered billfold. In unison they bent, grabbing for it, crashing heads together like prizefighters. "Leave it alone! It's mine!" she snarled, but his hand was both longer and faster, and he scooped the wallet from the deck.

She stood back, rubbing her forehead, while he counted the money, then whistled softly. "Are you a chambermaid who steals?" he laughed. "Or a paying passenger who lies?"

"Neither. I am Surlina Defore." She would say no more. He had not recognized her name the night before, so obviously he did not suspect she was the immensely rich Silver Belle. Still, it was useless to pretend she was a chambermaid. "As you see, I can afford to buy passage to New Orleans."

"Yes, you seem to have come into a goodly amount of Yankee money." He let the corners of his mouth turn upward. "Whatever you were doing aboard the *Radiant,* I'm sure it was proper. I apologize for my insults last night. By day I can plainly see you have far too much breeding to be a prostitute."

"How can you tell by looking?" Surlina asked. Watching him smile, watching the way his strong hands moved over the cat and around the coffee cup, watching how his gilded hair reflected the sunlight, she'd already forgiven him his teasing.

His voice glided from a throaty chuckle into outright laughter. "Oh, I can tell! You look to me like a woman made for love, all right, but not the tawdry kind any man can buy in the cribs of St. Charles Street. Your

79

face betrays you—too innocent, with your eyes still hungry, piercing a man's armor of indifference. Your cheeks flame too easily, telling me that you are interested in a way no whore ever is . . ." He trailed off when she turned her head aside.

Such intimate words—so accurate, Surlina feared, but how frivolous! She avoided his gaze.

"I've looked at many women—with lust, with pleasure, with affection. But I've never had one buck against me as you did last night. My knees went weak against your strength even as my body went hard against my will!"

"Stop! It's indecent to first apologize, then proudly recite your abominable behavior!" She faced Rainbeau with what she hoped was a look of injured virtue, but the twinkle in his gray eyes left her giggling instead. Oh God, why did she have to laugh! "You're not a bit sorry!" she flustered. "We won't talk of it anymore!"

"Perhaps we might try it again under less trying circumstances?" he asked, bluffing her into a corner where he took away her cup and moved terribly close, causing her to ripple inside. Then he casually altered the seductive drift of his voice. "Now, how about some breakfast? Come along to the galley. The rest of the crew deserves a look at a beautiful woman who dresses in shirts and britches as if they were a ball gown."

"I . . . I appreciate the garments, Captain Rainbeau," she said, softening her tone. "But I really hesitate to traipse your decks without a gown."

"Our supply of feminine togs is not abundant, though not hopeless, either. In your case, however, I think I prefer you unbound and uncovered." He ran his eyes over her, taking in the shape of her full breasts through the cotton shirt. The linen pants fit snugly over her hips, and he glanced at her derriere with a practiced eye. The subtly mocking, laughing way his eyes glowed upset her equilibrium. This man was used to looking at women not with tenderness, but with the expertise of an auctioneer. It disgusted her that he'd felt her legs the night before, had held her tight against him, straining through his chamois breeches as he rocked her hips like a common slut! And now he had the nerve to suggest that they might try it again sometime!

He seemed to remember his statement of a moment ago. "Reluctantly, I have to admit there is another woman aboard. My Aunt Dottie will put you to rights. I'll send her to outfit you. Then may I expect your company for corncakes and sausage?"

How courteous he could be when he tried! And how hungry she was! She nodded slightly, refusing to admit either her hunger or the way he charmed her with his rough talk, dimpled face or sultry voice.

Five minutes later, the cabin door swung wide and Surlina stood face to face with a wiry woman whose face seemed made of leather and whose arms held a heap of blouses, chemises, skirts, petticoats and slippers. The woman's face was barely visible above the pile, but it was smiling. "Howdy! I'm Dottie. Dottie Grace Rainbeau McDune, to be formal, but Dottie to you. Help yourself here to these duds. I've not a heap of use for 'em since I've took to the high seas with my nephew Julien and his riffraff." She dumped the load of garments onto the desk, then stood back, hands on her hips.

Surlina was amazed, both at the frisky look of the little woman and the loveliness of the clothes. The woman herself was dressed in khaki trousers, leather boots and a fringed suede jacket. She looked more like a trapper than somebody's aunt. "My goodness! Are you really Captain Rainbeau's aunt?" There was no family resemblance. Dottie had chopped gray hair, a quick, tough voice and calloused hands. She appeared to be well past fifty, with bright brown eyes which darted inquisitively.

Dottie's face was broad with intelligence and wit, plus an honest smile as she replied, "Yep, aunt by blood and love. Also chief cook and bottle-washer while my two boys are on this barge."

"Two?"

"You already met Julien, my straight-up-and-true nephew. His daddy Jonathan was my brother. I got a claim in kin to his cousin, too. Ramsey Arnauld's aboard for a few days, doing some of his secret stuff for the diplomatic corps. Oh, wait 'til you meet Ramsey. He makes Julien look back-country bayou, though between us girls, I'm guessing Julien's the better man —in bed, at least."

Surlina had heard of the South's fondness for extended families, but she'd never heard of aunts and cousins and nephews going to war together. As she chose a yellow skirt with a ruffled lace top, she asked, "Tell me more about the Rainbeaus. You sound like a most unusual family."

"I'll say! I'm one sister among five brothers—all dead before they were thirty-five!"

"How horrible!" cried Surlina. "All?"

"Dead through and through!" said Dottie, charging into the rumpled cabin energetically. She swatted the cat out of the way, made the bunk, put away her nephew's garments as Surlina shed them, all the while talking enthusiastically. "Yep, you've met up with a band of renegades now that you've met up with us bayou-bred Rainbeaus, lassie! I hear you bumped into Julien last night. Lucky he didn't spread you then and there. He's not one for waiting—that's for sure! Julien's a Rainbeau through and through, headed for a bad end!"

Surlina inquired quickly, "How old is *he?*"

"Thirty-three. Got about a couple of years left if the family curse holds out." Dottie did not seem particularly worried. She went on talking, humming snatches of a lively tune in between. "He came reporting to me this morning that you was a lady and a beautiful one who should have her pick of my garment chest."

Surlina felt more kindly toward the captain, though she still didn't take to his overt teasing about her sexual charms. "He'll probably come to a bad end at the hands of some angry husband," she laughed. "Does that trait run in the Rainbeau family, too?"

"Yep. Stealing other men's wives for sport is just one thing. Lots of semilegal horse trading for another.

82

The Rainbeau men put about as much gold into their horses as they do their women. 'A mount's a mount,' they say! That kind of talk comes from their Cajun blood. Oh, Rainbeau is a well-known name down in Bayou Teche country. There's even Rainbeau Bayou —runs right into downtown New Orleans and all the way to the home place of Whispers." She snorted and hitched up her trousers. "Hell, most of Louisiana was Rainbeau land before them dry-land planters showed up with their cotton and niggers."

"The Rainbeaus aren't farmers?"

"Sugar. I think that accounts for some of their sweet-talking ways with women!" Dottie laughed like a dog with a high-pitched bark.

Surlina's mind was still stuck on the story of five brothers dying violently before they were thirty-five. "Do you mind telling me about your brothers?"

"Heck, no! Most of 'em got what they deserved. I'm the only Rainbeau to see the sunset side of fifty in two generations!" She hefted herself atop the desk, swinging her legs, which were limber as a girl's. "You finish doing up the buttons and bows on that blouse, and I'll fill you in on the dastardly deeds of the Rainbeaus." Her voice twinkled with pride. "My brother Napoleon was the first to go. Galloped his black stallion up the middle of the marble stairs at the manor house. Broke both their necks. Terrence killed his bride on their wedding night and committed suicide. Oliver drove his team over the cliffs at Natchez. Clarendon—a duel. And Julien's father, Mister Jonathan, died in the saw-mill. That leaves me." She put her hands on her wide hips as if daring the world to intimidate her. "I'm just tetched in the head enough to go on living." She headed for the doorway, beckoning Surlina to follow, then leaned close to whisper, "I lead a sportin' life, lassie, and my hat's tipped to you for taking on the river and my nephew! You've just the kind of courage and fight he needs to simmer him down a notch. More power to you!" She gave Surlina a quick hug, patting her on the back like a genuinely affectionate aunt.

"Julien's lucky to have you along," Surlina smiled, "and I am too!"

"If'n we get along together, I might take you into some of my business dealings," hinted Dottie. "I do a little hunting in the woods when we stop, take on a wrestler now and then for arm fighting, buy and sell cigars in hundred-pound lots and run a little contraband cotton on the side."

"Contraband! That's punishable by death!"

"Not if you don't get caught." Dottie winked. "Ready for breakfast? And wipe that surprised look off your pretty face. You don't tell nobody my secrets, and I won't let on you took a shine to my nephew!"

"Me? A shine to that arrogant man? Don't be ridiculous!" As Surlina said the words, she realized they rang false. Why did her body play such tricks on her, reminding her abruptly of how it had felt to be caught by Julien's strong hands, pressed against his throbbing loins, ground against him till her hips turned warm. She promised to double her guard against a man who could elicit such a response from her against her will. It would probably be wise not to fall too firmly under Dottie's friendly spell, either. The woman might not be above conniving for the Surlina Silver or holding the Silver Belle hostage. No, it was wiser to keep her identity secret.

As Dottie led the way into the passageway, Julien rounded the corner abruptly as if revealing himself conspicuously when he might have been eavesdropping. Surlina saw him frown at Dottie. Dottie immediately scampered past him with a smirk. Next Julien raised his pale eyebrows. "What nonsense did she spread on you thick as molasses pie?"

Surlina knew better than to lie, but he did not seem on as sure a ground as he had earlier. Apparently he not only loved Dottie, but had some good reason to fear her. "She's quite a mother hen, isn't she? She's fixed me up with her lovely lace blouse and this pretty yellow skirt—"

"What did she tell you?" he demanded again, an edge of hardness sharpening his resonant voice.

84

"She talked about your family. About your home, Whispers."

"My home is the *Quail*. Nowhere else!"

Surlina couldn't fathom why he was so upset. "She told me about Rainbeau Bayou."

"Ninety percent of what she says is humbug!"

"And the other ten percent?"

"Outright lies. You mustn't believe the stories Dottie tells! She's old and confused."

Surlina was amazed at his malicious remark. Furthermore, she didn't believe it! Dottie seemed so vibrant, so energetic and full of life! "Then you didn't have a father and four uncles all of whom died young?"

His bronzed face clouded, handsome in its worried honesty. "That part is true."

"Then you are in terrible danger! You're thirty-three and—"

"—destined to live a long and happy life, Surlina." He interrupted her forcefully. After an uneasy pause, he held out his hands, palms up. "See? My life line runs long and true!"

"Oh, that gypsy fortunetelling is nonsense!"

"Is it? Let me see your hands." He reached for both her palms, letting them rest atop his own hands. "What I see here is a life of great adventure, of great passion and wealth. You love monkeys and snakes, collect salt cellars and sleep only on satin sheets. Am I on the right track?"

She laughed with him, realizing that he was simply distracting her. She gazed into his eyes, sensing the worry which lay behind them. No wonder Julien Rainbeau lived for the moment! In a couple of years, he might well be dead!

He lifted her hand to his lips, and suddenly his teasing voice was all tenderness. "Thank you. Thank you for the concern I see in your eyes, for the hope that I shall not come to an early end through my own foolishness."

A wave of longing swept through her, misting her eyes, weakening her knees. But she said only, "Be careful. Oh, please be careful."

85

"What advice in time of war! Here, here, let's forget this foolishness. Now that I have met you, I hope with all my heart that I have not already used up my best days." He dropped his voice to an insinuating moan. "Or nights."

What a devil he was to move so fast between tender honesty and raucous teasing! Glib and golden, that's what Julien Rainbeau was with his warm hands, mischievous eyes and smug little dimple in his chin. Well, she could give as well as take. "You talk much too fast for me. I've led a life away from men such as you —in mining camps miles from town, in a house with only an elderly father for company."

"That makes a much more convincing story than your being a chambermaid."

"You know nothing of me, Julien Rainbeau, and my common sense says to leave it at that!"

"I know a great deal about you merely from standing beside you for the last five minutes. I know you would not have braved the river without a compelling reason. Also, your wallet implies a young woman of sufficient means to be spoiled. You speak with the deliberateness of a man and the temper of a hellion. Obviously, you have the capacity to hurl defiance at any man you do not wholly desire. But if you should desire him . . . Oh God, yes, I also see in you the power to send a man either to heaven or hell by your touch."

He'd done it again! Talked circles around her with that effortless, teasing mouth, held her eyes seductively while his own hid behind a mask of impenetrability. Surlina knew she was breathing fast and begged her heart to slow down. "Breakfast," she ordered quickly. "All your joking has a certain novelty, but I really don't know how to respond to such remarks."

"No? Then how would you respond to a kiss?" Julien pulled her against him, lounging casually against the swaying bulkhead, holding her to his chest until she could hear his heartbeat. "Oh, your mouth is shaped more for passion than argument, I believe!" With that, he bent his mouth to hers, and she felt smothered in his voluptuous power.

His arms caressed her back, holding her to him as her breasts squeezed tight against his muscular chest. He pressed her lips under the cool moistness of his own parted mouth, seeking her tongue greedily. The soft flesh of her neck tingled. The sensations of warmth, of quickening, jolted her. Her legs began to desert her. "I'll swoon!" she gasped, pulling back breathless, her fingers touching her tingling lips.

To her shock, his manner was offhand. "You'll do," —he passed judgment, releasing her—"until you can be properly trained. You've the talent of an amateur. If I have time, I shall teach you to kiss properly."

The haughty, hot-eyed scoundrel! "The matter is done," she said flatly, chilling her voice to an even tone. "If I need instruction, it's from a far more accomplished teacher than you!"

"You didn't *like* my small token of affection? What a fine actress you are, then! I'd venture to guess now your round bottom is as warm as it was in the cane field!" He laughed hilariously. "Don't bother to look offended, my love! How flattered I am that you do not have ice in your veins and steel in your heart."

"If I had my dagger, you'd have steel in *your* heart!" She pushed her hair into place, alarmed at the heat holding her cheeks aglow. "I want none of your kisses and none of your breakfast!" It shocked her to think she was lying on both counts. She flung back her head and laughed at herself. "Oh, hell! I *do* want breakfast!"

He patted her back in a friendly gesture of camaraderie. "My God, at last! A *half*-honest woman!"

Julien set a brisk pace toward the galley while Surlina lagged behind, flustered and nervous. He had no sense of propriety at all, embracing her passionately, bullying her with his sarcasm, then displaying her to the men of the ship while her cheeks were still pink and her lips tingly. She took a deep breath and smoothed her skirt as they entered the narrow wardroom.

The room was crowded with men. Dottie presided over the gathering with a heavy black frying pan in one hand. Uncertain where she should go, Surlina stood aside as Julien moved across the deck, yanked on a canvas flap in the overhead and shouted to the above-deck, "Donlevy! Sit on that whistle! But don't cut back on the knots."

There was laughter from the wardroom congregation. "Captain's digestion's riled up again," snorted one.

Surlina was impressed by the joking informality of the crew toward their commander. As she heard the hissing safety valve die down, she thought how different this relaxed chain-of-command was from the briskly military operations of Sam Grant. What different men they were! Rainbeau so impulsive. Her longing for Sam had been so sure, so compelling; and her tangling with Julien was so spontaneous and made of wildfire. They were entirely different, and her response to each was entirely opposite. She thought, 'By God, I have sides to my nature I never knew!'

She was brought back to the chatter surrounding her; the men were still ribbing their captain. Julien rapped for order by striking his spoon against a metal plate. "Gentlemen, make yourselves presentable. We'll ask this young lady to sit down to corncakes and introductions." He motioned Surlina to sit on the bench to his right.

As she sat down, she brushed against Julien's muscular thigh, feeling his leg as clearly as if she'd grabbed it with her hands. He was already helping himself to sausage and pancakes, but he glanced at her, a surprised smile plying his lips, as if to acknowledge her brazen overture. Oh, he could read so damned much into an accidental touch!

Julien began the introductions by nodding toward a middle-aged man with a shabby brown coat and distant dark eyes. "This is Professor Boxt, our resident classics scholar. He's been prowling the backwoods of Louisiana, looking for plantation columns to draw."

"Sketch," corrected Professor Boxt, his eyes dancing at the chance to speak of his work. "I am collecting New World examples of Athenian and neoclassical statues, such as the hollow, hinged columns at Whispers."

"We found him adrift as we came upstream. He planned last night's raid."

Surlina bristled at the idea that she was confronting the man who had decreed the destruction of her steamer, yet she could say nothing. She put out her hand timidly to pick up a corncake.

"Go on, help yourself," Julien taunted sarcastically. "No servants are going to appear and lay a fresh cloth or bring cut flowers."

"Just coffee, please."

Julien leaned back. "Now, boys, this lady is Miss Surlina Defore, a woman who leaps to shore when grown men hold back afraid."

There were smiles and nods and "hello, ma'am's" in her direction. She tried to distinguish faces, but the crew seemed only a motley collection of raga-muffins ranging from youngsters to the middle-aged Professor Boxt. As the introductions were made, she studied Julien Rainbeau. This morning he looked well fed and well rested. He seemed utterly relaxed and comfortable as he sipped from a blue-enameled mug.

Julien redirected her attention to the greetings as a heavy set man with long jowls rose from the end of the table. He made a short bow over his bulging midriff, then settled back as Julien continued with the introductions; "Father Leonidas Polk."

Due to her convent upbringing, she managed an awkward half-seated curtsy, accompanied by the bobbing of her head. "A priest?" she asked outright.

"Episcopal," he answered. "Ordained of God to ride downriver with this rascal Rainbeau."

Julien said softly, "Father Leonidas is our guest, much to his dismay. He currently outranks everyone here. Father Leonidas Polk is Episcopal bishop of Louisiana and major-general of the Confederate Army." In mock bewilderment, he piously intoned, "How could such a man never have been to sea!"

"Much preferred it that way!" returned the clergy-man enthusiastically. "No offense, Rainbeau."

"Leonidas gets seasick. Curses like an old salt. Paying for his sins." Julien looked directly at Surlina. "How many other Episcopal bishops do you know who march ten thousand troops into neutral territory on a Sunday morning?"

In his own defense Father Polk stated, "It was too cold to preach . . . and Kentucky needed taking." Shouts of "Amen!" filled the room.

"Donlevy! Your turn!" Julien shouted.

Immediately the long-legged boy came bounding into the wardroom. He had the agility of a jackrabbit and a complementary twitchy nose. She recognized him as the gangling lad who had helped her the night before. He grabbed for the last of the corncakes as he seated himself. By the time he'd slid along the bench into seated position, his mouth was full.

"Haloo Donlevy," Julien introduced the boy formally. "A whiz at small-scale ambush and large-scale wagon pilfering."

Surlina glanced at Haloo again, trying to verify such questionable character traits. "How do you do?" she murmured.

Haloo barely nodded and munched corncakes at furious speed. Skittishly he lowered his eyes, apparently embarrassed to be greeted by a female.

"Now, here's a kid with the dew of the Ozarks still wet on his whiskers. Squirrel hunter and bushwhacker are his only credentials. He appeared on my ship's bridge one fine morning, announcing he wanted to 'fight bastards!'" Julien leaned back, watching Haloo and smiling with paternal fondness. "Yep, there he was, wild in the eye and full of corn whiskey. Had a Bowie knife in his teeth and a blunderbuss over the left shoulder. Naturally, I appointed him ordnance officer."

For some reason, Surlina felt sorry for Haloo. His Adam's apple leaped frantically whenever he swallowed. Black whiskers stood out from his spotty face. She felt a bit sorry for herself, too. How could this inexperienced gunner's mate help lead her anywhere but to certain disaster? What if there was activity on the river? The thought made her light-hearted. "Excuse me! I . . . I need air! May I go on deck, Captain?"

She slid stiffly off the bench, muscles still aching. Further, her back and hand retained the sore bruises of her meeting with Captain Rainbeau's boot, her mouth the imprint of his lips.

He showed her the same bluff concern as he had given Haloo. "Ah, Miss Surlina, haven't acquired your sea legs yet? Well, go ahead. But you'll find no easy ride on the *Quail*, not even topside."

Without good-byes, she fled the narrow room smelling of chicory and syrup and rushed through the dim passageway, eyes blurring, head down. Abruptly, she smacked into a dark furry creature. Instinct said she'd met a misplaced bear; reason said it was a shaggy giant. It didn't matter! "Pardon me," she panted, trying to push past.

"Hold on!" Julien's voice boomed behind her. "You've run into our engineer. Here, lift your eyes and say hello! This is Proctor O'Keefe, up from his hellhole to see the day."

No more introductions! Not right now! She gulped against her swimming stomach, attempting to focus on the weaving shoreline. Air! She must find fresh air! But all she inhaled was sweat-soaked leather of a jacket and the swirling fumes of alcohol which wafted from Proctor O'Keefe. He might be a whiz at engines, but his familiarity with bathing was clearly limited.

"Had your snoot in the sauce again, Proc?" asked Julien, launching a good-natured history of his engineer. His story, while moderately interesting, seemed to take forever. "Proctor's a bad fellow," joked Julien. "He plays gin rummy all night, nickel ante all day. Swills rotgut into that barrel belly, then runs my boilers as if they were cotton gins on the Yazoo landing." He leaned against the bulkhead and exchanged affectionate punches with Proctor. "Finest engineer in the fleet, Miss Defore."

"Yes, fine," she gulped.

Again, Surlina was impressed by the unorthodox rapport of captain and crew. To her surprise, she felt a growing pride in Julien. Here was a man of leadership, not merely some yahoo ringleader of joking and joshing. She suddenly felt reassured by the relaxed attitudes on the *Quail*. Somehow the special camaraderie meant special respect for Julien. Unquestioned loyalty. In amazement she, too, felt a tug of loyalty to him.

But she couldn't stand here a second longer! If she remained, she was certain she'd be ill. Using her hands, she thrashed past them, fleeing for the rail.

9

"*Mal de mer* must be a special hell reserved for women who leap from their own ships," muttered Surlina as she lay tossing in the bunk. For two days, off and on, she'd flinched at the odors and motions of the *Quail*. "All in your head," Dottie had insisted and brought her homemade remedies such as ammonia and peppermint. 'Surely today I'll be able to do more than stagger on deck with wobbly knees,' she thought.

She glanced around the little cabin, thinking of the things she wanted to do—investigate the rest of those lovely dresses Dottie had loaned her. There was something intriguing about a wiry old woman of sixty having stacks of frilly bonnets, patchwork skirts, silk blouses and a whole box of tortoise-shell hair combs! Dottie obviously had no use for the feminine attire; she always wore leather boots and khaki pants with a jacket laced like a scout.

Surlina loved pretty clothes, partly because she'd grown up wearing baggy trousers and men's flannel shirts in the Sierras, then utterly simple black two-piece shirtwaists at the convent.

Feeling only slightly more alive than dead, she steadied herself and decided to put on a dimity dress with several rows of ribbons around the skirt. She pulled the dress over her head and adjusted the wide shoulders. As she was tying up the ribbons at the skirt, a new wave of seasickness jolted her. Please, no more! She hesitated, rushed to the porthole, flung it open and let the misty morning air rush over her. From behind her, she heard a knock on the door. "Go away," she called. "Don't bother a dead woman!"

Despite her inhospitable greeting, she heard the door click, followed by the stamp of boots across the stateroom. Surlina turned her head enough to see Julien Rainbeau enter. That irritating man! His sun-tarnished hair gleamed like hazy mist on the yellow river; his smile was as bright as the sunlight and penetrated her with its warmth. She was astounded to see him dressed as if he planned a day in town. Her eyes lingered for only a moment on his lean figure. She must keep her focus on the horizon if she hoped to stave off the undulating motions in her midriff.

"We're off on a shopping trip," he greeted her. "I've come to collect your list of necessities."

"A shopping trip! Where in the world would you—"

"You may come with me. If you'll give up this faking of illness."

"Faking!" She was outraged that he had no sympathy for her distress. "I've been sick for two days, and you have seen fit to ignore my problems entirely! You have about as much compassion as . . . as . . . an Indian!" She gave him a black look. "I *am* sick." To prove her point, she took two wobbly steps and fell across the bunk, face down.

"You're not sick anymore. You're hungry."

"I'm sick!"

"Stop acting like a spoiled child, or I shall spank you! From now on, you can't be sick unless I say so! Now, sit up here and take your medicine. Dottie has sent you some chicory laced with bourbon and a cup of gumbo brimming with pepper sauce."

Surlina moaned at the idea of such a home remedy. In a moment she heard him moving about, stepping outside the door for a second, returning accompanied by the tantalizing yet nauseating smells of coffee, whiskey, fish stew and red pepper. She propped up on her elbow, unwilling to eat the concoctions but hoping to stabilize her head.

"Drink it," he urged. "The fire will burn out whatever's bothering you."

When he spoke to her tenderly, she thought she might do anything for him! She narrowed her eyes, hoping she might be able to swallow more easily if she didn't look at the green okra, red tomatoes and thick brown sauce. He raised the cup to her lips, steadying her with one hand around her neck. "Good," he soothed. "Very encouraging. With a little toddy, you'll find yourself back among the living!"

She sipped the next cup without protest, feeling the bourbon and chicory in her throat like warm syrup. Soon the warmth spread through her, making her slightly dizzy. She put her head back down on the hard pillow.

She felt her legs being jostled and realized that Julien had moved closer. Next she felt the touch of his hand against her back. He rubbed gently, making circles on her tensed shoulders and letting his fingers stroke her neck. What a healing combination back rubs, gumbo and bourbon made! Moment by moment she felt stronger. "You make a fine physician," she complimented him sincerely.

"And you make a pampered mistress who demands far too much of her present accommodations. Now, get up and put on some riding clothes. We're off on a reconnaissance of the Kentucky side."

He was asking too much. "I can't mount a horse. After the *Quail*, my legs and balance would be worthless!"

"Nonsense! You are simply full of caprice, woman! But you've seen the last of cabin service on this cruise. As of today you must begin to earn your keep!" Suddenly he leaned over and planted a kiss on the back of her neck.

Her surprise was compounded by the powerful effect the delicate touch had on her. Such softness! Such slight, lingering pressure! How much more intimate than being devoured face to face. She felt his warm breath near her ears, his fingers touching her hair. Then he placed a feathery kiss behind her ear, another near the temple. She felt herself quiver with excitement. How could she have come from near death to this degree of responsiveness in so short a time! Julien had a way with more than medicine, she smiled to herself.

When she did not withdraw, he took her arm, pushed the honeycomb green sleeve high around her shoulder, and planted a row of little kisses within the warm bend of her elbow. 'It's like a ceremony,' she thought, letting the sensations flow through her. She raised herself to meet him, flinging her arms around his neck, using her fingers to twist the shirt collar away from his skin so she could touch him directly, feel the strength of his spine and the smooth skin behind his ears. "You've saved my life!" she teased. "My dear doctor Rainbeau."

"Then surely you are indebted to me for one *real* kiss. The one I took the other morning did not satisfy either of us. You brushed it aside as if it had no consequence! And I was too intent on teasing you to show I cared." He let his arms slip around her, one resting lightly across the top of her shoulders, the other diagonally across her back, fingers curled around her waist. "This time I'm *asking*, Surlina. From now on, I'll not do anything you don't want me to do."

How charmingly suave! She wanted to kiss him, embrace him wholly, but she'd had no experience in meeting a man halfway.

While she was pondering her answer, he bent his head and placed kisses across the hollow of her throat, stringing them like a row of pearls one by one until he'd circled her ivory skin from ear to ear. He touched the soft lobes with the tip of his tongue, barely moistening them, sending new waves of desire through her. She was astonished at how simply he could possess her. He withdrew her hands from around his neck, stroking each finger with his warm breath, then nipping lightly at the tips. Her fingers began to burn. By the time he bent her back to the pillow, face toward his smiling lips, she felt inflamed.

95

"Yes, yes, Julien! Kiss me!"

Maddeningly, he merely stroked her cheeks, turning his hands so the caress was unhurried as he moved the dark curls away from her forehead. He lingered over her, touching her hairline with his tickling tongue. He spoke to her as if they could stay in this cozy bunk indefinitely. "Let us take time to know each other, Surlina. Fully. You streak through my senses like a shooting star; I cannot seem to capture you completely. Let me breathe in your scent of spice and lilac. Let me—"

She cut him off by raising her mouth to his, denying him nothing of her responses, gripping his shoulders between clenched hands until she felt her wrists throbbing. Something was happening inside her as well, a heaviness giving way to delight. She felt herself a statue suddenly come to life, suffused with a new sweetness in her mouth, nostrils, arms.

"Open your eyes!" he commanded. "Don't you want to see us? The way our eyes laugh and our ears redden and our lips lick playfully at each other? Never hold back from me, my darling! Give me everything! Your intensity! Your passion!" Then he kissed her again, seeking out her depths. His hands moved over her breasts, traveling across the thin dimity to cup each one. Her nipples stood rigid and the flesh around them felt tender, rising and falling as he began a tiny motion of lifting and releasing.

This time, when he parted his mouth from hers, he laughed with his old scoundrel tones. "By damn! I *shall* become a physician if this is the cure I can perform on young maidens!"

Surlina threw the pillow at his face, catching his wrist and twisting it. "No one would call for you! Who wants a surgeon who is a deceiver and a devil!" She escaped from him, pushing his strong shoulders playfully, scampering away as he lunged for her. "Now— out! The shopping trip you talked of does not include my virtue!" She laughed loudly, hearing her voice teasing as his. Oh, how well suited they were, able to torment with their jibes, wage battle with their eyes and surrender with their lips! Surely they'd never deny each other anything. "Are we stopping on the Kentucky shore near a telegraph office? I must send a message to my sister."

"My dear," he murmured, rising and straightening his shirt and adjusting the buttons of his vest, "I wouldn't trust you for a moment near a telegraph contraption! You'd have the *Quail* blown out of the water before we reached the next bend in the Mississippi!"

Surlina was horrified at the scorn and distrust he exuded. A few hot moments ago, she'd have trusted him with her chastity! No, no, he only wanted to use her, to draw her into his world of hostility. "I have no wish to accompany you on any raids, Julien Rainbeau! You're no more going shopping than to a parade! You're going *stealing*—and that's the straight and pure of it!"

He stood in the doorway, apparently half-angry and half-amused. "Surlina, you do not understand me at all. I am hardly of the charmed class of Southern aristocrats who drink juleps for breakfast and duel at dusk. I have *work* to do!"

"I know what you are! I've seen your planter's clothes, heard Dottie's stories of Whispers' sugar plantation."

"Did Dottie mention that Whispers' house and land belong to my cousin Ramsey Arnauld?"

The other nephew. Surlina remembered the name. "I thought he was on board. I haven't met him. And if he's related to you in your deceitful ways, I don't care to!"

Julien was thoughtful, stroking his chin with lean fingers. "We are worlds apart, Surlina; more than I thought. You climbed aboard this boat protesting you were a chambermaid. Yet every inch of you insists you are a woman of privilege and power. Well, I too am not what I appear. I belong to what the Yankees think does not even exist in the South—the working class." He picked up the half-empty cup and drained the cold chicory and bourbon. "My in-laws, Ramsey and his crew, are welcome to Whispers. My father did honest

97

labor in a sawmill, and I have made my way with the merchant fleet."

He leaned back, melancholy sloping his shoulders and a faraway look locking his eyes on the porthole and beyond. "Ah, yes, Whispers. I presume it's still there. But my ties to it through my childhood were all on my mother's side. She was a belle." He stood abruptly, a frown pulling the creases around his eyes downward. "She died when I was thirteen. Yellow fever. After that, I lived with my father at the sawmill."

"And the Naval Academy blanket?" She remembered the question she had meant to ask for days.

"Three years at Annapolis. Then economics dictated that I apprentice with the merchant fleet." Again he looked away. "There was an accident—"

"Landing party ready to go ashore," a voice rang out from the passageway. The noise startled them both.

'I am Surlina Defore, a neutral Missourian,' she told herself sternly. 'Whatever the *Quail*'s captain is up to on the Kentucky shore is not my affair!' Neutrality! She must cling to it; yet she felt it slipping away like yarn through a spinning wheel. How could her feelings vacillate so?

Surlina moved on deck to watch the glistening green shore through the sparkling spring mist. Less than five days ago, she'd danced with shy Sam Grant in the *Radiant* grand salon. Yet this morning she'd been quite content to let a Confederate river runner drive the seasickness from her body with his warm kisses. She thought guiltily of her father, perhaps in danger from failing health. Thad Muller wouldn't be above murder when he found Peter Defore without money to buy loyalty. Again she worried about her father's foolhardy idea of removing the silver.

If only she could have gone ashore and sent a telegram to Tandy! But that was silly. Tandy would surely show a cable to her husband. Then that damned Thayer Cabell would do everything in his power to secure the silver for the South. Each time Surlina held these discussions with herself, there was an inescapable

98

conclusion. She must rely only on herself, hurry to New Orleans and take charge of the Erlanger account.

She went to the rail on the port side, watching two rowboats toss on the yellow river. Julien and Dottie were in one.

Haloo Donlevy stopped by her side. "They should have took me if they wanted moonshine! I can smell a still a mile and three-quarters away!"

"Moonshine whiskey! Is that what they're after?"

He nodded. "They'll buy it, beg it, borrow it, steal it or kill for it. Turn around and trade it to anybody as wants it in return for a little spy work. A gulp or two of moonshine'll open a man's lips better'n a crowbar," volunteered Haloo.

She thought of herself swigging chicory and bourbon and then responding to Julien's advances. "A woman's too," Surlina agreed. "Who are the other two swindlers—the ones in the farthest rowboat?"

"That's master Ramsey Arnauld—the tall white man. And that little black boy is his fellow, Kuffy."

She squinted, trying to see the elegant Ramsey Arnauld, owner of Whispers. He must be a distinguished aristocrat, to take his slave along stealing!

Surlina turned her eyes to Julien again. As she watched him rowing for shore, his arm muscles bulging through his shirt, she smiled to herself. Julien Rainbeau somehow saw things other men's eyes missed. He'd somehow seen that an unlikely Ozark boy would make an ordnance officer. A classics professor found sketching in the swamps and an Irish cotton ginner would make sailors. An Episcopal bishop could be a man of battle as well as faith. And somehow Julien had seen in her the woman she'd always hoped to be. He'd seen it without being blinded by knowledge of her fortune. The wind stirred and left a rippling through her soul. When the time came to leave him, he'd see right through her!

While the *Quail* was anchored, several other landing parties paddled ashore. Proctor O'Keefe, a flask in his hip pocket and a gun in his hand, led a hunting expedition. Donlevy climbed atop the pilothouse and kept lookout, his rifle across his gangly legs. Professor Boxt quietly slipped away with three men in search of forage. Slowly Surlina began to understand that the *Quail* had no sure supply of anything—not food, armament, uniforms or sailors.

Before she could sit down to ponder her future, she heard Haloo's running footsteps. "Yankees! Yankees! Hard on shore!"

She stood transfixed, terrified that somehow Sam Grant's disorganized troops had caught up with her. For an instant she thought of diving overboard from the *Quail* as she had done from the *Radiant*. Fight—that's what she must do. Her folding dagger was in her cabin. She took off running, watching the shore.

A party of riders rushed headlong toward the ship, two tall soldiers and two short ones. Haloo and his sharpshooters were lining the rail, preparing to pepper the invaders.

The horses slowed, trying to get a footing in the looser gravel of the shoreline. "Ready!" cried Haloo, excitement making his voice rough as a rasp.

"Wait! No! That's Julien!" Surlina heard her words almost before she'd recognized the golden hair beneath the brimmed blue cap.

"Hold your fire!" Haloo ordered, studying the riders who were now hastily dismounting, slapping the horses to scatter them, then running toward the rowboats hidden in the weeds. "That's no enemy!" confirmed Haloo in amazement. Soon the entire crew lined the deck, cheering. Kuffy, the young black boy, was attired in full colonel's regalia, the pants rolled up around his bare ankles and the epaulets dangling over his narrow nine-year-old shoulders. Dottie's khaki pants shone out from under a dress cloak of Yankee blue. Ramsey and Julien wore Union jackets and clutched extra pairs of breeches under their arms. All four culprits floundered ankle-deep through the willows and water. From their haste, it seemed that the former owners of the clothes might not be far behind.

The adventurers paddled rapidly to the *Quail*, throwing the loot upward to waiting hands, scrambling aboard breathlessly.

"Round up the others," Julien called, leaping the boarding ladder. "We must head downriver at once!" He tossed his stolen jacket toward Surlina, who let it drop on the deck. She had no use for clothing which might contain lice or vermin. "Excellent camouflage, which you'll need before the night is out," he said quickly.

Everyone was straining to hear his news. "Activity over the second hill," he announced. "A camp, deserted at the moment. Probably a regrouping point. Cavalry units in the woods. We heard them and took leave with some of the extra horses."

"Forces in strength, Captain?" asked Haloo. "A fight in the offing?" His Adam's apple bobbed with excitement.

"No. I think we found ourselves in the middle of a scuffle between the Yankee army and some deserters. Look how these uniforms have been stripped of insignia and patches."

Deserters in the woods! Surlina shivered at the idea that Muller might have found friends along the Kentucky shore. Could he have made it this far? "Was there any sign of an old man?" she asked suddenly. "Someone aged and ill—" Her voice broke.

Julien's stare caused her to flinch. "You keep tabs on camps of deserters? Your interest runs to bands of renegades who rape and murder?"

"My father is traveling overland," she said weakly, afraid to tell more.

The hunting party hailed from shore, holding up rabbits and doves. "Signal the foraging party, too," Julien insisted. "With activity this close, we must make Caledonia Bend by dusk. We must warn the Confederate stronghold at Island Number Ten that trouble is on the way!"

By evening, the excitement aboard the *Quail* had dimmed to fretful watchfulness. Surlina tucked the Union jacket around her new outfit of Dottie's cast-off khaki trousers, long wool stockings and boots.

The *Quail* slowed in the fading light, making its way cautiously. A mist rose turning the decks slippery and cold. Everyone was busy, and Surlina was ignored in the bustle. "Where are we heading?" she asked Father Polk when she found him alone on the stern.

"Ultimately to Tiptonville, some thirty miles downriver, where the other Confederate ships will gather. But tonight, in accordance with our Captain's penchant for danger, we will circle back upstream to see what the Union fleet looks like."

"Upstream! Good God!" she uttered, forgetting to restrict her language. *"What the hell . . . !"*

"My feelings exactly," he assured her.

She was nervous the rest of the evening. Supper was an affair of turtle, turnip tops and hardtack biscuits. 'Dottie might be rated a marvelous cook aboard the *Quail* but she'd never win accolades in St. Louis restaurants,' thought Surlina, excusing herself after a few bites.

She heard music! She was certain she heard the lively sounds of an accordion as she made her way toward the bow. Who was lighting up this dim twilight with chords of a sweet Stephen Foster tune? How different from her ship's orchestra aboard the *Radiant,* but how wonderful! She followed the sound to a closed stateroom door.

At that moment, a tenor voice called, "Spies should not clomp their boots. Come in, whoever you are."

She entered, thinking perhaps she'd only peek, then was startled to see a handsome thin-faced man stretched languorously across the built-in couch. He did not look up except to cock his head, then continued playing deftly, his slim fingers touching the keys lightly. The instrument responded under his touch like a living thing, bending, sighing, singing. Every movement of his arms was sensuous, lithe and slow. Elegant. Disdainful. Aloof. A man in complete control of his instrument, forcing from it precisely the rhythm he wanted. His eyes were sea-green, like the ocean in winter, his lips thin like his neck. He seemed intent on only his music. But he motioned her to join him with his head, stating matter of factly, "So we meet at last. You're Surlina of the swampland above Cairo, I presume. I am Ramsey Darveau Basketby Arnauld of the bayous below New Orleans."

Ramsey. She'd known from his height and elegance it must be Julien's cousin—the one who owned the ancestral mansion; and the one who stood lowest in Dottie's estimation. What was it that attracted her and at the same time repelled her? He appeared so fastidious, almost prissy in the tidily arranged room. She felt prickles of antagonism raise the flesh on the back of her neck. At the same time, she felt that his stroking, sensitive hands might mold her to do his bidding.

She tried to make conversation. "So, you're the musical ghost of the *Quail!*" She didn't like the cool way his eyes roved over her, calmly and openly lingering on her ankles, hips, waist and breasts. "I'm surprised we haven't met until now. But I've missed most of the meals, getting my sea legs."

"I avoid the wardroom and that riffraff. Kuffy cooks for me. Simple things—an omelet, a mushroom pie, a bit of onion soup."

She was disgusted with his disdain for the rest of Julien's crew. Here was a man more intent on his own comforts than being part of a concentrated effort. She sensed he could be charming, urbane, sophisticated, ingratiating and utterly without principle! "You play beautifully," she acknowledged, indicating the accordion.

"And not only this," he replied. He fingered the

103

keyboard and let a few notes squeeze from the instrument. "I pluck these notes as I pluck life's other excitements." He pouted his lips and repeated pluck with lascivious, earthy insinuation. "Are you ripe for plucking, my budding beauty?"

"I see now that the diplomatic corps has a way with words," she said coldly.

He shrugged indifferently. "I usually have a way with women. Most find it more pleasant to join me than to resist." His calm sensuality fascinated her, reminding her of a snake sliding up on its prey.

"Wouldn't you care to be seated?" he said softly, patting his bulging pants to indicate the arrangement he had in mind.

Suddenly there was noise in the passageway, and the dark silhouette of a man filled the open entry. "Julien!" she cried with relief.

Julien's gray eyes took in the scene of Ramsey stretched on the couch, accordion at his side, aroused hardness in his trousers, Surlina standing facing him, her cheeks flushed. Her blurted comment, "I came to hear the music!" did nothing to allay his suspicions.

Ramsey made no effort to rise. "Would you like a drink, Cousin?"

"Such a gentleman!" snorted Julien, obviously straining to contain his anger. "Always the amenities!"

Surlina sensed more than competition between the men. They traded pleasant insults as if the jests were not to be taken seriously, but she felt them capable of killing each other under other circumstances. Ramsey lit a cigar, let it dangle provocatively from his thin lips, then used it to trace patterns in the air. He flipped an ash in Surlina's direction while addressing his question to Julien. "What have you required of this young sojourner as the price of passage?"

Surlina felt like an animal on the auction block, about to be presented to the highest bidder.

Ramsey continued in dulcet tones. "If you'd give her to me for a week, I think I could remove some of that annoying haughtiness from around her mouth and eyes."

"Ramsey, I've tolerated as much of your predatory jokes as I can. By God, I'll be glad to see you off the *Quail* and headed for Pittsburg Landing!"

Ramsey purred, "I do not think we have seen the full measure of this woman's capabilities."

"Enough!"

"Have you explored that exquisite flesh hiding beneath that abominable jacket? How were her breasts? Abundant and nourishing? Or stunted like the teats on a dried-up cow?"

"Stop it!" Surlina found her voice.

"There, there," soothed Ramsey. "No need to display your temper! Don't let this jesting between men—"

"Tomcats, you mean! Both of you!" She shouted back. "A pair of rutting tomcats!"

Abruptly Ramsey reached for his accordion and began a bawdy rendition of a popular song.

Surlina did not stay to hear more. She'd heard coarse talk in the mining camps, been exposed to the snickers and jibes of the workers in the shipyard sheds, but never had she encountered a man like Ramsey, who seemed to delight in crudeness covered with a veneer of breeding. Those leaf-green eyes were merciless in their probing, his thin lips cruel in their teasing.

She heard Julien and Ramsey continue to banter in satiric voices as she fled. "Let me have my way with her, Julien," sneered Ramsey. "I have never required innocence of my women. Nor docility. Nor timidity. Those qualities are much overrated . . . as you should know."

Julien's voice had a laughing hiss as he replied, "From her I would require much, much more! I warn you, Cousin, if you continue, prepare to have your dueling pistol in working order!"

When darkness fell, Julien tied the *Quail* to the shore. Despite the rain, everything movable was hauled on deck.

Surlina noticed that the impeccable Ramsey was absent from the night's dirty work. She was just as glad. She didn't care to confront his green eyes and insinuating tongue again. She thought him selfish not to lend a hand to the physical labor. Diplomatic corps! Ha!

She buried her budding hatred of Ramsey by flinging herself into clearing the galley of anything which might come loose in a battle. Dottie watched Surlina's furious activity for a moment, then inquired, "What's put the bee in your bustle, girlie?"

"Ramsey Darveau Basketby Arnauld!" Surlina recited, banging copper pots together like cymbals to indicate the clash that had infuriated her.

"He does that to people," laughed Dottie. "Look at him tonight—sleeping soundly while we tear down the ship around him."

"I don't like him," Surlina commented.

"Neither do I," said Julien, his voice startling her by its closeness. She turned to see him standing behind her, just outside the galley, rain streaking his face.

She stepped out into the rain beside him. "Then why do you tolerate him aboard? Do you have to provide him with transportation at the expense of your honor?"

"I'm merely captain of this ship, not master of my fate." He made a half-bow, imitating Ramsey's lithe diffidence. "I go where sent. I take whom I'm told to take. We'll be rid of him soon. He'll be off to Shiloh." He hurried away, calling "Underway in fifteen minutes. On course for Island Number Ten."

Surlina was staring after him when Father Polk approached her. "Do you realize how brave he is to make the dash upriver? What imagination! He proposes to pay a call on the Union fleet, circle them like a hawk, then fly to Island Number Ten with the warning."

"It sounds more foolhardy than brave."

"He's a daredevil, all right, but a brave and determined one. He endangers his command when, ultimately, it may not make any difference. Despite his brilliant ideas, he won't please his superiors."

Tartly she replied, "It does not please *me*."

From out of the fog came Julien's voice. "You do not care to die for the Confederate cause?"

"Absolutely not!" she assured him emphatically, unable to find him in the total darkness. "And furthermore, it never occurred to me that the way to New Orleans lay any direction except *down*stream."

At dawn, fog continued to shroud the immense, swollen river. Surlina was on deck, too excited to stay shielded. Haloo had rigged some ominous-appearing "scare guns"—stovepipes and logs which looked like mounted guns. Wet blankets covered the ammunition magazines.

Silent and shrouded in the fog, they steamed back and forth across the river.

"Be ready to step lively, boys," Julien suddenly shouted. "We're in for a warm reception." With that, he ordered "Hard aport," and the ship went reeling, throwing Surlina sideways into the pilothouse.

When she got up, she saw the Union ship as clearly as if the two were tied together. The *Quail* continued to peel around, then began to heave and yaw, making screeching sounds as it flirted with death.

Surlina felt a shudder over her head, followed by a crash as artillery answered the *Quail*'s audacious approach. She dropped to her knees, peered out again and found she could read *Benton* on the Union ship dead ahead. Again, Julien veered at the last moment, running so fast and close to the Yankee boat that it could not spin off a shot.

Then she heard an explosion nearby, smashing her teeth together and shaking her head as if it would never stop. When Surlina regained the use of her eyes, she saw fire. Already sailors were working to put it out. She rushed on deck to help, although smoke burnt her nostrils with its powdery odor. As she fought through the haze she stumbled over something. "Haloo!" Immediately she bent over the writhing form. "Quick! Help!" Surlina called, reaching for the boy to stop his thrashing. She rolled him onto his back. He doubled up in pain, but made no sound. His face was covered with deep scratches from the explosion and powder burns which scorched his flesh. She grabbed a wet blanket and threw it over him.

By the time others came to carry him below, Surlina realized that the ship was heading downriver once again. Safety! Success!

Captain Rainbeau was obviously thrilled with his escapade. Despite the continuing thunderstorms, he seemed incapable of slowing down. The *Quail* ran with throttles open, the safety valves hissing like a nest of snakes. In contrast to the noisy ship, the crew went about their duties in muffled quiet, their concern for Haloo apparent in the constant check kept on the galley where Dottie tended him.

When Island Number Ten appeared, Surlina saw black parapets looming through the drizzle like openings of caves. The walled fortifications rose straight up, surrounded by a maze of defensive breastworks. The *Quail* flashed its signals with red and green lanterns; then Professor Boxt came on deck to communicate with semaphore flags.

The bad news circled the ship the moment it came across the water: Father Polk was to go ashore to command a retreat.

"What will happen to him now?" Surlina asked Julien, waving good-bye to Father Polk as the dinghy pulled away.

"He will sacrifice himself. He is a big man, but his task is inhuman!"

11

"It's time we made haste to New Orleans!" Surlina ordered Julien after a serene day in which the *Quail* had moved barely ten miles downstream.

Julien spread his river charts across his desk, remarking smartly, "You are a notable grouch, Surlina Defore!"

"You promised! After Island Number Ten, you said we'd be heading for the Gulf." She was slightly uncertain how to hold him to his word. She feared he might pull into some secluded backwater and evict her in strange territory. "We're only a day south of Memphis! At this rate I'll see fall frost before I see the Crescent City. Oh, Julien, you don't understand how important it is to me to hurry!"

He looked at her with mischief in his gray eyes. The increasing warmth and humidity of the days made his sideburns curl charmingly. "Does your life depend on it?" he asked.

"No," she admitted. "But my father's might. For a man who seemed hell-bent on tearing the bottom from his ship to get a peek at the Union fleet, you now seem to have suffered a serious slowdown."

"You have still not revealed your real reasons for traveling to New Orleans. If you had been so intent on parting company with me, you could have gone ashore at Memphis."

"Hardly! With the railroad lines cut both directions from there, it's a city living inside a moat! I must go to New Orleans," she continued, "and you are taking an inordinate amount of time heading South! It's as if you are trying to prevent me from reaching there and aiding my father."

"I know nothing of those matters, as you have chosen not to confide in me. Even if you had, your personal timetables are of less concern than military ones. We shall continue to proceed slowly until word comes to send Ramsey ashore."

"Ramsey! Ramsey! Everyone acts as if he runs this show! What kind of hold does that overbearing man have on all of you?"

"He owns us, Surlina." Julien looked up from his charts. "He owns our land, our houses, our livestock. It was his money which bought and outfitted this boat. If we jump to do his bidding, it's a matter of self-preservation."

"He is an ass and should be treated as such."

Julien's laughter was like water gurgling from a spring. "Actually, I hardly know him, thank God!"

"But he's your cousin!"

109

"He's a descendant of Chateaubriand, 1791." He made Ramsey sound like a bottle of wine.

She dropped the subject, talking about the river, about him. "The Mississippi is more than some body of water. It has a spirit. And you, Julien . . . I'm only starting to understand your part in all this." She felt an upsurge of desire, wanted to caress him, hold him, understand him completely.

He looked up as she stifled the trembling which ran through her body. His eyes crinkled at the corners as if he were trying to make out the shape of shadows on the moon. He put out his hand and she reached for it, then froze, as he extended it past her, catching Squeebob. He held the cat in his arms, scratching its ears. "You have finally hit on a truth, Surlina. You *don't* understand my part in this war."

"I don't want to talk about war, Julien! Just get me to New Orleans!" She could hear her heart beating in her ears. Why did he hold that damned cat close against his heart when it was she who needed him! She lashed out at him to cover her feeling of rejection. "Something else bothers me, too. You only study the river charts one day ahead. Don't you want to know what's to follow?"

"I try not to peer around the bends of the future."

Surlina was worried: she thought it a dangerous—possibly fatal--weakness in his judgment. He seemed unable to contemplate the river as a whole that stretched two thousand miles south to the Gulf. He could only see the narrow span upon which he floated at the moment.

She sat down, chin in hands, then braced her elbows on the desk, her feet tapping a heavy rhythm, her eyes closed in concentration. Sam had been so different! He'd studied the river as if to digest every inch from Minnesota to Head of the Passes.

Yes, Julien was very different from the methodically brilliant Sam Grant. Yet she had found herself honestly responsive to both men, to the way they wielded authority, to the way they touched her physically. She remembered the steady desire Sam had fostered within

110

her, a well of emotion only he could fill. And now Julien, so earnestly daredevil, had brought fire to her blood with his kisses and yearning to her body with his intriguing hints of love.

"Strategy is what you need," she couldn't resist saying. "You must study your charts further ahead or—"

"Or end up as crow bait?" It seemed he refused to be serious, preferring to play with the cat. "Strategy. Let's see. Yours would be forthright and bold, obviously. Attack head-on. Mine, on the other hand, would seem devious and underhanded."

"You must change! Oh, Julien, you must! Or all Dottie's talk about being dead by thirty-five will come true." She put her hands out to him. "I can feel it!" She shivered convulsively, appalled to find that she actually feared the superstition. "Oh, God, I do believe it!"

"Fortunately, I don't!" He pushed aside the cat ignoring its mewing. Gently he drew Surlina into his arms. "Now our fortunes are inexorably twined. And while we are bound like this, it is time to ascertain your politics once and for all."

"I'm neutral," she said hastily, hoping to avoid discussion.

"That's what I expected of you, Surlina, ducking the issue. Oh, it's fine for me to fall tantalizingly in love with you, but you want everything on your own terms. I have no way of knowing if you're a spy sent to harass me with your charms."

"I'm neutral!"

"You could be wealthy, for all I know. Or you could be some wayward wife running away from an ogre who kept you in chains."

"Hardly," she laughed, hoping to tease him out of his questions. "I have nothing to confess as regards marriage or politics."

He was not to be put off. "Whose side are you on, Surlina? My question is straightforward, and so must your answer be. Whose side are you on?"

"No one's!"

111

He swept her against him greedily, like a man intent on exploiting a rich vein of gold. The rough stubble of his whiskers rasped her tender cheeks; his long golden eyelashes fluttered against her lids. He kissed her fiercely, with hunger and restlessness. Then he thrust her away. "Whose side are you on? Say out straight and clear, woman!"

"No one's!" She felt the tension between them stretched taut. "Oh, Julien! How can you touch me this way to my very core and yet demand what I cannot give!"

Again he kissed her, searching her body with his hands as if to find the secret spot of her vulnerability. She answered with the fire in her lips and the surging strength in her arms, clasping him to her with ardor. He wedded his thighs against her, the muscular power violating her resolve to resist him. She trembled with the frantic desire to hold him forever. She wanted him, he wanted her—how could anything keep them apart!

But even as she returned his fervent kisses, she knew the terrible answer. A hundred foolish reasons would interfere . . . and two good ones: love and money. Love and money would be incompatible when the fortune belonged to the Silver Belle and the need belonged to a Confederate river captain. She clung to him. "Julien, I do so need your arms around me, but I fear for us!"

"Darling, darling, don't be a coward. Our worst fears are imaginary, like that silly family curse on the Rainbeaus." His eyes were swimming in tenderness, gray as the sky when the last sunset ray fades to night. He jammed her against the wall, stripping the stiff cambric from her throat. He whispered, "Do you want me, Surlina? Are your emerald eyes dusky because of desire? Does your ivory throat turn pink because of me?" He held her tightly, till she felt his hardness wedging at the gauze petticoats.

"I want you," she whispered, "but—"

"No!" he roared. "Goddammit, want me without any ifs, ands, or buts!"

Suddenly Surlina was afraid she might never know

112

his lips lingering upon her nipples, his fiery tongue within her cleft. He would always be rich with lust and quick with anger, always just outside the limits of her understanding. She throbbed with the frustration of exhilaration gone awry.

For a moment he stood back, surveying her through slitted eyes. "Oh, I see, madam. You want me, but not as much as you want to argue politics."

He whirled on his heel, pausing only long enough at the door to plant an imaginary kiss on his palm and blow it into the cabin. Both she and the cat jumped, attempting to capture his fleeting affection.

The *Quail* sailed on top of a watery world. Arkansas and Mississippi rolled away behind the levees like wide bolts of green fabric striped with black bayous.

"Tell me more about Whispers," Surlina asked Dottie as they polished pots.

"Whispers sets with its face to the sea and its back to the bayou. Big house with a copper dome and tall, hollow statues around the porticos. No way in 'cept through the West Wind Gates. Osage orange grows all over the place. Smells like you done died and gone to heaven!" She stacked the copper lids, all the handles neatly upright. Then she offset her tidy instincts by spitting tobacco juice toward the porthole . . . and missing.

"Someday I'll come visit you there," vowed Surlina, using the bottom of a bright skillet as a mirror. She thought her face looked thinner on this diet of corn-meal and pepper sauce.

"Polish the pot, child! *You* don't need no tending to." Dottie sidled closer, making a shield of pans. "You captured that boy yet, Surlina?"

"If you mean Julien, he's more trouble than I can say grace over!"

Dottie nodded, adding, "Yep, tangle with him and you'd end up in more trouble than a sow with a lost piglet. You still in some race for New Orleans?"

"I must get there! My sister needs me," Surlina lied. "My father is ill and traveling overland. Dottie, could

113

an old man make it from Cairo to New Orleans in less than a month?"

"Sure. Provided he's in a coffin and don't have no need to eat! Speaking of eating, I think we need to vary the menu. Too many corncakes cloud the complexion. There'll be a woodyard stop at Greenville. I'm gonna get off there and fetch some eatables."

Promptly at two, when the *Quail* nudged the Greenville dock, Dottie packed off toward the nearest patch of timber, carrying her rifle.

When she returned a couple of hours later, she had an owl slung over her shoulder, and immediately called for Julien. Surlina eavesdropped.

"I got some mighty interesting information for you that I picked up while I was out hunting," Dottie told him as soon as he joined her.

"What's that, Dottie? I hope it's better than that thing you shot. Do you really expect us to eat that?"

"Yes, I do. Now hush up and listen," she ordered. "I met two fellers out there who told me a couple of things. Seems a bunch of deserters got together under some fella named Muller, and they've been terrorizing the riverbanks hereabouts."

Surlina, who had joined them, gasped. It went unnoticed, however, as Julien was listening intently to Dottie's next bit of news.

"They said Grant's been sent to command the Yankees at Shiloh."

"Grant!" Surlina's hands went to her mouth in a moment of surprise. "At Shiloh? Where's that?"

"A few miles south of Pittsburg Landing, on the Tennessee," Julien answered.

A flash of intuition told her she'd be safe from Muller with Sam Grant. Yet she had no idea how to get to Shiloh. Besides, she thought ruefully, her duty lay with Tandy in New Orleans. As she came to this conclusion, she noticed Dottie looking at her. In an effort to hide her interest in Sam Grant, Surlina asked, "Didn't you say Ramsey was going to Shiloh?"

"Right after supper," Julien said with a note of

satisfaction in his voice, apparently relieved to be getting rid of his cousin for the time being.

By suppertime, Surlina had composed herself. She had grouped her brunette curls into soft dark waves. Also, she had asked Kuffy to go ashore and find her some wildflowers.

He'd smiled and been delighted to go, telling her how much he missed the black earth and how much he feared the yellow river. She determined to tell Ramsey to send the little boy home where he belonged. Imagine dragging a nine-year-old child off to war! Kuffy had returned with wild purple violets and a dainty sprig of Queen Anne's lace. For supper she wore the bouquet at her waist.

True to her word, Dottie served the owl. Ramsey, who was making a rare appearance in the wardroom, blanched at the sight of the bird. "Unbearably tough," he commented when presented with a small piece. "Undeniably tainted." He laid down his fork and folded his hands.

The others ate timidly. Julien ducked his head and gobbled his portion in two bites, hardly stopping to chew.

"Another rumor of the day," he began, and all heads turned in his direction. "The talk in the Greenville tobacco shed was that Farragut is in the Gulf, already over the main bars and into the mouth of the river, fifty miles south of New Orleans."

Aghast at the idea that the city might fall before she could arrive, Surlina immediately joined the conversation. "Can he take New Orleans alone?" Suddenly she felt squeezed between two bad choices: change direction and attempt to find her father, or continue south and hope to spirit Tandy and the silver out before Farragut closed the escape route.

Ramsey said coolly, "The answer is yes. Farragut can indeed take New Orleans—like a man taking a woman against her will. New Orleans will scream, wring its hands, but eventually spread its legs."

Why did Ramsey always put everything in a sexual context! She raised her eyes to meet his, hoping to show she couldn't be shocked. He smiled at her with slightly parted lips, his cold eyes unblinking. 'He's like a marble statue,' she thought, 'all beautifully chiseled, but cold and indifferent.'

Julien was not aware of the little interchange and Surlina was glad. She'd much prefer Ramsey to dislike her openly rather than exude this devious hostility. His thin lips were almost the color of pale coral, his nails shiny with buffing, his eyelids as calm as a man intent on gazing at a woman. She did not want to think of what it would be like to lie in bed with him.

Instead, she forced her attention back to the discussion of Farragut's fleet. Julien's drawl was sharpened as he spoke with precision. "He has two fleets, actually. Twenty-four schooners and seventeen warships."

"Does New Orleans have *no* protection?" she cried, now genuinely worried about Tandy. And the silver was dear to her, too.

"Virtually no protection at all," answered Ramsey. "About like a virgin in a whorehouse—what she has won't last long. A man with a sudden desire and one thing on his mind can part her from her protection in moments." He sat back, curling his fingers around a cigarette, blowing smoke in the air. "She'll bleed, then embrace him."

Surlina turned on the bench, hoping to put Ramsey out of sight. "Julien, how long will it take Farragut to occupy the city?"

"Lovell has three thousand disorganized Confederate troops. Farragut has marines and the aid of his half-brother David Porter. The odds are with the Union."

She was impatient. "How long? Six months? Six weeks?"

"About a day and a half!"

"I must get there immediately! Ahead of Farragut."

He reached for her hand, then let his own hover above it. "I can get you there," he admitted, "but it will be impossible to get you out again."

She knew what he was saying with his questioning gray eyes—would she tend to her business in New

Orleans and then return? Suddenly the thought of taking Tandy to Europe hung like a noose around her neck. How miserable she was, concealing her real identity, and how hopeless she felt it would be to announce that she was the Silver Belle, the woman with enough wealth to influence the outcome of the war.

The moment of uncertainty passed. Julien glanced away abruptly as if he'd been rejected. 'No, no,' she thought, stung by his sudden avoidance of her eyes, 'don't put a veil between us!'

Ramsey interrupted her thoughts by making his formal good-byes. She murmured, "Safekeeping, Ramsey," without looking at him.

Julien's humming skipped like a stone across water. "Ha, ha, ha! Safekeeping! Don't worry about my cousin, Surlina! Ramsey's sense of warfare is perfect —for the last century, that is. Damn their thick skulls, the diplomatic corps still wants to fight set-piece battles, a la Napoleon!" He slapped Ramsey on the back. "Drill! Eighteenth-century drill! That's your idea of splendid warfare, isn't it?"

Surlina perked up, anxious to hear what the impeccable Ramsey would offer in defense of his antiquated ideas, but he got no chance. Julien continued musing aloud. "Drill is gone! You fools haven't realized it. Set-piece battles have passed into history."

"And what has taken its place?" she asked, intrigued by his military philosophy.

"Siege. Siege is the new word that will work in this war. Trenches. Making the most of civilization's advances. Using railroads, telegraphs, submarines, Gatling guns, land mines, nurses." He stopped, studied her a moment, then asked, "How keenly do these things interest you?"

She lied quickly, "Not at all! I am a neutral civilian."

"My God, woman! Don't bore me with that story again!" But as he took her arm, he let his eyes meet hers. His eyes shone as if a blindfold had suddenly been pulled away and he could see her clearly. As they

117

went on deck to bid Ramsey farewell, he kept his hand possessively around her sleeve. She sensed a new dimension to Julien—an aura of loss, that somehow he'd been a man deprived of things he'd held dear to his heart. She promised him with her whole being, 'You'll not lose me, my darling. You'll not lose me!'

12

At last! New Orleans lay only one more day downstream, around a few more of those wide arcs of water. Already the scent of the river had changed to one of brine, mixing its heavy waters full of silt with the surges of ocean which rushed inland to meet it. The delta country was crisscrossed with cypress groves, moss hanging from their stately branches like bridal veils. The sky clouded in the afternoon, then was washed by a violent thunderstorm which sent the *Quail* tossing. Afterward the sun set, resembling a thousand campfires. The night wrapped the river in elegant black satin. The lights of the city ahead appeared twinkling like stars rising from the earth. Surlina stood alone on the bow, watching the shoreline's flickers.

Julien came to stand beside her, quiet, a few polite paces away. His face seemed to have lost its tan in the white glare of the moonlight.

"What is it?" she asked, standing close to him.

"The ocean. Sometimes it is like a spray of memories hurtling at me." To her amazement, he began to talk of the sea, of the sourness of kelp, teeming fish, and stars, spindrift and sultry seasons. His brashness dropped away. No longer did he have the jocular crudeness of his crew, no more spinning yarns of sporting adventures on sea and shore. To her surprise, he was quite as serious as she.

"Why did you come back here?" she asked softly.

"You've spent your life at sea. Why come back here to fight?"

"There are people here, both living and dead, whom I love." His voice sounded as if it were hard to make such a confession. "In the end, I found I could not raise my hand against my birthplace."

"Don't talk politics tonight," she pleaded. "What rational man, North or South, would pride himself on striking his homeland? Or making a cargo of innocents like Kuffy?" Her carefully neutral voice nearly gave way as she thought of the true pawns in this conflict—the children like a little black boy carrying his elegant master's satchel, the misguided wives like Tandy carrying her head high with blind allegiance to a scoundrel husband, the Dottie McDunes forced to scavenge, scrape and steal to provide food.

"The man who stands his ground is the stronger," Julien said.

"Then you came back to bear arms because of geography? For places like Whispers? Can any amount of soil be worth the bloodshed you'll help perpetuate?"

Suddenly he was questioning her fiercely. "Who can say my love of nation is less because I could not strike my home ground?" He paced in long strides, arms swinging. "The South! The South!"

So, after all was said and done, he was as hotheaded a rebel as the rest! "Stop, Julien! I don't want to hear more!"

But he would not be stopped. "The South—God, yes, she's right—and for all the wrong reasons!"

"Don't talk of war! I know nothing of it and don't want to learn! I can't understand such division. I grew up in the territories, in isolated places so alien I shudder to remember them." She clasped her hands to her ears as if to avoid hearing. "I know nothing of this North and South business!"

"My South is a terrible place."

"Terrible?" She was shocked at the word coming from him. "What of its charm and wealth and gentility?"

He shrugged. "Magnolias, mammies and moon-

119

beams!" He laughed. "Ah, yes, fabled wealth, mythic adventure, native aristocracy . . ."

"None of these exists?"

He answered hesitantly, like a child slowly remembering a recitation. "No . . . all." He shifted his weight as if something had bruised him.

"I do not comprehend you. You fight for things which you spurn, which you say do not exist, which you scorn, like Whispers and Rainbeau Bayou, and men you despise, like Ramsey Arnauld!"

He took her hand. "Rainbeau Bayou is a back alley to the Mississippi. It's away from the mainstream. After this war my land will be set off as backwoods, too. Whispers will—"

"Take me there!" she interrupted. Surprised at her boldness, she recovered a bit. "I've nearly as much interest in seeing the West Wind Gates as Professor Boxt." She begged him silently, 'Oh, take me there, Julien! Don't let me go!'

He sounded disappointed as they walked along the deck. "You haven't heard me. Whispers won't be there after the war. Oh, it may well be standing, rows of statue columns and onion dome and shadowed porticoes. But there is no Carthage in the New World. Its spirit will be broken."

She shook her head. He was missing her message entirely! 'I love you, Julien! Can't you hear me?'

But he talked on, more forcefully now. "After this war, places like Whispers and people like Haloo—youngsters with wildfire in their eyes—and people a little tetched in the head like Aunt Dottie—they'll all be gone."

Surlina would not allow tears in her eyes, but they formed in her heart and made her voice crack. "What of yourself?"

His inscrutable mirth returned instantly. "If I'm not strung up by the neck, I shall go back to the merchant trade. Ask about me in ten years, my dear, and you shall hear of a middle-aged sea captain with a cat and pipe." He took both her hands and swung her

120

around like a minuet partner. "And as for you? Will you be the fat wife of a farmer?"

"I have business interests which I will pursue," she said briskly, rattling on quickly to avoid getting stuck in her emotional mire. It was safer to talk about him. "Surely you would prefer to command some ocean-going frigate now! Surely you do not prefer life on this . . . this *raft* in a muddy river with corncakes and owls to eat!" How undisturbed he'd been to think of her as the fat wife of a farmer! Was he simply going to let her go ashore with a brisk salute and a peck on the cheek?

At that moment, the nose of the *Quail* rounded the bend and the Crescent City shone along the starboard shore. So impressed was she by the sparkle and shine that she forgot her last question to Julien until he answered it.

"Prefer the *Quail?*" he mocked, feigning amazement as if unable to fathom her values. "In all honesty I can assure you I prefer many things to rain-soaked sorties, slippery decks, canvas cots and Dottie's coffee." He pretended to think, leaning away from her, stabbing a finger into the air. "Yes, the list is endless and sinful. I prefer dancing. Champagne. Racy French stories. Cigars—"

"Then why do you stay? Julien, darling, come with me to New Orleans! I have—"

"I have with my ship," he interrupted coldly, "as you have business interests. Consider this: my sailors slouch. They'll never master the art of proper saluting. They are farmers, plowboys, Ozark hillbillies. Not one of them has seen big cities or far-off oceans or glittering medals. But they will be the world's most devilish fighting men because they will dare the world and get away with it." He stopped abruptly. Distractedly, he spoke of the city ahead of them. "Unhappy New Orleans! Settled by convicts in chains, slaves in irons, victims of kidnappers and assorted other unwilling immigrants. It would not be wise to stay here long." He reached across the darkness between them to touch her face. "The way of prudence, and safety, for you lies

121

north. I have never discovered your true identity, but it's clear you're no southern belle."

She thought wistfully of her sworn duty to take Tandy to Europe. Then she thought with new panic of her father's mad idea to remove the silver from Erlanger's. "I shan't stay in the city long. But don't send me away from you tonight. You're so distant, so withdrawn!"

"I'll set you off at dawn."

"Where will you go, Julien?" She was longing to hold him, to cling to something in the tide she felt prying them apart.

"Wherever I'm sent."

It was the first time she had ever thought of him as being under military orders. He had seemed so much his own commander, but obviously his choices were not as free as she had supposed.

He growled, "What intimate questions you toss at me! Where will *I* go? How you tempt me to tell you, Surlina. But with tomorrow's dawn I might find my most personal secrets relayed to Farragut's fleet."

So the curtain of mistrust still hung between them. But this curtain lay immovable because she would not—could not—use the words to dissolve it.

Now his voice was calm. "The *Quail* will snoop through Rainbeau Bayou so as not to be detected, then put in at Whispers long enough for Dottie to set things to rights and Professor Boxt to sketch the West Wind Gates."

"Oh, Julien! We have so little time and there are so many things I should have said—"

"Perhaps our time will come," he said, silencing her with a gentle finger on her quivering lips.

Instantly, she was in his arms, pressing her lips to his with all her strength, seeking to arouse in him the trust she could not give with her words. She yielded, taking him into her mouth, sucking slightly as if the motion would blend them forever.

She let her head fall against his shoulder, docile and dreamy. With her eyes tilted upward, she was memorizing him. But she saw nothing of the dashing river captain she'd exchanged kisses and jests with a moment before. Now she saw only a melancholy man with the moon silhouetted behind him like an opal ball. A man whose countenance was somber, his eyes tender, his body trembling. Suddenly tears misted her vision, blotting away his profile. Unable to see him, it seemed she had lost him forever. His hopeful words, "Our time will come," would be crushed by the future! Only the present could exist. The tears cascaded down her cheeks as she lifted her head. "Our time must be now, Julien! Surely you want me, even as I ache for you!"

He scooped her into his arms. "I cannot hold you aboard against your will, my darling. I'll keep my word! I'll set you off at dawn! Just let me hold you tonight—"

"Yes! Oh, yes, Julien! Give me all your strength, your warmth, your love."

He carried her to the cabin, pushing the door inward with a flourish and letting it bang. She felt like a captive being carried aboard a pirate vessel. Suddenly she became aware that the noise of their lovemaking would cause gossip and embarrassed looks in the morning. She clasped her hands tight against his neck. "Can't we go ashore?"

He kept her in his arms but stopped all movement. Quietly he asked, "Have you changed your mind? One moment you urge me to the point that my body is fiery with desire for you. The next you are unhappy with our accommodations. If you will not have me, say so!"

"I will have you Julien! You will be my joy, my love! But I desire privacy—for the words I want to whisper, for the moments we are to share with no others."

He placed a delicate kiss on her ear. "We'll find ourselves a place away from prying eyes. There's a cotton storage shed at every riverbend. The bales are soft and can be spread like a quilt. Would you like that?"

She nodded.

"Then if we cry out in pleasure of each other, it

shall be to our ears alone," he murmured. He set her down in the cabin. "Pack the things you'll want. I'll see to anchoring."

She flitted about the darkened stateroom, unable to think clearly. What would she want? Oh, she couldn't even think logically! Already her skin was so sensitive that it seemed stretched over her like fine mesh canvas waiting for an artist's brush. Her tongue touched her lips and ripples shot through her like arrows.

Then she heard his footsteps and recognized his happy whistle which trailed off into humming. He appeared, grinning, a picnic basket over his arm, his Naval Academy blanket spilling from the cover. "I will cook dinner for you, too!" he promised, sounding boyish. "How do you like your venison?"

She teased him, "How do you like your women?" Suddenly it occurred to her that she knew so little, perhaps she wouldn't please him. "How do you treat your women?"

"Ask me again in the morning . . . if you've any questions left."

They laughed like children off on a holiday, lowering the skiff, telling only Haloo where to find them in case of emergency. He blushed beet-red in the moonlight, looking everywhere except at them as he helped steady the ropes.

Then they were off, rowing exuberantly, splashing each other in their haste, laughing as if a cloud of happiness had suddenly showered them with joy.

On shore, Surlina felt brave and adventuresome. When he accidentally bumped against her, she jumped. Julien blew her a kiss in the darkness. She felt her breasts distend the lace of her blouse. What a temptation to undress and run naked along the water's edge! 'Surlina, have you no shame? No! I have only love for this golden giant who calls my name so tenderly, brushes my lips with his velvet mouth, turns my flesh warm with his caresses.'

They ran to the cotton shed, where, after circling it, Julien forced the door with his shoulder. Inside, the smell was of a tightly locked parlor, musty but clean.

124

When her eyes grew accustomed to the darkness, she found the room nearly twenty feet across with birds' nests in the eaves and cotton bales standing in the corners like sentries holding up the roof. It was cheery once a lantern was lit, the shadows warming the walls of rough-hewn timbers, the trill of a cricket adding convivial noise. Surlina spread the gray wool blanket in the center of the floor and shoved a half-bale of cotton against the door. He teased her again, "Don't be so eager, my little wanton. Pick up that blanket and let's spread some of this loose cotton beneath it."

She was unsure what to do next. Should she undress? Clumsily, she put her fingers to the top of the lace mantelet. She turned her back and undid the mother-of-pearl buttons. Then she heard his voice. "Wait." She froze, waiting for his touch, but for several moments, all she heard was a scuffling noise. Finally, he tapped her shoulder. "Turn around."

He was nude. At first Surlina avoided looking at him completely. Then she reproached herself for such misbegotten modesty. This was the man she desired! This was the man to whom she would give herself willingly. She looked at him, enjoying the fine tightly curled golden hairs on his chest, the narrowness of his hips, the muscular ridges of his thigh. "You are elegant," she said without a blush.

He acknowledged his body's readiness with a downward nod. "And eager."

Her hands went up to the last of the mantelet buttons. "No," he said, "let me."

She was obedient, responding eagerly as he sought her throat with his kisses. He drew her down to the blanket, disheveling her curls with playful gusts of breath, catching the loose strands in his teeth, nipping at her ears.

He fastened his mouth over hers eagerly, grasping her tongue until she felt the current of her movements matching his. She let her body slide against him, eager to feel the softly curled hair of his chest beneath her kisses. He drew her gown lower around her shoulders, trapping her arms, then slowly kissed the shoulder-blades, the pale skin above her breasts, her long throat. He passed his hands along the soft curves of her breasts, moaned with delight, but did not expose her. Kneeling before her, he laid his head against her skin, the wavy sideburns of his golden hair touching her like feathers. The vibrations of her heart made it difficult for her to breathe.

Then he released the mantelet, drawing it gently over her head, lifting her arms along with the garment. He left it drawn over her head, not tightly, but like a loose blindfold. Her arms were upraised, her face covered, her breasts exposed. She felt the nipples tightening against his expected touch, the tips tingly with excitement.

"Lean toward me," he commanded. "Slowly."

First she felt his hands, catching her waist, guiding and steadying her. She wanted to sway, but his grasp was firm, allowing her to lean forward without side-to-side motion. Then there was a curious, cool touch and she suspended all movement. She felt his hands leave her ribs, then the brush of his fingers against her breasts, stroking upward, holding them firmly, bringing them together against him. His organ felt long and dry, except for the tip which he rubbed in circles around her nipples, gliding with a slippery substance.

The concentric motions were drawing her against him, making her breath hot within the material. Without a thought, she pulled away the material so as to see the erect masculine form tracing such patterns of delight on her body.

She ran her hands over his chest, touched his smiling mouth, brought her fingers across his proffered tongue, touched the tiny dark circles on his furry chest until they tightened and hardened. How wonderfully built he was! So responsive, so silky, so strong.

He groaned with pleasure. "You have no idea of your powers, Surlina!" He lay back, supine, pulling her across him till she straddled him, skirt still in place, but legs spread around his naked thighs. The hardness he transmitted was contagious; she felt desire

126

stinging her like a whip across her buttocks. Love flowed from her, making her slippery and thick.

"I'm ready," she cried, wanting him to take her.

But he held back, removing her skirt slowly as she stayed above him. He stroked her long legs, tracing the soft flesh of her hips between his thumb and middle finger. "You are smooth as ivory," he said, following the curve from waist to hip. "You are smooth as a mink. I could sink into you like diving into a fire—be completely consumed in one moment of ecstasy.

"Then do it, darling!"

He rolled easily taking her with him, positioning himself on top, stretched full length like a supple animal sleeping in the sun. The smell of their bodies was like seashells, the taste like salt and honey. He unfastened the garters which held her silken stockings, took her panties down gently, easing them over the curves of thighs and ankles, caressed her feet, blew warm tickling breath against the soles, traced the muscles of her calves with his fingers.

Her nerves felt as though they were at the point of bursting, her legs tormented for the feel of him within her. The tension of unsatisfied passion made her dizzy, wanting to make her reach out and shake him. "Now, Julien!"

He threw himself between her knees, spreading her legs with insistent stroking of his palms. His breath came in bursts, straining against the hurry his body demanded. His hand caressed her belly, traveled upward to hold each breast as he kissed, then sucked at their firm centers.

She arched beneath him, thrusting boldly toward his glistening organ. She heard herself half-sobbing with joy, but the sounds seemed far away. Her body was in turmoil, begging to be united with his.

He placed the tip at her entrance, letting it rest quiveringly as her flesh tightened around it. He pushed a bit further, urged by her ardent whisper of "Yes, yes."

Then there was resistance, and she saw his face

cloud with hesitation. His breath rattled as he shook with the spasms of forced restraint. "My God! Am I to be the first to know you completely? Oh, Surlina . . . you make me feel a god!"

Then he was deep inside her, the fast thrust like the dart of a streaking arrow, the hurt blending with the fire of healing. She was blinded with the staggering sensation of being lifted bodily from the blanket by his hands beneath her hips as he pitched into her. The sense of heat flowed through her like a geyser. She felt as if the rays of the sun had shone into her, concentrating all their power. The sounds she made seemed alien. She spoke with her body, following the rhythm he dictated with his thrusts.

The jerks and tremors grew more frantic, and she was unable to keep pace. Suddenly it felt as if the sea had spilled over within her as he cried out in passion. He buckled downward, searching out her lips as if maddened by the thrashing. Then he lay still, moaning, his wet face buried against her curls.

He praised her extravagantly, licking her breasts, smoothing back her hair, kissing her tenderly. "You're like the sweetness of wine! Oh, my precious, you're like the sea commanding a ship to its bidding."

She felt a tiny flexing of her muscles deep within, where she had not expected movement. "I am like the sky, about to crack," she murmured, lifting her legs around him. He lay within her, softer now, and she felt able to absorb him. To her surprise, she felt protective. There were many new things to be learned from the meaning of lover. This feeling of languidness—almost of intoxication—was pleasant, though there seemed to be soreness spreading a ring between her thighs. She was curious. "Did I bleed? The sounds . . . They surprised me. You . . . I knew you were strong, but it was as if you were armed with a spike of obsidian!"

He eased himself from her, lying at her side, his arm tucking her head to his shoulder. "And you were like the warmth of sunlight spilling through dark clouds. You pulled me, bent me to your will as no woman ever has!"

He rolled onto his back, his arms behind his head, smiling. "I brought champagne for a toast . . . but my knees are too weak to carry me to the picnic basket!"

She felt her muscles continuing to contract, as if repairing the damage where a secret battle had taken place. Conquered? No, she had no sense of desolation or violation. Twenty-six was a long time to wait when a woman was expected to marry at sixteen and be dead at forty! But how happy she was to have waited for Julien, how lucky to have found this man who touched her skillfully and called her precious. How rightfully their bodies cried out to each other, and how spiritually she now felt bound to him. Her throat constricted with the joy of knowing him, the fear of leaving him. Quietly, she began to cry.

Instantly he was soothing her, afraid she was in pain. He brought cotton moistened with cool dew and wiped her tears. He fashioned a gown of the gray blanket and draped it about her shoulders. From the picnic basket he produced ham and cheese, olives and champagne. He toasted her with lavish words, touching her cheek gingerly, as if she were made of porcelain. Through all this, she continued to weep intermittently, straightening her face long enough to smile radiantly at him, then disintegrating into sobs.

He was beside himself. "Have I hurt you? I'd never forgive myself!"

She shook her head and cried louder, apologizing at the same time. "I never cry!"

Finally he knelt, took her in his arms and comforted her by rocking silently. His touch melted her tears, steadied her heart, and filled her with strength. He whispered her name over and over again, as if wondering at its beauty, as if he'd never heard it until tonight. Then he eased her back to lie on the makeshift padding, his hands cradling her head. "Surlina, Surlina . . . how you have thrilled me! I have always wanted to make love to a woman who really wanted me. That

—more than your virginity—is the treasure you have given me. Oh, my darling, I worship you!"

She felt him against her, ready to make love again. This time, the terrible urgency was gone. Now his tenderness shone through, the long strokes of his hands spreading her thighs gently, reassuring her. Now, she, too, had time to test each sensation—the taste of the charming dimple in his chin, the musky smell of his skin. The moistness of her skin allowed a sense of friction as he slowly began to move into her. Again she felt a warmth within her, as if a sudden fever had gripped her body. A pressure was building up, different from the storm of wild caresses which had thrilled her before.

Now she knew she could never resist his touch. Surlina let the movements within her core spread outward, tilting her hips, tensing her legs, flexing against him. She gripped his wrists with her hands, buried her mouth against his lips, raised her knees.

He groaned with pleasure, attempting to restrain his own movements. "Shape me to you," he whispered, sensitively matching her rhythm.

She felt a forcing within her that was new. The urgency was hers.

"Now!" he cried, and pressed her hips together against him. A violent shudder swept through her, then pinpointed into bright throbs.

A moment later, flooded with pleasure, she cried out, "Oh, Julien! Oh!"

This time she did not cry. She laughed, wild, delighted, shaken with triumph. She felt a delicious fatigue grasp at her senses.

"We should rest," he said, spreading the blanket over them.

"No, no . . ." she protested, not wanting to lose the moments of touching, of closeness, of knowing. But already her mind was drowsing, lost in the haze of exhaustion which had followed exhilaration. "No . . ." She tried to compose words to tell him of her newfound happiness. She felt her eyes close, her body snuggle into the hollow of his chest, her consciousness slipping away. Yet her mind stayed awake long enough to think how little he really knew about her while at the same time he'd known her in a way no man ever had. He had not accepted her because she was the Silver Belle. He'd simply known her as a woman and yes, oh dear God, yes, he'd accepted her as such.

13

Even at daybreak, the road into New Orleans was teeming with traffic. Surlina bounced in the carriage as the driver worked his way among gangs of black laborers, men on horses, other carriages and wagon teams. She'd told him to hurry and he was obeying, the sight of her Yankee greenback dollar urging him along.

She sat rigid, bracing her body against the bumps, aware of the tingling soreness with each jolt. She smoothed her skirts, keeping her mind off Julien for fear she'd lose her nerve and run back to his secure embrace. How could she leave him! And yet she'd done it, going quietly, hardly speaking to him, not trusting herself to look at him even for a second.

She forced herself to watch the levee road. Squatty palmettoes cast bright shadows as the sun rose higher. The sweaty bands of blacks, wearing vivid bandanas around their heads, swore at the early-morning heat as they headed toward the wharves. The warm April breeze touched her face like a damp cloth.

She called to the driver, "Hurry, now! Pontalba Apartments. Do you remember?"

He nodded and flicked his whip across the horse. "Yes'm! But you don't need to rush into town. The whole town's getting fixed to come out! Why you come visiting when Farragut's planning to pay us a call?" When she didn't answer, he laid another slap of the cattail reed across the horse's flanks and glanced at the

131

greenback Yankee dollar; her affairs were none of his interest.

As she reached the center of the city where Tandy and Cabell lived, the pace of activity increased. The city was scurrying, not yet in the full panic of a battle, but with the grim knowledge that war was about to settle upon its shoulders. War was coming, and coming fast; and people, frightened and disorganized, were rushing headlong out of town. The fruit market was swarming, Negro women carrying bushel baskets atop their heads, the smell of bananas and citrus thick in the air.

By the time the carriage had bounced into the narrow, crowded streets of the Vieux Carré, Surlina was mopping her forehead and pushing the wrist tapes upward on her arms. She inspected her blouse. Dismally, she noted that she'd selected an old stained garment. Washed by Aunt Dottie's exotic bleaches of lye soap and owl grease, the garment still bore traces of Dottie's habit of spitting tobacco juice. What would Tandy think?

At Jackson Square, the carriage halted, unable to move because of a traffic jam. Surlina glanced to her right, admiring the magnificent St. Louis Cathedral. To both sides of it she saw apartments with latticework balconies. One of these half-hidden houses was Tandy's. "Which one is the Pontalba Apartments?"

The driver pointed across the packed square to the cloistered buildings on the far side. "About a block, if you've a mind to fight the crowd, ma'am."

She didn't bother to tell him she'd fought several other obstacles in order to arrive in New Orleans. She climbed down, paid the fare and set out. On the street, the smell of the river was close again. She could hear it against the levee, a block to her left. She could see the moorings, smell coffee and banana boats and see a whole fleet of sternwheelers. The idea of a blockade seemed ridiculous with this many ships obviously able to slip into port. What of Farragut's fleet? Did it really lie only a day away beyond the two flimsy downstream forts? Suddenly she felt her mind click with a new idea. Ports, boats, blockades notwithstanding, she could always *buy* a ship, and sail to Europe! And leave Julien, her mind nagged, threatening her logical plans with illogical tears.

First she must collect Tandy. She traipsed through the street, hearing frantic talk. "Yankees will be in these streets within a week! They'll blast the Cathedral to rubble! Murder children in their beds! Rape the women!" She lifted her skirt to avoid the water standing in the deep gutters and set her sights on the frame and red brick apartments.

Number four Pontalba lay behind an entryway barricaded by wisps of bougainvillea. The tightly woven foliage slid along the brick walls, framing either side of the cypress doorway. She jangled the bell, then used the knocker as well, for emphasis. A bird, disturbed by her racket, whistled disapproval from among the branches.

Tandy herself answered the door, her eyes fluttering along with her voice as she cried in obvious amazement, "Surlina! My stars up in heaven!"

"Is father here, Tandy?"

"Goodness, no! Of course not!"

So she had beaten him to New Orleans after all! Yet she must not dally; she would go to Erlanger's this very afternoon. For the moment, however, she could rejoice in seeing her sister. "Tandy! Tandy! You've not changed a bit!" She hugged her younger sister, noting the same slender waist, brown curls, eyes so pale blue they seemed veiled. Even the charming, tentative voice had not changed. Tandy still sounded twelve years old when she spoke.

As soon as they were settled on the damask sofa, Tandy cried again, "Suh-leena! Suh-leena," adding the strangled syllables of southern accent to her own entranced speech. "Whatever brings you here?" She put her dainty hands to her cheeks as if her face might break apart in wonder.

Surlina impatiently tried to give an explanation without lying but without revealing everything that had happened. "Tandy, I think you may have more unexpected visitors. Father is coming to New Orleans, too!" She rushed on before the startled Tandy could inquire about forgiveness after being disowned. "I have traveled by ship, but he is coming overland. His health is not good. If he does not arrive in the next few days, there may be cause for concern."

Tandy accepted the news with equanimity, merely fanning her oval face and puckering her mouth. "Well, I shall make him welcome when he gets here, though I cannot vouch for good behavior from my husband."

Surlina did not want to talk of Thayer Cabell. Yet. Quickly, she turned the conversation to topics she normally avoided through sheer boredom. Tandy rang for tea, and a massive silver service was laid quickly on the rosewood table.

Suddenly Surlina realized that time was precious. "Tandy, I have not traveled from St. Louis merely to play tea party with you! I have come to collect you and get us out of the country."

"Good heavens, Surlina!" Tandy fluttered her eyelashes in rapid motion and shook her curls. "Why, I'll have to ask Cabell!"

"All right. Where is he?"

"Upstairs at a meeting." She made no move to rise from the silken couch.

Surlina saw exactly how matters lay. If anyone was to ask Cabell anything, it would be she!

She tucked in her blouse as if putting on armor. She had met her brother-in-law only once. Now she intended to barge into his meeting and state her case. As she marched steadily up the stairs, she remembered his foppish Continental style, his false gestures of aristocracy, his florid face. She hadn't lost her prejudices! Her father had called Cabell a revolutionary by trade. His dealings in cotton, tea, spices, and tobacco were those of a trader intent on supplying the nations of Europe with their delicacies while supplying the Confederacy with finance. With his French Royalist family background, his attitude was that what the South most needed was a king!

She stopped at the top of the stairs, listening to loud

male voices which came through the second closed door on the right. Obviously the heated discussion concerned the arrival of Farragut's naval forces. She recognized Cabell's voice by its distinctive falsetto ring.

He was full of flowery, useless words. "We should grieve for this beautiful city, my fellow Orleanians," he exhorted the others loudly. "Every patriot is called upon to wring his heart in the face of this disaster which carves our very entrails! This very day, tyranny makes ready to march in our streets. Iniquity stamps her heavy boots, muddying our great river. Violence sits on hungry haunches upon our doorsteps. We mourn! We mourn, my brethren, in shame!"

'What a pompous ass he is,' Surlina thought, her hand upraised to knock on the door and silence his tirade. At that moment, she heard noises in the courtyard below. She crossed the hall and looked through the narrow window. Four men were busily hoisting a banner which read, "Public Meeting for Enlistment of Private Sailors." On a quickly erected platform, an elegantly attired merchant officer paraded—all swords and sash and gold lace. D'Orsay pumps and top hat and tie.

Her amused admiration gave way to wonder as he began to shout a message of sabotage. "Crew members of boats in the harbor! Listen lively! There's a new life awaiting you as patriots and privateers!"

The words jolted her heart as she thought of Julien. Surely no man had bought *his* splendid loyalty! Ramsey Arnauld's money might have provided the *Quail*, but Julien had not given up the merchant trade because of emotional exhortations like those she was listening to. And Sam—even though he'd admitted war had been a "godsend" for a man making eight hundred dollars a year, surely he hadn't donned a uniform with mercenary thoughts in mind. Only now did she realize how the Surlina Silver had protected her for so many years. It was her job to protect it! She stiffened her resolve to follow her father's wishes.

The elegant orator was shouting, flinging his top hat into the air and catching it, begging crew members

135

of any boats in the harbor to sign with him. He asked them openly to relocate—to abandon their employers and ship with him as privateers.

She stood at the window, fascinated. Beyond curiosity, however, she calculated the information might be useful. She, too, could outfit a ship to take her to Europe. Apparently New Orleans was full of men of amenable loyalties. For a certain price, a crew could be recruited. She must delay no longer. She turned her back, determined to barge in on Cabell immediately, but Tandy was coming up the stairs, resting every second step, her small hand placed over her heart. Her breathing was shallow and labored. Poor Tandy! It seemed the muggy southern climate had not agreed with her. Surlina pointed to the scene outside the balcony. "Tandy, did you hear that speech? How can that bragging fool talk that way?"

"Rafe Semmes is a gallant man!" Tandy puffed in his defense. "He speaks no differently than the other one hundred seventy thousand citizens of our Crescent City! We stand together. We shall never surrender!"

"Oh my God, Cabell has infected you, too!" Surlina was appalled. "Tandy, don't spout ridiculous nonsense with Farragut steaming in the unguarded back door to the city. You sound a fool!"

In reply, Tandy stuck her pert nose in the air and flounced past her sister. She opened the double louvered doors to what was apparently an upstairs sitting room, seated herself in a green velvet lounge chair and took up her embroidery.

Surlina remained in the doorway. "Don't sit down and start sewing some useless frill! Pack your trunk! Europe is the place for us. I promised Father I would fetch you out of this hellhole. I'll go to Erlanger's and then we—"

"I shall go nowhere unless dear Cabell consents."

"Tandy, you must think for yourself! Don't sit on your velvet ass and wait for the grown-ups to tell you what to do. You must quit this playing dress-up and sewing fine seams!"

Tandy merely ducked her head and continued her

neat stitching. "Sister, sweet sister! What can I say that you'd understand? These are the things I like!"

Unexpectedly, Thayer Cabell entered the room. He was as exaggerated in person as his voice had sounded through the closed door. His thick black hair fell over his inordinately high forehead. He wore a patterned waistcoat and a stiff linen shirt. To Surlina he appeared grand, foreign and annoying. He had thick lips which she could not imagine anyone wanting to kiss, a paunchy midriff and thin, beanpole legs. Dandified, assessed Surlina, and oh yes, every bit of seventeen years Tandy's senior. But worst were his grim eyes, which Surlina classified as small and mean.

"Dear husband," gushed Tandy, "look who is here! It's sister Surlina! All the way from St. Louis just to visit me because she was worried! Isn't that sweet?"

Thayer Cabell thrust his fat neck forward, obviously shocked at the sight of their visitor. "My God, why?" he muttered, then seized her hand in greeting.

Surlina mumbled hello, let him brush her fingertips with a European kiss and made a one-sentence statement of her mission. Something was lacking about him, despite his appearance of wealth and manners. True, he had lately returned from France, where he'd helped negotiate the South's cotton loan with Trenholm, Fraser, but she still couldn't believe he possessed intelligence and discretion.

"We'll book passage to Europe," Surlina explained. "Or, that failing, I shall buy a ship and set sail."

His face puffed like an adder, turning pink, red and purple in splotches which overran each other. "Christ Jesus, woman! Where do you get the gall to speak to me as though you're issuing orders?"

"I *am* issuing orders. I have my father's orders concerning Tandy and myself. My plans do not include you, so you may continue to rant and rave, as long as you show me the courtesy I deserve." She looked him straight in the eye. Men like Thayer Cabell tolerated women only as servants to their wills and needs. She gathered her courage. "We are not well acquainted,
137

but you'll find I am quite different from Tandy. You will have to treat me differently, too."

"Yes, yes," he muttered, wiping his face by blotting it daintily. "It's custom to treat sisters differently from wives. I shall treat you quite differently from my dear, sainted Tandy!"

Obviously, they did not understand each other at all. "I will go to Erlanger's this afternoon to withdraw the silver. We will wait for Father as long as we can, but the fast approach of battle makes it imperative we leave within days." She felt her heart miss a beat. How could she keep making the statement with her voice so clear when inside the words split her like an earthquake. She felt her knees wobble and put her hand out to Tandy for support. Tandy smiled, touched her hand, then went back to embroidering an exquisitely intricate sundial.

Cabell marched up and down, rolling his head. "Let's not be hasty. Perhaps there are other ways you could aid Tandy. Perhaps your silver could be better used to—"

She quoted her father, "The Surlina Silver will never finance bloodshed! This war will last years, God help us all, and I'll not prolong it one minute by financing it!"

He strode the length of the room, running his hands down the sides of his waistcoat, making streaks as he raised the nap the wrong way. He blustered, "Why, this war won't last! The fight will be over in a week —a four-day week—when Semmes takes to the seas!" He poured whiskey from a glass decanter and held it below his nose like smelling salts.

Tandy rose quietly and closed the window. Surlina saw a mist was falling. In a moment it had turned to rain, which fell straight down noiselessly.

"This war won't end in a week or a year. Surely you know that is ridiculous," Surlina contradicted.

"I know certain facts, Miss Surlina. I know, for instance, what resources the South has." He inhaled, as if puffing himself up. "The South has willpower! And

138

everyone knows one brave boy in gray can outfight ten of them Bill Yanks!"

"Firepower—not willpower—wins wars."

He seemed startled that a woman would argue with him. He snorted hastily and blew his nose on a silk monogrammed handkerchief. Lowering his voice to a sarcastic, instructional tone he might use on a wayward puppy, he insisted, "My dear, history proves—"

"History proves not a damned thing," she cut him off. "In fact, my dear Cabell, history lies!" She flung the words at him like a fusillade. "It ignores the facts because men like you repeatedly ignore the facts."

Overcome by all the argument, Tandy excused herself to rest.

Surlina reasoned that with Tandy out of earshot, perhaps Cabell would listen to logic. Surely he would see the sense of her plan.

But he did not. "A thousand times no. I will not hear of my wife making a perilous journey on the high seas. Not Tandy. Not my paragon of virtue and saintly dear wife."

"Cabell, you talk like an idiot. Come to your senses. The climate here is obviously not good for Tandy. And kept in a gilded cage like this apartment, she won't have the faintest chance of surviving when the Yankees strike." Surlina fanned herself with Tandy's embroidery. The closed room seemed to steam. "Don't you realize there's going to be *bloodshed* here in a few days . . . maybe tomorrow, certainly as soon as Forts Jackson and St. Philip fall."

"They shan't fall. They will *never* surrender."

"Farragut and Porter are set to attack. Please think of Tandy."

Thayer seemed incapable of such a generous act. He continued to shout nonsense as he moved Tandy's needlework aside, flung open the windows and drank another glass of whiskey. "True things remain and certain things are true! The South will never submit! Cotton is King!"

Surlina could take no more time with this man. He was worse than she'd remembered. "I must make ar-

139

rangements. Tandy must come with me to safety."
Suddenly she remembered Julien's whispering to her,
"The way of prudence and safety for you lies North."
She softened her stand. "She *could* come with me to
St. Louis."

Tandy entered the room and smiled wanly. "Move
about? Why, possibly we will, for the duration of this
. . . uh . . . this late unpleasantness." She nodded
desultorily as if dreaming of a splendid outing for a
picnic.

Surlina realized that the mood in the room had
changed. Cabell was smiling at her, extending both
blotchy hands, showing his yellow teeth behind those
fat lips. "I have all but forgotten my role as host in
this diatribe of disagreement. Come, turn around, Surlina, and let me kiss your cheeks in proper greeting.
Let's have no more talk of destiny or departure." He
spun her around and planted slobbery kisses on both
cheeks. She reared back, startled, her eyes daring him
to touch her again.

He moved to his wife and stood behind her, holding
her shoulders as if he could physically twist or bend
her in any direction. "Now, Tandy dearest, we must
entertain your sister at dinner. Let's see . . . for tonight's menu . . ."

"I am going to Erlanger's," Surlina announced.
"Anything you plan for supper will be fine."

"Perhaps I should accompany you."

"And take possession of the silver for the South?"

"Only a certain class of women goes about the
streets unescorted." The haughty look became a questioning leer. "You have traveled the length of the great
river *alone?*"

"In the company of river pirates," she said sweetly,
hoping to alarm him further.

He flicked his mustache tips like a tomcat wiggling
his whiskers, obviously seeing her in a new light. Perhaps she was a female who could be made use of physically. There were rules about these things, of course,
but there were always foreign diplomats who needed

140

entertainment, who enjoyed slender hands and full breasts and a certain amount of fight.

As though she had read his thoughts, Surlina dashed down the stairs, through the courtyard and out into the rain.

14

Jackson Square remained crowded despite the downpour. Surlina turned down Rue Chartres. Erlanger's lay beyond Canal, the wide boulevard which separated the American section from the Vieux Carré. She had seen pictures of the great international banking house with its circling drive and thick iron gates. Anyone would be able to direct her to such an imposing edifice of stacked marble, Grecian columns and stone lions. As she walked along, jostled by the crowds, she wondered if the columns of Erlanger's would rate a sketch from Professor Boxt. Oh, she already missed the lively crew of the *Quail,* even though she'd promised herself not to think of them. A few memories of Dottie's jokes, Haloo's blushes or Julien's kisses, and she'd toss away her resolve to go to Europe.

She concentrated on the jumbled intersections which were thronged with citizens. Traffic was weaving in both directions, some people apparently fleeing downtown, others struggling to make their way there.

The rain grew heavier as she neared the broad avenue named Canal. Now the pall of smoke mixed with water. The city seemed to be burning itself. Surlina could see stacks of cotton bales smoldering in the drizzle. At every street corner men stood atop each other's shoulders, laughing, talking, shouting. On every corner, the refrain was the same: "Three cheers for Jeff Davis! Three cheers for Beauregard! Three groans for Lincoln!"

She had stopped across the street from such a group,

watching their antics and thinking what a rambunctious and foolish city this was, when suddenly she saw a high armored wagon attempting to pass. The horses were whipped by the team of drivers, but the clogged streets made movement slow. She spotted another wagon turning a corner a block away. As they drew closer, she made a horrifying discovery. These heavily guarded wagons bore the name Erlander's Banque Internationale. "What is happening here?" she cried. "What are those Erlanger's wagons about?"

A nearby man answered her politely. "Aye, they are loading the gold and silver of the city onto boats. It'll be shipped upriver, and then to Richmond. The Confederacy has commandeered it all!"

Her startled reaction was selfish. "Not *my* silver!" No one could commandeer the Surlina Silver! She rushed toward the banking house, losing a slipper on an uneven curb. Her hair streamed back from her wet face.

She ran the last half-block toward the bank. As she approached, her eyes scanned for evidence that her silver was still intact. But the citadel seemed closed. No, not closed, for the iron gates were standing wide open. Surlina raced through, rushing up the circle's cobblestones. As she got closer she could see that the windows of the bank were broken and the double doors ajar at the corner entrance. The inside appeared dark, as if this were only a shell of a building. Outside the doorway the circle was full of carts, mules, horses and wagons. She realized in dismay that all the banking world intended to run inland in front of Farragut's forces. Well, she'd run nowhere! Oh, if her father could only have gotten here sooner! 'Oh, Father, I pray you have arrived before me! Your instincts were right again!'

Surlina hurried through the door. Inside, she found an almost empty room. The audit books lay in heaps on the floor. Bills of lading were shredded in mounds. Tellers' cages had been smashed. The doorway to the vaults stood open and unprotected.

Obviously a fight had been waged, but who had been

the participants? "Where is Erlanger?" she demanded loudly. "I must see Jean Erlanger at once!"

A disoriented clerk pointed an idle thumb toward the second story. Quickly she rushed to the winding staircase. A guard lay sprawled at the turn, dead, his open eyes affixed on the painted ceiling. Without stopping, she jumped over him, blending a curse with a prayer.

Jean Erlanger was a man of great reputation, purportedly as skilled and famous as his father before him in money matters. She burst through the door into his private office, saying, "I am Surlina Defore."

"You are too late."

She saw a man slumped forward on his desk, a pistol in his hand. On the desk were scattered bills of several foreign currencies along with wadded ship ladings. Overhead a skylight tile was missing; rain fell onto the marble floor.

The man slowly raised his head. He was round faced, like a moon with misplaced eyes. For an instant he reminded her of the owl Aunt Dottie McDune had served for dinner. Then he sat back in his leather chair, staring. "The end of the House of Erlanger's," he muttered. With hands atop his bald spot, he shook his head. "Oh, I am so sorry about the . . ." His gaze took in the littered desk and missing skylight. ". . . about the facility."

"Has my account suffered?"

He rose, shouting. "Yes! From your own capricious scheme!" His voice rose to a wail and his owl eyes fluttered. "I was shocked by your foolhardy and secretive plan to—"

"—What plan?" She interrupted wildly, eyes narrowing and throat constricting. "What plan? I've sent you no orders." Suspicion bit into her hands like cold fangs. She locked her hands together. "I have communicated *nothing* to Erlangers! Has my father—?"

"—Yes, we have your father's written orders, of course. But the plan was stated as having your express approval by the courier who—"

"Courier? I've sent no messenger to you!" A frenzy

143

shook her—chicanery by her father, deceit by Thad Muller, a plot by the Union, double-crossing by Thayer Cabell. "What courier?" she demanded again.

Erlanger's eyes widened until black flecks of fear floated in the pupils. "The courier who brought us your father's message—the letter with the double wax seals."

So it was probably Thad Muller, after all. How had he managed to arrive before her?

Before she could describe Muller, Erlanger put his hand out to her, his face blanching the color of eggshell. "Oh, Miss Defore! The courier also brought us terrible news . . . of your father's death."

The words struck through her heart like a sword, then were immediately tempered by the thought that Muller might be lying. Tears welled up in her eyes, despite her faint hope. "My father was ill," she admitted, her teeth chattering as if a sudden coldness had descended. "But there is also a possibility this courier only meant you to believe my father had died." She dabbed her eyes with her sleeve, which was already wet, then described Muller. "I think *he* has my father hostage at least . . . if not dead." A new wave of sorrow rushed at her as she thought of Peter Defore left alone in the countryside to die.

Erlanger poured glasses of water for them both, but neither drank. They sat in stunned silence until she pointed at the pistol on the desk. "For your own protection?"

He looked startled, then nodded, as if he'd only now discovered the gun. He put it hastily into a drawer. He seemed to move numbly, as if capable only of responding to things she pointed out to him. He rocked his head in his hands. "The end of the House of Erlanger!"

Surlina realized he was not altogether coherent. Gathering her wits, she asked for details of the letter.

"It was a packet of instructions," he answered, peering at her curiously, as if she should be privy to the contents. "Certainly we checked the signature. It matched the one of your father's which we have on

144

file." A bit of pride crept back into his wretched tone. "Everything was in order!"

"Yes, I'm sure the signature was genuine," she said, remembering her father's letter writing aboard the *Radiant*. "But what were his orders?"

"Why, that the plan had your approval and that your arrival should be expected!"

She smiled. What confidence her father had that she'd arrive in New Orleans just as he'd ordered her to do. He could not have known of Julien Rainbeau, of the sudden passion and commitment she'd shared. Somehow her father had believed she'd make it to Erlanger's. Her father, Tandy, the treasure: all had played a role in her decision to leave Julien—indeed, to dive overboard from the *Radiant* and leave Sam— and now it was all for naught! She moaned in despair. "So Thad Muller ends up with the Surlina Silver!"

"Why, no! Of course not! This Muller merely delivered the sealed packet, then left."

"You didn't deliver the silver to him?"

Erlanger sniffed, as if her ideas of banking left much to be desired. "The ingots were removed in accordance with your wishes."

"*My* wishes?"

"As expressed in your father's letter! Miss Defore, please do not act ignorant of this matter. We only followed explicit orders."

The veins in her temple throbbed as she leaned toward him. "Where is the silver?"

"Sent to the forge!"

"My God, has it been *melted?*"

"Of course! As you ordered!" He became distraught, pulling off his bowtie, growing red in the dark circles beneath his eyes. "Melted and cast as a pair of gates."

Gates! She stood quietly, trying to comprehend such an odd plan. Of what use were silver gates? She stared at him. "A pair of gates?"

He grew frighteningly still, his eyelids fluttering weakly over round eyes. "Yes," he sighed. "An ordinary pair of carriage gates, though larger than most,

145

of course. Cast as gates. Painted black. Those were our instructions, and we followed them to the letter."

She ran to the window, flushed with sudden inspiration. "Those are the silver gates?" she questioned joyously, indicating the ones at the beginning of the drive. Without waiting for an answer, she ran to Erlanger and hugged him. "Congratulations! How clever! My silver is removed from your bank, melted, then returned to hang at the entrance! How amazingly safe!" She laughed excitedly. "Was that Father's idea, too? Keeping his dearest possessions in full public view? What a brilliant disguise! Camouflage at its finest!" She danced around, laughing with delight.

Slowly the connection penetrated Erlanger's mind. "These gates?" he asked haltingly, stumbling toward the window. "Oh, no, most assuredly not! My dear Miss Defore, I feel I must set the record straight. Your silver is gone. To the best of my knowledge, your father is dead. You do not want to accept either fact, but that is the sum of things."

"No, no," she argued. My father is not dead! He . . . he . . ." She was overcome with the fear that Erlanger might be correct. She tried the other subject. "Even if these gates are not the silver ones, then surely you have them hidden elsewhere!"

The banker slumped back into his chair, holding onto the edge of his desk with both hands. Loose currency fluttered to the floor as a gust of wind swirled into the room. Rain dripped steadily through the skylight, splattering the marble floor.

"Mr. Erlanger, we've both taken quite a blow but let's not believe it fatal. You have the bank. I have my gates, if you'll only disclose their whereabouts to me. I'll live to see my fortune repossessed and Thad Muller hanged. And you'll live to see Erlanger's proud name restored."

He put his head down and began to sob.

She was horrified at his breakdown, but frustrated by his refusal to tell her the location of the silver gates. She patted his bald head, coaxing, "Where are my gates, sir?"

"I do not know."

"Find them!" she burst out before thinking. Then she stifled her impetuous demand, pulling a chair to the side of the shaking man and quizzing him gently. "Tell me everything."

"The gates were prepared as ordered."

"Yes, yes."

"Put on a double wagon with double-strength bottom."

"Go on."

"Railroad ties were loaded over them to protect and conceal them. We were to hold them at the departure pier until your arrival."

"Which pier?"

"The wagon was stolen last night!"

She yanked his head up to look him straight in the horrified face. "Did you leave them unprotected?"

Quietly he sat up, took the gun from the drawer, and spun the chamber. "You impugn the integrity of Erlanger's! We had the finest undercover guards in the entire South posted by the pier!"

"And what became of these finest undercover guards in the entire South?"

"Vanished."

"One double-bottom wagon loaded with railroad ties and two of the finest undercover guards in the entire South simply disappeared. In the company of Thad Muller, I well imagine! If he has harmed my father and stolen my silver, I shall never forgive him! Vengeance and death won't be sufficient for that vermin!" She fixed her mind to do mathematical calculations. How long a head start did Muller have with the wagon? Which direction would he go with it? Sailing to Europe now being financially impossible, what loyalty did she continue to have to Tandy? "How much is left in the Defore account? A few hundred dollars? A few thousand? I wish to withdraw the balance."

He waved the gun overhead. "Miss Defore! There isn't ten dollars—greenback or Confederate—left in this entire establishment!"

It all seemed to hit her at once. She was no longer the Silver Belle! And perhaps she had lost her father as well as the fortune. For a moment she felt defeated. Then she remembered how she'd discovered the vastly rich vein of ore—by walking alone into new territory, by letting her liking for the rocks with the pretty blue streaks in them entice her to carry them back to the camp.

Very well, she would find the silver again—by looking high and low for her father, the Mullermen, the gates. New Orleans merely had a civil war on its hands! She had a battle for inheritance, revenge and her namesake. "Good-bye, Mr. Erlanger, until we meet again in happier times." She picked up a few bills of foreign currency from the floor.

He did not unfix his gaze. She was halfway down the broad staircase when the shot pierced the building with its brutal echoes. Skylight tiles dropped to the main floor. Stunned, she covered her face with her hands. Two men rushed past her, up the stairs, questioning her with screwed-up faces. She shook her head at them, but did not turn back. She did not doubt that Jean Erlanger was slumped in his leather chair, a bloodstain on his left breast.

She kicked a loose cobblestone, watched it roll beneath the massive iron gates which guarded the once-mighty banking edifice. She felt badly that Jean Erlanger had not summoned the strength to see things through. "The end of the House of Erlanger, but only the beginning of my search for the Surlina gates."

Surlina was certain a man was following her as she left the cobblestone circle at Erlanger's and hurried along the boardwalk. A black man fell into step beside her for a moment, looked at her, then fell behind a few paces. She wished she knew another route back to Tandy's, but the narrow streets of the Vieux Carré twisted and turned.

She shoved through the crowd, ducking low as she crossed a dark alley, hoping to elude the man. But when she glanced back hurriedly, he was making his way through the wet gutters. His appearance was that of a strong young field hand.

The man was still there, keeping less than a half-block between them. Perhaps she could lose him in the maze of market stands. She wove a diagonal path among the tiny shops where buying, selling, bartering, haggling and arguing were going on in several languages. When she looked for her tag-along, he was gone. Had she been mistaken? Or had she been swift enough to lose him in this tangle of humanity?

She looked around carefully for the young black she had suspected of following her. In the crowd, there were many Negroes, dark-skinned Portuguese, Spaniards, Creoles and Indians. He could blend with the crowd simply by standing still. She wished her dress were a more neutral color than this blouse with the stains and the skirt with red ruffle trim. For a moment she longed for the comfort of the trousers and battle jacket she'd worn aboard the *Quail*, or the plaid shawl and chambermaid's skirt she'd worn to dance with Sam.

Rapidly, she checked the street, darted across and ran for Tandy's house. She heard the heavy clatter of footsteps behind her and ran faster. Clutching her handbag tightly under her arm, she fled around the sharp alleyway bend by the square, ready to dart into the safety of Tandy's sturdy brick entryway. A wrong turn! These ridiculous alleys were like a maze! Breathless, she ducked behind the fancy grillwork of an iron fence, flattening herself below the level of the brick supporting wall.

It was exceptionally quiet. Too quiet. The noises of the market had been comforting. Now she heard nothing and was frightened. Cautiously she turned her head, still crouching by the wall, afraid to stand up and see if anyone suspicious was in this narrow alleyway with her.

She seemed to be in a courtyard, ringed by the brick wall with the ornamental ironwork atop it. Gradually, it dawned on Surlina that she was surrounded by crypts in one of New Orleans' above-ground cemeteries. Her ears strained for sounds, but all seemed safe. Slowly, she got up.

Out of nowhere, it seemed, the huge black man leaped toward her. Seizing her wrists, he pulled her through the gateway of the iron fence. Surlina screamed, more out of anger over her own stupidity than fear. It quickly became apparent that battling with him was futile.

"You Miss Surlina?" he asked once she had calmed down a bit.

"How do you know my name? I don't know you." Until this moment, she had suspected he was probably a looter who had seen her at Erlanger's.

"Your pa done told me to look for you. He say you be goin' to the bank."

"My father, Peter Defore?" Was this some horrid joke?

"He ol' man. He tell me what you look like." Suddenly the black man became very agitated, looking about in all directions. "I gotta go quick. If'n they catch me by a white woman, I be in big trouble." He started to edge away from Surlina, terror clearly written in his eyes.

"Wait, wait! Did my father tell you anything else? Where is he?"

"He be north at the lake."

Suddenly a carriage pulled around the corner. The horses reared and the driver halted them just short of where Surlina and the slave stood. The driver's face showed anger at both having made the wrong turn and at seeing the pair together. He raised his whip, "Ho! Get away there!"

The black man ran away instantly, jumping the ornamental fence, darting through the row of crypts and disappearing down the alleyway.

It all happened so quickly that Surlina never got the chance to ask what her father may have wanted to say or learn exactly where he was.

The carriage driver was astonished to find that he was no hero in her estimation. Instead, he was tongue-lashed for his interference. He drove on, mumbling in confusion.

After he was gone, she walked through the grave-yard. There was no sign of the black man. Sorrowfully, she turned back to the streets which converged on the Pontalba Apartments.

15

Surlina and Tandy greeted each other at supper with mutual exclamation: "I have important news for you!" They stood together at the foyer to the dining courtyard, whispering in the evening hush. The sky had cleared, leaving a sultry sunset, humidity thick as fog and the chirping of mockingbirds.

"Tell me your news first," insisted Tandy. "What have you found out?"

"I've learned Father may be near here. Is there a lake nearby?"

"Of course! Lake Pontchartrain is four miles to the north. What's he doing there?"

"I'm not sure." There was no point in alarming Tandy; it was sufficient to give hope that their father was alive. She gave her fragile sister a quick hug. "Now, what's your news?"

Tandy stood tall, arranging her frilly lace handkerchief in the pocket of her beautiful costume. Surlina had to admire the effort Tandy put in to make an appearance. Of course, she'd had years of experience making costumes for her dolls. Surlina wondered if her sister would every truly grow up.

"Oh, Surlina, we are to have a dinner guest—a most important member of the diplomatic corps. Thayer is bringing him home from the council meeting to dine with us."

Surlina's heart sank—diplomatic corps. "Who is it, Tandy?"

151

There was no time for an answer, as Surlina immediately heard Cabell's distinctive falsetto and his companion's coldly commanding reply. Ramsey! Surlina gulped, shut her eyes, then steadied herself to deal with Ramsey. By now he'd be aware of precisely who she was. She acknowledged his presence by looking directly into his sea-green eyes, pretending surprise and delight that their paths should cross again.

He moved immediately to kiss her hand, capturing it between his long, sensual fingers. His eyes twinkled with an "I have the upper hand now" message, but his words were charming, exuding civilization and restraint. "My pleasure is boundless to have you as a dinner partner. You ravish my senses, Miss Defore!"

Oh, that rogue! Such smooth talk, such polite nonsense! She'd not be fooled by his gentlemanly manners. She'd seen him in action. No, it would take more than this thin varnish of charm to blot out his foul suggestions aboard the *Quail*. As he offered his arm to escort her to the table, she murmured, "I thought you were bound for Shiloh. Or did you find the action too hot?"

He smiled warmly, forgiving her insults with his eyes. "A change of plans. I hope you will pardon that I did not die in that fearsome bloodbath. As for you, you seem to have undergone a change of identity since I last saw you." They were standing beside their places now, but he kept her arm tucked through his possessively. "You played your role quite well. I suspected you of several things, but never of being the Silver Belle."

"The scene I beheld at Erlanger's indicates that I am no longer the Silver Belle," she replied. "At best my ingots have been commandeered to Richmond; at worst they have fallen into the hands of Mullermen."

"In any event, you will be hell-bent to retrieve them!"

It embarrassed her for Ramsey to understand her so well. She shook her hand loose and seated herself before he had time to assist her. Instead of conversing with him, she engaged in the inanities which passed for repartee with Tandy.

Finally, with the after-dinner mints, Cabell and Ramsey excused themselves. "It's back to work for us," insisted Cabell, nodding at Ramsey. "Another secret go-round of the council." They put their heads together and whispered like a couple of old women, then apologized again and made their departure.

"Thank heaven he's gone!" blurted Surlina as soon as Ramsey was out the door. "That ill-tempered swine! That dog of low degree!" She wasted no more time on Ramsey's pedigree. She had business to attend to. "I am going out, Tandy."

"Heaven forbid! You must not! Only men are allowed on the streets after dark, and there is a ten o'clock curfew even for them!" She paled behind her powdered cheeks, looking faint as a faded painting. "Surlina," she begged, clutching her sister's hands, "put whatever troubles you have in the hands of my husband. He can assist you, I'm sure!"

"Assist me out of my inheritance," she replied. No, she must not offend Tandy by impugning Thayer Cabell. He was a dangerous man, to be sure, and not to be taken lightly. "He is too busy to help me," she said tactfully. "Why, serving on the Council of New Orleans must keep him dreadfully busy!"

Tandy, smiling agreement, did not press the argument. "But you must not go out. Besides the curfew, this is Saturday night! The blacks will be dancing in Congo Square!" She shivered and looked toward the shutters. "Nice women don't even like to hear their music."

"Tandy, I'll go in disguise and plug my ears, then! But I must go. It concerns Father." She broke away before Tandy could protest.

Hurriedly she ran to her room, donned the tobacco-stained blouse, pulled her trousers on, rummaged a gray flannel jacket from the well-stocked guest-room closet, then borrowed the fine beaver hat Thayer Cabell had left in the downstairs foyer. She caught sight of her image in the downstairs triple mirror. She'd never pass muster with Tandy! But she'd be able to walk the streets, alleys, swamps and backroads of the parish

153

without coming to a bad end. As for the music from Congo Square . . . Well, Tandy had simply whetted her interest when she'd spoken of dancing.

Surlina was barely a mile toward her goal of the lakefront when she encountered resistance in the form of Confederate defense lines. "Halt! Who goes there?" demanded a sentry. Surlina found herself thoroughly inspected, her disguise laughed at, and her plans terminated. "No, ma'am, you ain't going through these lines! That's orders."

Dismayed, she tried a bribe. "I have silver," she offered, "if you'll let me through to find it."

"Can't you do no better'n a story than that, ma'am? Can't you make it gold at least?" He bit into a plug of chewing tobacco and looked at her in disgust.

"I want to speak to your commanding officer!"

"That's General Lovell, ma'am. He's here somewhere all right, stringing troops round the lake six deep!"

"Point him out to me."

"Sure admire your spunk, ma'am. That's him, on the gray mare at the end of the column."

She ran to the man in charge, pulled his horse's reins and entreated him to let her pass through the lines.

Lovell was curt. "Miss, I am a man with too much to do in too little time. This perimeter is secure. State your business in going beyond it."

"I am a neutral citizen."

"I have no way of knowing that."

"My business is personal."

"You'll need an official pass. A writ signed by both the diplomatic corps and the Council of New Orleans."

For once, she was pleased to know Ramsey and Thayer. She rushed back into town, determined to get the pass.

16

By morning the city was sealed, with Lovell's forces on the lakeside and Farragut's forces on the riverfront. For four days the city sat in limbo; no one was allowed in or out. The council met incessantly from dawn to sunset without ordering Lovell either to fight or retreat. Surlina begged Cabell to sign a pass for her. "I must attempt to meet my father," she said, telling him no more than necessary.

"He will be in greater safety behind the lake," replied Thayer. "Maybe, when we rendezvous northward, you will have a chance to inquire of his whereabouts."

"Rendezvous? You mean when you give up this silly fight and refugee?"

Cabell would not admit that he and Tandy would leave the city. He constantly wet his lips with his swollen tongue whenever surrender was mentioned. He went about his meetings with an air of bluster, as if Farragut and Porter's fleets were mosquitoes to be slapped away if they became bothersome.

And he was not alone in his inability to face reality. Despite the presence of Union marines, the city had not lowered its flag. No official could be found who would hand over the surrender papers. Therefore, the fleet stayed anchored by the customhouse while the town remained defiant.

The impasse could not last. Yet Surlina was afraid it might last long enough to deny her all hope of finding her father and tracing the double wagon with double-strength bottom which carried the silver gates. She fretted, fussed and fumed—mostly at Tandy, since Cabell stayed away at meetings.

Tandy spent her days resting and desultorily packing a few things for a possible departure. Mainly she embroidered banners with fanciful decorations of southern stars and bars around the edges.

All the playacting came to a halt with the reality of gunfire on the Sunday morning that New Orleans put on its church clothes and, instead of flocking to St. Louis Cathedral, went en masse to the riverfront and hurled vituperation at the anchored Union fleet.

Surlina heard the splatter of shots and rushed to the balcony. Tandy came onto the balcony in her dressing gown, screwed her little oval face into a pout of disappointment and said nothing. Cabell trailed along behind her, fire in his eyes, a snifter of cognac in his hand. He rolled the dark liquid while his bean-pole legs swayed. "An army of occupation," he snorted contemptuously.

"A well-armed army of occupation," Surlina corrected him. "Moving against a city of civilians! Damn you, Cabell! Can't you resist the urge to play Napoleon? Can't you get my sister to finish packing?"

"Look! They're torching the wharves!" he cried triumphantly. "This will show Farragut that we don't accept his so-called armistice!"

"We must get Tandy to safety! See that crowd? Soon they'll overflow the square, the levee and all the roads northward. It seems that General Lovell's troops have already slipped away during the night. If we don't leave the city within the hour—"

Her frantic protests were cut off by jeers from the throng, followed by a fusillade of cannon fire from the frigates.

Surlina watched as boatloads of Federal Marines approached the landings. Crowds stood at the water's edge, hurling stones, rotten fruit and curses. The smoke from numerous fires clouded the air as a wealth of cotton went up in flames. The aromatic stench of burning coffee, bananas, tea, spices and olive oil mixed with the pungent aroma of gunpowder. In Jackson Square, directly below her, red-faced civilians worked frantically, heaping munitions, guns and caissons into piles ready for exploding.

The crowd turned to rioters as the marines marched

156

onto New Orleans soil. Cabell's loud curses flowed from the balcony like the braying of a donkey. Surlina saw that the path of the marines would lie directly beneath the balcony. She hoped that her hotheaded brother-in-law would have the sense to quiet down.

Surlina ran to Tandy's room. "My Lord in heaven, woman! Quit packing! Can't you leave anything behind?" She grabbed the latest embroidery creation and flung it from the open trunk. "Tandy, we are not traveling by steamer! This trunk is useless! A small bag is all you can take!"

"Perhaps we can find a riverboat. I need my things, Surlina. I shan't leave without them." Tandy folded her hands, apparently unfazed by the sounds of warfare outside the window.

"No boats!" shouted Surlina, wondering why she bothered to explain. "We're going overland, but not if we don't leave immediately!"

Tandy's tears brimmed like dew on her curly eyelashes. She clasped her embroidery hoop against her bosom.

"Dear God!" Surlina swore and dashed back to the balcony to check the square. The marines were headed for the flagpole atop the customhouse, charging forward to remove the defiant Stars and Bars and replace it with the Stars and Stripes. Cabell began to shout, florid and vehement, leaning far out over the balcony railing, shaking a fist at the advance guards. "Rally round, citizens! We should shout our oaths down upon their heads! We should kick dirt from every town balcony. We should shoot the man who lowers our flag! We should fight as long as there is a rooftop from which to hoist our flag!"

Surlina dashed at him, trying to cut off his mouthings. Such proclamations would make all of them hopelessly unsafe in New Orleans. As she pulled him backward, she saw the Union columns entering the square. Farragut and Porter led one procession, General Ben Butler the other. The jeers of the crowd rose to hurricane strength. Shrill whistles sounded like bombs. "Dixie" was sung from a thousand boisterous throats.

157

Shockingly, it was the young women who shouted the most extreme epithets. Tandy came onto the porch and said nothing, only folded and refolded her lace handkerchief into squares. Cabell snorted obscenely, slapped at a bold mosquito, missed, and knocked his cognac snifter off the railing.

Surlina forced herself not to chide him, to ignore Tandy, to steel her heart to be calm. 'If I am swept up in this confrontation, I will never see my silver again,' she thought. 'I'll never see Julien again if I become a hostage to Confederate plans without my consent. I'll never see Father if I lose my status as a neutral. I must stay completely out of this war!'

In the back of her mind, she thought of Sam marching determinedly south while Julien Rainbeau's tattered river defense force headed north. They were inevitably bound for collision. 'Oh, Surlina! What a mockery you make of neutrality, worrying first about Sam Grant and then about Julien Rainbeau! You can do nothing for either! Put yourself to good use, woman, and keep this foul oaf of a brother-in-law out of trouble with the law.'

As the marines approached, she watched Cabell carefully. His face was blotched with anger. He wasn't above drawing a gun and firing. His mouth poured more obscenities at the approaching Union officers.

Surlina studied the two naval officers heading the near column. Porter and Farragut marched shoulder to shoulder, erect, eyes ahead, stiff-backed, pausing only when necessary for their way to be cleared through the hostile citizens. Cabell yelled at them, "We shall fight on! We shall fight till hell freezes over . . . and then on the ice!"

Surlina snapped at him. "Cursing doesn't make you a warrior. Shut up!"

To her amazement, he darted inside. Hoping he would stay there, she turned her attention to the crowd again. The Union soldiers were behaving surprisingly well, treading slowly in well-cut uniforms displaying markings of the Illinois 21st, the Ohio 7th and Missouri 8th. A few units looked as disheveled as the men

158

aboard the *Quail,* ragamuffins displaying no spit and polish at all.

Spittle was flying onto the heads of the passing marines and onto the Union flag. Again she felt that this war eluded her. She remained certain of an underlying unity, that a nation which had been wedded and welded could not be pried apart by decree. Then she heard the shrill feminine voices screaming, "Women of the South. First to rebel, last to succumb!"

Feeling more secure since she was alone, she leaned over the railing to see the famous naval officers up close as they came by.

Suddenly Surlina felt a presence beside her. As she glanced up, she realized that Cabell was back, holding a bucket. The smell caught her nostrils as she jerked her head away from the odor of slop, sour milk and vegetable peelings from the kitchen.

As he hoisted the bucket, she caught at his sleeve, "Stop!"

With one hand he shoved her aside as the other arm swung the pail over the railing. His aim was deliberate and accurate. The slop fell directly onto the heads and gilt and blue coats of Farragut and Porter.

Horrified, she stood watching as the stream of liquid flew into the faces of the two men. Farragut stopped dead in his tracks, hands to face, stone-still and obstinate. Porter tensed, then squatted, reflexing to fight. Spluttering, fighting to keep his eyes open, he attempted to wrestle his saber from its sheath.

The commotion was instant. "Up there! I saw it! She did it! She's the one!"

In the next moment Surlina was aware of drawn swords and guns pointing upward. She turned to Cabell. He was gone! She was quite alone on the balcony—with the bucket sitting in plain view.

Above the racket, she heard cheers drowning out the soldiers' hoarse shouts. "Hooray for the Dixie belle! Courageous girl!" A mad scramble ensued beneath the balcony as troops attempted to gain entry. "Seize her! Arrest that woman!" One marine began climbing the column. Southern hands pulled him down. There was

159

pounding on the door below. Two soldiers were boosting each other into a palmetto tree, attempting to gain entry.

Surlina ran inside, down the stairs, burst into the sitting room and shouted for Tandy. She yelled for Cabell, too, furious that he had been cowardly enough to duck away after his rash action. She found him bundling Tandy out the back entrance into a carriage waiting in the alleyway.

"Come quickly," begged Tandy. "Hurry! Get in!"

"Where are you going?" She made an instant, unreasoned decision. "Cabell, you must stay! You must tell them I didn't throw that slop! Tell them I'm neutral!"

"Don't be a fool!" He swung into the carriage, urging the coachman forward.

"Where are you going?" she cried again.

Tandy, already pale from the exertion, cried, "Vicksburg!" as the coach rattled away. "Come when you can!"

The coach rattled around the corner out of sight just as federal soldiers came swooping into the back alleyway from the other end. "Halt!" they cried to her.

Surlina faced them obstinately. "I am going nowhere," she announced. "I have done nothing. I am a neutral citizen, Surlina Defore of St. Louis."

She was cut off as two marines grabbed her arms. They held her fast, arms to her sides, as they marched her through the house and out the front door. As she emerged onto the square, a cheer went up from other balconies. "Daughter of the South! Hurrah for Confederate womanhood!"

During the next hour Surlina was pushed, shoved, questioned and marched. She repeated only her name and neutrality. Already a plan was forming in the back of her brain. She had a friend in the Union Army, a man of dignity and honesty, a man of compassion and calmness, a man who would believe her. Sam. If she could send word to him at Shiloh, she was certain he would respond. He might even help her locate the silver gates. He had no love for Muller, as she remembered vividly.

"Leave me alone!" she shouted as a marine opened a cell door at the parish jail. She threw back her head and walked inside. Sam Grant. He was her best chance ... perhaps her only one.

"Another bowl of watery rice! Rats live better than this out in the gutters," complained Surlina, pushing away another jailhouse meal.

One of her cellmates, Thievin' Ann, a pickpocket with long, slim fingers, reached for her bowl. "Give it to me! I'm hungry enough to eat my own grandmother!"

Surlina looked at the other women in the cell as she passed the soupy-gray rice to Thievin' Ann. In the last ten days Surlina had learned most of their stories. Dauphine was the beggarwoman, thrown in jail because she had no place else to go. Rhoda was the prostitute accused of overcharging the victorious Yankee customers. She described herself as "fair but frail," made no apologies for her white sateen corset which she wore as a blouse, and regaled the other women with lurid tales of New Orleans's red-light district.

In the ten days Surlina had passed with these women, she'd made one true friend—a woman much like herself in spirit and independence. This was Patt, a young widow from upstate Mississippi who had summarily hacked up a Union captain who had come calling at her door. As Patt told the story, "An ax was handy, and he wasn't."

"Any news of General Butler?" Surlina asked, curious about the man who would handle her trial.

"He has set himself up a wine celler and a harem," Rhoda answered.

The other women gasped, but Surlina laughed. "Next we'll hear stories that he has opened kegs of whiskey and let it run in the gutters!" she scoffed.

"Things like that happen, though," Patt observed. "The Union soldiers scampered through my house, carrying off sugar, flour, salt and the kitchen curtains!"

161

She smiled. "But General Grant made them return the curtains."

Surlina grabbed her shoulder. "Grant? Sam Grant? *The* Sam Grant?" She had almost blurted *my* Sam Grant. She hustled Patt to the far side of the cell, shielding their conversation by turning aside and raising her hands. "I must send word to him of my whereabouts. When you are sent north for trial, you must contact him for me."

"Of course," Patt agreed, shaking her sunstreaked hair. "He seemed a fair man and generous, sending back my kitchen curtains even after I'd deprived his captain of a head. I informed him that his soldiers must not take what's mine."

If Sam were so fair to her friend, surely he'd help her find her silver as well. "Patt," she whispered, "we must get you out of this jail. Volunteer for an early trial. Demand to be sent to Grant's jurisdiction."

The women put their plan into action that afternoon by having Rhoda bribe the guard for writing materials. Rhoda then traded him kisses and a free feel of her sateen corset to dispatch the letter north to Grant's headquarters near Corinth.

Days passed and Surlina grew increasingly alarmed. "No word! We'll both rot in jail," she wailed after no reply had been received in two weeks. She lay on the cot, face down, mired in gloom. Twenty-four days in jail! Long enough to grow wan, her complexion sallow, her black cell clothes loose and baggy. Long enough for her father to have lost hope, long enough for Muller to have salvaged the silver gates, long enough for Butler to have put fear and trembling into the citizens of New Orleans.

Then Patt was ordered sent north with the next exchange of prisoners. As the women embraced, Surlina whispered, "Remember, talk to no one but Sam. Tell him I'm falsely accused and falsely held." She squeezed her friend's hands.

That night Surlina lay awake, wondering if Patt would ever reach Sam or if the whole roundabout maneuver would only end in a shambles. She wasn't sure what she expected Sam to do, but she had faith that he wouldn't leave her languishing in the parish jail.

But languish she did, through another entire week, watching with hope each time the guard came near, her heart thudding with disappointment as the rumors of Butler's coarse dealings with the city multiplied.

Dauphine was sent back to the streets. Rhoda decided to be taken before Butler so that she could become one of his women.

Thievin' Ann stole the guard's pay envelope from his hip pocket, then paid her fine with the money and was released. Surlina was left alone in the cell with plenty of gray army blankets, all the cots she could use and time to regret her decision to leave St. Louis.

The guard hollered at her, "Visitor! Your fiancé is here! Two minutes! Hurry up!"

She ran to the cell bars as he fumbled with the keys.

Stepping out from the dimness of the corridor was an immense man with huge arm muscles and enormous feet. He opened his arms for an embrace.

Surlina felt herself gathered in like a small child. The man's clasp was like a vise. Then, in a moment of shock, Surlina sensed that the stranger intended to kiss her full on the mouth. She pulled back, trying to break his clutch, but the giant seized her tighter, bringing their mouths tightly together.

Surlina felt the warm fat lips, then a sharp, insistent poking. Involuntarily, she opened her mouth. A tiny capsule was thrust in. The kiss was suddenly over. The man drew back, smiling. Surlina deposited the mysterious capsule beneath her tongue, saying nothing. He broke into bright conversation about home and friends, then informed the guard he was through. Surlina coughed, depositing the capsule in her hand, and docilely returned to her cot.

She rolled herself in a wool blanket as if planning to sleep, her excitement building as she worked the container open. In the near darkness caused by keeping the blanket over her head and her back to the bars, she withdrew the tiny slip of tightly rolled parchment, which slowly uncurled in her hand like a leaf.

Scratched in pencil were a few words, which set her trembling with relief. "Can't do more than speed your trial. Sam." Oh, he'd not failed her after all!

17

Surlina rehearsed her defense as she walked toward General Ben Butler's headquarters. The forest of tents made a city all their own in this swampland west of New Orleans. The sky was strung with clouds, promising thunderstorms during this May night. Behind her lay the city, silent under twilight curfew—a city which had never formally surrendered. She stepped around a rut full of water, mosquitoes lying black on the surface. Why would the army decide to establish headquarters in a swamp? Oh, yes, she remembered, the land had belonged to some Confederate whom Butler wished to humiliate.

Flies buzzed in the evening stillness while a cavalry unit went about the task of feeding the horses. "How many men in this camp?" she asked her accompanying guard.

"Twenty-five hundred. And about as many horses." He edged closer and dropped his voice. "What you done to rate a personal hearing—at night?"

A good question. One she'd pondered since early afternoon when word had come for her to be transferred from jail to Butler's headquarters. Perhaps Sam's message had reached Butler and he was acting on the request for speed. 'I'll apologize,' she decided. 'Not for myself but for Thayer Cabell's abominable manners! I must be ladylike and sorry for any transgressions, then turn the tables and quiz my interrogator about Thad Muller.' She shivered in the May heat, just thinking of that illiterate Indiana bean farmer! Instead of answering the guard's question, she asked him, "Where's the prison?"

"Maybe you won't end up there," he replied hopefully. He stopped before a long series of connecting tent rooms. "Here's Butler's tent. Wish you luck."

She entered the tent by ducking under the tied-up flap. Inside the first canvas room was an adjutant, busy with papers. He glanced up, chuckled, closed his file and stood. "Miss Defore? For a *personal* hearing with the general?" When she nodded, he chuckled again, low and leering, and motioned her inside, then made a hasty exit.

No good was going to come of this meeting! Surlina hesitated a moment before going in, adjusting her jail uniform. She spotted a fresh daisy in a glass on the adjutant's desk and quietly appropriated it for her buttonhole. Flowers and music! How she loved them . . . and how long since she'd been free to enjoy either.

Surlina walked into the inner room, facing the infamous officer across his campaign desk. Instantly she appraised him as overtired and short-tempered. His uniform was slack, his eyes baggy, his jowls drooping; a tick of weariness twitched his little finger on the left hand. 'Perhaps he is too tired to care about my minor sins,' she hoped. He did not look up, so she bestowed a smile on the young aide seated in the corner with a sheaf of documents on his lap.

She stepped forward, stated her name and listened as the particulars of her case were read aloud. All the while she kept her eyes directly on Butler. He listened, sometimes tapping a pencil, sometimes locking his red hands together, occasionally twisting an onyx ring. He had a delicate face, marred by sideburns which jutted out from his chin in coarse patches.

He looked up inquiringly. "So, at last, I meet the Queen of Southern Slop."

"I am a neutral citizen of St. Louis."

He rose, walked around and appraised her face and figure openly. "You look to me like a fair-skinned, dark-eyed, bewitchin' young chicken about ripe for

165

pluckin' and eatin'." He pushed her hair behind her ears. "Too bad your actions belie your tenderness."

"Some of the actions of your army are hardly commendable either, General Butler!" She immediately wished she had not taken him to task.

He continued to circle Surlina. Except for his face, he was a heavy man. Perhaps his boots pinched his feet; she noticed he limped. Her remark about his army seemed less to annoy him than sadden him. "My army has much in common with Wellington's. Both scraped together from the scum of the earth." He paused, taking a measurement of her bosom with his eyes. "But the reception of this city was nothing short of treason." He grabbed her upper arm, pinching it painfully. "You filthy devil in the guise of a fair-skinned maiden!"

"Don't you dare touch me!" she snapped, then attempted to ease away from him, wondering how to fathom and manipulate him. He stood back, an acquisitive leer playing over his lips as his big tongue licked the corners of his mouth.

Finally, he spoke. "Perhaps I shall find it in my heart to forgive you. Maybe you were only plying your avocation, like a woman of the streets."

"I shall not pardon *you* for that last remark."

Abruptly the game was over. He returned to his seat and plopped down heavily. "Miss Defore, your fame has preceded you. You seem to bring havoc to Union generals you encounter. I've heard from Grant about the *Radiant*—"

"Sam? Oh, yes, I know him!" Her cry was enthusiastic as she attempted to convey they were old friends from long ago. "How has he been? Where is he now?"

Butler looked at her suspiciously.

She decided to play dumb. "Is Sam here?"

He fell for the ploy, shuffling his boots together, then limping to one side. "Here? Of course not! He's at Corinth, still licking his wounds from Shiloh!" He hobbled around the tent, smacking a fist into an open palm, gloating. "Yes, there he was, at a wilderness meetinghouse with everything exposed to his blood-

166

thirsty enemies except his private parts!" Boisterous laughter, reeking of jealousy, poured from his throat, making his purple veins quiver. "That old fool! Surprised on his horse's behind, that's what he was! Mark my words, miss. He won't last long in this man's army."

How could she explain Sam to his enemies when she could hardly explain him to herself. He had an air about him, that was all—an air of fate. She had looked for another word, not believing in fate; but it was this aura of destiny that hovered over his hunched shoulders. Quietly she said, "Sam is a great man. It is inevitable that history will recognize him."

Had she overplayed her part? Something had alerted Butler, for he cocked his head, stroked his chin and pulled at his onyx ring. "Sam told me to hear *your* case, not *his* defenses," he said briskly. "You're awfully eager to cast him as a hero, aren't you? Why would the Silver Belle bestow a steamer on a backwoods brigadier?" His eyes twinkled with anticipation, saliva beading his thick lips. "Tell me, is ol' Sam not the monogamous soldier he purports to be?"

She'd heard the old adage about the best defense being a good offense. Surlina boldly decided to attack her captor, singing him a ditty she'd learned in jail. "Maybe I can amuse the Union general with a song to the tune of 'Yankee Doodle,' " she said sweetly, then began before he could answer. "Old Butler stays in Fort Monroe . . . and listens to the battle . . . and then the Southerners whip him back . . . just like a drove of cattle."

Anger bristled his sideburns straight out from his head. He bared his teeth. "That is sufficient!" He sat heavily in his desk chair.

"You don't like music? Why, General, how dreary! Then I shall have to save my vocal pearls to cast before other swine, I suppose."

"You slut! You bitch!" He bolted upward, knocking his chair backward, slammed into the desk and sent it crashing. He grabbed her shoulders, stripped away the daisy, mashing it beneath his boots. She flinched beneath his hands. He tightened his grip, digging into her

167

shoulder blades like twisting a knife blade. "I know all about you, Surlina Defore! You're the Silver Belle, the old maid who needs a good man to take the kinks out of her bustle."

"And I know about you, Ben Butler! You're the cross-eyed politician who bought himself a generalship!" While she stood her ground with him, her heart fearfully skipped beats. Despite his sagging face, he was a man of strength. "Turn me loose! You're hurting me!"

He let up on the pressure but kept his hands on her. "I have been sent to rule with an iron hand. I think I would enjoy using it on you. I have complete power here."

"Yet you cannot control the city you were sent to govern!" She bit her lip, angry that her temper should defeat her vow of neutrality. "I apologize, General. I do not doubt your absolute authority."

He picked his ruler out of the desk debris, tapped her curls with it, touched her wrists, her waist, bent forward and tapped her knees. "Young lady, I can do whatever I want with you."

"You cannot inspect me like a horse. Kindly put away that ruler."

"I can hang you, for example. How would you feel with the coarse hemp tightening about that ivory throat?" He attempted to stroke her neck, but she slapped his hand away.

"I can imprison you," he suggested, his tone rising. "How would you feel withering to skin and bones behind bars? No fat on your handsome cheeks. Those abundant breasts shrinking to the size of the tits on a goat!" His hand came up, but he did not try to touch her chest.

"Or," he remarked in a tone full of insinuation, "I can rape you. How would you feel with me pushing my knee between your thighs, grunting with pleasure as I give you pain?" He whirled around and tossed the ruler high in the air. "I can do all these things! All for sufficient reason . . . or *no* reason!"

Surlina shut her eyes, wishing for once she were back

168

at the convent. 'I'll let the words tumble through my brain without actually hearing them,' she promised herself, then stood silent and rigid under his verbal assault.

When the barrage had stopped, she opened her eyes. Butler smiled at her, licked his lips, then stepped to the tent flap and let the material down with finesse, making the closing look unobtrusive. She trembled involuntarily. She stalled for time. "General, I am hungry—almost faint."

"A little weakness on your part would be most becoming," he retorted as he gestured for her to sit on the cot. She moved toward it but avoided sitting. He pranced openly now, his eyes nearly closed so she could not meet and defy them. His darting tongue left little flecks of tobacco juice on his lips.

She was aware how slave women must have felt on the auction blocks. "Keep your eyes to yourself, sir. Keep your eyes to yourself, and I shall save my slop for more worthy hogs."

Butler forced himself against her then. With one swarthy hand he stifled her outcry while the other arm sent her backward. "No more talking! You must bargain with me now!"

"You have nothing I want."

"No? Not a pair of black gates which are rumored to be of interest to you?"

She was stunned. "What?"

"I have taken possession of a wagon—an extremely heavy wagon heaped high with wheels and railroad ties. Do you know what this wagon might contain?"

"How did you get it?" she cried. "From Muller?"

"Let us say only that a certain soldier attempted to desert the United States Army. In the first place, he was not a very smart man to want to do this. Second, after remaining at large despite all Grant's goosey efforts, this same deserting soldier attempted to drive a wagon through *my* lines. Naturally, he was caught, the wagon confiscated and—"

"Thad Muller! What have you done with him? I am so grateful you have captured that brute!" Her praise was heartfelt. "Let me talk to him! I think he knows where my father is."

"You'll have a dead-end conversation with Muller. He was hanged from the gallows yesterday by orders of the general commanding." He preened, executing a little bow. "That's me."

"I want to see the body! I want the satisfaction of seeing his broken neck, seeing that ugly fish-face tattoo erased by the red marks of the noose!"

"My God in heaven, woman! What a garish mind you have! So, a little blood and gore only heightens your appetite? Some men are like that, too. Come off the field of battle with their organs hard and their swords bloody." Butler swore softly, lust dilating his pupils. "By God, we'll just give this a go. You hie off and fill your eyes with a corpse! I'll have supper sent. I don't want a girl to get all drawn up in the gut and go slack on me before she should!"

Surlina was having second thoughts about viewing Muller's body, but it would buy her time away from Butler. She followed the general's directions and waited for the aide to escort her to the makeshift morgue.

All during the walk she thought about the silver gates. Butler had seem intrigued, calling them heavy black gates. Apparently he had no real idea of their value. She steadied herself to enter the embalmer's area, a tent with a wooden worktable in front, vials of formaldehyde and vinegar handy in glass cases. Despite the smell, she wanted to verify that Thad Muller was truly dead. "Yes, take me inside," she said, drawing a deep breath.

The odor permeated her nostrils, washing over her in a sudden gust. The smell of death was lightly covered by floral perfume. She spotted the scent bottle unstoppered in the corner cabinet—Dr. Fontaine's Balm of a Thousand Flowers. But ten thousand flowers could not mask the stench of dead bodies. She raised her cuff to her face and breathed through the material. Her impulse was to bolt from the tent, fling herself into the fresh air and take her chances in running away.

The embalmer, a slight, stooped man with cheeks as pallid as the dead he tended, led Surlina to a row of wooden coffins. "Just finished nailing this one shut," he grumbled, "now you want me to pry him open again! You here to claim him?"

"No! I'm no relation of Thad Muller!"

"We'll ship him home to Connecticut then, like his papers show."

"Connecticut? Muller's from Indiana—an Indiana farmer."

The embalmer shook his head. " 'Taint so. Says Connecticut clear as printing on his papers."

"Then the papers are forgeries! He's a thief, murderer, outlyer and deserter all right, but he's harassed my path ever since leaving Indiana, not Connecticut." She wasn't sure why she was so insistent Muller's body be returned to the proper state. Why did they bother to ship criminals home when soldiers who died in battle were buried in common graves? She had lost all interest in seeing the corpse. "I've changed my mind. I don't want to view the body."

"Hold on there. I think you better. It wouldn't be the first time we found a mix-up in papers meant a mix-up in corpses." He attacked the coffin lid, yanking the nails out with the hammer claw, sticking the used nails into his mouth.

Surlina rolled her hands into tight balls, feeling her stomach curl in apprehension as he lifted the lid. Surlina could not bear to breathe and at the last instant shut her eyes tightly. When she could hold her breath no longer, she gulped air, took a quick squint at the naked man laid out in the box, then squealed. "Christ! That's not Muller!"

"Well, that's the man we hung for Muller." He slammed down the lid. "Then who is it?"

"Sweet Jesus, I don't know!" She was beside herself, darting for the outdoors while cursing the embalmer, the army and especially General Butler for hanging the wrong man! She heard the embalmer trailing after her and shouted at him, "Get away from me! Keep away!" Surlina dashed for Butler's tent, heard the heavy foot-

171

steps fall away as the embalmer gave up the chase, then wondered how wise it would be to confront Butler with his mistake. He'd hanged someone, all right, probably a deserter and bandit. A Mullerman, true, but maybe all members of the renegades carried papers proclaiming themselves Muller. Thad Muller was too damned smart to be caught by the army! He was too damned clever to be caught driving a slow-moving wagon. She'd have to catch him herself if she wanted to see him dangle from a rope!

Butler was standing in front of his tent, directing the serving of supper. Mess boys hurried in and out carrying trays, steamer dishes, an iced bucket of champagne. He'd obviously planned a feast while her appetite had been ruined. She stopped running, attempting to overcome her squeamishness. If Muller was still at large, he'd surely be after the silver gates. Her main concern must be to get free, take possession of the silver, then find her father. Butler was the key to the puzzle. Somewhere on this sprawling post of men and horses was a double-bottom wagon heaped with wheels, railroad ties, and one immense pair of black carriage gates. As another bottle of champagne was taken inside the tent, an idea formed in Surlina's mind. If Butler drank enough champagne, he might well tell her where the wagon was. She plastered a pleasant look on her face while her insides remained shaky.

The moment he saw her, Butler dismissed all the orderlies. Without mentioning Muller, he nodded at her, swiftly opened the sparkling wine, filled his glass and drained it. Butler then refilled it and offered her one. Surlina accepted. He toasted her with lifted eyebrows. "Bottoms up, dearie?" He walked past her, swatting her rump with his open palm.

All right, he had the silver, which she wanted. What else did she have to offer in trade? She seated herself primly to a meal of beefsteak, cornbread, collard greens and pinto beans. A huge jug of catsup accompanied the meal along with salt and pepper. The whole idea of eating seemed repulsive, yet she must feign interest in wining and dining. She sipped the champagne, nodding her approval.

"If you're starving, dig right in," he commanded. "I prefer to take my ease for a while." He sat on the edge of the cot, watching her like a stallion eyeing a mare. "You don't look dressed proper to me," Butler decided. "My last dinner partner ended up eating naked as the bird on her plate." He finished his wine and refilled the glass again.

"I'm quite comfortable."

"Be more comfortable over here. Come, set beside me."

She moved as ordered, conscious of the creeping fear which raised goose bumps on her arms.

She sat just out of his reach, turning to face him, launching a conversation which she hoped implied by its civil tone that they would chat long into the night. "I am so pleased that you intercepted Muller and his wagon," she lied. "Did you put the railroad ties and wheels to good use? What else did you say was in the wagon? Gates? Carriage gates?"

He drank steadily. "All put to good use, yes, indeed! Railroad ties make great footbridges in this gumbo swamp! An army always needs new wheels on its wagons. All put to good use, yes sirree!" He went to the champagne bottle, found it empty and uncorked the second.

"And the gates," she prompted. "What use did you make of ordinary carriage gates?"

He laughed cryptically. "Does the Silver Belle have more than a casual interest in the possessions of an outlyer?"

"Tell me where the gates are!" she demanded.

"Settle down! Those gates are out of your reach. They're headed into the bayou country. We'll use them at the next plantation where we set up headquarters." He was caught up in his grandiose plans. "I intend to use only the finest homes as my personal headquarters. Those are imposing gates. They'll look well with my name welded to their arches."

Surlina was convinced that he did not realize the

173

fortune which lay beneath the simple black paint. Or, if he did, this was his way of keeping the silver in his possession until the war was over. Damn! Another enemy to contend with. Thad Muller still loose in the countryside, her father unaccounted for, Tandy refugeeing in Vicksburg, and now Ben Butler intending to use her gates to decorate his bayou headquarters! Suddenly she felt terribly tired, as if unable to fight all the obstacles. When he put his wineglass aside and undid the top fastener of her black blouse, she simply let her shoulders slump and did not resist.

"The path of least resistance is always easiest," he murmured, encouraged by her docility. He undid a second button, then grinned happily, catching hold of the ruffle on her chemise. "What! Frilly lingerie decorates the iron maiden? By God, I have underestimated you, Miss Silver Belle! We shall have a lot of fun, you and I!"

Surlina was not sure she could fight him away, but she could at least deprive him of seeing any response from her. She edged further to the end of the cot as he plopped down beside her, tugging off his boots and hose, then loosening his belt. She quickly poured the last of the champagne for him.

She lowered her voice, trying to sound coy. "We're in need of more champagne, don't you think?"

"By damn, we are!" He rose tipsily, looking into the cooler for another bottle. When he found none, he tugged his trousers upward and wove his way to the tent flap, apparently going in personal pursuit of the cool wine.

The minute he left, she was on her feet, searching, though she had nothing precise in mind. Surlina froze as the tent canvas rustled. Whirling, she saw a sergeant with a handful of rolled documents in his hands. While she knew her own eyes were wide with surprise, his were totally astounded. He immediately turned red in the face while she felt her blush extend to the lace atop her breasts. The poor man dropped the maps, grabbed her supper tray and backed out of the tent.

She flew to the documents, unrolling the first one

with greedy hands. It was a map of the city. No good. Her hands left sweat marks as she tried to reroll it. Never mind; she let it drop and grabbed the next cylinder. Ah, yes, this was better, a plan of the low country to the west. There, marked with a star, in black ink she read the words, "Regimental Headquarters: Butler." Then she gasped involuntarily. The star marking the bayou headquarters was at the plantation she most wanted to visit—Whispers.

Surlina had an inkling how fast things would move now. With New Orleans under the Stars and Stripes once more, Union forces were free to fan out like spokes on a wheel. Farragut's forces were already headed upriver, with Vicksburg as their target. Butler had earmarked Whispers as his next headquarters— had probably sent wagons ahead with his possessions, including her silver.

For a moment, she worried about the safety of the plantation, about Ramsey's great house, Dottie, Kuffy, and most of all, Julien.

She ran to the supper table, grabbed the steak knife, and hastily cut away the portion of the map showing the location of Whispers. On impulse, she stuck the dinner knife in her waistband, feeling the point against her hip. She stuffed the piece of paper into her chemise and hastily rebuttoned her blouse.

Blowing out the lantern, she moved stealthily in the darkness, appropriating Butler's money belt from the desk drawer, then silently lifting the flap to peer out. The general could not be far away. Sentries would be patrolling. She crept through the tent doorway, hunching low, and slipped behind the general's black stallion, grateful for his sheltering bulk and color. Deftly she untied him, gliding toward the rear of the tent. As she reached the darkness at the perimeter, she slung herself across the horse's back, clutched his reins and neck and dug her heels into his flanks. "Go!"

Her dash across the sentry line was haphazard. Guided only by a few lanterns and the lovely lure of total darkness beyond the pickets, she trotted the horse carefully. Then, as she broke into a gallop, a final sentry rose up, looming large by the ditch. "Halt! Who goes there?" he cried. Surlina kicked hard into the stallion's side. Like a winged horse of mythology, it leaped both soldier and ditch.

"Deserter! Stop, thief!"

As Surlina glanced back, she could see no lanterns moving toward her, though there was one sharp report of a rifle.

She rode hard, hearing only the sound of reins slapping the horse's neck, the wind rushing past her face and her own delighted laughter.

18

By dawn the horse's flanks were lathered and his mouth drooling foam with the exertion. Surlina, too, was grime covered and panting with the stiffness of too much motion. She dismounted, but with each step she ached from having ridden astride.

Twice during the night she had paused, trying to find out if she were pursued. She doubted that she would be. Butler could certainly send forces after her on grounds of horse thieving, but Surlina didn't think he would. Instead, he would head straight for Whispers, to cut off her chance of regaining the gates.

After she had watered the stallion and let him cool down, she walked him slowly along the levee. It would be best to leave the main road during daylight. A consultation with the dusty map assured her that any road would do. They were few and far between in bayou country, and all led to Whispers. What she really needed was a boat! Whispers sat in a wilderness of water, ten times more approachable by bayou than by land.

The first road leading west was merely a rut-covered trail. Surlina turned the horse down it, seeing she would have to walk as the foliage grew too dense and low

176

for her to ride. Moist vines created a stormlike darkness, with wetness and warmth remaining, but light failing.

As she penetrated deeper into the swamp, a stagnant odor rose from the still water in the bayous. Bird chirps and jumping frogs broke the silence.

Suddenly, splashing echoed in the dense environment. She darted behind a tree, hoping the black horse would blend with the foliage. Surlina held her breath as the swishing sound occurred again. From around the bayou's bend she spotted a lone Negro boy in a canoe, hitting the water's scum with his fishing line.

She stepped out of hiding, almost slipping down the mossy bank. "Ahoy! Which way to Whispers on the Rainbeau?"

The boy stood up in the pirogue, eyes startled, paddle in one hand, fishing pole in the other. The boat began to rock, threatening to dump him. Then his face lighted up with a huge smile, nostrils flaring, teeth gleaming. "That *you?* The lady what likes the flowers?"

"Kuffy!" She ran down the embankment, catching hold of willows to keep from falling in the green water. "Oh, you looked so small in that boat all by yourself! My goodness, sit down before you fall overboard!"

He complied, grinning happily, then paddled toward her. "I'm catching fish for Aunt Dottie. She's promised a mess of eatables for supper at the big house since all the men from the *Quail* are coming over from the secret place."

Surlina's heart trilled like a songbird. Julien would be there! The little boat touched shore, and she stepped in unsteadily, abandoning Butler's black stallion to find his way back to the army. "Who is at Whispers?" she asked quickly.

"They is all to home," Kuffy confided, dipping the paddle noiselessly into the bayou, turning the boat around. "Home!" he breathed again, and she saw how happy the child was to be back at Whispers instead of running about the war-torn countryside in the company of Ramsey Arnauld.

The boat glided along the dark water, the foliage

177

meeting overhead, creating a tunnel. "Do you have a family, Kuffy?" It appalled her that she'd never thought of the child as being more than an extension of Ramsey.

"No mama," he replied. "No more. But she told me the story 'bout me and King Jesus Man both being born in the cow barn. Me and King Jesus Baby, we both slept in the hay, mama taught me."

Surlina smiled maternally at the little boy who fancied himself so lucky. "Kuffy, is everyone all right at Whispers? Has there been any trouble? Any Yankees?"

"No soldiers this day," he said happily. "Aunt Dottie shooed some bluecoats away yesterday, though. She say they don't want trouble. Mostly we just tend to what needs doing, dig a well, shoot turkeys, chop cane stalks. Dottie say, 'keep your nose clean' and the army won't bother us."

Surlina thought fondly of Dottie; then her heart sang louder at the thought of seeing Julien.

Without warning, the forest seemed to break apart as a rifle shot cracked the heavy air. The noise crackled across the bow of the pirogue, sending both occupants leaping to the bottom. Surlina flattened herself over Kuffy and the flopping fish, squashing everything in a frantic attempt to get out of danger. An instant later, she heard a loud holler—a victory whoop—then barroom language. Surlina straightened up a bit to peer over the bow.

"Dottie! My God, what are you shooting at?"

Dottie did not seem surprised, merely motioned her to keep low, then aimed the gun again, almost directly overhead. Another roar issued from the gun, followed by a thud, a crashing of branches, and a tremendous splash in the bayou. Surlina glimpsed falling yellow fur, paws and large teeth. She gasped in fear. "What was that? God, Dottie, you'll kill us all!"

Dottie was laughing merrily, splashing into the scum after the trophy. Her long arms were clad in buckskins, the fringe waving as she thrashed through the knee-deep water. "Eatables! Bobcat for grub! A skin of meat for the supper sitting!" She used the rifle butt to club

178

the animal before lifting it from the swamp. She hoisted the animal over her shoulders, looking strong enough to carry anything home from the woods.

Surlina was amazed. Dottie, obviously proud of her accomplishment, clambered up the muddy bank with ease, her thick ankles squishing in the wet boots. "My mule, Murray, is down the ruts apiece. Climb out of that ridiculous crouch, Surlina, and walk a spell with me."

Surlina nodded and Kuffy helped her out, his eyes still wide with bewilderment at Dottie's antics. "I'll fish some more," he ventured and looked to Dottie for encouragement. She nodded and he paddled away rapidly.

Dottie dragged the bobcat down the trail by his tail, slung him over the mule's back. Next she turned her attention to Surlina. "So look who's come calling at Whispers' back door!"

"Dottie, who's here that can help defend the plantation? Yankees are headed this way. Whispers is marked to be General Butler's new regimental headquarters."

"Not anymore, it ain't," snorted Dottie. "I done held them advance scouts off to a standstill and a fare-thee-well!" She dusted her hands as if the fight had been weighted heavily in her favor.

At the same time that Surlina was glad for the safety of Whispers, her hopes for the silver gates sank. She kept pace with Dottie. "Several supply wagons were coming. One in particular had a pair of carriage gates in it."

"Yep. Done shooed that bunch away, too."

"No! Where?"

"Don't rightly care, long as it ain't here." She shook her head. "Them passel of Basketby-Arnauld women and babies couldn't defend a dandelion against sunstroke! And Ramsey—he's of the opinion he can talk 'em to death!"

"Those black gates!" wailed Surlina. "Think now, where could they have taken them?"

"Why the snit over gates? You being the Silver Belle, buy some more!" Dottie made it obvious she knew Surlina's identity now. "Well, I did hear one young feller—only trying to do his job, I reckon—allow as how he would ship the supplies upriver with Farragut. Said if Farragut didn't want 'em, *he* could send 'em to Grant's army below Memphis."

Surlina was thrilled at the idea that by some convolution, Sam might end up with her gates. 'Surely he would give them back to me,' she thought. Strangely, she realized she never thought of Sam without the next moment thinking of Julien. "Aunt Dottie, is Julien at home, too?"

"Yes and no. He and Professor Boxt and the boys are working on the *Quail*'s rigging over in Bayou Teche, laying low while the big river is full of gunboats. Today, though, Julien had to go off to a regular true-up war council. It was a sight to see, him all decked out to meet with Jeff Davis and Ramsey, of course, and some feller named Thayer Cabell."

"Cabell! That's my—" Surlina stopped herself, unwilling to claim relation with Thayer Cabell. Also, she was uncertain how much Dottie already knew. One thing for certain, she couldn't imagine Julien Rainbeau taking orders from the likes of Cabell.

"Julien will be home for supper, provided he gets his ears loose from all the blowhards."

They had arrived at a clearing. Forest gave way to lush lawns, and topping a rise stood a magnificent home of wood, stone and statue. The fabled onion dome sat atop the house, glistening copper-bright through its weathered casing of blue-green.

"Whispers! It's so lovely," Surlina said, hushed by its beauty.

Dottie quizzed her as she brought the mule to a halt. "How'd you like New Orleans? Take in all the sights? Tend to all your business?"

"I was not well received." Surlina didn't explain, but thought to extend her apologies for appearing here without warning. "I know I'm not expected—"

"That's true enough," interrupted Dottie. "Nothing much is, these days. Nothing much is." With a toss of her gray hair, she indicated that Surlina should go ahead to the house. "Your welcome will be warmer than a June night when Julien gets back! He nearly busted a gut when he found out you could buy and sell him ten times over." She seemed to want to pry, but restrained herself with a curse. "Oh, shoot, an old lady should button her lip and let you hot-blooded young folks do the unbuttoning!" She winked. "You and Julien gonna sear the sheets tonight? Or hide out in the cotton barn like you did last time?"

Oh, no secrets were safe with Dottie! Surlina said honestly, "The silver stands between us now. I cherish the memory of that night, but there will never again be that innocence between us." She felt sadness etching its pall over her. Never again could she present him with her virginity; never again could she trust him not to be acting under orders to obtain her fortune. She felt the brimming of unwanted tears against her lashes. "I might as well leave, Dottie, nothing can ever be the same."

Dottie handed Surlina a dirty handkerchief. "If I was you, I'd do less sniffling and more courting. Give Julien time, some soft words, and half your pillow. Things tend to look better in the moonlight than in the harsh light of day."

Left on her own to discover Whispers, Surlina crept toward the house, admiring each new vista, startled by the size of the West Wind Gates. She could see why Professor Boxt had traveled cross-continent to sketch them. They stood tall as three men, wide as a gunboat and were faithful replicas of their namesakes which had guarded Troy.

The esplanade of oaks and cypresses stopped at the courtyards. There, cedars ringed the croquet court, the sundial and the island. Four little footbridges ran across a clear stream which formed a moat around the main house. The only connection to a true road was through the West Wind Gates which faced the sea-wall.

Surlina walked quietly, seeming to absorb some of the dignity of the formal gardens, lulled by the scent of Osage orange. Now she could identify the hollow, hinged statue columns around the wide porticoes. Faith, Hope, Charity, the Three Graces, the Fates, all accounted for in statue form, their heads detailed with lifelike eyes, hair and lips. Massive brick, mortar and post columns rose at the corners and wings, doing the real work of supporting the second and third stories. Between the statues, ivy had put out tendrils, making it appear as though the goddesses were holding hands around the house. Red-brick corner planters gave additional strength. There were two porch swings, gutters full of magnolia leaves and a pack of dogs lying stolid and smart with their noses tucked up on their front paws. Surlina was totally charmed.

She ascended the steps, found the inevitable creaking board and looked for the statue named Hope. She made her way twice around the house without spotting it. The second time she passed the front entry, the door swung open.

A house servant in full evening dress bowed to her. "Welcome to Whispers. Your calling card, miss?" He acted as if she had been expected for a long time.

"I . . . I have no card."

"Then do you have luggage for the night? Big box, little box, bandbox or bundle?"

"No. No luggage." She wished that Dottie had come along to vouch for her. "May I come in? I am a friend of Mr. Rainbeau's."

There was a moment of strained silence, then the servant led the way through a silent house. Less grand than the imposing exterior, it was elegant but tattered. Her impulse was to open windows and give everything a good airing.

As they moved along the dim hallways, she tried to look unobtrusively for members of Julien's family.

She caught sight of no one and before long the slave stopped at a white door, turned the knob and indicated she should enter. Inside was a sitting parlor done in chintzes and gay striped wallpaper, and a smaller room, apparently a tiny chapel with a maple kneeling bench, Bible on a stand and a single rush-back chair. The bedroom was tremendous with a fireplace

182

on the inner wall and a row of windows. She looked out on a private garden.

Outside a stooped and white-haired Negro was patiently sifting the dirt. Surlina was strangely moved by the scene. It made her want to take off her shoes and rush to the yard to feel the earth between her toes, to be a child again. She wanted, for a moment, to be like Tandy, capable of little-girl fantasies with dolls and tea parties, and forget the responsibilities of silver, family duty, fragile loyalty and love. Oh, this place was alluring in its simplicity and beauty. Julien had scorned it . . . then come back to fight for it. She understood him better, seeing him in the light of his home ground.

A knock at the door indicated the bath water had arrived. Four giant women settled two steaming tubs on a raised platform. One pointed to Surlina's jail uniform. "The sooner that's buried, the better!"

Surlina laughed and shed the garments, wrapping herself in a proffered sheet. The slaves spread towels, a vial of scented bath oil, cakes of barleycorn soap and glycerin lotion on the platform. She thanked them, then sent them away, assuring them she could bathe herself.

Oh, the luxury of hot water! Her tired body slipped into the first tub with a grateful shudder. 'I'll soak forever,' Surlina thought, melting into a daze of wonderful sensations. 'I'll be clean! Wear fresh clothes! And I'll see Julien.' A cloud seemed to darken her mental horizon, so she slipped lower in the tub, letting all the worries of the future wash away.

After she'd rinsed and dried, Surlina was astonished at how wonderful she felt. She made herself at home in the room, inspecting the pinewood bed. It was heaped with eyelet covers and pillow shams which spoke of somebody's months of patient embroidery. In the armoire, she found starched and ironed clothing. She rummaged through them, fascinated by what seemed to have been left by some former belle. She selected a cool calico frock.

She was still going through the shoes and dresses,

trying to figure out to whom they might belong, when there was a knock at the door.

It was Dottie, now attired in a clean pair of men's breeches, complete with suspenders, a handsome bandana knotted at her throat blending with the plaid shirt she wore. With a wave of her hand, she ushered Surlina into the gallery hallway. "Come and meet Julien's kinfolks." Surlina was already nodding happily when Dottie added, "and his baby."

A gasp of astonishment was followed by silence. Finally Surlina's words tumbled out. "Julien's *child?* He's *married?*"

Dottie nodded nonchalantly, tossed open the portico doors to a small room and stood aside. The playroom was bright with white curtains and late-afternoon sunshine. A little girl of about four jumped up at the sight of Aunt Dottie. The child came running, flinging her arms upward, red shoes skipping over the braided rug, ruffled pantalets flipping as she jumped up to hug the leathery old lady.

In the next instant the child cried out in delight, "Daddy!"

Turning, Surlina saw Julien approaching, his face reflecting the child's exultant welcome.

A wave of longing swept through her at the beauty of his blond hair, gray eyes, dimpled chin and trim body. Impulse said, 'Run to him, kiss him with fervor and trust.' Instinct said, 'Hold back, wait and see!' She started to smile. He rushed past her, barely nodding in her direction.

Dottie hurriedly handed his child to him and rushed away, as if not caring to witness whatever scene was going to be played. Surlina stood back, impressed again at the handsomeness of the father and daughter. To her eyes, Julien was every bit as strikingly beautiful as his golden-haired, dimpled and diminutive daughter, who braced herself in the crook of his arm. She hugged him, ducking her head and shyly calling, "Papa, Sir, I love you!"

He kissed the girl, then put her down. "Good evening, Miss Defore."

"Why didn't you tell me you were married?"

"Why didn't you tell me you were the infamous Silver Belle, the girl whose fortune might finance the whole war?"

"I didn't care to."

"Neither did I."

She summoned her courage. "My silver makes no difference—if indeed I can lay my hands on it again."

"Nor does my personal life to you! My wife died four years ago."

At that moment Dottie reappeared, announced dinner and took the little girl's hand. "Come, Laurel, we'll lead the way." She made herding motions to Julien and Surlina. They remained obstinate as statues, eyeing each other with open hostility. Dottie insisted, "You two will have to fight later. Come to supper. How about a mite of truce time?"

Julien offered Surlina his arm. She declined with a look of apprehension, falling in step behind him as if to keep him under surveillance. How could she have loved this man who now acted like a complete stranger? She would never repeat the experience of having her caution blown away by soft kisses! She was so intent on her thoughts of damning him that she did not realize he had stopped. She bumped into him, full force.

He whirled, caught her against him and kissed her as if to punish her. His lips were hard, demanding and proud. He pushed the calico from her shoulders and buried his mouth against her throat.

She pulled away, not sure whether she felt her cheeks flaming from annoyance or arousal. He wanted to hurt her—that much was clear! Why would that stir her so unexpectedly? Shocked, she almost wanted to have him take her against her will, to feel his potency without having to give of herself. She stiffened, her hand going to her throat. When she spoke, she was horrified to hear her voice quiver with emotion. "Why did you do that?"

His resonant voice resounded in the still house. "Merely to find out if you had blood in your veins or

185

chalk. I am ravenously hungry for the taste of flesh —icy cold, silver gilded, treasonous flesh!" His eyes shone. He was waiting for her to move.

She waited, too. "The nature of your hunger will have to be satisfied elsewhere, Julien Rainbeau!" She thought of Sam, of his anguished berating of himself as she'd waited in jail. Now Julien leaped at chances to accuse her. "My silver is my flesh and soul! I have nothing for you!"

"As I thought," he said sarcastically. He threw open the doors to the downstairs parlor. It was filled to capacity with mostly elderly women, all dressed in black. Her hands were icy. She swallowed hard, following him into the room, hoping she'd be able to act natural during the round of introductions.

The oldest of the crones was Grandmere—all pretension and bustle in her hoopskirt. Like the statues ringing the house, the other women came in sets: there were the jewels: Opal, Pearl and Ruby, then Faith, Hope, and Charity. Harmony, Joy and Spring, though younger, were in their mid-fifties.

Julien made light comments about each of his aunts. "They all have tendencies. Faith has a tendency to drink. Opal has a tendency to faint. Even Grandmere —she has a tendency to decline." He was charmingly mischievous, obviously the delight of the old ladies.

Altogether, Surlina found the women as quaint and queer a group as she'd ever beheld. By the time she had made the circle of introductions, each woman had tapped her hand, patted her wrist or stroked her forearm. They meant it endearingly, she supposed, but she wanted to flee from their touch. And flee from Julien, so debonair and joking, so coolly polite behind his facade of warmth.

Fortunately, a younger collection of cousins and in-laws arrived, enlivening the atmosphere and sparing Surlina the necessity of dealing strictly with either the old women or Julien. To her chagrin, Ramsey appeared, striding into the room carrying a violin.

He bowed, holding the instrument aloft in his artistic, slim hands. "Will you join me in the music room while Julien holds court here among the kin-folks? They dote on his tales of derring-do. But let us take our leave of such childish pastimes. We shall listen to music and enjoy *other* activities."

Surlina didn't trust him for a moment, but she smiled and took his arm, more angry with Julien than afraid of Ramsey. He seemed less threatening than aboard the *Quail,* yet she was certain there was more on his mind than music.

He ushered her into a room which held black-lacquered benches, an ebony grand piano, two harps, and, on a small enameled table, a collection of flutes, pipes, whistles and recorders. Riffling the music atop the piano, he began to play "What Joy is Mine," a Bach chorale she recognized from convent years. Some-how, sacred music from Ramsey's bow seemed sacrileg-ious. "Play something lively," she insisted. "I'd like to dance out on the portico, spinning around the columns, taking off my shoes and racing across that dewy lawn," she giggled. "This afternoon, I even wanted to go out and play barefoot in the courtyard."

"How changeable you are! Tonight I saw you looking daggers at my handsome cousin."

"Let's not discuss Julien Rainbeau!"

"Such perfidy from the Silver Belle! Ah, well, I'd just as soon damn him to perdition myself! So! If you are over your infatuation with him, I shall play a tune of congratulation. Then we shall stroll upon the grounds and find a corsage for you, my beauty."

She knew instinctively it would be destructive to fall under his spell. Urbane Ramsey of the diplomatic corps —oh, yes, just the man to flirt with her, play her moods like the strings of that violin, then spirit away her secrets. "I know you were at a meeting today, Ramsey. With Jeff Davis, Thayer Cabell and Julien. Was I a topic of discussion?"

"How you flatter yourself, Surlina! It is my regret to have to inform you that you are far down on the list of lost causes the South endorses. After your antics with Farragut and Porter—"

"Cabell threw that slop, not I!"

"Your protest brings color to your cheeks and makes your emerald eyes shoot fire. Then after your episode in jail—"

"If I ever get a chance to put a dagger in your evil heart, Ramsey, I pray God I do not fail."

"Enough of this playful talk, kitten." He silenced her with a loud squawk of the bow across the violin strings. "We are more alike than not, Surlina. We both intend to keep what is ours. Julien is an impediment to us both, with his meandering talk of loyalty and his scandalous love of danger. You and I should be allies . . . not enemies."

"I suspect your plans for me as well as my silver, Ramsey. You'd use Julien to seduce me, then use him for your own aims." She turned to leave the room, only to find Julien standing in the doorway, laughing silently. He rocked, holding his hands to his sides, obviously overcome by the discussion he'd overheard. "Get out of my way!" she ordered.

"Wait, wait!" he cried, catching her arm. "How am I to seduce a maiden who runs away like a timid chipmunk?" He stroked her slender hand, and she felt herself turn pliable and warm under his touch. "Honest, I have only come to escort you to supper! Our guests from the *Quail* have arrived and are anxious to see you. They have missed you."

She questioned him with her eyes. 'And *you* have not missed me, Julien?' Her voice quavered. "I've missed them, too. Haloo, Professor Boxt, Proctor O'Keefe . . . all of them."

They moved down the gallery, leaving Ramsey behind. "And did you never think of *me* again, Surlina? After that night . . . ?" His voice was low, almost shy, as if afraid of her answer or her silence.

How could she tell him! 'Oh, my darling, you've been in my thoughts every hour, every minute, since that night we spent in each other's arms!'

Before she could form the proper syllables, they had reached the dining room and her chance was lost. She felt him draw away, chastened by her silence. 'He has too much pride to let down his defenses again. I can't

188

seem to do anything right since setting foot at Whispers! Surlina looked at him, stricken with remorse for not reassuring him of her longing, but he had already turned away.

Surlina was seated along the side of the long table, where all the women took their places. She was slightly surprised at the dining room, with its grand furnishings and elegant china. But, again, Surlina had the feeling of fading greatness about the house as if it were mainly Dottie's gumption holding the place together.

Dottie, however, seemed to take the challenge in stride. "Eat hearty," she urged everyone.

Surlina sat on the left side, next to Laurel and Grandmere. Julien and Ramsey, the only two family men present, sat at opposite ends of the table as if balancing it. She watched Julien. Obviously preoccupied, he ate little and held himself removed from the conversation. As she remembered, he once had said that Whispers was a world in which he didn't belong. Apparently he chose to withdraw, for his charm belonged here perfectly.

As supper ended, the women in black expressed their eagerness to hear tales of war from the two men. Apparently they could not see that Ramsey, the sophisticated diplomat, and Julien, the scrappy river rat, had no desire to speak. Julien especially seemed ill at ease. 'He's more comfortable on a ship,' Surlina realized, 'with wind in his face and spray wetting down his sparkling hair.' Suddenly she was pleased that he would never be a Southern planter. She felt him too powerful, too alert, to have no ambitions beyond the merchant service, but clearly his plans did not lie with Whispers. She was glad.

Ramsey excused himself and left the room.

Julien was left to bear the brunt of his relatives' questioning. He was already staring out the doorway, apparently far away in thought. "How far did you go this time, dear boy? Yes, tell us! How far up the coast?" asked Grandmere.

These old women were feeding on him like a crowd of leeches! How tightly cloistered they were in this

189

little enclave, referring to the Mississippi River as "the coast."

As Dottie began to help Kuffy and the other slaves remove the dinner plates, Grandmere gave her a look of disapproval. Dottie said, "I don't hold with no slavin' or mammying or pickaninnying," and continued carrying plates to the kitchen.

"The Bible is full of slavery," said Grandmere imperiously, stopping the house servants in their tracks.

"Yeah," Dottie agreed, "and full of adultery and concubines."

After a while, Dottie returned, bringing raspberry-leaf tea and cacao-mint coffee for after-dinner drinks. Then she sat back down and urged, "Go on, Julien."

As Julien discussed the influence of geography on the South, Surlina was once more under his spell. 'My Julien,' she thought. Somehow she must make him understand: the silver was hers, and she intended to retrieve it and *keep* it. But it need make no difference in their feelings for each other.

Aunt Dottie brought in a large orange cake and put it in front of Julien. He peered at the concoction, which seemed to be covered with frizzled orange hair. "What the hell is this, Dottie? Bobcat soufflé?"

She sniffed, "Carrot and potato cake," and handed him a long knife to cut it.

He toyed with the blade, his eyes still clouded with the concentration of lecturing to his unbelieving in-laws. He drew a long swath through the frosting. "Now, this is the way the pattern looks. Each time I take the *Quail* north, I cannot go as far. Nor return as far south. The Union troops are like a great snake, coiling around the river, squeezing it dry."

Surlina broke in, anticipating far ahead of where the others' minds were. "The final squeeze—where will it come?"

He took the knife tip and drew two S bends through the carrot trimmings. "The river is the belt of the confederacy. Here, like a buckle on the belt, sits one defensible city." He plunged the knife deep into the cake. "Vicksburg."

The assembled ladies cried out in proper horror at his violence toward their dessert. But obviously he did not care, and neither did Surlina. She echoed his belief, seeing instantly he was right. "Vicksburg. It will all end there."

Grandmere challenged him. "Why Vicksburg?"

"Because the Mississippi flows through her like a single artery. Cut that one vessel, and you've cut to the heart." He slashed the cake several times, turning it to ruins.

Dottie took away his knife, scolding him gently. "Julien, you've quite made your point. We'll keep our skirts clear of the city on the hill."

He rose, pushing back his chair in scraping haste to get away. "We'll all meet again with our backs to the river at Vicksburg." He stalked from the room.

Surlina would have jumped up and followed him, but she sensed that there would only be more disagreement between them. Fidgeting, she sat through a process of dipping pecan halves into a pot of boiling syrup. All the women were adamant that they would never refugee to Vicksburg or anywhere else. They nodded wisely to each other, looking like a collection of nuns.

As soon as it was polite, Surlina excused herself, feeling sorry for Laurel, who was left sitting on Grandmere's lap. Poor baby, doomed to grow up in this unwieldy antique mansion.

Surlina rushed to find Julien, not wanting the evening to end with this nagging bitterness between them. She circled the parlor, the music room, the gallery. Finally she went out onto the veranda. He was sitting on the west portico, far back in a woven willow chair. She opened the conversation neutrally. "This is such an interesting porch, with its hinged columns."

He did not respond. After a few moments of moody silence, he said, "I met Thayer Cabell today. He is an ass."

"Amen to that!" At last they'd found common ground. "I cannot abide the man! But I love my sister, and she is determined to stand by him, sacrificing life, limb and honor to the Confederacy."

"A proper lady. Exactly what the South will not need in the future!" His voice lost its usual musical quality. It was blunted with dullness. Why did he maintain this unaccountable, withdrawn facade? Did Whispers always affect him like this? Or was *she* the cause of his resentment and melancholy? Surlina stood at attention as he spoke again. "Why did you come here?"

She owed him honesty, at least. "I came looking for my silver." Suddenly she felt overwhelmed with all the escapades she'd endured on behalf of the treasure . . . and it still lay beyond her grasp. "Julien, I must find it! I need it! For my father, for my sister—"

"For your own greed."

"How little you understand of that fortune, Julien. That treasure is named for me because I found it as a child. Everything I ever got—all the fame, glory, good food, fine clothes, business dealings—came about because of that silver. I'll not give up what is rightfully mine!"

"Bravo!" He clapped his hands desultorily.

She felt embarrassed at her spirited defense of money. Oh, she wanted to yank him out of that chair and dash his head against the columns.

"Surlina," he said wearily, "I'll tell you once and for all: your silver is not your treasure."

"How silly! Of course it—"

"No, my darling. Your wonderful spirit is your treasure. Your sparkling green eyes. Your cascade of brown curls framing that fair face. Look—there in the gallery—that grandfather clock is not time. This terrible house is not the South. A galloping horse's shadow is not a horse. And the silver is not your treasure."

Aghast, she cried, "Never will I give it up! Never to North or South, blue or gray, Mullermen or—"

"Or me?" He jumped from the chair, stark anger written across his features. "Good night, Surlina. Sweet silver dreams." The words were light, but his tone was grim. He whirled on his heel and was gone, leaping the portico railing, dashing across the sloping lawn, out the West Wind Gates.

Stunned, she felt anger rising inside her. For a moment, she thought of running after him, demanding that he understand her need for the silver. No! She would not go running after any man—certainly not Julien Rainbeau, who made her forgetful of everything except his own physical presence. What had she expected to find here? Passion and fulfillment? She now seemed doomed to end with anxiety and frustration.

She walked along the portico, oppressed by the humid night. The smell of honeysuckle tangled with the bayou brackishness. A frog croaked his greeting to the darkness; night lilies opened shimmery beneath the crescent moon.

She sat in the chair where Julien had been. His scent enveloped her as if she'd lain her head in his lap. Why did this unreasoning pride keep them apart? She looked at the columns, motionless and formal with their ivy headdresses. They seemed to watch her, as if they'd heard all the arguments for and against love for generations and never been indiscreet.

Moving to the massive cornerpost, she leaned against its strength. So much solid force to Whispers, so much emptiness! Like herself, where Julien was concerned. Away from him, she felt sure of herself, able to seek out the gates, do battle with Mullermen or General Butler. But by his side, her logic gave way to the spell of his resonant laughter, the softly curling sideburns, the creases around his somber eyes.

It hurt her to the core that she was the one keeping them apart. 'If we are to share more than heated words in this life, then I must make the first move,' she decided.

Surlina went to his room, asking directions from Kuffy. 'Don't be away long, Julien,' she begged, watching for signs of him from the window. She found a pewter-handled comb and fluffed her curls. Sometimes she envied women who had longer, straight hair. How pleasant it must feel to unplait the silken hair and let it hang over naked shoulders. She stretched

193

her curls, but they would do no more than cover her forehead and neck.

No sign of Julien. From far away a bobwhite trilled its short syllables, reminding her of the *Quail*. She undressed and crawled into his bed. "Come to me, Julien," she whispered. "Come to me. Leave the sea and its siren songs. Come to me. I am your true love."

She slept fitfully, wakened by nightmares of pursuit by Muller and Butler, her father's death, Tandy's health, the gates lost forever, Julien lost forever. Her hands searched the bed, needing the strength of his arms and the power of his manhood. But she found only emptiness.

Then suddenly it was morning. The sun exploded into the room. She felt warmth, opened her eyes to daylight and found Julien bending across the bed. She sat up, throwing her arms open to him. "Oh, Julien! I waited—"

He cut her off with caresses, little fluttery kisses on her eyelids, her forehead, her cheeks, throat and ears.

"I had terrible dreams!" she wailed, locking her arms around his soft flannel shirt.

"I'm here now, darling. Here to keep you safe from dreams, from my own foolishness. Oh, Surlina, forgive me for my arrogance! I am caught up in this war—this place—until my mind cannot think of love. I discredit everyone's motives, even my own, when all I want is to have you!" He knelt by the side of the bed, undoing his clothes, then climbed in beside her.

Instantly she was in his arms, hungry for his fresh skin, his clean taste, his tongue upon her lips and breasts. She felt the curves of his body, the suppleness of his spine, the firmness of his hips and the softness of his cornsilk hair.

They touched, rolled apart, falling back upon each other with the quick, hot breathing of a person about to sob. The fire of desire penetrated Surlina's brain and made her feel light-headed. She caressed his shoulders, twining the curly hairs of his chest around her fingers. He pressed his lips to her nipples, waited,

194

then sucked gently, pulling the dark shapes to hard points in his mouth.

The round touch of his fingertip pressed between her legs. She opened to him, like a valley, opening her mouth to his kiss at the same time. He lingered, stroking his hand smoothly over the curve of her thighs, her knees, her calves. When he tickled her feet, she giggled and he kissed her all over again, tickling behind her ears, against her spine, over her belly.

Now her desire fastened on feeling him within her. Stirred by the beating of her heart, she pulled him toward her. He straddled her, towering erect and slippery, then crouched, thrust in, out, then stopped.

"Oh, no! Don't stop!" she whimpered, clutching at him, her hands hard against his tight hips.

"A moment," he murmured, shutting his eyes and throwing back his head. "A moment or I shall lose control and deprive us both. I have dreamed of you so long!"

She touched him, caressing him with her hands.

Then he rolled her backward, thrusting eagerly, keeping his weight balanced on hands spread far apart on the mattress. She tried to push against him, capture all his sweetness within her, but he moved too fast, driving her into a frenzy. He fell against her, hands cupped beneath her spine, spreading her buttocks, stroking and squeezing till she cried out in little gasps of delight.

"Turn over. Look in the mirror there," he whispered. She restrained herself from moving as he swung her around, raising her toward him, positioning her so she could see. How lovely they looked, shiny with glistening sweat, their mouths red and cheeks rosy. How perfectly their bodies locked together, he taking her from behind, hands folding around her breasts as their rhythm began anew.

Now she felt filled completely, little spasms of pleasure uniting into a bigger throb of insistence. For a second, her motions seemed poised on a high cliff; then, abandoning all reserve, she left herself fall against him.

Her head fell limply forward, her hips gliding to a stop in his lap. She felt his response deep within, heard the long moan of release, absorbed the contractions as part of her. She moved around him slowly, in a circle, until they collapsed together against the pillows.

She touched his face, seeing him anew in the light of love. "Last night, when I was waiting for you—hoping for you—then I looked in the mirror and wished I had straight hair."

He kissed her curly hair, assuring her it was perfect.

"Where were you last night, Julien?"

He sighed contentedly. "Somewhere much less comfortable, now that I have learned what was waiting here for my comfort and pleasure. What I have learned this morning of your passion and honesty more than repays me for the risks I took on your behalf last night."

"Risks? My behalf?" She sat up, fearful of his penchant for danger.

"I have been on a goose chase which has yielded a golden egg, my darling. I have found your enemy, Thad Muller, hiding in the swamps! And I have news of your father . . . He is alive!"

"Oh, tell me! Tell me!"

He jumped from the bed, snatching up his clothes. "After breakfast. You have exhausted me so I cannot speak without sustaining myself on ham, biscuits and red-eye gravy!" He took a playful swat at her. "You have exhausted me beautifully, my love!"

"Will your strength return?" she teased.

"Peace, woman! I'd rather take on Muller and his band of outlaws than tangle with you again—"

She cut off his complaint with a kiss, loving the way he melted against her body in a swoon of strength and delight.

19

When breakfast was over, Julien offered Surlina his arm. "Let's take the morning air before I report to work."

As they set off across the broad lawns, she begged, "Tell me of my father. Where did you find him? Near New Orleans?"

"I only heard of him—that he is alive but ill and plans to journey upriver to Vicksburg, where your sister has taken refuge."

"Thank God! Then he isn't a hostage of Mullermen."

"Indeed not! From what I heard from the river men, he was far too crafty for that bag of outlyers."

"I have been so worried!" She felt certain that her father would meet Tandy in Vicksburg. Soon she must make Vicksburg her goal, too. "And Thad Muller? Did you actually have a run-in with that farmer-turned-thief?"

He is up to his usual tricks, looting along the river, terrorizing Union outposts and Confederate strongholds. He has raided a supply train of wagons headed for Farragut and Porter upriver."

"Supply wagons! Christ Jesus! Surely not the wagon which held my gates!"

Julien looked at her in confusion. "What's this about gates?"

So he did not know all her secrets! For a moment, Surlina thought of passing off the mention as unimportant. Yet he had brought her news of her father, had taken risks on her behalf. "In New Orleans, I found that my silver had been melted and reshaped as carriage gates. I traced them to Butler's camp, then to the supply train heading north to rendezvous with Farragut. The army wagonmaster is quite unaware

197

that beneath the black paint lies a fortune. But Muller is aware—or so it would seem!"

She was confounded when he began to laugh. "Silver gates! Why, darling, next you'll regale me with stories of ermine toads and diamond trees. Come. I will show you where my father's sawmill stood."

She followed his steps in silence, hurt that he hadn't taken her story seriously, relieved in a curious way that he had not swooped down selfishly on the truth. Obviously, silver gates—if they existed—did not lure him.

They passed the croquet court, then turned into a pathway almost hidden by flowering dogwood and redbud trees. Trumpet vines laced through the branches, spilling orange flowers among the purple and white buds. The foliage closed behind them like dropping a net over their heads. In another moment, the civilized landscape of Whispers was blotted out completely. Enthralled, Surlina felt a primeval lushness of magnolia, wisteria, and camellias reach out like long, stroking fingers.

As they crossed a fallen tree, she put out her hand to him and was pleased he did not let it loose once they were headed down the path again.

"Julien, if you found yourself very thirsty . . . ?"

"Yes? I should likely break out the spirits jug."

"No." She told him the story of the dipper and the well. "Would you drink the dipper? Or pour it back?"

He answered instantly, without a hint of indecision. "Why, drink down the dipper, of course! And then use my wits to find more." He laughed happily.

She wanted to pull him close, to hold him tenderly, to make him understand the danger of his quick decision to always opt for sure things. But he pointed ahead and cried, "Ah, here we are at the sawmill."

The site was unrecognizable. Only his careful tracking of the foundation, precise pointing at the waterfall cleft and quiet description made her see it at all. He sat on the stacked stone of a long-ago wall. "This was my father's livelihood. He was never intimidated by my mother's family, although she stayed a Basketby-Arnauld forever. Jonathan ran his sawmill, saw me

198

through three years of Annapolis . . ." He walked the edges of a rotting board. "It was then the sawmill was lost."

"Lost?"

"It took a final victim into its teeth—my father—then was still forever."

Surlina winced, imagining Jonathan Rainbeau sucked into the swirling saws.

Julien pushed aside pine branches, scuffing at the base of the tree with his moccasin toe until he had dug up layers of rancid sawdust. "So fast! The sharp cry. The clean cut. Sudden blood atop the water. Then bubbles, fast-flowing river and gone . . . gone." The look on his face was more wistful than angry. "The mill was not abandoned. It simply went . . . like my father. Not to any greedy banker with a mortgage or the covetous hand of Ramsey Arnauld or even to any hated Yankee traders. Simply back to forest, to yellow sunlight through black branches and jackrabbits nibbling at pine pitch and maybe an Indian poking his fish trap at the edge of the creek."

"You are very different here than aboard the *Quail*, or in the dining room of Whispers."

"And I was different before the war." He stood close to her, his hands poised above her shoulders but not touching.

He seemed willing to speak of his past, so she asked him about his wife. "Can you talk of her?"

"She was my darling golden girl, obediently sitting by the fire for hours, combing her hair, making little curls with her fingers and patting them in place by her ears. She was the perfect ornament for a place like Whispers." His smile was nostalgically pleasant, steeped in memory, but without apparent grief or longing. "A delightful, simple girl. She'd prance and scamper, fetch my slippers and pipe, and if I spoke, she'd turn up those soft, unquestioning eyes."

His portrait did not evoke jealousy. "She gave you pleasure."

"Certainly," he agreed, then stretched his arms above his head as if needing to outgrow the memory. "But I

199

needed a great deal more." He broke off a cattail reed.
"As you do." With hard pinches, he broke the fur
from the hard brown head of the cattail. "Hindsight is
quite a mixed blessing. I would not have changed my
wife . . . and I mourned her honestly." He threw the
reed away like a spear. "But miss her?" He shook his
head; not guiltily, but not proudly.

"What of Laurel?"

"Doomed, I fear, to be a Rainbeau-Arnauld in the
grand manner—that most fatal of Southern ideals: a
proper lady."

Suddenly he leaped away, snatching a log from
the ground, uttering a cry of alarm. She whirled as the
wood came down with crushing force against a wide
stone. Then she gasped, realizing Julien had killed a
snake. The head, yellowish and wide, was pinned firmly beneath his club. Before it had finished writhing, he
tossed it into the stream.

She bounded to him, rushing into his arms. He
pinned her to him. No more nonchalance on his part,
no more dormant promises from her. "Oh, stay with
me, Surlina! Stay, darling! Stay!"

The words sounded miraculous to her, as impossible
as the marvelous sounds they made in bed together. She
returned his embrace, her mouth tender as if licking
his secret wounds. She felt small and weak, though not
in some wily feminine way. He simply overpowered
her with the rising passions he could generate within
her breasts, lips, legs and heart.

He caressed her breasts, ran his hands over the
divided skirt, seeking an opening. "Will you stay with
me?" he whispered. "Will we be together?"

For a moment she thought, 'Always, I'll stay always.'
Then she broke the embrace, questioning him with a
trembling voice. "Stay here? At Whispers? I cannot!
You cannot!"

But he begged her again, ardently, his eyes gray-
blue with their energy of desire. "Oh, stay, Surlina!
Throw away your cloak of silver pride. Destroy that
mask that marks you as the Silver Belle! Stay with me,
darling!"

She moaned with the agony of pleasure and impossibility. She felt smooth against him, like a polished stone. It was as if her true and loving nature had slept all these years, only to be awakened by his kisses. For another moment, their embrace seemed complete. Then she broke the magic by being practical. "There'd be no peace for us, Julien, neither here nor aboard the *Quail*. The silver would lie like an anchor on my conscience. But, darling, I love you! Oh, how I love you!"

Abruptly he stepped away, harsh and commanding, slapping his trouser legs with a willow branch. "I could order you to stay."

She was jolted by his quick shift in manner and tone. Suddenly he was a stranger again, commanding her like some recruit sailor! "Pardon me, Captain Rainbeau," she said, daring to laugh aloud. "But submitting to orders has never been my way."

"Submit?" He snickered coarsely. "Oh, kindly spare me the melodramatics of female simpering, Surlina!" He stamped away through the underbrush, forcing her to follow or be left. He strode rapidly, not looking back. "Submission? Ha! I can do without any feminine feigning. No, thanks! I'll pass on swoons and heaving bosoms and closed eyes which hide contempt!" He raced along the path, anger bristling from his back.

At the playground clearing, he whirled on her. "No," he said quietly, using the word as a threat. "No. I asked you once. I'm in no position to play endless variations of asking again."

She fell back, dumbfounded and bitter. Did he really want—expect—her to stay? Or did he merely want to antagonize and taunt her with his own inability to remain. What did "stay" imply? Marriage? All she was sure of was that if she loved this man, she couldn't pretend indifference. If she needed him, she'd have to admit it. And if this lingering ache of something unfinished between them would not go away, then she'd have to take desperate chances to follow him.

She walked along until she came to the freshly sifted dirt of the croquet court. On impulse, she took off her shoes and plodded along in the gray soil, packed and fine as ashes. She took tiny heel-to-toe footsteps, like a baby practicing the new art of walking. A dog, lying serenely sleepy, rolled over in friendly greeting and offered his stomach to be scratched.

She sat by the big dog, remembering how only twenty-four hours ago she had considered flopping onto the tent cot with Butler in order to sacrifice honor to silver. Now she was equally unwilling to sacrifice her silver for Julien's mercurial passion.

As she looked up, she saw him moving away from the house, down the hill toward the bayou. He had changed to his work clothes. Again her heart fluttered. Surely he was not the most handsome man she had ever met, but he was certainly the most compelling. With his somber gray eyes and musical voice, laughing mouth and golden sideburns which would never slick into military obedience, he would always be deprived of the title of gentleman. As she would never be the South's epitome of proper lady. But flair and authority, those qualities which Bishop Polk had pinpointed as being uniquely Julien's, he had those in abundance! He was marked indelibly, branded by those very traits of spontaneity and command. Leader. Commander. Captain. The names and titles and authority would always fit him.

And she? Was she as irrefutably marked by her silver? What had happened to neutrality? She remembered Sam's admonishing her, "Don't wait until the choices are made for you! No choice, in itself, is a choice."

Then, would she stay?

Only for tonight.

20

She saw Julien once, late in the afternoon, chopping wood with a brightly polished ax. She walked to where he was splintering the hard bois d'arc logs, watching his muscles bulge with every overhead swing of the blade. Sweat ran down his face, his hair wet and matted like moss, his gray eyes faded to black dots of exertion. Why did he work harder than any slave?

"It's honest work. You'll not find me sitting on my velvet ass counting *my* money!"

"Why do you do this to me?" she asked, disappointed.

He cursed violently, slung the ax away into the pile of logs, shoved her roughly to the ground and fell atop her, his breath raging, arms squeezing the life from her. "I regret that I love you! I repudiate the power you have over me! And I refuse to destroy myself for you!" He yanked hard on her hair. Holding her face between his hands like a vise, he kissed her as if slapping her with his mouth.

"Stop it!" She struggled, frightened by his violence. She beat at his chest with angry fists, shoving and slapping as she pushed her way to a sitting position. "You've gone mad! Your family will think I'm some common camp girl to be flung in the dirt!" She flustered her way to her feet, dusting away the wood chips which clung to her hair.

"Let them think what they will." He retrieved the ax, holding it across his chest like a shield. "I owe them no excuses for how I live. Neither do you." He swung the blade with perfect precision, creasing a line in the earth inches from her toes.

As he raised the ax to swing again, she fled in terror. He was absolutely and doubtlessly insane!

After supper, it was apparent that a long round of family good-byes were to be said in the music room.

Grandmere held forth with imperial announcements, her spectacles slipping down her nose. "If things take a tendency to disintegrate, then we will refugee to Jackson, taking little Laurel with us. Dottie is embarking on a mission to Memphis in the morning."

Suddenly there was a noise in the gallery, and all eyes moved expectantly toward the door. Julien rushed in, a great smile on his tanned face, a pack over his shoulders. "Presents for everyone!" he announced, and the old ladies squealed with delight. They giggled and twittered as he dispensed little tokens: bonnet ribbons, a crewelwork sash, a cameo breastpin, little pillboxes enameled in mauve, satin pillow cases, French novels. Surlina caught his eye and he winked, admitting what she suspected—that the gifts were all stolen. No matter. The aunts were wildly appreciative.

When he came to Surlina, he placed a single kiss in her palm, bent low and murmured, "I wish it were the moonlight, the sunlight and the starshine of a thousand days and nights together."

Then he laughed and moved on, leaving her hand hot and tingly and her heart overcome with sadness. He presented Ramsey with a substitute cigar of grapevine and dried sumac leaves, then took over one of the rocking chairs, holding a fat aunt on his lap.

She kissed his forehead. "Now, dear boy, where will you be off to next?"

A glance passed between Julien and Ramsey. Ramsey smiled indulgently at his cousins and aunts. "Have you no respect for military secrets?"

"No," admitted the aunt, standing up beside her nephew. "Where are you off to, Julien?"

Ramsey rescued Julien from having to make an outright refusal to answer. "Why, Julien's reconnaissance up and down the Mississippi is so secret, we say even Robert E. Lee and Jeff Davis have no idea where his gunboat will be thundering off to next."

Julien lit one of the fake cigars, leaned back and

blew puffs of smoke in the air. Chuckling, he added, "All I leave behind me is a trail of smoke!"

The old women went back to their music, playing happily at enjoying the war. Julien reached over and took Surlina's hand, blew another ring of smoke upward. In an instant of intimate communication, she saw the message in his eyes. 'That's not all he'll leave behind. He'll leave me, too.'

21

She made up her mind to leave first. She went to her room and packed a small satchel. The table knife she'd stolen from Butler's tent went into the bottom of the bag. Then the general's money belt which she'd found held nearly two hundred Yankee dollars. She took a few practical outfits from the armoire. Shoes. A pair of boots. She wouldn't need much—just enough to see her to Vicksburg. She must contact Tandy, see if their father had arrived, find out if Muller had succeeded in stealing her gates or if they'd been given to Farragut's upriver force. She closed the satchel, not daring for a moment to think of Julien.

She'd go tonight, while her courage was high, not waiting for dawn when she'd have to tear her heart apart by watching *him* go.

She heard a tapping, and looked toward the door expectantly, then realized the random noise was at the window. She listened as the noise stopped, came again, then died away.

She moved across the room with light steps. Pressing her face against the window, she heard the pings and hisses again. Rain. Lovely, scented, spring rain, drifting in from the Gulf. A fog lay against the bayou shores like a wisp of white smoke, leaving the cypresses draped with Spanish moss towering above the grayness like paint brushes. The soft grayness reminded her of Julien's eyes.

A tapping at the door sent shivers through her. 'Please . . . let it be Julien. No, don't let it be!' She hesitated. The knock sounded again, softly, like leaves rustling. She waited another moment, then cracked the door only an inch. "Go away."

"But I have brought you a present," whispered Julien. She could see him standing in the darkened hallway, a long section of material across his outstretched arms. "It's a gift for you," he repeated.

"Stolen, no doubt," she whispered back, not anxious to rouse the household.

He walked forward and she had no choice but to open the door or have him crash through it. He strode into the bedroom, tossed the gift on the bed, let down the mosquito netting, opened the window and blew out the single candle on the nightstand. "It's a nightgown."

She went to the pinewood bed, pulling the material from under the netting. The rain hissed at the open window, splattering the marble sill. She looked at the gift, then at his eyes, hoping to see how much sincerity lay behind the token. Damn him! His eyes still held as proud and annoying a gleam as when he'd thrown her to the ground by the woodpile. She felt very vulnerable standing with the nightdress in her hands, so she laid it across the back of an upholstered chair.

He picked the gown up, moved behind her, held it to her shoulders as if measuring. She could feel him close, smelling of lotion and soap, the soft touch of his fingertips grazing her shoulder. Turning to face him, she fought to keep control in her voice. "It's lovely, Julien! Thank you very much." She focused her attention solely on the gown, not daring to respond to him.

"*You* are lovely, Surlina."

"*You* are a great flatterer, Julien. I heard you at work tonight in the music room, charming all your relatives."

He sighed. "And all the while, my heart was aching

to throw you down in the woodyard again!" He captured her hands to his lips, teasing the sensitive pads of her fingers with his tongue. Then his voice turned serious. "Oh, Surlina, it would take a great deal of war to blot out the instinct a man has for falling in love with a beautiful woman."

Words so thrilling to her heart, so touching in their honesty—but so damaging to her resolve. She pulled her hands away, placed the gown on the chair again where it dangled like a question mark between them.

He caught her chin in his palm, lifting her face lightly toward his. "Don't be so serious, darling!" He picked up the gown again, tossing it to her.

She held the silk against her face. Suddenly she was filled with yearning. "Before you, I never knew loneliness, as I never knew what it was like to be together. I never knew emptiness, as I had no idea of completion."

His arms enveloped her like a mantle, holding her close as if to prolong this night forever. The mysterious glow from the garden torches touched the room with shadows. Her ear, against his throat, could hear his heartbeats rising to a crescendo.

"Come, Surlina," he whispered. "Make me your love."

She lifted her arms around his neck, yielding her body to the desire which seemed to rise like a fountain. She moistened her lips, wanting to kiss him like the rain. "When I am with you like this, I feel new. Clean. As if I could never lie. Never hurt anyone. As if I could fly to the moon and bring you back its silver shine!" Silver! Instantly, she knew she'd said the fatal word.

He drew her to the chair, sat down, tugged her until she sat on his lap, head against his shoulder. "For all you mean to me, darling, I cherish you. For all you hope in the future, I hope with you. But—" He paused and she felt wariness creep into his body, his hands tightening around her wrists, his muscular thighs tensing beneath her hips. "But the silver is not my concern."

"Julien, promise me you'll help me find my gates!"

She took the terrible risk of asking him by blurting the question without taking a breath.

He chuckled uneasily, kissing her on the nose. "Is it promises you want from me? Ah, Surlina, promises are something I do not easily make . . . nor lightly break." He bent forward, laying his head against her breasts. "I promise only to love you."

Oh, surely that would be enough to keep her always from harm, need or sorrow! It would be enough to lose herself in his love, renew herself in his strength, re-create her soul from his tenderness. She felt him clutching at her, needing promises from her lips. She laughed with joy. "Let me put on the nightgown, Julien. Then we will laugh over our good fortune in finding each other!"

She heard him inhale, breath trembling, then he pressed his lips to hers so softly it seemed lovelier and warmer than flickers from a perfumed lamp. Her body no longer questioned him; her mind was at ease. "Tell me again," she begged. "Tell me again that you love me."

He said forcefully, "There can be *no one* for me, if not you!"

She turned as she stood up, the silken gown rustling in her hands. But when she'd quickly shed her clothes, she only held the cool material against her body.

He moved to the bed, then questioned her. "Don't you know how to put it on?"

"Yes," she said, quivering with excitement.

"Then pray do so, darling, so I shall have the pleasure of taking it off again."

She threw the silk over her head, sliding her arms through the loose sleeves. Looking in the mirror, she could see herself dimly. Her dark hair stood out in contrast to the creamy silk which flowed from neck to toes. And when she moved, it thrilled her to feel the swish of the gown following her steps. She pirouetted, vividly aware of the sensations of nerves, moisture, heat and flesh that were sculpting her like a knife.

She lifted the skirt, jumped on the bed beside him and stretched full length atop him, bringing her mouth to meet his lips, her breasts hard against his chest, her thighs encasing his hardness. At that moment she was overcome with tenderness. Nothing she could give him was good enough! She wanted to yield utterly, to let him penetrate her innermost places, let him possess her entirely.

She heard the rain beating on the sill, smelled the fragrance of his thick golden hair, tasted the ripe moisture of his mouth. The bed sank beneath their weight, hollowing out a valley which cupped them together. The silk grew warm, glistening in the torchlight like her skin. He pulled the gown tight across her breasts, molding it to her hips until every curve was outlined.

"You're extraordinary," he said, stroking her throat, tracing circles around her nipples through the silk, kissing her hair. "You're like a tide which pulls me steadily to you." He met her mouth and pulled her tongue between his lips, sucking gently. "Your eyes shine like satin. They are dark and moist, watching my every move."

He lifted the gown high around her shoulders, leaving the embroidered roses of its neckline across the hollow of her throat. She took her arms from the sleeves and he folded the gown back across her neck like a scarf.

Now their bodies met without restraint, obedient, vibrating. Her legs parted; they rolled; he lying fully across her. She rippled with each caress, breathing fast, alert to each motion of his fingers and tongue. He touched her triangle of dark hair, dipped a finger into her moisture, then touched her in a new spot. She tensed, dazzled by the sensation, then sighed in a long breath of pleasure. He made circles, pressing against the firm-textured place first with his finger, then by using the tip of his erect penis.

She began to burn, as if laying naked in the summer sun. She pulled away, for fear she could not bear the delight of her feelings any longer. "Oh, Julien, no . . . no more . . . I can't . . ."

"But you can! Beautifully. Wonderfully. Give yourself to me fully, Surlina. Let your hips buck beneath me and your skin sing as I touch you. Let your rosy lips open and suck me in like a whirlpool." He pushed against her then, swaying, all his strength centered in the one muscle.

She felt the contractions of her body encircle him, then unite like flames devouring a pine bough. Inside, she seemed a tightly wound spring about to fly loose. Her breathing was violent as she worked against him. "Don't turn back," he whispered hoarsely, pumping faster, squeezing at her breasts as if to draw nectar from them.

His words were like a catalyst, giving her permission to move ahead into the great light she felt just beyond her. "It's like the wind pushing me," she murmured. "Like an orchestra bringing all its instruments in tune!" She slid around him, lifting her hips from the bed to hold the sensations centered deep in her womb. She felt the heated liquid, heard the lapping sounds, throbbed with the deep thrusts of his body, then felt herself flattening out as if seared with a branding iron. The little spasms grew, climaxing in a great shudder which convulsed her from head to toe. Suddenly she lay still.

She began to apologize, "I went off and left you! Oh, Julien, I'm so sorry!"

He silenced her with a hand across her mouth, jamming himself harder and deeper into her. It was as if he would never be satisfied until he broke her in two. She felt him rigid all over, his arm muscles bulging as they'd done when he chopped wood. He forced her upward, to a half-sitting position, continuing to move like an animal releasing pent-up savagery. Then he cried out, an inertness passing through him like a blow, and he fell, panting, burying her beneath him.

'Pray God you give me a son!' she thought, then melted with surprise. It was the first time she'd admitted such terms of commitment. Instantly she felt paralyzed, shamed and intimidated that she should have such longing for a permanent part of him.

"What is it?" She heard his voice close and worried. "You seem a volcano, about to erupt."

"Julien! Julien! I must have you always!"

"Always and forever," he whispered back seriously. He hovered over her, moving the sheet to cover her legs, drawing down the silk gown like a cocoon. "Always and forever."

She felt the drift of sleep waft over her as if she were drugged. She curled against him, content. "Always," she murmured and then dropped away into unconsciousness as he added the gentle refrain, ". . . and forever."

22

When she awoke with a startled sense of coldness, she reached for the warmth of Julien's body. She sat up, apprehensive of the emptiness of the bed, aware that the door stood slightly ajar. The room was quite empty, the window closed, the rain drizzling steadily, the mosquito netting folded on the chair, Julien and his clothes gone.

Instantly she was out of bed, hurrying toward the door, peering down the hall, seeing the flicker of a newly lit lantern extend from the library hall. Clad only in the beige silk nightgown, she scampered down the gallery, pulling back to the shadows outside the library when she recognized the murmur of male voices lowered in subdued argument.

Peeking through the crack, she saw Julien and Ramsey facing each other angrily. Julien's back was turned, but he radiated antagonism with his stiff shoulders, swinging arms, and legs planted far apart. Ramsey, lithe and relaxed, lay propped on a chaise, one leg dangling, lazily tapping the floor.

Julien's voice carried like a major chord, full of moody misgiving. "I could not."

Adamant, Ramsey folded his arms. "You had your

orders. Strict, confidential, clear orders from the highest council."

"I could not ask it of her."

"You mean *would* not. Oh, hell, Julien, admit it! You're not the man for this job. By God, I wish I were six foot six, three hundred pounds, and had a dozen pricks! I'd mount her like a bull, bellowing with rage and frothing at the mouth!"

"That's enough!"

"No, it's not enough! Not when you waste our time seducing women only for your own pleasure and forget that the silver must be saved for the Confederacy!" He tossed a stack of books to the floor. "Courtship is entirely valid as a tool of war. You were told explicitly what to do at the meeting. Now you renege!"

"Surlina is not your concern."

"And must not be yours any longer, either. Now, how much faith do you put in this story of silver gates?"

Surlina stifled a gasp. So Ramsey knew about the gates! Julien must have told him! And now they had the gall to sit in the library discussing her like a sack of grain. She strained to catch every word, engraving their businesslike tones deep in her brain.

"The treasure is either bound upriver for Farragut, destined overland for Grant, or residing in the coffers of the Mullermen."

"And your meeting with Muller? What arrangements were you able to make?"

"Only that he would supply us with information on troop movements in return for safe passage to Vicksburg."

"If he's hell-bent on getting upriver, then his raid on the supply wagons must not have been profitable. So! You'll take him on the *Quail,* of course."

Surlina shuddered at the implications of Muller in cahoots with Julien.

Ramsey went on coolly. "In the meantime, we will dispatch our own raiders northward. Muller will get the credit for attacking the supply wagons again! Be sure you keep him aboard long enough for our force to do its work. I, of course, will see to it that our Silver Belle enjoys all the pleasures of Whispers."

Julien shook his head almost imperceptibly, his voice tightening. "If you lay a hand on her, Cousin, I'll—"

"What? Don't bother me with stories of honor! I know you're a rounder. *You* know *I* am! We will share this little tart between us like the whores we used to buy in Natchez-under-the-Hill. Tell me, will she take it lying down? Or should I tie her upright to the bed-post for the first few thrusts of my sword?"

Julien spun around, fury creasing his face. "We've sparred long enough. I have a ship to command! But I promise you . . . if you bed her, I'll call you out!"

Surlina pulled back into the darkness as he charged through the door. He darted down the hallway, never glancing back, letting the door slam as he exited from the house.

She took the stairs in double bounds, fury overcoming her shame at being duped. When his eyes had danced with passion and his fingers had spread her legs, was he thinking only of his orders from the Confederacy? Well, double-damn him!

Suddenly, at the top of the stairway, she switched directions, running around the balcony to Dottie's sleeping porch. She flailed at the door. "Dottie, get up! It's Surlina! May I travel to Memphis with you?"

Feet scurried, the door rattled and Dottie peered out, her gray hair done up in a lacy bonnet. She had on long red underwear and a pistol belt. "What time is it?"

"Four in the morning, I think."

"And you want to travel north with me?"

"Yes! I must! Julien has gone off to steal my silver, and Ramsey is going to keep me a prisoner here! You must smuggle me out in your cotton wagon!"

Dottie looked at her in amazement, thumbs tucked under the pistol belt. "Julien and Ramsey up to more of their shenanigans, eh? Memphis, you say? Well, pack your satchel, girlie! Let's be far up the road by first light!"

23

By midmorning Surlina, Dottie, Kuffy, and Murray the mule were barely past the bayou cutoff and onto the main road. "Christ, this dumb mule of yours is worse than a snail! I'm afraid someone will come after us!"

"Not likely, considering I left notes all over the place that you was down at the landing weeping good-byes in Julien's ears and Kuffy and me had gone to town for wagon supplies. They won't suspect the truth till middle of the afternoon." Dottie perched happily atop the immense wagon, singing to her mule, spitting tobacco juice and admonishing Kuffy to keep his eyes open for "eatables."

"Dottie, please! Won't this beast move a bit faster?"

"Murray and me travel at our own speed. Now, here's the ground rules for traveling in my company. I chaw tobaccy. I spit. I cuss. I drink corn whiskey when I can get it and moonshine when I can't. I pee in the bayou and don't wash my socks a-tall."

Surlina laughed, but still wished Murray would pick up the pace. She grabbed the whip and laid two hard strokes across the mule's back.

Dottie wrestled the whip away. "Stop that! Murray's a tender-mouthed mule! Can't nobody work him but me. He don't trot unless I whistle."

"Oh, hell, he can't trot at all," sulked Surlina, pushing the sunbonnet back from her sweaty face.

In response, Dottie put two fingers to her teeth, blew out her cheeks like a bellows and emitted an ear-splitting whistle. Murray promptly dashed down the road. Surlina had to grab the seat handle to avoid tumbling. Kuffy turned a somersault atop the cotton.

"Murray can move, all right," Dottie confirmed proudly. She slowed him to his usual lackadaisical

214

speed. "When I give him the signal, he can nigh well outrun a jackass to a sack of greens. Now, as for you, Miss Surlina, you ain't about to outrun your memories of my nephew by whipping my mule."

Dottie was right, but Surlina refused to admit it. She centered her mind on one thing: escaping Ramsey's reach. Then she'd decide on a plan of action. She probably couldn't intercept Julien's raiders before they hit Vicksburg and the Union supply wagons. If she went to Vicksburg though, she'd find herself back in the clutches of Thayer Cabell. Her best hope was that the gates had already been shipped upriver to Farragut and then overland to Sam Grant.

A tremor passed through her as she thought fondly of Sam, wondering if he'd been restored to command yet or was still languishing from the debacle at Shiloh. "How far north will we have to go to encounter Union lines?"

"Why? You thinking of going over to the enemy?"

"I've told you over and over: I'm neutral!"

"All right," laughed Dottie, pulling up to a crossroad store. "Take some of them neutral dollars out of your money-belt. We've got to buy some goods."

Dottie planned to camouflage the cotton wagon by making it look like a peddler's traveling warehouse. For two hours she supervised the spending of Surlina's money and the rearranging of the sideboards. First, the contraband cotton bales went in the bottom, nestled between hay bales. On top went everything Dottie could lay her hands on. Hay, pots, pans, raggedy clothes from a trashcan, shawls from the dry-goods counter, two striped mattresses, a dozen sunbonnets, discarded stovepipes she found leaning against the crossroad marker and Kuffy's bedroll. Five hundred pounds heavier in the wagon and forty-five dollars lighter in the money-belt, they set rolling again.

"Now," laughed Dottie, heading down a back trail, away from the main road. "Which of us do you suppose is the poorer? You with all your money melted into gates or me with contraband bales in my wagon? Every bale we're setting on is worth one everlasting, hell-raising fortune. If I can get 'em far as Yazoo landing, they'll bring twelve thousand dollars. And on the wharf at Memphis they'll be cash to the tune of a hundred and twenty thousand greenbacks!" She cackled with gleeful greed.

Surlina admired the crotchety old lady for her willingness to take matters into her own hands. While Dottie didn't hold with "no slavin' or seceshin' " she had a strong streak of the same trait which seemed to ail the whole South—a perverse and deep seated go-it-alone pride. But while everyone else was wringing their hands, muttering about "beauty and chivalry" and refugeeing to Richmond, crusty old Dottie was toting cotton bales to Memphis beneath a wagonload of junk.

Suddenly Surlina was knocked from her reverie by Dottie's alarmed whisper. "Uh-oh—company."

Surlina sat up straight, her eyes blinking in fright. A figure on horseback was approaching at a gallop. She squinted against the sun while fumbling for her knife. "Turn around. Go back. There might be more!"

"Hell, no," argued Dottie calmly. "I'm going straight through and get speedy results." She glanced back. "Get Kuffy out of sight."

Surlina could see details now. "That's a Union uniform! Must be a scout."

"He'd best stand aside for Dottie McDune! When I start throwing lead, it'll be too late for him to learn to dodge."

"You can't shoot him!"

Dottie only laughed, pulling Murray to a halt. "Surlina, get in the wagon and pull on a shawl and some old clothes. When I tell you to, moan out loud and clear. I don't mean no high-toned opry singing! Moan, understand?"

Surlina rolled into the wagon opening, scratching for the dirty shawl as the soldier approached. "Dottie, what are you—"

"Lay down and get to belly-achin'! One scout won't likely bother himself about an old lady and a case of sickness."

Surlina stretched out atop a stained mattress, squint-

216

ing through the canvas slits. As the soldier halted, gun in hand, she began to moan softly. She pulled the bonnet low across her face, hoping she looked as sick as she was starting to feel.

The soldier held his horse steady with some trouble as he brandished his pistol above his head. He appeared young, with scraped cheeks from cold-water shaving and glossy fine brown hair. He motioned the cotton wagon to a halt and announced, "No throughway! My orders are to let no one pass this road. Confiscate all wagons and livestock."

Dottie nodded in agreement. "Fair enough." She commenced climbing from the driver's perch. "In fact, I'm greatly relieved to be confiscated. Now my sick niece will be put in the Union hospital. Take a heap of worrying off my shoulders!"

Surlina moaned loudly.

Dottie enthused, "I'm sure beholden to you, sonny. Yellow fever ain't my cup of tea."

The soldier lurched backward on his horse. "Yellow fever!" Frantically he motioned Dottie back onto the wagon. Surlina let out a full-bodied groan.

Dottie urged the young man to come closer. "Here, take a look!" She lifted the canvas flap. Surlina flopped her arms listlessly and made retching noises.

The formerly stalwart boy now frowned in consternation. "Orders is orders."

"You're right welcome to the wagon and mule," interrupted Dottie. "Here, just lend me a hand, and we'll stretch my niece out here aside the bayou."

"No," he replied quickly. "I'll just unhitch the mule and take him!"

"Be doing me a favor," agreed Dottie. "This puddin'-foot animal is plumb worthless." She clucked her tongue in sorrow. "Sure hate to saddle you with this slack-jawed, lame-brained hayburner of a mule."

The soldier unhitched Murray with speed and determination while Dottie sat impassively on the seat. "You're doing me quite a favor," she told him again. "But say, fella, could you lend me a hand before you go? I suspect I'll be needing to dig a grave between here and the Natchez Trace. Could you spell me on the shovel?"

The soldier declined the gravedigging. He led the mule a few paces and tied him to the saddle horn of his own mount. He swatted the mule's rump. "Let's go." Murray balked. After considerable urging, the mule took two steps, balked again, moved another step and stopped. A choice curse issued from the scout's mouth and he whacked the mule across the ears.

"Hey!" fumed Dottie, "Murray's a tender-mouth mule! You watch your language and how you tug on him!" She sat back, crossed her arms and tapped her foot. "You know, come to think of it, you'd best not drag that mule back into your camp. Why, my niece was a-riding him all day yesterday, just as she took sick. Yellow fever's mighty contagious!"

The boy continued sweating and straining, gritting his teeth. "Orders is orders!"

"You better think twice or three times about dragging contamination back to your camp."

"This . . . mule . . . is my . . . prisoner!" The soldier yanked hard on the mule's bit. Dottie issued a last warning. "I told you Murray's a tender-mouth mule. You saw that bit in across his tongue once more, and he'll proceed to show you how the cow ate the cabbage." With that she climbed down, walked slowly over to the mule, swatted him on the rump and pronounced, "Git." Murray picked up one leg and then the other for a dozen steps. "Move on along there now, sonny, 'cause I'm going to let my niece out of the wagon to rest in the shade."

Surlina was helped by Dottie's firm dragging motions to the shelter of a cottonwood tree. "There, there," soothed Dottie, wiping the younger woman's forehead with a tobacco-stained bandana.

At Surlina's appearance, the soldier hurriedly mounted his horse, towing Murray like an iceberg. As soon as he was out of earshot, Surlina demanded, "And do we now pull this wagon to Memphis ourselves?" She flung the shawl away.

218

"Home afore dark," muttered Dottie. "That's the rule."

"Rule for what?"

"For tender-mouthed mules and virgins, providing you want to keep them thataway." Dottie pointed to a small hill down the road. "See the second rise beyond the saplings? When he clears there, we'll play a game." With that, she got her gear together to fish for crawdads. She handed Kuffy a line and motioned him to get busy.

After half an hour's work, they feasted on a dozen tails. Then Dottie asked, "Our brave soldier boy done cleared the top of the hill yet?"

Both women stood, squinting against the sun. The boy was now afoot, trying to lead both balky animals.

"Time for action," crowed Dottie. She cupped her hands, pouted her lips, puffed air into her cheeks like a bullfrog, then let loose an ear-splitting whistle.

Suddenly Murray began to behave like a stallion. He rose on his hind legs, pawing the air and snorting. The horse reared back, too, alarmed. The soldier lost both reins, grabbed for them, then jumped toward the horse, trying to retrieve a handhold, but it took off for higher ground. He heaved himself toward Murray, catching his mane tentatively as the mule again pawed the air. Murray raced back the way he had recently traversed so slowly.

Within two minutes, spurred on by Dottie's whistles, Murray, in a lather, raced up, the soldier, who had lost his gun in the process, still clinging to his mane. Dottie greeted the scout with her pistol to his face. "You damned fool! Running my poor mule! I've half a mind to horsewhip you."

The soldier stared open-mouthed at Surlina, who was standing healthily upright. Apparently he was a brave boy, for he refused to be intimidated by his loss of horse and gun. "That mule is confiscated property," he argued to Dottie.

"That mule is now *my* prisoner of war," corrected Dottie. She poked the boy in the chest and ordered him to turn around. Then, with a prod of the gun in the buttocks, she ordered, "Let's see how fast *you* can run.

Head on out, sonny, 'cause my ears is laid back nigh as far as my mule's!"

The soldier was off and running in an instant, high-stepping the road and dashing for the cover of a cottonwood grove. Surlina laughed until her sides ached. Dottie patted Murray and began picking cockleburs from his matted coat. The mule merely whinnied, sounding to Surlina exactly like an overgrown dog.

"Dottie! Stop the wagon! Look at that pair of gates! I want to inspect them!" Surlina was clambering over the side of the wagon before Dottie had pulled to a halt.

"Lord-a-mercy, woman! You've dived off this wagon to look at gates every ten miles! We been on the road a month, and I'll bet you've sidled up to nearly forty pairs of gates—and all for nothing."

Surlina took her knife, dull from carving on various plantation gates, and sawed at the metal. Solid iron. Disappointed, she returned to the wagon and swung aboard. "You won't have to put up with me much longer," she said cheerfully. "We'll be in Memphis by this time tomorrow." She counted backward on her fingers, figuring out the date they'd left Whispers and how many days they'd been traveling at night and hiding during the day, trying to avoid Confederates, Union troops and Mullermen. "Why, tomorrow's the Fourth of July!"

"Be parades in Memphis, I 'spect," allowed Dottie, a smile on her face. "Ought to be some mighty fine poker games, too. I think Kuffy and me will bunk in the wagon, save our pennies for penny ante and keep a watch on our contraband till I can get me a cotton trader's pass."

"Not me!" vowed Surlina. "It's the Gayoso Hotel for me!" she promised herself, and lay awake that night dreaming of clean sheets, a hot bath, and clothes which didn't smell like tobacco and mules. She arose the next morning, took a cursory bath in the nearby creek and combed her hair for the first time in days.

Memphis! It loomed on the horizon like a grand metropolis, flags flying, banners crisscrossing the streets between second-story windows, crowds shouting in the streets. "Gone all out for the Fourth," decided Dottie and clucked to Murray to move along smartly.

As they entered the streets, Surlina had an eerie feeling of being back in New Orleans. The city was obviously under Union control, but the crowds were Confederate and unruly. All the federal finery was for show, as the city expressed contempt by locking soldiers out of saloons, refusing to serve them, stable or shoe their horses, or allow them entry to private homes. All Tennessee must be contested territory, Surlina figured. No telling who had her gates in an area so laced with disputed commands.

She swung her satchel off the seat, announcing loudly, "Fare thee well! True to my word, it's the Gayoso for me!"

"We'll be at the stable by the river if you need us," shouted Dottie. "Good luck to you, girlie!"

Surlina pushed through the crowd, hefting her valise close against her. It held her most valued possessions —the kitchen knife, Butler's money belt, her clothes and shoes. She crossed the broad avenue where she could see the hotel at the end of the block.

Suddenly, in the crowd on the porch of the Gayoso, she spotted a familiar face. Was it Sam? She stopped, uncertain. The man was in civilian attire and wedged inconspicuously among taller men. 'He's lost weight, and he looks dreadfully tired. But, yes, it's Sam!' She summoned her voice and called to him. "Sam! Sam!" She pushed toward him, taking his appearance in more fully. He was more stooped than she remembered, his shoulders rounded in a dusty brown cloth jacket. He had a heavier beard, bushy and more red than brown at the ends. Even his chestnut hair seemed thicker. "Sam!" He looked directly at her without spotting her. She saw his clouded blue eyes and her heart sank. His cheeks had always been so rosy, his robin's-egg-blue eyes so clear! What had happened?

"Sam! Here! It's me!"

He reacted to the sound of his name, scanning the crowd, looking confused. Then, suddenly, he looked directly at her. His jaw dropped sharply, his mouth parted in surprise, and shock widened his eyes. His lips formed a smile and he bounded down the steps, shoving his way through the crowd.

"Oh, Sam!" She hugged him exuberantly.

He held her arm tightly, the Adam's apple in his throat bobbing up and down. Finally, he croaked, "I heard you were shot trying to escape Ben Butler's camp!"

"They shot at me," she laughed, "but even Union pickets miss once in a while!"

He still could not believe she was safe. He kept shaking his head. "And Butler's horse was stolen— came back two days later without a rider."

"True," she agreed, pleased to learn that the black stallion had found his way home safely. "I found him an excellent mount, speedy and durable." She giggled. "And I found Butler's hospitality rude and undignified, though his money belt repaid me for the time I wasted in his unpleasant company." She twirled around, knocking into people, giddy with relief at finding Sam, able to laugh at her troubles long ago in New Orleans. "Oh, Sam, isn't this a wonderful party Memphis is having! Tonight you shall be my dancing partner, and we shall take to the ballroom of the Gayoso like we did to the grand salon of the *Radiant*."

His eyes twinkled for a moment, then hid behind the pall of worry. "I have had more trouble than—"

"No more trouble than I!" she interrupted. "But now our troubles are over! I want no more of them. I want you to dance with me and—" She stopped, aware of his somber countenance. "You're so serious and I'm so giddy. I've nearly forgotten my true intent. Sam, have you any gates in your command?"

"What? I can't hear you in this noisy crowd."

She dragged him away, holding his arm earnestly. "Sam, have you any gates in your command?" she repeated.

Abruptly he pulled away, turning his face, his eyes downcast. "Surlina, at the moment, I have not even a command!"

Her heart fell. She'd come all this way, hoping, assuming, and now he knew nothing! Then she remembered she had never actually told him of the debacle at Erlanger's and the melted silver. Certainly General Butler would not reveal his suspicions. Thad Muller wouldn't report to any Union headquarters with his theories, and Julien Rainbeau was intent on raiding the supply wagons himself. She thought of all the people involved and decided that her best hope lay with Sam. "Your reports about me being shot were wrong. But the reports about Muller's capture were also wrong. They hanged the wrong man."

"Son-of-a-bitch!"

It was the first time she'd heard him curse. He seemed changed; less orderly, more like a common soldier. She recited the details of the silver gates and ended with the rumor she had clung to for over a month: the gates had been sent north to Farragut and then overland to Memphis. "I was so certain they were bound for your army, Sam!"

"My army? Surlina, you haven't heard a word I've said. My army is in a state of transition—with Halleck in command and me left behind the lines gathering dust. All I have left is the steamer you gave me."

"But Sam," she exclaimed, "I thought the *Radiant* sank!"

His weariness seemed to dissolve for an instant. "The ship is here, Surlina. Would you like to see it? I renamed it for you—the *Tigress*—for the way you acted when we first met."

"Can we dance in the grand salon?"

"Only by pushing aside horses and hay, I'm afraid."

She shook her head, hating to see the desecration of the gorgeous *Radiant* in its new role as cavalry stable. But he took her arm and set out toward the river. His mind was obviously on the humiliation of having no army. He complained, "That damned Halleck! With him in command, this war will last a hundred years! Why, he is burrowing like a mole toward Holly Springs. Constructing earthworks in front of him every time he advances an inch!"

223

"And you languish on the hotel railings, acting as if you have nothing to do! Oh, Sam, help me find my gates! Help me hunt my silver! That's something you can do!"

He nodded docilely. They were walking toward the steamer, which she could see had been repainted and repaired with alterations to both decks. "Will the war end soon?" she asked, "even with Halleck and acres of breastworks?"

He stopped on the landing, seeming to ponder her questions. He spoke as if they shared a common interest in military strategy. "Two years ago I would have said, yes, it will end in thirty days. But the fighting at Shiloh cured me of such assumptions. Never has there been anything like the bloodiness there! Never has there been a war like the guerrilla war in Missouri! Never anything like the bitterness in Tennessee." He shook his head, eyes weighted almost shut, shoulders rounded forward with an invisible force. "It will eventually end, I fear, with a nation physically exhausted and morally numbed."

She shivered with the chill of his prophecy. Inside, she was shocked at his unhappiness, horrified at the physical toll she could see it had taken on him.

"Like a sheep, I have been shorn of my surmises," he said. "And my command."

Perhaps he was momentarily without his army, but command was still his. She could read it in his eyes, which were hurting to resume leadership. He had the instinct for wielding power. It was part of his being, a peculiar and personal trait. She felt a complex emotion, one she could not fully explain, only that there was an air of inevitability about the two of them as well as about his destiny.

Now she could see the decks of the *Tigress,* dull against the dull river water. Sam hailed a sentry, saying they were coming aboard. She held back. "I really don't want to—" she broke off, unable to explain.

He took her elbow, supportive, as if just now recognizing the impact the ship had on her. "Let's ride then. Away from town. Where it's peaceful."

She nodded consent and he asked the sentry to saddle two horses and bring them around. From far inside the steamer she heard the calliope playing "Yankee Doodle." She smiled at Sam, humming the music. "*One* of the songs you know." He colored slightly.

When the horses were ready, she noticed that the saddle blankets were made of the floral carpet which had graced the staterooms. He held her horse while she mounted, riding sidesaddle. Then they were off, passing the picket line at the end of the levee, streaking for the wooded hills to the east. Surlina laughed and let the air rush through her hair, tossing back her head and barely holding the reins. The summer field was full of black-eyed Susans and delicate Queen Anne's lace, puffy milkweeds and sky-blue bellflowers. "Stop! I want to pick some wildflowers," she called. "The last flower I had was a daisy I stole from Butler's desk."

He held the reins of both horses, watching her flitting like a butterfly, exclaiming over her bouquet. When she came back, both hands full, he asked, "Do you remember the lilacs I picked for you?"

"How sweet they smelled! How polite you were . . . and generous! Sam, I have never known a man like you. Your mind seems to stretch out infinitely yet retain an enormous file for details. You stole my steamer, then brought me lilacs."

"You *gave* me the steamer," he teased. "I distinctly remember."

She tucked handfuls of flowers in the buttonholes of his brown jacket until he begged her to stop.

"Now you are decorated to my satisfaction," she laughed, plopping a last black-eyed Susan into his beard. He yanked the flower away, scandalized at the idea of a general wearing wildflowers.

He took her face between his hands and held her gently. "The summer light enhances you, Surlina. Let me look at you, memorize you like this field of flowers. You have a special color I want to remember: a shadow of pink on your fair skin, a smudge of pride in the way you jut your chin, a shading of mischief in your emerald eyes." He looked away, then back, holding her eyes in a gaze of longing. "My God, I cannot remember feeling this happy in months!"

She brought her mouth up to his instinctively, brushing his lips like a shadow passing over the moon. "Sam, Sam, happiness is yours for the asking." She thought, '*I* am yours for the asking,' but was too surprised to tell him aloud. A peacefulness spread through her, compounded by the lazy warmth of the afternoon and the sense of anticipation she felt between them. She scrambled across the field, plucking daisies, calling, "I shall weave a daisy chain and handcuff you to me!"

He shook his head, amused but reserved, and sat down with his back to a small stump. The horses, tethered together, stood nearby, munching the long grass.

She came back to him with her skirt full of daisies and her petticoat showing. Silently, she dropped to her knees, showering him with flowers. He chuckled, picked a clover stem and sucked on it. She stretched languidly in the sweet grass and laid her head on his arm. Tenderly he stroked her forehead, pushing away the curls.

For a moment she felt wanton, then callous. She wanted kisses and caresses, yes, but she wanted to seek his help in finding the silver gates as well. Would she be as cruel as Julien, trading information for temptation? Of course, Julien had admitted he'd drink the quick dipper of water and use his wits to find more—just as he'd probably used her passion and would now use his wits to find another woman. Surely Sam would see she was right in the long run. He believed in long-range plans and strategy. 'Freely given,' she thought. 'I want his information to be freely given, even as I want my affection for him to be freely offered.'

"Will you let me tell you the story of my treasure gates? Then, when you know everything, perhaps you will help me find them. I know you were fond of my father. I know you would prefer Thad Muller in prison."

"Muller is a blot on the record of my brigade! I'd use the hemp liberally on him!"

226

"And perhaps your sense of honor will extend to seeing justice done concerning my silver—even if you choose not to help me for my own sake."

He stood abruptly, stamped his boots, faced away as if he could not bear to look at her, as if it were utterly necessary to make his pronouncement to empty space. "Surlina, how little you realize of how close I would come to doing as you ask. How close I would come to being my own undoing and that of my army . . . if I had one. Every moment I spend with you puts me on increasingly dangerous ground. Why, this very afternoon I've run away from town to go prancing and picking flowers!"

"I *like* flowers!" she pouted.

"And silver."

"And you." She put her arms out, seeking his embrace. "Oh, hold me, Sam. We've never had the time to simply hold each other. There's no hurry now. Finally, there's time for us. We'll finish our dancing and play that chess game we always talked about. We'll—"

"Did you come back to me only because of the gates, Surlina?" He took her in his arms, looking desperate for assurance. "Are you leading me into an ambush? Am I consorting with the enemy?"

She shuddered. "You hurt me more than if you had struck me." His suspicions filled her with dread. "You think it treason to embrace me? Then turn me loose. Send me away! Throw me in the brig as you once tried to do!"

He clasped her to him tighter. He seemed cornered, eyes darting from the stump to the horses to the horizon and back to her. His lips touched her mouth, then fastened hard against her. His hands moved to encircle her waist, then dropped to caress her hips, traveled up to touch her blouse and cradle her breast. "We *will* have time," he vowed softly.

A bugle split the air, drowning out the sound of whippoorwills and jaybirds, breaking the spell of flowery meadows. "We have to go back now, don't we?" she asked.

He nodded and picked up the reins to the horses.

They walked the steeds side by side, talking softly, as companions and friends. Suddenly she realized that his logical, assertive mind had been pondering the problem of the gates all along. He posed a new hypothesis. "What if the gates do not exist, Surlina?"

"But of course they do!"

"Erlanger might have invented the story of melted silver merely to hide his own losses or corruption. I do not think *you* invented the tale, dearest. Only that you might have believed it without foundation. Have you ever seen the gates?"

"No."

"Then they may prove elusive—to you, your father, Thad Muller, Butler and everyone else who tries to get his hands on them."

"Julien Rainbeau. Add his name to the list. He's one more man out to find them. He's planning to have raiders attack the supply wagons, making it look like the work of Mullermen."

"We can send a telegraph message to warn the quartermaster. Perhaps a warm reception can be arranged for this Rainbeau fellow."

Surlina felt guilt and remorse. How could she sleep with Julien, want a son from him, then calmly recite his plans to a Union general? Why, the same way he could sleep with her, beg passion from her body, then calmly recite her secrets to Ramsey!

"As for Muller," Sam went on, "I'll put a squad on his trail again, if I can get permission from Halleck. We'll gamble that Halleck is fool enough to believe this story of gates. A little long-range planning should bag Muller like a rabbit."

How right she'd been to seek Sam's aid! With pride ringing in her voice, she said, "That's how you fight your battles, isn't it? Strategy. Planning. No spur-of-the-moment feints and dashes."

"Yes," he laughed. "The object is defeat."

She matched his laugh, teasing him with a smile. "And if I were your quarry, Sam? Would you defeat me?" She dug her heel against her horse's side and reined him to a gallop.

228

She heard the horse behind her hesitate, then change stride to catch up. She looked around and saw Sam roaring with laughter, chasing after her. He rode with the ease and natural grace of a man used to the saddle, blending his movements with those of the powerful animal. Back inside the picket lines, Surlina slowed her steed. They cooled the horses by walking them by the riverbank. At the steamer, she dismounted, resting her hands lightly across his shoulders, looking expectantly into his eyes. "I will be staying at the Gayoso, Sam. Will you let me know the results of your telegraph work?"

"I'll bring you word tonight," he replied.

She left him at the steamer, feeling immense relief.

At the hotel, the lobby was full of boisterous celebrants of Independence Day. A rowdy group of Southerners sang, "Jeff Davis is coming, yo ho, yo ho," while nearby Union sympathizers chorused, "We'll hang Jeff Davis from a sour apple tree!" Wall posters recruited for both North and South, offering "chances for travel."

By the time she'd had a bath and supper, the singers were slowing down. By ten o'clock Surlina heard sweet melodies. At midnight, melancholy filled the downstairs. Now the choruses sang, "Mother, Do You Think of Me?"

Upstairs in her room, she listened to the singing while idly brushing her hair. Should she give up and go to sleep? No. Sam was a man of his word. If he'd promised to bring her word tonight, he'd not fail. She looked at herself in the reflecting glass, pinched her cheeks to make them rosier, then kicked off her slippers.

The instant she heard the knock at the door, she was running toward it, smiling. Opening it, she was pleased to see that although the hour was late, Sam looked more refreshed. Maybe he just needed something to do. She motioned him inside. He remained in the hallway, hat in hand, cigar stub between his teeth. Was he too bashful to come into her room? She smiled demurely and moved into the hall beside him, leaving the door ajar.

"Sam Grant reporting as ordered," he jested. "Your trail is not cold. The gates exist. Farragut's communiqué calls them 'carriage movables.' They arrived at his command in mid-June, but when he left the upper river, he sent them overland."

"I knew you could find out!" Surlina exulted. She ignored the thoughtful frown which made creases around his blue eyes. With no particular army duties, he should be getting plenty of sleep. Why did he seem so restless and unkempt? She pushed aside her concern for him in the flurry of excitement she felt about his news. "And what is their overland destination?"

"Holly Springs, with Halleck. He's establishing a supply dump there, along with his ammunition and provisions for a thousand years!"

"Send a message quickly. Have the gates sent here. To me. Holly Springs is not far—barely in Mississippi."

"Anything sent to you from a Union supply dump would arouse suspicion. Your plan would mean certain confiscation."

"Then have them sent to you." She reproached herself for not thinking of that. "*You* will not take them away from me."

"The gates are only en route to Holly Springs. They have not arrived."

"Sweet Jesus, no! On the road somewhere? Prey to Muller and Rainbeau and all the other rabble of the river?" Well, at least she had Sam Grant chasing them now. "I know you'll find them and return them to me."

"Only ask me to find them, Surlina! Don't ask me to present them to you," he pleaded with her, using his eyes to stab her into silence. "At this point you have only asked me for information. But make no mistake. If I had command, and if I had the gates, and if they truly turned out to be silver, then I—"

"You'd give them to me, Sam! I know you would!" She whispered to him fiercely, as if to hypnotize him.

His voice seemed kindly. "Surlina, dearest, you do not yet understand the reasons for this war."

"Nor do I want to!"

230

Now anger flared the blue of his eyes and contracted the pupils. "Your only standard—the only colors you have raised—have been silver."

"You know it is my only concern!"

"My concern is the nation. You must open your eyes, Surlina. The prosperity of the nation is your prosperity, its health, your health."

She flounced away, hurt and defiant. She taunted him with the only words she knew could wound him. "So, General, with no command, you think now to take command of my silver!" She whirled to face him, crimson with disgust. "As you have seen in the lobby of the Gayoso tonight, your guns cannot purchase loyalty." She opened her door and marched inside, leaving it wide open behind her, waiting for him to enter.

"Guns cannot purchase loyalty, but silver cannot purchase you peace." She heard footsteps, then his voice fading down the hall. "The barriers between us are more than gates. Good night, Surlina."

For a moment her pride prevented her from turning and calling his name. Then she cast aside all thoughts of right and wrong, wars and treasures. She ran after him, her bare feet moving silently. She caught up with Sam at the end of the hall, halting him from behind, putting her arms around his waist and stopping him with a jerk.

Burying her head against his back, she sobbed, "Sam, Sam! Don't go in anger! Don't leave me like this."

When he turned and took her in his arms, he was pale. Quietly, he made a simple confession. "I am in love with you and you know it. There can be nothing more terrible for either of us." Every word seemed to cost him endless soul searching and a massive effort. "What you mistake for my anger, Surlina, is my overwhelming emotion, which terrifies me to the core. What you see as my rejection of you is my protection. If I should wear my feelings on my sleeve, it would mean only harm for you!"

Surlina was thrilled by his admission of passion,

stunned by his logic. How could he stand there passively when the ache in her heart was making goose bumps flare up along her arms? "Then are we always to be apart? Never to know the trust and joy of a night together?" She meant to keep her voice discreet and her stance neutral, but her body was refusing to remain impersonal. "Oh, Sam, stay with me tonight! I need you. I want you."

"I love you," he repeated, in a whisper which held as much rage as ardor. Then he broke the embrace, pulling away as if drawn by a team of oxen. "Maybe another time, another place. Perhaps never."

"Perhaps never?" Her voice echoed with incredulity.

"Perhaps war and fate will cheat us of what we want. But if they do, understand forever that I love you and I ache for the completion of our flesh with all my heart." He tore down the stairs before Surlina could react.

She put her face in her hands and stumbled back to the empty room. To lose Sam, when she'd only found him, was too much. She flung herself on the bed and cried until her throat was raw. From downstairs she heard the sweet strains of the late-night singing. Awake, incredibly lonely, red-eyed and sniffling, she went to the stairs to hear the music better.

From the top step, she could see down into the lobby. To her surprise, Sam was seated in the shadows of the corner. He was alone at a table, a bottle of whiskey and glass his only companions. He looked miserable, he was drinking steadily and without delight.

Horrified, she trudged back to her room, not letting her eyes glance back at the staircase. "Oh, Sam, I've lost you," she moaned and began to cry again.

When Surlina awoke at daybreak to noise at her door, her first thought was 'Sam! You've come back!' Then she heard the raspy voice calling her name and moaned. "Go away, Dottie!"

"Open up or I'll shoot my way in!"

Surlina unlatched the chain and peered into the hall. There stood Dottie, in buckskins and suede tunic, one

232

hand on a brand new long rifle, the other on Kuffy's shoulder.

Dottie leaned on her gun, polishing its brass patchbox with her suede sleeve. "Had a tiff with your general friend, eh?" When there was no answer, Dottie added, "You know the general I'm talking about—that little bearded fellow, Sam Grant."

Surlina backed up, sat on the edge of the featherbed, reached for the hairbrush and began whacking her head in such a certain display of anger that her words sounded ridiculous. "No. We are quite good friends."

"Good friends?" Dottie smacked the side of her leather britches. "I've done a mite of reconnaissance on my own, and it's your good friend who supplies the cotton trader permits. Now, if the general in Memphis wanted to supply me with a cotton trader's pass—"

"You could, no doubt, supply the contraband cotton," interrupted Surlina impatiently. She jumped off the bed and began to dress rapidly.

"I certainly could," agreed Dottie, "and you could supply the general!"

"Sam Grant would not do it!" Surlina was surprised at her faith in him. "He would never profit from this war. I know him."

Dottie's eyes were openly snickering. She appraised Surlina head to toe. "You know him as well as you know Julien?"

"Get out of here!"

"Oh, hellfire, Surlina. Will you kindly quit tearing out your hair and putting your clothes on backward? I've come to deliver myself of two messages, not preach."

"Say anything you want . . . on your way out."

"I've already been to Grant's river steamer office, asked him for a permit and he's turned me down flat."

"Ha! I knew he would!"

"He sent you something," teased Dottie. "When I said I was a friend of yours, he choked up and started being accommodating."

"What?" Surlina put on a placating smile. "What did he send me? Give it to me!"

Suddenly Dottie turned to Kuffy. "First, the slave network is working. Kuffy got word for you last night from your sister. That's my other news."

"Tandy? But how? She's in Vicksburg."

"Yes, Tandy Cabell, in Vicksburg, said to tell you she's sick. The news came over the jumbo drums. You know those tin kettles the blacks do the African talk on."

"Tandy's sick? What's wrong?" She searched Kuffy's face for clues, concerned about her sister.

Both Dottie and Kuffy shook their heads and shrugged. "Don't know more," offered Kuffy. "She say for you to come."

"I can't," Surlina thought aloud. "I have to pay a call on Halleck in Holly Springs." She had just thought of the idea and it seemed sensible.

"Good luck to you then," said Dottie shooing Kuffy toward the door. "The boy and I are off to join up with them that's glad to see us!" She withdrew a slip of paper and waved it enticingly. "Grant sent you this."

Surlina pounced like a buzzard. "A pass!" Voraciously she read the words which authorized the bearer to proceed to headquarters on demand. "Oh, he read my mind! He knew I'd head for Holly Springs!" She held the pass against her heart, delighted.

"There's a message which accompanies your paper," said Dottie. "Something more you're not expecting."

"Yes? Tell me quickly!"

"Grant moves south." She gave her report, saluted the wall, booted Kuffy out of the room and closed the door as she left.

Surlina ran after them, demanding, "Grant moves south? What does that mean? Is he back in command? Is he after the gates? Tell me!"

But Dottie and Kuffy trotted down the stairs. Obviously they knew even less than she. All right. Grant moves south. Tandy is sick in Vicksburg. The pass to headquarters. Gates at Holly Springs, hopefully. Yes, it would work to take the train south to Vicksburg, check on Tandy, then proceed to Holly Springs. At the rate Halleck was advancing, he wouldn't get there until fall.

She rushed into her room and started tossing things toward her satchel. Grant moves south? So would Surlina Defore.

24

The train to Vicksburg, a narrow-gauge railroad, jostled and shrieked while making little forward progress. It stopped every fifteen minutes for water, to let cows cross the tracks, to repair rutted roadbeds or dismembered ties. Here, a low-water bridge was underwater. There, the water tower was empty.

The distance from Memphis to Vicksburg was only 175 miles, but by rail it became a journey through Tennessee, Mississippi, Arkansas and Louisiana, the final leg being a raft trip across the Mississippi River and a flight of three hundred steps up Vicksburg's cliffs. Surlina felt grimy. She had worn her traveling outfit for two days.

The train stopped again and she peered out the window. What now? Suddenly she saw a band of riders galloping downhill, heard shots and yells. She dived for the dirty train floor, following the example of the other passengers. All was quiet for a moment, then the rumor was whispered up and down the aisle. "Renegades. Robbers. Outlyers. Mullermen! Quick, take off your rings and watches! Hide your money!"

Mullermen! She was so incensed at the idea she stood up to get a better view. My God! There he was —Thad Muller—riding at the head of the column, waving his renegades forward.

He rode past her, then reined his horse so violently that the animal reared and pawed the air. He whirled his steed and leaned toward the passenger car windows.

Frightened he might have seen and recognized her, she ducked down, crawled into the aisle and ran for the women's toilet.

Inside the small stall, she locked the latch, worried it wouldn't hold against any real force. So Muller was still at large, terrorizing the countryside. For an instant she mentally berated Sam for his inability to capture Muller. And Julien! Had *he* blithely turned this thief loose to loot after their journey upriver together? Men were nothing but a pack of groveling dogs!

Surlina heard the robbers clambering through the train, demanding jewelry, wallets and food bundles. Apparently they weren't eating too well these days. She stiffened as the latch rattled, but no one attempted to force the handle. Her courage was deserting her moment by moment as she huddled beneath the wash-basin, blocking the door further by holding her feet against it. Part of her wanted to do battle with Muller —make him pay for holding her father hostage, for trying to steal the silver, for engineering the original spy work which had cost them the *Radiant*.

Suddenly the door jarred, then crunched inward as a man came hurtling through, tearing the flimsy wood from its hinges and jamming her legs in the process. She cried out, scrambling to her feet, digging for her knife. Instantly he had her pinned against the wall, her wrist securely held, his putrid breath close against her face. "Muller!"

He stuck the door back on its posts. "Didn't think no plywood was going to keep me out, did you, Silver Belle? No more than when you threw me out of your hifalutin' St. Louis living room! Thad Muller always comes back!" He twisted the knife from her hand and held it to her throat. With his other hand, he yanked her curls. Suddenly he sliced off a lock of her hair, chopping it violently and bluntly. "Give me a souvenir, Silver Belle!" Then as she flattened herself hard against the flimsy wall, he grinned and licked his thick lips. "Give me a kiss! Not any of them nose-in-the-air, slap-in-the-face kisses neither!"

Surlina let out a wrathful shriek and clawed at him.

He slapped her face with the side of his hand, then bent his mouth toward hers, open, wet, smelling of whiskey. She spit at him. Wrestling her against the window shade, he raised the knife. Panicked that he would kill her, she sank limply to her knees.

"That's better," he gloated and sliced another curl from the top of her head, tilting her neck down till it touched her breastbone. "While you're down there where you belong, you can still give me that kiss!" He kept the knife atop her skull, pressing her head forward while the other hand fumbled with his trousers. "That tongue of yours likes to give such hot lashings, let me feel it where it'll do some good!"

She fell forward, tackling him around the knees, but he did not lose his balance as she'd hoped. He laughed, brought his knee upward in a rough kick to her chest, then shoved her backward again. Exposing himself, he dangled his organ like a red and veiny turkey neck. "I'll give you a souvenir, too, Silver Belle! You ended up with the silver, but—"

"I don't have it any more than you!" she cried out angrily. Instantly she was furious with herself for admitting she didn't have it. Now he'd be back on the scent like a bloodhound.

He seemed startled, then bent down, grabbing her chin, making her look directly into his pitted face. "Where is it? Tell me or die! Your father promised me my share, then double-crossed me! You'll not play me for a fool as well."

"The Union Army has it! And that's one place you can't go snooping, you filthy bastard!"

She heard scuffling noises outside the door. "Anyone in there?" called a male voice. She opened her mouth to scream. Muller's fist jammed against her teeth, rocking her back violently and snapping her neck. She bit at his hand, thrashing her head against the taste of blood in her mouth. The sounds in the hall grew louder. A man shouted, "All right in there, ma'am?" She saw a look of fear cross Muller's face. Hastily he jerked up the window shade, twisted the handle and pushed the glass outward. He scrambled to his feet, not bothering to

237

button his trousers, and dived through the narrow window opening.

He hit the gravel railbed, yelped, then ran for the woods, pants flapping.

Surlina leaned out the broken window and spit blood and curses at him. The train jostled and resumed its journey. From the hall she heard the passengers scrambling from their hiding places, women swooning and children crying. She put a hand to her mouth. Her tongue was cut where she'd bit it, her gums sore, but no permanent damage. She almost felt like jamming her own fist down her throat for blurting to Muller the availability of the silver.

Two hours later, Surlina was on the Vicksburg riverfront. No hordes of flatboats jamming the docks, no swarms of sailors joking and lounging, no slaves sweating and swearing. She tidied herself after the rocking raft trip across the river, then shook her curls into as much order as they would assume after the impromptu haircut by Muller. Looking up the hundreds of steps which led to the fortresslike city on the hill, she dusted her wrapper and slung her satchel across her back.

Halfway up the narrow wooden stairs, she had to stop and rest. She shed her cape, dismayed to find her dress damp under the arms from her exertions. Altogether she felt disreputable. 'When Tandy sees me, she will probably slam the door in my face,' she thought.

While catching her breath, she watched the wide river. There were no signs of any shipping on the river, no trace of Farragut's fleet, Confederate gunboats or merchant steamers. She straggled up the rest of the stairs, developing a dislike for the sandstone cliff. What kind of town wanted its head in the air and its feet in the river! Atop the mountain she found a city of wide streets, green summer lawns, tidy white frame houses and a magnificent red-brick courthouse, the Confederate flag towering on a fifty-foot spire. Every street corner rewarded citizens with breathtaking views of the river.

She stopped a passerby and inquired if he knew the

238

address of Thayer Cabell. "Harrison Street, two blocks down," he pointed and bowed.

She found the house with no trouble. A modest home, not nearly as splendid as the Pontalba Apartments in New Orleans. It was a one-story frame and needed a new coat of white paint. She was let in without question by a black maid. The living room was appalling to someone who fancied herself neutral. While the maid went to rouse Tandy from a rest, Surlina examined the framed needlepoint banners made up of thousands of patient stitches. Tandy must have stayed up many a night hating Yankees to have sewed all these things!

On the piano stood sheet music entitled "Farewell to the Star Spangled Banner," arranged for pianoforte and guitar. Apart from the piano, however, the furniture was meager. The woolen carpet was worn in a path toward the door and frayed at the edges. The cane-back chairs were neither sturdy nor fashionable. Tandy and Cabell were refugeeing in proper impoverished spirit.

The house was quiet except for the maid scurrying between rooms. Surlina listened for sounds of her father. Perhaps he was asleep. The atmosphere seemed as if this were a place for only the ill and aged.

"Surlina! Oh my stars, thank goodness you've come! I'm in here, Sister! Please come in!"

At the sound of Tandy's excited welcome, Surlina went into the bedroom. Her sister was propped up among dozens of pillows like a chirpy, thin bird. Her dainty hands darted out and she continued her happy feeble greetings. Surlina appraised the patient. She had a glassy shine to her complexion, and when Surlina sat on the edge of the bed and hugged her, Surlina felt Tandy's' bony ribs and shoulders beneath the dressing gown. Thoughts of dysentery, malaria, jaundice and tuberculosis, all prevalent in this land in summer, made Surlina feel doubly protective of her sister.

She stood back, taking into consideration the pale white nails, the prison pallor of the skin and the wavy brown hair wound around Tandy's throat like a muffler.

239

Her sister's nightcap was a contraption of sections of the Confederate flag woven among lace and smocking. "My God, Tandy do you wear Dixie pantalets as well?"

The sisters shared a laugh, Tandy ending hers with a cough. Surlina asked, "Are you better? It worries me greatly for you to be ill!"

"Much better! Only sorrow weighs my heart now."

"Sorrow?"

Tandy blushed, nodding uncertainly and reaching out both hands to draw Surlina close for her news. Tandy had miscarried.

Surlina inadvertently let her horrified thoughts escape into words. "What a time to be pregnant! I didn't know Cabell had it in him! Well, at least he thinks of something other than the United Southern Action once in a while! Oh, I'm sorry," she apologized, realizing how unsympathetic she'd sounded. "I was just shocked. You've been married five years, you know, and no sign of a baby until—" She was getting in worse trouble, making Tandy tremble. She apologized again, softly, then hugged her timid sister with genuine compassion. "It's sad you lost the baby. But I'm proud you're doing so well. With me here to look after you and Father —where is Father?"

"At the courthouse. Helping Thayer make arrangements for the ball tonight."

It took Surlina a moment to digest such strange news. "Father and Cabell are speaking to each other? Father who is elderly and ill is out gallivanting, helping plan a *dance?*"

Tandy pulled her down to share the secrets. "It is wonderful, Surlina! Father and Thayer are thicker than —no, not thieves, of course! Thicker than blood brothers. You will be amazed at the complex schemes they have for Vicksburg's defense."

"What happened to Father's loudly proclaimed neutrality? Am I the only one left in this family with any sense?"

"We forgive you," Tandy said seriously. Then her cheeks began to blush with excitement as she told of the ball to be held on the courthouse lawn. "It's a benefit. Father thought it up as a way to raise money for our brave firefighter's brigade."

Surlina remained astonished. It was not like Peter Defore to promote moneymaking schemes to benefit anyone except himself. His hatred of Cabell had been thorough and undisguised. She couldn't believe he wasn't up to some roundabout deviltry. "Tandy, the last time I saw Father, he could hardly hold his head up. Does he plan to dance the bamboula tonight, too?"

"We are all going! You, too, now that you are here!" She climbed out of bed, her wobbly, thin legs managing to get her to the armoire where she began looking at dresses. "This wonderful city has four cisterns on the courthouse lawn. Every man owns his own leather bucket. And tonight we'll raise money to buy buckets for the younger boys since so many of our gallant men are away. Isn't it wonderful?"

"It is somewhat short of wonderful." Surlina unbuttoned her shoes and kicked them off, wiggling her toes. She began to unbutton her bodice, inquiring, "Tandy, is there hope for taking a bath . . . or is all the water saved for firefighting?" She went on undressing.

Tandy turned aside, apparently embarrassed at the sight of her sister's petticoats. Surlina paid no attention, borrowed one of her frilly nightcaps and deftly hid her massacred curls from Tandy's sight. "I well imagine this city does cry out for a party after spending the last months in the company of Farragut's fleet."

"Sixty-seven days. That's how long Farragut was here!" Tandy took a small copybook from her bedside table. "Twenty-five thousand shells. Twenty-five hundred marines, most of whom became ill. They tried to dig a canal."

Surlina went into the bathroom and proceeded to pump water. "But they'll be back. I've heard smart men on both sides of this war say that the battle for the river will be fought at Vicksburg."

Tandy, childlike in her enthusiasm, could not be convinced. "Why, any child could see water wasn't

241

going to run uphill in that canal!" Surlina bustled about, finding a bath brush, a small sliver of yellow soap and a threadbare towel.

As Surlina took her toothbrush from her satchel, a bar of chocolate she had brought with her fell onto the bed. Tandy lurched, her hand grabbing for the candy; then she drew back, excusing herself.

"Do you want it, Tandy? Go ahead. I bought it in Memphis, planning to nibble it on the train, but I . . ." She remembered Muller and his gaping, wet mouth and gaping trousers and concluded, ". . . but I lost my appetite. Chocolate is getting scarce in Memphis. Shoes, too. Most of the sugar and salt has to be smuggled into the Gayoso dining room. Tea is—"

"In Vicksburg shoes cost a hundred and twenty-five dollars, Surlina! There is *no* sugar or salt. *No* tea. Didn't you see the empty riverboat sheds? The deserted docks? The Union blocks the river, and the Mullermen block the countryside! This town is desperate."

Surlina quickly pushed the chocolate at her sister, watching with new understanding as Tandy's thin arms and shaky hands grabbed the prize. "Tandy, what *do* you eat?"

"I haven't been too hungry," mumbled Tandy, devouring the chocolate. "I've been sick. Not hungry at all." Her composure cracked a bit; it was obvious she was lying. "Oh, Surlina, it wouldn't help if we had suitcases full of that Confederate paper money! Flour costs two hundred dollars a barrel!"

"What do you live on?"

"Boiled bark makes tea. Rice is still available at three dollars a pound. Oatmeal. Straw."

"No wonder you miscarried!" Surlina felt ashamed of herself for being so well fed. "I didn't know."

"No one does!" Tandy drew herself erect, cramming the last of the candy in her mouth. "Especially not those damned Yankees!" Tears came to her eyes. She flung back her head, replacing the wetness with icy determination. "I am proud to be hungry! I shall be proud to starve for the cause, just as dear Thayer would be proud to die!"

Surlina settled into the cold bathwater, doubting greatly that Cabell had any intention of dying for the Confederacy. "Has Cabell a way to provide for you? Or have all his cotton-trading dreams faded?"

"We are very happy," Tandy said defensively. "Cabell and Father are full of plans!"

"What are you going to do about food?"

Tandy curled up like a little kitten on the dressing bench, unconcerned. "We'll manage."

Surlina was fired with disgust. "Oh! Are you going to lie in bed and rest your way into poverty? Going to let blowhard Cabell dream you into starvation?"

There was a charged pause while Tandy studied her nails and Surlina scrubbed her neck. Finally Tandy asked shyly, "Did you bring anything with you? Any . . . any money?"

Surlina answered lightly, "If you mean that worthless specie the South is passing off as money—no." She reached for the towel.

"No silver? Or greenbacks?" Suddenly Tandy's frail voice rose. "Oh, Surlina, I have not had any medicine! Or coffee! Or meat in so long!"

Surlina dried herself hurriedly, turning to comfort her sister. As she wiped Tandy's face, she catalogued their needs. "Food. Medicine. Money." Where to get them? The silver gates. She must redouble her efforts to get to Holly Springs. She hugged Tandy, leading her back to bed. "I will find the silver. I have vowed to do it! But until then, we shall all have to work hard for our meat and bread. Do you understand what I'm saying? You and Cabell, and Father if he is able, must all go to work. I'll do my part."

"Work? Like in a store?" Tandy sat back gingerly, looking accomplished in all the ways that didn't matter. Surlina knew of no way to be tactful. Couldn't this featherbrained sister realize what work meant? Tandy had never worked, not in the Sierra camp with the long tom or sluice boxes, not at the convent with the schoolbooks, and certainly not since being a wife in that gilded New Orleans apartment. "Yes, Tandy. Work. In a factory, perhaps. Or on a farm. You could

243

organize refugee tents. Count change at the farmer's market. Dig niter in the Yazoo caves. W-O-R-K!"

Tandy's solemn little face peered into the future with round, unbelieving eyes. "Me, Tandy Cabell? Why, of course, I'd be glad to! But . . . but what will happen to the way we've lived? What about the . . . the . . . social structure of the South?"

"What about your own survival?"

Tandy retreated to rhetoric. "We shall never surrender."

"You won't have to. You'll disintegrate first."

Surlina decided to go to the firefighters' ball for two reasons. She wanted to keep a careful eye on her father and Cabell. And she actually yearned to put on dancing slippers and wear flowers in her hair and glide to the sweep of music.

She finished lacing herself into one of Tandy's much-too-small corsets, leaving red ridges on her fingers as she attempted to tug the strings together enough to tie. For slippers she'd rigged a pair of boudoir velvet shoes which had seen better days, then bound them with black crisscrossed ribbons, tying the satin high around her ankle. She took apart two dozen rose stems to camouflage the holes in her hair. Damn Muller!

She adjusted her dress. Whirling, she tested it. Very danceable. The dark pink color reflected the glimmer of the roses in her hair. How different she felt from the grimy girl who'd spent three days on a train!

She thought of Father as she finished dressing. What an amazing man he was! He'd come back from the courthouse looking frisky despite his watery eyes and trembly hands. When he'd seen Surlina, there had been a blink, then a smile and laughter on his lips. They'd exclaimed over each other but not really had a chance to talk. He'd simply said, "The man or woman who can outplan Peter Defore ain't been born yet!" Then, tiredness catching up with him despite his willpower, he'd fallen asleep. She didn't doubt for a moment that he had better schemes in mind than taking up ballroom dancing!

Surlina finished powdering her face, her toes already tapping. She looked out the window, noticing the courthouse dome already lit with lanterns, the Confederate flag illuminated bright as day. A courthouse ball during wartime! How flagrantly peaceful.

She was ready before Tandy, naturally, and while she dreaded spending time with Thayer Cabell, she went into the parlor. She hoped to impress upon him the need for honest work in this era of muddled finances.

He was seated with a Sir Walter Scott novel spread on his knees. As he held his glass—two fingers of bourbon over slivers of precious ice— he seemed an English squire three centuries removed from his proper element. He seemed to have gained weight. How could he grow fat in a hungry land? He placed the leatherbound book on the table, looked at her politely and inquired, "What would you think of organizing a Vicksburg Jousting Society?"

She ignored him. "Cabell, have you planted yourself in Vicksburg for the duration?"

"I am rooted in the South!"

She laughed at his statement—the famous spy greeting which had become so common that it was used in jest on the streets. She answered with the next line, "These are ponderous times."

"We hope for better."

"In whom shall we trust?" Surlina did not go on with the charade. She, for one, intended to trust only herself. As to whom Cabell might trust, the matter was open to conjecture. She attempted to talk practical matters. "Can you make crop here, Cabell?"

"Make crop?" He seemed to envision cut flowers for the table.

"Yes. Plant a garden. Grow things. Be a farmer— of necessity."

"There will be no necessity. The river is open again, all the way to Baton Rouge. This very night the river fleet has brought a barge upstream, laden with goods!"

As usual, she was angry with him. After all, she planned to do everything she could to recover the silver. He should make some effort, too. The matter was left in the air as Tandy joined them.

"How happy I am to have my whole family together," murmured Tandy. "Father said for us to go ahead. He is more tired than he expected from working at the courthouse. Pat Martha, the maid, will help him dress and fetch a carriage for him later." She took Cabell's arm, looking wan behind the white face powder. Her neck tendons stuck out, and her hands seemed afflicted with a permanent tremor.

Surlina was disgusted that Cabell apparently saw nothing amiss. How could he have the gall to lay himself on frail Tandy, spurt his seed into her and then ignore her obvious failing of health?

"Are we ready?" inquired Cabell and offered each lady an arm. In silence they walked out to the carriage. Surlina knew she should now put silver, hunger and warfare out of her mind. But she felt a keen righteousness in holding her brother-in-law's feet to the holy fire. "Cabell, Vicksburg will be taken. Some night while you are muttering about chivalry or conniving with river pirates, the city will surrender."

He laughed so loudly that he spooked the horses as he climbed in. "We laughed at Farragut's surrender demand in June!"

Tandy spoke up proudly. "Cabell helped Governor Autry prepare the answer." She quoted the text, as if the words would be her next rendering in stitchery. "Mississippians don't know and refuse to learn how to surrender to an enemy."

"Fine," declared Surlina, "but the city will still be taken. Even Julien Rainbeau admitted that." It was the first time she'd spoken Julien's name without total hatred.

"Only foot by foot," snapped Cabell. He seemed as rash in defense of this town as he'd been in New Orleans throwing slop. "This town will only be sacrificed foot by foot—with the citizens proud to do so!"

He swelled out in girth, as if puffing up like a bullfrog gave him the right to expand his views.

"How do you intend to eat?" she nagged him again.

"I do not intend to answer frivolous questions from women!"

Surlina found him intolerable. Only love for her sister would keep her in Vicksburg a moment! She'd tell him nothing of her plans to go to Holly Springs. Two blocks away from the courthouse, the streets were full of people. The townsfolk were abuzz with the news that a privateer had come in from the bayous. "More loot is coming up from the docks now! Aye, she's a sturdy little packet boat! Be ready to bid for the goods!" The throng ran toward the courthouse lawn. "Hurrah for the river runners!"

Surlina appraised the offerings brought by the Confederates. On the tables were tea, wine, perfume, satin yard goods, brandy and Medjool dates.

Ever practical, Surlina lamented aloud, "Why did they not bring ammunition and quinine?"

At that moment there was a burst of applause. She turned as those around her whispered, "Yes, it's the captain who brought in the goods from the bayous! Isn't he handsome?"

She looked at the man and yes, he was handsome, as he had ever been. The daring river pirate was the same man who haunted her memory—Julien Rainbeau. Tonight he looked stunning in his powder blue silk shirt, shiny black shoes and black cloth pants. Apparently he had helped himself to some of the loot. For once his moss-gray eyes did not seem so daringly proud.

A wave of heat struck her face as she remembered how she'd been seduced by his charm and easy words. She turned to dart away. But Cabell's loud voice hailed him with praise. "Oh congratulations there, Rainbeau! What an accomplishment!"

Julien's thick eyebrows knitted as his frown possessed his entire face. "Accomplishment? Sir, I wish I had never heard of that stinking ship of contraband!"

There was a quick murmur of disapproval from the

247

crowd. Surlina stepped back again, trying to stay out of his sight. Cabell argued, "But these were Yankee goods! We have every right to them!"

Julien put up his hands to stop the argument, looking tired and harassed. "All right. I have followed my orders. The goods are yours, Vicksburg. They're still spoiled goods. Can't you see you heap your sins and expunge your guilts on Yankee heads while you slit your own throats?"

Cabell, obviously not understanding, raised his arm in mid-air to slap Julien's back in camaraderie. Captain Rainbeau, however, spun out of reach and in so doing came face to face with Surlina.

There was a frozen instant of recognition. Then he bowed low, and as he rose, he kissed her hand.

With the simple touch of his warm lips to her skin, she felt a net thrown around her heart again. Panicky, she fought him away. "Always so courteous, Captain Rainbeau?" she asked. "Always quick to kiss a lady's hand and desert her in the night?"

Before Julien could respond, a photographer approached, wanting to capture the daring riverboat captain's likeness with one of the newfangled Brady machines. Surlina stood aside as he posed, watching him with a mixture of longing and hurt. He was so glorious—tall, slender, vain enough to smooth his splendidly curling sideburns. After the powder flash, he immediately took her arm again. "Ah, Surlina, what new twists have the Fates braided into my life that I should find you in Vicksburg?"

"I am pursuing business matters. The same ones you left Whispers in the middle of the night to pursue."

"The business of the silver gates."

"Julien, have you heard more of them?" Her quick enthusiasm jumped out unbidden.

He faced her squarely. "No. And you have not given them up?"

"Never!"

"Then, madam, like the river at the delta and Farragut's fleet at Vicksburg's bluffs, we remain at an impasse." He smiled and took her in his arms as the orchestra began. "But not, I hope, at an end."

Surlina could not answer. She mistrusted him but felt the same hot desire for him. She danced at a frigid distance from him, granting Julien no reception at all. They were constantly interrupted by well-wishers saying thank you to the dashing Captain Rainbeau. One clapped his shoulders. "A glorious victory, sir!"

"At best all I make is mischief," he replied. Yet the crowd persisted, like charming children, not understanding the game they were playing.

She asked him the question she feared. "Can this city be put under siege?"

"Any city can be."

"But will they risk it?"

"It will take a large land force. I doubt it for the moment. But Vicksburg is tempting."

"And the silver, Julien . . . Will you now change your mind and help me recover it instead of dealing with Muller and sending raiders?"

"Ah, my darling, *you* are tempting, too. My efforts with the raiders and my sojourn with Muller brought me nothing except trouble."

"I must buy time to find the gates. I must buy time to outwit Muller. I must find time to outwit you!"

He pulled her against him. "Time is precisely the thing we find in short supply. The South has little time, Surlina. We have even less. Come, darling, let us forsake this rabble."

Her heart began to beat boldly even as the heat of humiliation closed her eyes. He was up to his old tricks. By whose orders did he speak charmingly to her tonight? Surlina looked at him steadily. "Julien, you seduced me purposely at Whispers. I heard you and Ramsey discuss it, as if I meant nothing."

"Yes, a duty I did not choose and one which I dispatched poorly, I fear."

She was too stunned to cry out. Why couldn't he have lied, she wondered? Why did he have to admit . . . ? "Only a duty? Our night at Whispers, with the creamy silk nightgown and the pinewood bed and

249

the rain against the window and your lips against my breast and—"

"That I leave you to judge," he said gently. His hands came forward, holding her face. His gray eyes glowed as his fingers slipped around her throat. "Only I beg you, do not judge that night as harshly as you judge me now." He brought his face low, next to hers, smelling of salt and clean-shaven skin. "For I did love you then . . . and I ache for you now." He barely kissed her ear. "Always and forever. Don't you remember?"

She flung her arms around him and in full view of the citizenry of Vicksburg, she kissed him greedily.

He laughed loudly and waltzed her to the punch bowl. "Now you know why I love you. I would never vote for the shrinking violet as the national emblem of womanhood!" He grabbed the dipper deftly away from a servant. He filled it with punch and held it aloft, full and dripping. "Now, as you once asked me, what does the smart man do? Drink it down quickly and enjoy—or pour it back?"

She understood his implications. Julien might profess love, but only for a moment was he inviting her back into his heart.

"Julien, the time is so wrong." She thought of her need to visit Holly Springs, of Sam whispering "perhaps never."

He continued to hold the dipper aloft. "Do not let this war rob us of each other. Have you forgotten I'm the one who reached out to you? Loved you for your own sake?"

Still she hesitated. "The time is so bad."

"We shall have no other."

She clearly saw the longing in his eyes, the determination in his voice, the eagerness in his body. She seized the dipper and gulped, then looked up and offered it to him, smiling and expectant.

He threw back his head and pushed the punch ladle away. "No need, my dear. You already have me eating out of your hand."

When they were away from the crowd, Surlina asked

him, "Where will we go?" It was one thing to be unconventional and kiss him in public view, quite another to share a bed with him either abroad the *Quail* or at Tandy's house.

"My current accommodations are rustic, but serviceable." He led the way down the hundreds of steps toward the river. "A tent under a cypress tree on a sandbar in the Mississippi . . . and a moonlit night."

She was thrilled at such a romantic notion.

"Come along," he urged, holding out his hand. "And quietly. These woods are full of deserters. More men hiding out from both sides than fighting!"

They crept from the steps to the rowboat, from the rowboat to the sandbar and along the underbrush toward his tent. Surlina strained her ears to capture the night sounds: crickets, whippoorwills and mourning doves, the steady slap, slap of the river shore, rustles of raccoons in the cane at the sandbar edge. Surely there were no Mullermen on this private island of Julien's! With a sudden shiver, she envisioned Thad Muller attacking them during a moment of intimacy, killing Julien and raping her. She held tightly to Julien for safety. "You'll keep a close watch, won't you?"

"The only thing that will annoy us will be mosquitoes," he whispered back, slapping an insect from his neck. "But I will keep my pistol handy." He tugged her against him playfully. "And I will keep you close."

Her senses began to tingle. 'I will think only with my heart tonight,' she vowed. 'Schemes and silver, spying and revenge are work for the brain during daylight. The moonlight is meant to speak to the body.' She took a deep breath and let the damp air fill her lungs.

Julien's tent was a single sheet of canvas propped in a triangle over a metal rod. It looked like a small pointed ship anchored on the flat sandbar. Julien inspected the tent, hung his pistol on a sloping branch, then spread a pallet on the soft ivy which covered the ground under the willows.

She sat down, a tremor of anticipation passing through her.

He took the roses from Surlina's curls one by one, holding them to his nostrils, then shredding the petals and scattering the scent over the blanket. He pulled back, his hands raised in surprise. "Surlina! What has happened to your hair?"

"I cut it," she lied. Then, to cover any further questions she added, "You'll also find a bruise on my ribs. I fell in the train aisle on my way to Vicksburg." She kept her voice calm, swallowing hard against the fury which welled up in her throat when she thought of Muller.

"You're not a very convincing liar," he said gently, running his hands through the blunt shafts of hair. "No woman would butcher herself this way, except maybe Dottie. She slices that gray hair of hers with a straight razor."

"Yes!" Surlina cried, capturing his comment for camouflage. "Dottie cut my hair! We were in Memphis, and she convinced me she could trim it. I should have known better!" She tussled his hair and smoothed his curling sideburns to focus the attention away from herself. He said nothing, sensing she did not want to explain any further, then kissed the top of her head as if to heal it.

She laughed, leaning into his arms. "Once you cured me of seasickness by rubbing my back. Now I fully believe your kisses will restore my curls."

"Another of love's mysteries," he said quietly. "Like the way thinking of you when I am alone on the *Quail* restores my sanity. Like the memory of your arms around my neck binds me up and gives me strength."

Surlina felt a misty film forming in her eyes. "How I've missed you! Oh, Julien, I hated you! Hated you and loved you at the same time! Wanted never to see you again, and at the same time I was aching to cling to you!"

He embraced her as if to shield every inch of her, bringing his lips to her forehead, then kissing the end of her nose, nibbling her lips, then dropping warm, breathy kisses against her throat. His hands swept up and down her body as if relearning every curve. Then

252

he cocked his head and frowned. "My God, Surlina, when did you take to wearing corsets? What other armor do you have under that gown—sidearms, spurs and sabers?"

"I dressed for a courthouse ball," she reminded him, "not a rendezvous with a river pirate."

"I want nothing between us," he said, undoing the ribbons and lowering the flaring neckline until the fullness of her breasts rested above the corset line. "Tonight we lie open to the sky and open to each other. No clothing. No coverings."

As he undressed her, he seemed unhurried, kissing each part of her body as he uncovered it, letting his hands glide and caress until she felt warmed by his dancing fingers.

"Oh, Julien, lie to me if you have to! Tell me those wonderful lies you whispered in the pinewood bed! Tell me I'm the only woman you want!" She trembled, sitting against his shoulders, feeling him flinch as she spoke.

"There'll be no lies between us, just as there'll be no coverings." He held her close, stroking her back with firm, comforting movements. "You are the melody of this night, Surlina. My dark, haunting song. Let me watch you, see your throat ripple with tiny waves when I kiss you. Move your strong arms around me. Hold me to you like a seashell holds its pearl. And when I tell you of my love, perhaps it will not be with words . . . but it will never be a lie!"

He kissed her passionately, as if to cure them both of lovesickness by burning them in the fires of their own desire. 'Yes, bind me to you!' she thought, and took him eagerly into her mouth, moving her tongue against his in a circular motion. She felt delight sweep through her blood like fever, her heartbeat fast in her chest, the flowering sensation between her legs. "Let me touch you," she whispered and slid his shirt upward to kiss the golden coiled hairs of his chest, lick at the nipples which responded readily.

He shed the rest of his clothing and she touched him with greedy hands, flinging herself over him like a mantle, burying her breasts against him, her curls, her lips. She stroked his stomach, then kneaded his muscular thighs, clasping his erect organ between her palms and caressing the taut flesh until she felt tiny spasms within him. He groaned with pleasure when she bent to kiss him. How vulnerable he was to harm; yet she felt only an overwhelming desire to give him tenderness. She let her tongue travel over the sweet saltiness of the tip, caressing the little cleft with gentle licks which made him toss and moan. All the while, within herself, she felt a tightening, as if all her being were straining toward him.

He struggled to roll, taking her with him. "Let me give you the joy you give me," he said, disposing of the last of her garments. She looked at the stars and thought, 'oh, yes, I would be open to you like the sky! I would stay as tight to you as a sword in a scabbard. I want you hard against me.'

His hair held the scent of salt and jasmine as he bent between her legs. She touched the gilded strands, twisting them in her fingers. "How glad I am to have you here."

"Here?" he teased and kissed her mound. She felt a flutter within her womb. Rhythmic. Sweet. A feeling that she might be able to take off and skim the ground as she stretched up to take his kisses. The sensations of his finger were like a wire stretching tighter and tighter, pulling her to him. "Thank God you are a real woman," he praised her, "one who squirms and stretches and tightens, not one who faints and whines and has no more wit than a sea bird. Give yourself to me, Surlina. Give me all your sweetness."

He moved down hard upon her, testing the entry and exclaiming with pleasure when he found her roused and moist. She felt every nerve on edge.

He thrust partially, waited for her to close around him; then dilated her fully, sweeping his arms around her back, raising her breasts toward his eager mouth. He rode high and hard, leaning back on his knees, lifting her hips to meet him.

She whimpered, feeling the pain of consummation

burning her too soon. She squeezed her thighs and hips trying to stifle his tide which was carrying her away too fast. But he spread her legs again. "Open, my beloved. Open as the sky above us. Open as the river around us."

She widened, straining to catch each tingle of sensation. He ran his hands through her dark curls. "Glossy as a raven's feathers." He stabbed at her throat with his tongue. "More glorious than a tossing sea." He traced her throbbing veins downward to her breasts and encompassed the nipples with his lips, licking the points to trembling hardness. He made ecstatic little sounds with each thrust.

She felt a rising cadence within, one which could not be postponed. It was a cascade of feelings, straining through her with fierce onset. "Oh, Oh, Julien!" she cried out, then felt exploded as if a hurricane had blown within her, knocking flesh, blood, bone and muscle asunder. The intensity seemed immense, flooding her with sudden convulsions of pleasure which almost reached the proportion of pain. She writhed and twisted, rushing to capture the fullness while struggling to end the fury. For an instant she felt poised to dive over a cliff. Then, with the swift downward plunge of his body, she let herself go, hurtling with him into a frenzy of completion, clawing, crying, clamping her legs around him high above his waist.

Then the hurricane's scream within her died away and a peacefulness set like a tranquil sunset sky. She opened her eyes and saw him smiling at her tenderly. He touched her fingertips with his, letting them barely meet. "We're whole," he said in awe. "I feel as if we broke apart into a thousand pieces, then met and formed a new whole. Oh, Surlina, you're incredible!"

She lay there with her hands behind her head, basking in the contentment of his homage. He laid his head upon her belly, like a child going to sleep face down in a feather pillow. His hands came up and fondled her breasts, sliding downward to fold around them and lie silent like a fire flickering down to embers.

She murmured happy words. "The night is like a melody."

"You are the melody," he whispered again, but she silenced him with a finger across his lips. No, it wasn't she; it was the river, the moonlight, the cicadas, the cedar fires, the sand and, most of all, strong, sure, sweet, sweet Julien.

While he slept, nestled against her back, she studied the sky. Her eyes watched the moon, following its course through the patchwork glow of clouds. The sycamores of the shoreline touched their branches together, nodding in the night breeze. Giant cypress roots, standing exposed in the water, formed arches like silver gates. Silver gates. Her mind had done it again. Now, when she least wanted to think of it, her mind simply rained ideas.

She reached to shake Julien, whispering to him in a flurry of excitement. A plan! A way for them to stay together and yet retrieve her treasure! "Julien, wake up! Are there back rivers toward Holly Springs?" He barely raised his head, grunted and burrowed against her again. "Julien! Can the *Quail* go through the shallows? Through the bayous that run into the Sunflower or the Yazoo? Wake up! Can you get me close to Holly Springs by boat?" When he did not respond, she picked up a twig and poked his shoulder until he awoke.

Standing, he picked up their clothes and gestured toward the tent. "The dew will fall shortly. Let's move to the cot." Inside, he lit a lantern and sat down on the taut canvas. "Now, what were you trying to tell me?"

She sat down beside him, turning to tuck her knees up on the cot so she could face him. "Julien, I want to go with you on the *Quail*—up the backwaters as close to Holly Springs as you can get me."

"Holly Springs? The Union supply station?" He traced circles on her arm as if making question marks. "What's there for you?"

She summoned her courage. "My gates."

He burst out laughing, pulling her against him and

256

kissing her between gusts of merriment. "Oh, Surlina! Why can't you be something indecent, like fat or featherheaded? Why must you be the Silver Belle?"

How could he think her request amusing? She returned his kisses playfully, but felt the keen stroking of his lips would shortly make her pant with desire. "Will you take me with you?"

He answered her indirectly, in a voice which was tired and melancholy. "This was the first time we could rest, Surlina. The first time we could sleep together, lie side by side with the breeze blowing through the piney woods and no one to intrude. We could have slept. Talked if we wished. Lain awake all night if we needed, with your face against my shoulder, my lips to your breast, heart beating against heart. But now you choose to plunge us into chaos over that damnable silver! I wish I knew nothing of it!"

"But you do know of it. And you must help me get it back." She lay quietly in his arms, awaiting his vow to help her. He stroked her cheeks with his fingertips. He was gentle, gluing himself to her slowly, the hairs of his chest against her ribs, the hardness between his thighs strong against her. Then as he bent near, he held her back like an arch, bending her away, kissing her long and deeply, until she recoiled like a spring under him. The peaks of feeling built inside her and ardently she cried out, "I must have you again, Julien! Yes, hard in me, I must have you!"

Then, shattering her warmth, he pulled away, hurtling himself from her body and completely off the cot. "No! The silver is still between us—harder than I will ever be!"

She felt desperate, degraded by the desire he could stir in her so easily, humiliated by his ability to withdraw. "No, don't do this to us," she pleaded. She held out her arms, seemingly holding out her soul to him. "Please help me! We can take the silver and use it together! Buy a way out of this damnable war!"

He flinched as if she'd offered him a cup of poison. His jaw shook with angry efforts at control as he silently handed her clothing to her. By the lantern

257

glow she saw the hurt in his eyes. His voice limped, rage mixed with tenderness. "Don't make whores of us both, Surlina. It is bad enough that you go chasing over the countryside lusting for silver. At least give me credit for having thoughts of love for you which extend beyond your fortune." He grabbed her shoulders and shook her fiercely. "Give me credit for having husbandly thoughts as well as a lover's." Abruptly he turned away, pulling his clothes on with haste. "My only promise was to love you. On that I would never renege." He faced her again, dropping to one knee, clasping her around the legs. "Oh, Surlina, I want to bind our hearts and bodies together in wedlock . . . not chain us together in silver handcuffs!"

Her mind was lost in confusion. Hadn't he tried to intercept the supply wagons for the Confederacy? Hadn't he conspired with Ramsey and consorted with Muller?

She hadn't realized she was crying until he said, "Dry your tears, darling. We are neither one worth them!" He lifted the tent flap as the first streaks of orange hinted of sunrise. A chill wind blew from the river, rustling the water and promising a gusty day. The waning moon dipped behind the hawthorns like a bird diving out of sight.

25

As the noose drew tighter around Vicksburg, Surlina nursed her father and Tandy while her own discontent grew into rage. There *were* ways from Vicksburg to Holly Springs and she was tired of dawdling!

Surlina went to the public library and studied a map of the countryside. She learned the names: Mint Spring, Big Bayou, Stout's Marsh, Friar's Mire, Hayne's Bluffs, Baldwin's Ferry and Jackson Road. Somewhere out there were her silver gates—unless, of course, they'd been captured by Thad Muller. Or Sam Grant. Or Julien Rainbeau. Hell, no one could be trusted! Certainly not her father, though she longed to seek his advice. But he was continually secreted in the parlor with Cabell, their eyes red from too much whiskey and cigar smoke, their energy consumed in devious plots and counterplots for Vicksburg's defense. When Surlina spoke to him briefly about recovering the silver, he encouraged her, but without his old sense of vehemence. "When the time's right," was all he said, leaving her to wonder if he had schemes of his own and was only lying low in the shadow of Cabell's rhetoric.

Meanwhile, Vicksburg's food supply ran from low to desperate. Word of the plight of the town was sent to the Confederate Ranger Force in Texas. A week later, there was late-night hollering, then lanterns by the river, an immense clattering of horses and bellowing of cows. The news spread through the town in minutes. The Ranger force had arrived to supply hungry Vicksburg with a whole herd of beef. Surlina and Cabell joined the crowd that lined the riverfront. The Rangers herded the cattle into the water and swam them across the river. As the muddy, cursing cowboys reined their horses onto the Vicksburg side, Surlina caught a glimpse of a familiar face. Excusing herself from Cabell, she ran after a sweaty, river-soaked rider with a strange mount. "Dottie! I know that's you on the mule! Stop, for heaven's sake!"

Murray the mule halted, snorting and rippling his flanks. Dottie peered out from under a felt hat with a Texas roll to the brim. She wiped the tobacco juice from her lips and grinned. "Howdy, Surlina."

Surlina hugged the wiry old lady and gave Murray an affectionate pat. Providence had intervened. "Are you going back to Texas with the Rangers?"

"Nope. One cattle drive's enough, even for Dottie McDune!"

"Would you like to go to Holly Springs with me?"

"Why not? Where's that?"

"It's one hundred fifty-two miles northeast of here

259

through swamps, marshes, bogs, bayous and backwaters!" She hesitated, "And Mullermen, too!"

"Sounds just like my cup of tea," whistled Dottie. "My wagon's on the other side of the river. We'll float it across tomorrow and set up the sutler trade again."

"Is Kuffy with you?"

"Had to send him home to Whispers. Ramsey's a-fixing to go campaigning again. Kuffy has to go along and poach his eggs and wipe his ass."

"I miss him—Kuffy, not Ramsey!"

"Likewise."

"Dottie, come to Harrison Street with me. I want you to meet my sister, Tandy. Her husband is in the category of blowhards like Ramsey, but you'll like my father."

"Lord God in the starry heavens, Surlina! Your kin would nigh come apart at the hinges if you drag in a tobaccy-spittin' crone and a mule! No, me and Murray will swim back across the Mississip and keep a watch on the wagon. You find me tomorrow when you're ready to head for the hinterlands."

Next day, Surlina found Dottie engaged in wholesale barter. She'd traded her Texas brim hat for a case of citronella candles. She gave part interest in a future bale of contraband cotton in exchange for a restaurant-sized coffee maker. She explained succinctly, "Ain't enough goods in this whole county to outfit a trader's wagon. So we'll open us a mobile coffee canteen. You're the woodchopper."

They pulled out on the Jackson Road, making efforts to encounter armies of both sides and doing a lively business. The first day they sold thirty gallons of coffee an hour from the big woodburning boilers. The next three days they averaged ten gallons a day as the troops thinned out.

Then they ran out of coffee, one week to the day they'd left Vicksburg. At sunset, Dottie announced, "That's it!"

"What now?" asked Surlina. She was tired of wielding the ax in the forest anyway. Her hands were calloused and her arms sore.

"I'll think of something. Right now we'd best get to sleep."

That night, Surlina was startled awake by scratching noises. Dottie's voice echoed in the darkness and a gun clicked. "Hold it right there!" Hurriedly Surlina lit the lantern and peered out. At the back of the wagon was a young soldier, still bent in the middle, attempting to fill his canteen from the coffee urn. Dottie had a rifle in his back.

Dottie spoke slowly to the soldier whose questioning face was that of a surprised bully. "Ain't going to do you no good cause there ain't nothing there. You a soldier?"

He grew meek at the inquisition, apparently reassured at the obvious question. "Yes, ma'am!"

"A volunteer?"

"Yes'm!"

"Well, well, well," cackled Dottie. "So you're one of them fellers who up and offered to die for your country! Promised to lay down your life, hunh? I'll be right proud to give you that chance!" She poked the rifle barrel under his chin. "How's your fighting instincts about now?"

"Evaporatin' like steam from a teakettle, ma'am."

Surlina intervened. "Let him go, Dottie."

"And have him straggling around the countryside, making trouble for crazy old ladies?" She sat down, squatting on her haunches. "You ever tended a still, soldier boy?"

Surlina grasped the idea instantly. "No, Dottie! No moonshine whiskey!"

The young soldier answered solemnly, "No, ma'am! My ma don't hold to likker."

"Good for your ma," said Dottie. "But anyways I got a recipe. We're gonna make army juice since we're out of coffee." She moved closer to Surlina's lantern, unbuttoned four pocket flaps before she found a worn piece of paper. Then she read slowly, "Bark juice, tarwater, turpentine, brown sugar, lamp oil and rubbing alcohol."

Surlina was adamant. "That will kill people!"

261

"Maybe a casualty here and there," Dottie admitted, smiling. "But there's more ways to kill a cat than kiss him to death!"

Suddenly the soldier lurched for Dottie's gun, grabbing the barrel and twisting it away from her, his frantic arms pumping like a well handle. As he backed away, he swung the gun level at the two women. "Now the tables have turned!"

Dottie howled with laughter. "Sonny, you better take another gander at that musket. It can't hurt nobody. Squint your eyes again at that corncob plug on the end."

He edged backward, examining the plug with darting, wary eyes. "What's it for?"

Dottie sighed, "You're either a city tyke or a mighty young soldier boy not to know how to plug a day's ration of rum in a musket. Now, don't pull that plug unless you're dying of thirst."

He was insistent. "I can't have nothing to do with alcohol, ma'am! I'm attached to General Grant's staff and his aide, Mr. Rawlins, won't allow—"

"Grant's staff?" Surlina interrupted. "Where is his headquarters?"

He considered a moment, resting the useless gun against his leg. Guide service would be preferable to a life as Dottie's moonshine partner. "Why, I'd be proud to show you the way. The general's setting up a new headquarters at the plantation by the river. The one with the big water tower and the hillside full of rosebushes. Rosie Mound's its name." He stuck his hands in his pockets and shifted his shoulders in an adolescent swagger. "Course, I don't know 'bout me draggin' in no nameless females off the roads—"

Surlina drew her well-worn pass from her satchel. "Rest assured, your general will be happy enough to see *me*."

"Surlina," reminded Dottie. "We ain't halfway to Holly Springs. You striking off into the boondocks again at the mention of Sam Grant's name?"

"I may not need to go to Holly Springs!" She smiled as anticipation warmed her. "But I do need to see Sam

Grant," she admitted. She looked at the soldier. "Let's go." Dottie stood aside with a sigh.

Rosie Mound Plantation sat behind enormous black gates which Surlina inspected with enthusiasm. The gates showed no signs of newness. She walked on toward the great house, surprised at how suddenly autumn had canceled the last remnants of summer. The morning air was crisp. After her all-night journey, she had passed from tiredness to a second wind of alertness.

It was apparent that she had practically beaten Sam to his new headquarters. Wagons, horses, tents, sentries, piles of supplies and soldiers created a jumble in every direction, spilling along the main entrance road, across the lawns, behind the hedges and over the low-lying hills on both sides of the house.

She spotted Sam sitting at a makeshift desk which was no more than a board across two barrels. Without hesitation, she called his name and waved. He looked up and leaped around the end of the table, bounded down the steps and upset a pot of greenery.

Then the other men at the table came hurrying down the steps. Sam introduced her: Rawlins, Sherman, Dana, Eaton and other names she promptly forgot. Rawlins impressed her, fussing with needle, pins and button. She also looked carefully at the man the newspapers usually insisted was crazy—William Tecumseh Sherman. Well, Sherman did indeed have a wild look about him! His eyes were bloodshot, his red and copper sideburns sticking out like fans. His attitude was anything but reassuring.

He welcomed her perfunctorily, scowling, "Grant has neither time nor interest in petty problems, miss." He made it clear he had neither time nor interest in her either. When Sam quietly remarked that he would see her at dinner and pointedly reminded his staff to set a place for her, Sherman and Rawlins exchanged ominous glances. Obviously she was not welcome at Rosie Mound. Well, Sherman and Rawlins could rot in hell! She'd come to see Sam, not them.

Inside the mansion, a little brown housemaid showed her to an upstairs bedroom which faced west. She watched more wagons arriving, disgorging every imaginable paraphenalia of an army post. It was clear that Sam was moving in for an extended stay in this part of the country. Yet Rosie Mound, of itself, was hardly an objective. Vicksburg. Of course. The thought struck her with terror. How divided I am, she chastised herself, pulled between her fear for Tandy's safety and the assumption that Grant could overwhelm the city. Again, her tug-of-war with herself began, the feeling she stood as an island between Sam and Julien, North and South.

In the afternoon she slept, then bathed and experimented with ways to conceal the last blunt stubs of hair. Most of her curls had grown back, soft and auburn, but one annoying spot on the crown of her head stuck up starkly. She also gave considerable attention to her costume for dinner. It must be selected with care, pretty enough to please Sam, demure enough not to offend Rawlins, striking enough to show Sherman she was a force to be dealt with, not insulted and ignored. She settled on an elegantly simple white muslin dress. She went downstairs early for dinner. Rawlins stamped about the dining room, inspecting silver and napkins, crystal and chairs. He made a great show of turning all the wineglasses upside-down.

Then Sam entered! She felt the thrill of his nearness as he offered her his arm. No more a shabby brigadier, his uniform was nicely cut, clean, tailored of good wool. Now he had a major general's bright stars, his boots were buffed to glossiness and he held out his arm to her in a gesture of confidence.

She smiled, sweeping into the room like the queen of England rather than a war-buffeted, currently penniless silver princess. He noticed the upended wine goblets. Remarking in an aside to his aide, he pointed out, "Mr. Rawlins, I doubt there is anything inherently evil in the fermentation of Mississippi grapes." Grudgingly, Rawlins repositioned the glasses.

Surlina feared Sherman and Rawlins would drag Sam away after dinner. Oh, that Sherman was such a talker! He spoke eloquently, describing his last battle as "plunging into billows of blood." Then he launched into a picturesque description of bayous in the moonlight.

How romantic, she thought, casting a sidelong glance at Sam. Would they find any time alone together at Rosie Mound? Or would they be forever chaperoned by his irritating staff? She daydreamed lazily, envisioning herself dancing with Sam on the porticoes, lying in his arms, pressing her lips to his, asking his help in retrieving her silver.

However, Sherman would not let the conversation veer from one course: Vicksburg. The men went on discussing possible routes. She was dying to drag Sam away, to learn the details of when the army had finally restored his command, what had happened to Halleck and the supply dump at Holly Springs.

As the meal ended, she felt pleasantly warmed by the mellow wine. Neither food nor alcohol seemed to have an effect on Sam. He continued to ask questions of his staff, nodding politely in reply, never raising his voice. Sherman, on the other hand, was nearly in a frenzy by the time the meal was over. He called for a map of Vicksburg, spread it atop the table and pounded it with flat-handed thumps. After studying it for ten minutes, he tossed it on the floor in disgust, stamping it with his boot heel. "Vicksburg! What a burr under our saddle! Remove that one sticker, and it's smooth riding!"

She was reminded of the time at Whispers when Julien had stabbed the carrot cake and made the identical point. The war for the river would focus on Vicksburg. The time had come.

The memory of Whispers made her compare it to Rosie Mound. This lovely plantation seemed almost new. Rosie Mound was a place where war had intruded genteelly. Surlina was delighted to be in its comfortable environment. She was also impressed with the amount of food on the table. Meat pies, turkey, ham, oysters and cucumbers. Onions, mutton chops, liver, shrimp in a rich tomato sauce, cornbread, sweet

265

potatoes and venison. The wine was dark and slightly bubbly, like the burgundy she'd tasted in France.

As the talk of strategy and objectives droned on around her, she began to devise her own plan of divide and conquer. Separate Sam from his devoted staff! Separate him in a clever way which would not alienate his helpers. She remembered, to her regret, that he had a wife and four children somewhere back in Illinois. Perhaps a question of domesticity would reassure Sherman and Rawlins that she was no threat to their general. She turned directly to Sam and waved her hand as if flicking away the war. "And how is your family, General?"

He looked puzzled, then pleased. "All well, thank you. My eldest son, Fred, is champing at the bit to join me for the Vicksburg campaign. He was with me on the Tennessee River, and I fear it has only whetted his appetite for adventure."

Sherman seemed placated by her interest in children. "I have a family of four, also," he said.

For a moment Surlina was burned by guilt. Here she was conspiring to get Sam alone when his familial loyalty was obvious. All's fair in love and war? Hardly. But a wife and four children did seem unfair competition!

Surlina toyed with a bowl of brandied pears during the prolonged dessert. Sherman continued to eat voraciously, gnawing turkey legs and gulping down vast quantities of fresh milk 'Even afterward,' she thought, 'when war ends, he'll still be a war-maker.' In contrast, Sam would still be a man! Again she felt a tender quivering in her heart for him. Would she get the chance to tell him? She looked toward him, hoping to catch his eye and signal a hint.

He was finishing his coffee. As he lit a cigar, he eyed the heaping bowls of food still on the table. "This land is so hospitable. An army does not need supply lines in such generous terrain."

The others sat dumbfounded. Sherman disputed him with his own logic. "By the same token, Vicksburg could defend itself indefinitely." He bit into the last turkey leg. "You couldn't maintain an army forever—not even on the abundant poultry of northern Mississippi."

"Then don't forget the old axiom: any fort will surrender after forty-five days."

Surlina disagreed. "Gentlemen, there is a fallacy in your lesson books. This entire land might scorch itself before it would feed your armies. As for Vicksburg, it might see to it there was nothing left to surrender after forty-five days."

Sam turned sideways in his chair, alert, leaning toward her with obvious interest. "You might be right, especially since it takes four million blacks to feed five million whites here, and the slaves are beginning to desert."

"I watched what happened in New Orleans," she said. "I heard Vicksburg laugh at Farragut's surrender demands and spit in his canal."

Sherman leaped up, upsetting his milk. "Madam, you are indeed too Southern in-your sympathies for me!"

"I remain neutral. Sam knows that."

She saw the sudden spark of anger in Grant's eyes. "Do you still pay lip service to that myth?" Sam said coldly. "Then you are a traitor in both directions!"

Wide-eyed, she sat silently, horrified by his indictment. Feeling dismissed, she excused herself.

Sam rose with her. "Fresh air would do us good," he said mildly, making it obvious he was no longer angry with her. He offered his arm and a smile.

She hesitated for an uneasy second, not certain she wasn't still angry with him. Then she clasped her fingers lightly around his sleeve. He looked the part of commanding general now with his shiny brass buttons, the clear, certain eyes and steady gait. What she'd seen in Memphis was obviously in the past. Now his eyes communicated with hers directly as he led the way out of the dining room. He picked up another cigar, looked at her expectantly, than placed it in his pocket with a chuckle.

Once they were outside, Sam gestured across the

lawns and toward the hills beyond the quarters. "Let's make a little inspection trip. I've not had a chance to reconnoiter the grounds."

Surlina bided her time, waiting for the right moment to discuss the possibility that her silver gates lay somewhere on the premises among the loads of army supplies. "How long will this be headquarters?"

"I suspect we'll move before we actually get settled." Sam seemed gracious, patient and reserved tonight. Was this the same man who'd named the *Tigress* in her honor? What about the way he'd blushed when she'd tucked a daisy in his beard? And the way he'd held her to him on the deck of the *Radiant* and in the corridor of the Gayoso? She recognized deep within her the same steady hunger which had begun aboard the steamer, and now resumed with gnawing force. There was a certain spot of emptiness within her that only he could assuage.

Surlina was startled as she realized he was talking. He was telling her the names of flowers, grasses and shrubs as they walked along the path—the gramas and hellebores and verbenas. His knowledge of botany was a surprise. He took out a yellow notebook from his breast pocket and jotted something down.

"Your sketchbook?" she quizzed him, again admiring his wide range of interests. "Let me borrow your notebook, Sam. I'd like to sketch that magnificent buttonwood tree."

He obligingly tore out a page for her and handed her the short fat pencil. Quickly she drew his profile.

The loud cry of a bluejay startled them both. Sam, who had walked ahead, looked up as if to tell how much time had passed, then walked quickly back to her. "What have we here?" he asked, looking at her sketch. A small smile played around his lips. "Nicely done," he complimented her, "but it displeases me."

She thought he saw faults in her lines and shadings. "In what way?"

"I wish it were of *you*. Then I should find myself a locket and keep it."

What a sweet, surprising thing for him to say! Another reminder that behind the stern exterior lay a man with a sense of humor and tenderness. She felt light-headed, but she kept her voice coquettish. "No, no, you cannot have it! It is mine! I shall buy *myself* a locket and wear it."

"Tigress!" he said in a tone of amusement and exasperation. She saw the vitality in his blue eyes, the way they moved over her with an implicit message of hope.

She pressed the sketch to her heart, then tucked it deftly into her bodice, letting the edge barely protrude. "There! Now, you see! General Sherman can't change my mind and you can't change my heart!" She leaned slightly toward him and popped a frisky kiss on his cheek.

He blinked, trying to keep feeling from his eyes, but his body betrayed him. Leaning closer to her, warm and eager, he caught her hands and drew her to him as if the magnetism between them was irresistible. "I hoped you'd come here, Surlina. I dreamed of it, reproaching myself for daring to want your youth and beauty. And now you've arrived, more vibrant and captivating than I dreamed." He held her face in his hands, then gently—almost shyly—kissed her forehead, eyelids, and cheeks.

"Oh, hurry up and kiss me, Sam! And do it right!" She threw her arms around his neck recklessly.

This time he pulled her against him with power and determination, his arms firmly encasing her waist, lips meeting and probing her mouth, thighs pressed against her muslin flounces.

When their eyes met, she saw the stark, hungry reflection of her own longing, realized he sensed it and was unable to fully admit it. "This is a strange day for me, Surlina," he began slowly. He took her hand, putting his own over it, walking in cadenced steps. "Eating plentifully when all around us are hungry. And strange again to have you here, to be walking with you." He halted, "It's quite new to me to find myself happy while under the permanent shadow of war clouds. I wonder if I dare risk it."

269

It was a long speech. She did not detract from its value by answering. Facing him, their eyes on the same level, Surlina drew both his hands out from his waist and whispered, "Your secret tigress will always love you!" She could not say more, could not admit his small, surprised admission of happiness thrilled her. She pulled her sketch of him from against her breast, kissed it and folded it tight in her hand, knowing she would never part with it.

The lovely intimacy of the evening was broken by horse's hooves pounding to the top of the hill. It was Sherman again. As ever, he was impatient to do battle as he reported sabotage near the Tallahatchie River crossing. "The gunboats are through upstream! And a group of damned secesh women detained my soldiers for most of the afternoon!" He wanted to go immediately to inspect the situation and urged Grant to accompany him.

"All right, all right," agreed Sam, though Surlina detected reluctance in his voice. She felt the frivolous intimacy between them dissolving, being replaced by the cold noose of destiny.

26

Grant and Sherman were gone all night and far into the next afternoon. Surlina spent the day outdoors at Rosie Mound, raking leaves, snooping through the army wagons, making friends with the gate guards and impatiently awaiting Sam's return. The late afternoon was drizzly, with fall winds which sent the pin oak and sycamore leaves dueling.

She had already had supper alone when the generals and their aides returned. The entire retinue went immediately into conference, scraping muddy boots up the beautiful mahogany staircase, rattling chairs across the polished floors, tossing swords onto the inlaid tables. The hour grew late with no sign of the men disbanding. Surlina lingered downstairs, hoping Sam would come back down. From her own intelligence gathering, she'd found out Halleck had left an enormous supply dump at Holly Springs. The gates might well be among the thousands of pounds of tools, wagons and railroad gear. On the other hand, enormous amounts of supplies had been distributed to forward headquarters such as Rosie Mound. She retained hope the silver might be lurking on the premises.

She jumped up from the piano bench when she heard doors opening and boots tramping. She ran to the bottom of the staircase, aware of the stares of Rawlins, Eaton and Sherman, but determined not to miss Sam. When he did not come downstairs, she gathered her skirts in her hands and raced up the stairs two at a time. At the top she took a moment to smooth her curls over her ears, adjust her skirt and retie the armband on her tunic.

Suddenly Sam came through the conference-room door. Tired and rumpled, he had one hand to his left temple. His boots were caked with mud, his trousers creased and his jacket hung limp. Her first reaction, on seeing his bloodshot eyes and wet lips, was that he was ill. Then when he brushed past her, apparently unaware of her presence, she thought he was concentrating.

She spoke his name softly and tapped his shoulder. He turned, looked at her without really seeing her, but mumbled her name in recognition. His hand went to his jacket breastpocket. He drew out a small box and held it out to her, all the while rubbing his left temple with one hand.

She was mystified. Opening the tiny box, she was stunned to see a delicate golden chain with a carved cameo silhouette. The locket had a gilded mesh frame and raised black figures of a man and woman atop the white ivory background. "How lovely! Oh, I shall treasure it always!" Again, without putting it in words, she felt keen desire for him. It was steady, surging, not racing and diving like her passion for Julien. No, here

271

was a demand for love that would remain unchallenged and constant. She opened her arms to him. "Thank you, Sam, it's so—"

"There was trouble on the river." Obviously, he was unaware of her brewing desires and uninterested in her thanks for the trinket. He cleared his throat and held up his hand for silence. "Surlina, there are gunboats which may well come through the backwaters and attack us here. The Mullermen are operating with impunity in these parts again. Rumors are afloat of raids. I think your story of silver gates has finally surfaced, and the war is on for them."

She was pleased he had not berated her about the subject, merely informed her. But she was aghast at the possibility that *everyone* knew where they were except her! "Are they at Holly Springs?"

"In the vicinity."

"Well! Whatever that means in terms of geography, it means I shall soon have my silver back."

"It means nothing of the sort, Surlina. Quit crowing like a rooster, woman!" He corrected her harshly, as if she were a child. "It means your talk about remaining neutral is total poppycock now. Both sides intend to duel for that fortune."

"They can't! It's personal property to be used as my father and I see fit." She decided to gamble and beseech him openly. "Get it for me, Sam! I know you can!"

"Can or will? Never mind! I do not have it . . . yet. But if it comes into my possession, I cannot return it to you."

He'd wounded her deeply. Her response was to mount an attack of her own. "For a man of few words, you've outdone yourself. Let me recount a few words I've heard about you. They call you plenty of other things besides the general commanding." She rushed on, afraid to stop and examine her accusation. "They call you the Bastard of Belmont. The Drunkard of Donelson! The Toad of the Tennessee!"

He lapsed into the quiet, familiar stance of dignity. "I am aware." He rubbed his head with both hands, obviously caught in a headache of large-scale proportions.

She was immediately sorry for her personal invective. Further, she was curious about his pride. "Don't those epithets bother you, Sam?"

"Yes. The words sting me to the core. As a man . . . I hurt, but as a military commander, I take no notice."

"Then you are two men!" Suddenly she understood him. When he wasn't on the battlefield, he was human; a man who suffered aches and pains, a man who would remember to find her a locket. Then why would he not help her recover her fortune and treat it as an area outside his military responsibility? Why couldn't she deal only with Sam and not with this damned general! "And I know neither man."

He sensed the insinuation. "Sometimes, like yesterday evening, when I am with you . . . many things seemed far-off and unimportant."

"Yet now you rank *me* as unimportant. You've decided to forget me! Sam, let us choose to forget this war! That's what keeps us apart, not silver or Sherman or gunboats!"

"I remember now, you are the lady who never liked making decisions." He laid a tender hand on her shoulder, rubbing gently. "But no, I cannot choose to forget. Each hour, like the events upriver right this moment, narrows my choices further. I am down to one choice now, Surlina, and it is not concerned with silver or lockets or ourselves."

She shivered with foreknowledge. He sounded too deadly calm. A decision had been made in that conference, apart from gates or Mullermen. She put her certainty into words. "You plan to attack Vicksburg immediately!" She panicked at the idea of Tandy and her father caught up in battle.

"Clear the river or lose the war!"

She knew he was now out of reach of her pleas. His eyes were already on a distant horizon. "Vicksburg is the key, as you always said."

"Surlina, you must abandon any idea that I might

273

aid you. I have gone far beyond propriety in loving you. I have tested—"

"You know nothing of love! All you've done is kiss me with guilt on your lips and lies in your heart!" Surlina tore away before she flailed at him with bare fists. One moment he'd been a man she loved, the next instant merely a military commander she dared not approach. She rushed out onto the second-story balcony, slamming the double doors behind her.

She listened as Sam's footsteps retreated. 'Very well,' she told herself, 'I can't help loving him, but just as certainly I can no longer seek his help. And it doesn't matter.' She moved down the outer staircase.

She raced outside to the pile of leaves she had raked during the day. It was still smoldering, with a patient slave sitting nearby with a bucket of water. Surlina grabbed the long-handled rake with the tin spokes and beat the fire madly, whipping and spinning the embers, flushing the flames into new life.

The slave sprang out of the shadows. "Please, miss." He moved toward her but dared not touch her or wrestle away her rake. His voice begged, "If you light up the prowlers, they'll be forced to attack!"

"Prowlers! Near the plantation? Are they merely more Union troops going about storing things? Or are they Confederates spying on Grant's headquarters? Or do they wear civilian clothes—red bandannas around their necks?"

He shook his head. "Nobody for sure. We keep watch best we can! This light don't help—no, sir!"

Again her willful temper had made trouble. She'd better see if she could do some good. She turned back to the house to find Sam. Surlina routed him from a downstairs meeting, boldly barging in and whispering in his ear. "The slaves insist there are prowlers near the water tower. It could be Mullermen."

Sam sprang up, not disputing her integrity or questioning her report. "Possible prowlers. Sherman, take a squad. Here's hot work for you!"

The cavalrymen were off in a thunder of horse's hooves and flashing swords. She watched it all from the balcony. The shouts. Flashes. Screams of bullets and furious whiz of rifles. Sherman's fast-riding soldiers made short work of rounding up about a dozen stragglers left near the water tower, lassoing men from their steeds, shooting those who dashed for the woods.

Suddenly the fight was over. Men had died tonight because she'd told Sam of intruders. Men she didn't even know—neither friends nor enemies—but fellow human beings. 'No, no it's not my fault,' she argued with herself. 'Isn't this war? Besides, they might have been Mullermen, outside the protection of any law.' She felt better thinking perhaps one of the herd of prisoners approaching the house might be Thad Muller with his fish-face tattoo enclosed by a rope and his thick wet lips now dripping the saliva of fear. She remembered with revulsion his fumbling for her body on the train. If she were responsible for his death, she'd be glad!

Surlina leaned over the railing as the riders returned to the courtyard. Several dead bodies were slung over saddles. In an awful instant of heart-wrenching recognition, she identified a body. She did not cry out—could not—as her heart pounded and her breath would not come.

"Father! Oh my God, it's my Father!" She ran across the courtyard, fearing she might faint as she approached the lifeless form slung face down over the horse. The white hair of Peter Defore fell forward with his arms, his sickly body twisted grotesquely in the upside-down position. A single bullet hole through the neck spread a stain down his jacket front. One of his suspenders had come undone and flapped against the horse, making the animal twitch.

Now the courtyard was full of shouts and orders. She heard Sam's voice directing further forays. Surlina turned toward him, frozen in her grief, unable to call to him. When he glanced up and saw her, he jerked in horror, then came bounding across to where she stood with her hand on the chest of her dead father.

Instantly he took her in his arms and held her head against his shoulder. She heard him call for help, order

275

the body taken down and covered. A wave of bitter helplessness rose up in her and she went slack against him. "I've killed my father!"

"These were Mullermen! What was he doing with them?" His voice was not questioning her in particular, simply the circumstance.

Tears trickled out slowly from behind her sudden shocked numbness. "He's dead because of me!"

She felt Sam's hand stroking her neck gently. "It's no one's fault. I ordered the ambush. If someone is to take the blame, let it be me." She felt his head bow against her shoulder, heard the husky murmur in his throat. "I'm so sorry, Surlina. So sorry."

Her grief spilled over as he led her back to the house. "What was he doing there in the woods? Oh, I told my sister not to let him leave Vicksburg! This war is so unfair—North, South, armies, enemies! I have no use for any of you!" She struggled to get the words said between clenched teeth.

Sam let her sob against his shoulder, strong arms comforting her, his face turned aside overseeing operations.

She held her head up. "I will have no more of it!"

"Yet we must, dearest. The bloodshed—rightly or wrongly—is far from over. Even when we see our brothers and fathers sacrificed, it is not over." He took her into the house and made sure she was not left alone. In less than an hour he was back with papers in hand and a small glass of brandy for her. He sat down opposite the couch where she was lying. She struggled to sit up. She knew there were arrangements to be made.

"Where do you want your father buried, Surlina? It will be very difficult to send the body back to St. Louis, you realize."

"Vicksburg. Where Tandy is. No, maybe here is best."

"I think you're right. We'll have a burial service in the morning if it's all right with you."

She held his hand tenderly against her cheek, drained now of tears. How grateful she was for his sturdiness, his compassion. He moved around the alcove sitting room, turning the gas light down to a mere glow, covering her with an afghan. He bent low and lightly kissed her forehead. "I grieve with you, Surlina. Let me sit here with you tonight, close, able to hold you if you want me to, able to dry your tears if you need me to."

She murmured a simple, "Thank you," acknowledging she didn't want to be alone. 'How strong he is to take on my burdens,' she thought. 'How loving and kind to weep for an old man he hardly knew. And how deeply he must care for me.'

Peter Defore was laid to rest the next day. There were no flowers except the few stalks of Indian paintbrush Surlina picked from the fence row. Surlina felt she moved as if in a dream as the body was lowered, the earth replaced, the ground tamped down.

Surlina became convinced the burden for their father's death lay with Thayer Cabell. Cabell would have access to reports of the silver possibly being at Rosie Mound. He would have learned of the Mullermen's plans for a raid. And he would have been the one to suggest Peter Defore might once again deal with Muller in return for the gates. Given a whiff of adventure and a hint of the silver, Peter Defore would have been only too eager to journey forth.

Surlina stood staunchly quiet. She saw it all: Cabell had sent her father with Muller, hoping they'd find the treasure, then planned to take Peter's fortune for the Confederacy. Men like Cabell never did their own dirty work!

But now her father was dead and buried. 'I'll have to send a note to Tandy, telling her about Father. I only wish I had the nerve to tell her about her husband,' she thought, moving away from the grave with Sam by her side. The silver gates were probably here at Rosie Mound. The Mullermen would not be back with the tightened security she knew Sam would enforce. Surlina was more determined now than ever to find them.

Several mornings later she dressed in calico work

clothes and made the rounds of the sentries, collecting information on the perimeter defenses, the guard points and the pass words. "No, ma'am," they told her willingly, "no signs of Mullermen. Business as usual with the gunboats in the river and snipers in the woods, but no activity close to the headquarters."

Relieved that her gates had not made an appearance, Surlina went back to the big house, changed and went down to breakfast. She saw instantly that while many of the staff were present, Sam was absent.

She said hello, and several men nodded. The chaplain returned her greeting politely. Sherman raised his head only long enough to glare his disapproval of her. She hated him. As she helped herself to buckwheat cakes, she inquired where Sam was. Curtly, Rawlins told her, "He is ill," glaring as if she were responsible for sapping the general's strength and his will to command by being on the premises.

"I'll take him a breakfast tray," she said and left the room before anyone could object. She walked to the kitchen wing behind the main house. She had been looking for an excuse to prowl in the kitchens and quarters, to make decent inquiries concerning any gates which might be among the army's supplies. Telegraphs notwithstanding, the best news grapevine in the world was still the slave network.

Surlina stopped to adjust her skirts by the small swinging gate leading to the kitchens. No bit of metal was too small to overlook! Then she scurried along the cobblestone path worn smooth by the soles of countless slaves serving countless meals.

After knocking politely, she entered the kitchen. The head cook introduced himself. He was a thin-faced, long-necked black of gaunt proportions. Dressed in a dark-striped shirt and white apron, he resembled a fugitive from a chain gang. After she had asked him to make up a breakfast tray for the general, she drew him aside and said quietly, "And tell me, are there any new gates?"

"No, ma'am," he hesitated, apparently thinking it

278

was something she wished served. "But I can sure whip some out in short fashion."

"No, no, nothing to eat! I mean, are there any more big black carriage gates? Any more roads into the main area of Rosie Mound?"

He shook his gnarled head. She pushed him further. "Are there any old sets of gates then? Any smaller ones? Perhaps a pair sent here by the army and stored away?"

His downcast eyes, shuffling feet and darting glance out the greasy window made her suspicious. "Tell me immediately," she ordered sternly. She knew nothing of beating slaves or bossing servants, but felt she could learn quickly.

"For sure, before the army come, we took up all the missus' fine dish and mirror. We took the best rugs up. We took the fine lamp. Then burrowed it all in the hillside. 'Bout that time a wagonful of stuff come. Somebody say it from the army. But the missus just say to put it in the hillside, too. There was big crates —look mightily near as big as wagons—"

"Crates? Which hill? Where's it buried?" She was crazy with excitement, glancing out the door trying to decide which low slope held the treasures. Maybe it was in the river levee! My God, how could there be so many hills she hadn't noticed before? "Which hillside? Tell me!"

"You won't break the missus' fine dish or mirror? She come back from Natchez two days away."

She gave her solemn promise not to disturb anything. He gave a slight jerk of his head. "In the hummock that gives this place its name—the mound of roses—the one with the water pipes sitting on top. The one everybody tromp up and down."

She had to control her mouth from twitching into a wide smile. Now she had the silver! In the hillside under the water tower! All she had to do was spirit it out from under the watchful eye of the Union Army and out of the clutches of the plantation owner. She forced a serious look onto her face. "Thank you for

279

fixing the breakfast tray. The general will be very pleased."

She carried the tray herself, back through the house and up the stairs. She knocked lightly on Sam's bedroom door, afraid he might be asleep. A grunt of acknowledgment led her to enter hesitantly. She saw his hunched figure in the chair by the bed. He was sitting alone in the darkened room with his feet in what smelled to be a pan of mustard water.

As she came across the room, he blinked, a hand went to his forehead and he struggled to stand.

"No, don't," she said quickly, putting the tray on the bedstand. "I've brought you breakfast." She touched his shoulder gently. "Here, eat this toast. Try some tea."

He waved it away. "I'm not hungry."

She peered at his miserable figure, the strained face and squinted eyes. "You've had a sleepless night. What's wrong? Is it strategy, Sam?"

"Sit down, Surlina. I cannot talk right now. My head is pounding."

A creak of the door made them both jump. A black appeared, hunched over, nearly prostrate as he crept into the room. She recognized the cook from the kitchen. Perhaps he'd come to report her snooping! But he immediately began beseeching Grant in whispers, "Please to take me wid you. Oh, please take me wid you folks. Oh, I be glad to tote and fetch and wait on you folks!"

"Can't," said Sam abruptly, cutting off further argument.

The old Negro remained crouched, crushed with disappointment. He finally backed out.

Surlina was in sympathy with the old slave who yearned for freedom and the man who couldn't grant it. "The poor slaves! They're becoming the heart of this war, after all." She thought of Kuffy, still burdened with Ramsey's elegant campaign gear.

"The very soul and center. And no one, North *or* South, knows what to do with them." He buried his head in his hands. "All *I* know is every time Sherman's

280

cavalry sweeps out, they bring in fifty prisoners and ten miles of blacks."

She moved to stand behind him, massaging his neck, trying to unknot the muscles.

He continued, "I have a plan. Unbeknownst to Chaplain Eaton. I intend to lay all these darkies on his shoulders." His own shoulders shrugged with weariness. Then he brushed aside her hand. "I must get up. I cannot afford to be sick."

She secretly agreed. Neither of them could afford to spend idle time at Rosie Mound, though she hated to leave this cozy room. Again she glanced around.

"I like this room," she said cheerily. "It would be the perfect place to stay on a rainy day, listening to the drips on the window and contentedly working."

"Why, Surlina, you've never struck me as the domestic type." His voice sounded stronger. Perhaps she had at least distracted him from his misery.

"Oh, even a tigress likes to cook and sew occasionally," she said, thinking she might take up the habits someday. "I managed to get you a breakfast tray already today. Maybe I shall even sew a button on your jacket! You won't be shocked if that's the sum of my domestic talents, will you?" She buried her head against his back, nuzzling him playfully.

He reached behind him and gently maneuvered her around to face him. She kissed him tenderly, afraid she'd hurt him. He breathed in awe, "Oh, Surlina, you make me feel that war is far away instead of outside this door."

"While we are together, it *is* far away. While we are together, I'll be jealous of nothing but our precious time! The other lips you've kissed don't bother me. But these few days, I'm jealous of them!"

"Then let's make short work of this day! Tonight will be ours alone!" He grimaced with pain but moved with determination to dress in full uniform.

When he had finished pulling on his boots, she picked up the tray from the bed table. But as she offered it to him, there was a clattering outside on the

281

stairs. The door swung open and there stood Sherman, surveying the domesticity and scowling.

The wild general reported at once, still peeling off his riding gloves. "It's that rascal Rainbeau again! He's over the river and bent on mischief."

"Julien Rainbeau?" she gasped. "He's near here?"

"Yes, indeed," retorted Sherman, pounding a fist into a palm. "Now mind your female manners and butt out of military discourse!"

She sucked in her breath apprehensively. Sherman stomped through the room, opening curtains and windows. "More activity near the water tower last night, too. No signs of Mullermen. Rainbeau again! That damned hellion! I'll swear he gets credit for every bit of mischief done in this hornet's nest. By God! There can be no peace till Rainbeau is dead!"

Grant folded his arms, taking the emotional report and whittling it down to factual size. "Rainbeau and his fleet? He's a good man—no doubt about it. I suspect anytime there's a particularly nasty job to be done, the Confederacy sends for Captain Rainbeau."

Surlina was jolted as if a lightning bolt had struck her. How beautifully simple! She ran from the room, leaving the surprised generals. *Send for Julien!* Precisely what she would do.

27

Surlina composed her words economically, then bribed the cook who wanted his freedom to make sure Captain Rainbeau personally received the communication. In return she promised to put in a good word for the slave with Chaplain Eaton.

She wondered if Julien would shrug off her idea as a trap or laugh at her needs. She fretted all day, stationing herself at an upstairs window where she could spot all comers and goers at Rosie Mound.

A creaking of carriage wheels renewed her hopes. She peered closely at the approaching wagon, disappointed to see only a sturdy farm woman in a sunshade hat and red shawl. Surlina started to pace back and forth, trying to work off her impatience.

Moments later there was a knock at the door. "The missus in the carriage wants to see you," a housemaid said upon entering.

Curious, Surlina ran down to the yard where the wagon was pulled up under a cypress tree. As she walked toward the vehicle, she watched for signs of danger. Nothing seemed amiss, however.

Slowly a big hand pulled back a towel covering a basket. Deep within lay a pistol. Surlina jerked back, then peered more closely at the face hidden in the shade of the sunbonnet. "Julien? Is that you?"

His voice, so clear and melodious, gave him away the instant he spoke. "I hear milady requires a fleet at her disposal." He leaned out of the wagon and attempted to put his arms around her.

She was unsure whether to throw her arms around him for coming to her aid or shy away for fear of revealing his identity. He scooted over on the wagon seat, held out his hand and she scrambled in beside him. What a risk he'd taken to come in person! She pointed to the hill. "Julien, can you reduce that to smithereens?" She went on excitedly. "What kind of fleet have you? Gunboats? Mortars?"

"I have the *Quail*. Nothing else."

"Only *one* boat! That's not a fleet!"

He trotted the horse to the shade of the barn's overhanging roof. There he attempted to kiss her, his eyes twinkling and mouth grinning.

She pushed him away angrily. She was not sure what she had expected. Why, Sherman had talked as if the backwaters were teeming with ironclads! "One miserable boat!"

"Quite so," he agreed. "But hell, woman, there's only one miserable war!"

"Julien, my gates are here!" she cried, not wanting to flirt with him. "Right here! Inside that little hill

283

under the tower. I'm certain of it. They are in crates, and they were buried there with the good mirrors and rugs and you must help me get them out and—"

Suddenly he was serious. "So, congratulations. You've found them."

"Julien, I want you to steal those gates!"

He mimicked her perfectly, adding a little pout at the end. "Steal the gates, oh, yes, please do, Julien." Again he attempted to kiss her.

She sprang from the protection of the carriage seat, facing him from the ground where she planted her feet apart and took him to task. "A man I consider quite intelligent told someone this very morning that anytime there was an important job to be done, the Confederacy sent for you. Julien, now *I* have sent for you. Can't you do it?"

Julien leaned back, hands absently playing with the pistol in the basket. He watched her intently. She felt the sweep of his eyes over her body, felt the intrusion of emotion into their discussion. Surlina stamped her foot in the dust of the barnyard, furious with herself. "I see! When the chips are down, you can't do it!"

She could tell from his expression that she'd hit a sore point. But the silver was hers and she meant to have it even if it cost her Sam's good will and Julien's desire.

"I understand," he said clearly, his voice reflecting the attempt to control his temper. "Like everyone else, you want to hand me your problems." He stepped out of the wagon, throwing the sunbonnet onto the seat. His gold hair gleamed in the evening. "Send for Julien! Why not? Everybody does it. Got a problem? Send for Julien. Something especially nasty to be done? Something inconclusive or distasteful or dangerous? Then by all means, send for Julien!" He began to lope around the chicken yard, scattering roosters and hens in his path.

She attempted to shush his bellowing. "You promised to help me . . . once."

He stopped by her side, silenced. "No," he said softly, "I only promised to love you." The reflection

284

seemed to cost him something. He stood with his arms limply at his sides. "Which, goddamnit, I still do."

He pushed her halfway into the chicken shed, shielded from view, then kissed her mightily. She thought him extraordinarily silly and handsome in his calico frock, with his wonderful masculine hands against her back and tempting, warm lips against her mouth. As she felt his full power against her, she wondered at the mystery of expectation this man produced within her. He was so incisive, going straight to her heart the same way his tongue went straight to her lips and his hand went straight to her breast. She felt a tingling sensation turn her nipples hard, her breath to raggedness, her determination to defeat.

It was impossible not to caress him. Her legs parted slightly and his hand skimmed beneath her skirt. He moved his hands up and down her legs, rapidly. Immediately, she felt responsive, and her thighs pressed against him, wanting to see if his body was crying out, too.

"Take your clothes off," he suggested huskily.

"Julien!" After she'd blurted her reprimand, she saw he was laughing.

"Then shuck your ideas," he suggested.

She shook her head stubbornly, seeing they were back to serious discussion. She tidied herself and stepped back outside.

"If I can't lay you and I can't obey you, I might as well say adieu." He picked up the sunbonnet and waved it.

"No, wait! Now you know where the silver is! You may steal it for the Confederacy!" She was stunned by the black look on his face.

"Surlina, give up the silver."

She felt the executioner's dark hood over her future. Finally, he had asked her outright to give up the gates.

While she was pondering, he burst out laughing. "Oh, well, I see that for you this war comes with a money-back guarantee!" He swung her around and kissed her cheeks, apparently past the point of remonstrations. "I suppose I shall never deny you any whim.

Now, precisely what is it you wish me to do after I commit grand theft?"

"Take the gates aboard the *Quail*. Take them to Vicksburg for me."

"Wait a minute! For all your consorting with Union generals . . ." He paused, his eyebrows questioning and obviously hoping for a denial. When he received only a blank stare, he finished, "Your logistics are poor. Shall I walk up in the middle of the night, without benefit of lantern, I assume, and dig through several tons of earth on that mound of roses? Single-handedly, mind you, I drag out these gates weighing thousands of pounds. Next, haul them through the swamp. Then, wrestle them onto my poor broken-backed *Quail*. Presuming she's still afloat, you then want me to steam grandly to Vicksburg. Is that all?" He cocked his head and winked.

She did not like his impish behavior but she had to answer, "Yes, that's about it."

"By God, why not! Send for Julien!"

She grabbed him by the sleeve. She could see now how foolish her plan was. "All right, scram!"

"Will you go to Natchez and wait to hear from me?"

"Natchez! That's two hundred miles from here."

"Take this wagon. Go right now—before nightfall. The railroad is open south of Oxford. Go to Natchez and wait. It may be several weeks until you hear from me. There is work to be done here." He handed her the reins.

"Yes! I'll go! I'll wait for you, Julien!"

His hand touched her cheek for only a moment, traveling lightly across her nose, settling on her lips. "How long would you wait, Surlina? How long could I expect you to wait for me if you did not think I was the key to your beloved gates?"

He slapped the reins into her hands and darted toward the fence before she found her voice to answer.

28

Surlina spent Thanksgiving in Natchez in a dilapidated rooming house where the holiday meal consisted of stringy turkey, sweet potatoes, hominy and a pie made of equal parts of yams and cinnamon. Chill gusts raked the great river to a froth and shook the last leaves from the tree branches. Nearly a month! Would Julien never come? She repeated her vow to herself, 'I will wait,' yet it was with increasing impatience and more than a shade of doubt.

After the meal she dressed in an impractical gown and went into the garden to commiserate with the gray afternoon. Standing among the swirling leaves, watching the storm clouds, she felt useless. "I will wait for Julien," she promised, but her determination was wavering. Despondently, Surlina went back inside to her room with the saggy bed and peeling wallpaper. She shucked off the dress and put on a practical white blouse and black riding clothes. There was a knock at her door, followed by a bell sounding in the hallway. "Suppertime! Suppertime!" She wasn't hungry, but she went downstairs.

Standing at her place by the long boardinghouse table, she saw a guest. A priest! He was already in an attitude of prayer, face down, eyes closed, the long vestment and hood shielding his features. She folded her hands and stood respectfully with head down, anxious to get on with the meal.

As the voice droned on, it suddenly seemed familiar. She studied the thin jowls, the pointed chin and peculiarly reedy voice. She was sure now. Despite his cleanliness and formal attire, this was Bishop Leonidas Polk. Her mouth opened and her eyes widened in silent recognition.

Without missing a syllable, Bishop Polk nodded at

her. He raised his hand as if to bless the food, then pointed at the back door. Continuing the prayer, he circled the table, making individual blessings, urging the group, "Close your eyes and open your hearts."

While the congregation of boardinghouse regulars prayed, Surlina questioned Polk with her eyes. He nudged her elbow and nodded slightly toward the exit. Silently she lowered her head, quietly slipping a tableknife into her pocket, and tiptoed away from the table. Polk slowly worked his way backward, edging toward the door.

Swiftly, silently, they slipped away, he shedding his vestments in the alcove, she grabbing a leftover turkey leg as sustenance for whatever adventures lay ahead. Then they dashed out the rear entrance, tearing across the yard in haste and leaving the picket gate swinging wildly behind them.

No baggage, no cloak, no good-byes. Racing along the street, they ducked between houses, jumping fences, darting into the narrow alleyways which led downhill. The cold November air slapped the wide legs of the divided skirt against her ankles. Down the muddy path she sped, through the seamy district of Natchez-under-the-hill where gamblers and whores lived. Finally they were at the landing.

Beneath the frozen willows and tamarisks at water's edge, she spotted a rowboat. Crouched low, huddled over the oar as if it were a source of warmth, sat Donlevy. As they ran to the river's edge, he jumped out and stood shivering in knee deep water, steadying the boat against the current's pull while they boarded.

Quickly they pushed off, rowing into the white-capped river. Despite being breathless with cold and exertion, she asked him, "How did it go at Rosie Mound?"

Haloo drawled, " 'Bout fair to middlin', I'd say."

Polk said sternly, "They were greatly outnumbered."

Haloo shrugged as he tugged his oar. "Aw, Cap'n Rainbeau says we don't like to fight a-tall unless'n it's agin' twicet our numbers!"

She looked to Polk for a factual explanation. He remained mysteriously quiet, a smile playing across his features. "Let us say that General Grant will be looking for a new headquarters."

She shouted over the roar of the wind. "The gates? Did Julien get them?"

Neither man would answer. Finally Haloo stammered, "The *Quail* is setting a mite lower in the water these days."

She pounced on the startled boy and gave him a big hug.

At the instant the rowboat was roped to the *Quail's* slippery side, Surlina clambered aboard. Suddenly she stopped, dumbfounded. *There they were!* My God, they were huge! So much bigger than she'd imagined! How could they have dragged these monsters aboard? She knelt to touch them. She could almost feel the warmth of shining silver beneath the paint.

At that moment she saw Julien come striding forward. His walk was brisk, his eyes cold and his manner direct as he spoke to her. "You owe Rosie Mound Plantation one water tower, six cases of gooseberry wine, a Syrian carpet and a set of French mirrors."

Surlina began thanking him profusely, praising him extravagantly. Her hands still held the gates, seemingly unable to let go. She pulled herself upright. "I appreciate your efforts, Captain Rainbeau." Then her wild eagerness took control again. "Oh, Julien, do you have a saw aboard? Can we cut through the bars right now? I want to see my silver!"

Julien merely nodded and asked Haloo to fetch a hacksaw. Then he left without saying a word.

'I believe he's jealous!' she thought. 'How childish!' She turned away from the spot where he'd stood, giving all her attention and encouragement to Haloo. The boy worked with a steady cutting motion.

Her tension seemed to creak and rise with the squealing of the saw against metal. "Hurry!" she urged.

"Too hard," said Haloo. "Cain't be silver."

"Lay a shoulder in there!" Surlina ordered, wanting to seize the saw from him. She bent closer, demanding for herself the first glorious view of shimmery metal lurking beneath the black coating of paint.

Haloo was sweating despite the chill weather. Cursing under his breath, he worked until she could see the bulge of his arm muscles and throb in his neck veins. "Too hard," he panted.

"Let me see!" Again she dropped to her hands and knees. She dug her fingers into the bar, forcing her nails into the tiny nick the saw had made. The cut was only a half-inch deep and all she could see was black. It was impossible to feel or tell anything! Her fingers seemed to vibrate as she pinched at the metal.

Haloo crouched down beside her. "Ain't silver. Them are iron from start to finish."

She moaned defiance against the horrible words. From behind her, she heard Julien's voice talking to a crewman about mechanical matters. She leaped up and faced him, devastated. "These gates are solid iron. You have brought me the wrong ones!"

"I brought you the *only* ones." He appeared controlled but she thought she heard a small sigh of relief escape his lips. "Now what would madam like done with her iron gates?"

"Hell's bells! Commit their bodies to the deep! Ship them to Tredegar and melt them for ammunition! Throw them overboard! I don't care!"

"Now will you give up the chase?" Julien asked.

"Never!" As a furious afterthought, she yelled, "And stop this boat! I want off!"

He chuckled then, the first break in his frozen demeanor. When he opened his arms to her, she collapsed in his embrace like a child clinging to a stern parent after a spanking. He led the way to his stateroom. When she entered, she moved Squeebob aside in a sweeping motion of her hand, then fell across the bed, head buried in her arms, tears of unhappiness overflowing despite her sniffling attempts to control them.

She heard Julien close the door. His boots scraped the floor as he pulled out the desk chair. He spoke quietly, as if talking to himself. "I've thought about it for months, and I still don't understand. *Why* do you need that fortune so badly? Certainly you're not a woman of fabulous gilded desires. You subsist on hardtack and wear ordinary riding breeches and traipse about with a worn satchel. You're not charitable, either. Nor a gambler. So why do you need it?"

"It's mine!" There was no way to reason with him and she had no desire to try. She repeated illogically, "It's mine!"

"Surlina, last week I had to cut off a sailor's arm. I amputated with that hacksaw you and Haloo used today."

She flinched, unsure why he had so abruptly changed subjects. She looked at him expectantly, letting some of the childish petulance drain from her clenched muscles.

"The man cursed me. But I reasoned that if I sawed off his arm, despite his screams, I'd save his life. He reasoned that without his arm, he didn't care to live." Julien drew his chair closer to her bunk so their faces were nearly touching.

"Did he live?" she asked.

"Yes." He set his face against her flushed cheek. "And you will live without the silver—but first you must decide you want to."

She shook her head and drew away from his contact. Huddled on the bunk, she pondered his story. Suddenly he rose, frowning. "You sit there worrying—obviously unable to make up your mind. Surlina, I have been a failure at many things but I have always understood your need for the silver. You don't."

"You're jealous, Julien! You're threatened by my silver."

"Absolutely."

"You want me to give it up just to prove some silly point about your pride."

"Pride? Perhaps." He stood stolid, the dimple decorating his chin, his hair more yellow now, the creases around his eyes deeper. She sensed the toll he was paying to be a warrior.

291

She pulled her knees up and clasped her hands around them, resting her chin atop her legs. At the moment, it seemed plausible to give up the chase. But what about tomorrow?

It seemed he was reading her mind. "End the chase here, Surlina. I will not sacrifice myself on an altar of silver. Don't burn yourself on a pyre of greed." He sat on the bunk beside her, tilting her chin upward so that she looked directly at him. "Can't you see you've lived behind gates all your life? Convent bars. Your father's tyranny. Society's expectations of a silver belle. All I'm asking you to do is to fling away the gates and walk out—free!"

"What about Muller? What about Cabell and Ramsey? Do you think for a moment they'll stop chasing the silver? What about Sam Grant? And Halleck? You think everyone's going to haul out truce flags?"

"I don't give a damn in this world what they do!" He was furious, hitting the pillow against the bulkhead, kicking at the cat with his boot. "But *I'll* not be cuckolded by a damn pile of money!"

Suddenly he slammed her to the bunk, pinning her shoulders with his hands, kissing her as if to suffocate her. She tossed against his assault, sensing the hurt he sought to inflict. His lips, which she had known to be so warm and tender, were now cruelly hard. His body, which had covered her with compelling vigor, now pummeled her. The gray eyes were fiery with desire to give pain.

His hands yanked at her body, not in caresses, but in wild possessiveness, stripping the fasteners from the blouse, grabbing the waistband of the skirt and tearing. His hands were damp, unfamiliar, his lips fevered as he brought himself across her again, biting away the thin camisole which covered her breasts. She felt him out of control, savage, as if the tension within him was unbearable.

All at once, she went slack under him. "I'll not fight you," she whispered. "You're shaming yourself, acting like a wild animal! Ramsey said you were a common—"

292

He cut off her protests with a slap. The sting of hurt banished all her efforts to keep still. She clawed at his neck, bit at his hand, kicked against his legs. Despite the violence, she was struck by the sight of his face—he looked miserable, but he fought her to a trembling, thrashing standstill.

Words were useless, fighting nearly so. He was intent on rape and her best interest was in protecting herself, not causing further harm. She steeled herself against his assault, cowering against the bulkhead for the few seconds it took him to shed his clothes. She already felt violated by his rage. His swollen organ between her thighs would only confirm it. He sagged against her, every muscle writhing, shuddering with need. The light from the porthole struck his sideburns and made him seem afire as he ripped away her last garment.

Then he was atop her, giving no touch of gentleness or tender arousal. Straining to batter her into submission, he charged against her, snarling. Sweat rolling down his face, he buried himself into her like a dagger. She cried out, but he impaled her again, wedging her arms tight against her body, forcing her mouth open with his tongue. He stabbed at her, crashing and pitching like a ship out of control in a hurricane's blackness. His eyes blinked open for a moment. Then, with a sudden backward snap of his head, he seemed to awaken from his frenzy.

He fell forward heavily, the spasms wrenching his body up and down. Then, swiftly, he withdrew, staggered from the bunk and crashed against the desk. Swearing, slapping his palms together, he ranted like an enraged madman. "I didn't mean to! I'd kill myself before I'd hurt you! By God, I'll cut out my heart and—"

Overwhelmed, she spontaneously put out her arms to him. He shrank from her touch, his head in his hands, moaning. He grabbed his clothes and yanked them over his trembling body. Unable to face her, he mumbled, "I'll send your dinner to the cabin. You can

293

go ashore with Bishop Polk in Vicksburg. I'll never force myself or my views on you again!"

"Julien! Don't run away!"

But he moved out the door and slammed it as if he hoped never to see her again.

Two days later, when the *Quail* tied up beneath Vicksburg's red bluffs, Surlina still had not seen him. She sent word with Haloo that she wanted to say good-bye. Julien did not appear on deck. She delayed as long as possible but Bishop Polk had an appointment with General Pemberton and he urged her to come with him.

She took a last glance back at the sturdy gray packet boat before turning her thoughts to Tandy, and climbing up the steps toward town.

Bishop Polk saluted the city. "Hail, Vicksburg—the city that has set her cap to change the course of the war!"

Surlina felt choked with disgust. She thought of Tandy and Cabell and all the other misguided citizens, ready to die to hold the fortress.

"These bluffs look impossible to assault! No army could climb them. Are there other routes of attack?"

"Every which way, actually," Polk replied, assuming his stance as Confederate major general. He was puffing with exertion from the climb and indicated that they should rest a moment. He picked up a loose rock and carved a map in the soft stone cliff. "If you don't mind leeches and snakes, you can come up that way through the bayous. If you don't mind ticks and mosquitoes, you can get here overland. Then there's the canal. In fact, if you have immense amounts of manpower and great indifference to casualties, you can even climb the cliffs on which we stand."

Surlina resumed hiking up the steps. Indifference to casualties! Precisely what it would take to overpower Vicksburg. And she knew just the man who would have that queer lack of concern for dying men: William Tecumseh Sherman. "What will you tell General Pemberton about Vicksburg's chances?"

"I will state the facts. It is Grant's plan to close the river here. It is the Confederacy's will to keep it open. The collision in aims will make Vicksburg a Waterloo for someone." He stamped up the steps two by two. "I'll tell Pemberton what common sense tells me. By damn, the Yankees will have hell to pay getting into this city."

"But Sherman is just the man to try it!"

"Yes, he'll come. And the lists of dead and dying will be longer than the Mississippi River."

Surlina didn't doubt that siege was bearing down rapidly. She must get Tandy out of Vicksburg. Silver gates or no, they must attempt to get back to St. Louis. She remembered Sam Grant's axiom: "After forty-five days, *any* fort will surrender." She looked up as they crested the top of the cliff. The town hadn't surrendered yet—that was certain! It was decorated for Christmas with tinsel on the lamp posts and garlands on the street markers.

They sat down to rest. Surlina roused her courage to speak of the subject which had been on her mind for the last three days. "I should not have asked Captain Rainbeau to steal the gates for me." She tried to address the subject neutrally and think of Julien only by his military title.

Polk replied, "Perhaps you should not have, although I have often thought Julien would happily steal anything." Abruptly he took her hand. "Do you love him, Surlina?"

She hesitated, anguished by her own uncertainty. "I have angered him . . . to . . . to the point of indifference with me. Perhaps even hatred."

"He will recover. Neither of you has the ability to remain indifferent about anything. If Julien is intractable with you, it is his way of balancing his care of his men and ship. Julien is a genuine rebel, and he wages unconventional warfare."

"And he's doing a good job," she cried out, eager to praise him. "Isn't he?"

"No. Julien Rainbeau will probably be the youngest and only commander ever publicly asked to leave the

Confederate River Defense Force." He smiled. "His superiors are confounded by his swashbuckling raids, his lack of spit and polish aboard the *Quail*." He searched the horizon, avoiding her eyes, as if he hated to speak. "I suspect he will be relieved of command at the council's next meeting."

"But, why?" She was outraged and incredulous.

"He is impetuous, daring and *awesome*. A man who has twice defied the council because of you! Surlina, he has risked *everything!*"

'And then uses his wits to get more,' she thought, overwhelmed with tenderness.

Polk continued, "Julien wants freedom to move up and down the river, through oceans, over continents. He fears being tied to one port."

"Or my silver."

"It would weigh him like an anchor."

"That's such puny arrogance," she snapped.

"Would you want him without his vivid temper and lively strength? Ah, Surlina, you two are alike, so much so you know of no way of meeting except head-on."

He had expressed her thoughts exactly. She was silenced by sorrow. They started walking into the main street.

"Julien is dangerous. And brilliant. But he has not mastered the politics. As well as being an outright pest to his superiors, he is dangerous to himself." Polk continued. "He has a serious flaw in his makeup—he does not know himself." He stopped on the corner of Harrison Street, obviously intending they should go separate ways. "If you love him, Surlina, you will have to give up certain things, for you are asking him to surrender one set of values without giving him time to seek another. You keep silver as your idol. Laying your hands on those gates has become your religion."

Humbled, she admitted, "I no longer know how to give them up." She'd alienated Julien, driven him to assault her physically and then hide from her in shame and hatred. As for Sam, she'd wedged the silver between them, engineered the destruction of his headquarters and left him without so much as a backward glance. In a way, she still felt guilt over her father's death. The only clear emotion she retained was hatred of Thad Muller. Everything that had happened since that spring day in St. Louis had been set in motion by him!

29

"He's gone," Tandy cried, collapsing into Surlina's arms in the doorway.

"Who's gone?" asked Surlina, wondering if the blustery Thayer Cabell had perhaps blown away due to his own windiness. Or perhaps someone had displayed the good sense to kidnap him! She entered the house on Harrison Street pleased to find her brother-in-law absent and her sister looking well.

"With Van Dorn's raiders! Oh, Surlina, he should not have gone!"

"Raiders? Where?"

"They've gone to Holly Springs to blow up Grant's supply lines. He shouldn't have gone! Not now! Not since I'm—" She rushed back through the living room and collapsed on the velvet couch. "Not now that I'm—"

"You're what?" Surlina sank down next to her sister, suspecting the worst. "Oh, Tandy! You're not pregnant again! Not so soon!"

The sudden blush, the shy smile behind the dainty hand and the fluttering eyelids confirmed the news. Surlina blurted out, "How could you?" Instantly she saw the crestfallen slump of Tandy's shoulders and the stricken look in her eyes. "I didn't mean to hurt your feelings. I only meant you had such a hard time, losing the baby last time, I thought you'd avoid that beast like . . ." She gave up. Hugging Tandy close, she murmured, "There, there, it's all right."

"Without dear Cabell here, I'm so worried!"

Surlina gave Tandy an affectionate pat. "Now, don't worry about Cabell. He will be in no danger of getting himself near any minié balls."

"Sweet Surlina, you do not understand my husband. He's a brave man and a gentle one." She kept her gaze on her lap. "You do not know of married love." She began to sniffle daintily.

There was no answer. It was obvious Tandy was trying to extend genuine pity to an elderly spinster sister. Surlina knew it would embarrass Tandy far more to talk of nights of passion with Julien or the steady hunger she felt for Sam than to remain silent.

Tandy cried persistently and with consternation, making no effort to stop. "I'm pregnant, and Cabell is leaving."

"Leaving? The Van Dorn raiders won't be gone long."

"No, leaving."

Surlina suspected the worst. Cabell would probably flee to some other safe spot now that the siege of Vicksburg seemed imminent. "Where's he off to this time? Does he expect to drag you along?"

"England."

"My God!"

Tandy raised her eyes, brightening with pride. "He's going alone, at the personal request of Jefferson Davis. They've been at Brierfield all week working out the arrangements. He is to see Lord John Russell and Palmerston to seek their aid for the South!"

Surlina searched for something gracious to say. Cabell in England playing diplomat! He would do nothing more than lead the South on another detour from reason. Both Jefferson Davis and Thayer Cabell were fools if they thought Russell or Palmerston could be seduced into any North American adventuring. However, there was no point in saying such things to Tandy. In a way, Surlina was envious of her sister's limited perception of what was coming in this war. She stroked Tandy's baby-fine hair and leaned against her narrow shoulders. "All right, Tandy, it appears we

shall have to keep house ourselves here in Vicksburg."
She couldn't risk Tandy's pregnancy by a perilous trip
back to St. Louis.

Tandy didn't move, apparently deep in a trance of
nostalgia. "I long for the old days, Surlina, when we
were little girls in the convent. Don't you remember
those as the good times?"

Surlina shook her head gently, for she remembered
those years as they actually had been—years of isola-
tion and despair. She remembered the mining camps,
living pillar to post, as bitter and hard. But Tandy
remembered it all differently, through a veil of forget-
fulness. Of course, Tandy thought of war unrealisti-
cally, too, still calling the scenes of death and battle
"mischief" and "unpleasantness." Surlina had stripped
herself of such theatrical masks. She saw war as brutal.
Destructive. Ugly. And the result of this particular war
was likely to last well beyond their lifetimes.

It was time to set priorities. "When does Cabell go
to England?"

"He goes in January—less than a month."

"And when is your baby due?"

"The end of June."

"He may well not be back!" Surlina was indignant.
"How can he leave you?"

"He must go! It's for the Cause."

"You realize we are stuck in Vicksburg? There's
no way I can get you to New Orleans or St. Louis. In
a few more weeks, there won't even be railroads or
ferries in and out of this city."

Tandy quizzed her with a little smile. "So?"

Surlina stood, rolling up her sleeves as if to set to
work. "So, Tandy dear, the choice is made. I'll clear
my mind of everything but your welfare. I'll stay right
here in Vicksburg with you and when you give birth,
I promise you it'll be to the bouncingest baby ever to
breathe south of the Mason-Dixon line!"

An air of holiday expectancy hung over Vicksburg
as rumors of Christmas, parties, spies and Van Dorn's
raiders kept everyone watching the river, the cliffs
and the Jackson Road. Would the cavalrymen make

it home for Christmas? Would they succeed in cutting the Union supply lines . . . and maybe grabbing a few things which could be put under the holiday tree as gifts? Children out of school played in the caves along the cliffs, fancying themselves scouts. People chatted in the streets, afraid to move inside and miss a possible homecoming. Tandy was so eager for news that she popped outside at the slightest noise.

Surlina tried to keep her mind on the household. She gave Pat Martha a new list of duties, oversaw the making of fruitcakes and even attempted to sit and knit alongside Tandy.

By the time she'd been in Vicksburg ten days, Surlina felt she would certainly go crazy. She dreaded Cabell's return. His presence would put her over the brink for sure! After supper, when Tandy put on her coat and tied the double-layered bonnet tightly beneath her thin chin, and came into the living room, Surlina was beside herself. "Don't stay up tonight! Go to bed!"

Tandy merely sniffed, flung open both dining- and living-room windows and sat down, staring out into the December night. When Surlina could not force her sister to close the windows, she gave in, put on her own winter coat, dragged the blankets off the bed and bundled them both up to wait. "This smacks suspiciously of being stupid!" she told Tandy, then pulled down one of Cabell's leather-bound volumes of Swift and began to read.

After two chapters, Surlina dozed off. There were no noises to disturb her, no shouts through the open window, no horse's hooves clinking against pebbled streets.

She was roused awake by Tandy's urgent whisper, "Listen! Listen! I hear it!"

Surlina sat up, shaking herself into alertness like a dog coming out of water. The mantel clock struck midnight. She cocked her head, straining to find the direction of some elusive sound. At first she heard only night noises, the wind and pine branches sighing. Then, from far off, she recognized a steady churning sound.

"A train!" Now the noise was louder, the certain

chuff-chuff of a locomotive. "They've brought in the train! The *Mississippi Central!*" Tandy bounded up, clapping her hands.

The sisters danced an impromptu jig. Tandy, already tightening her bonnet strings, implored, "Let's go meet it!"

By the time they rushed into the street, it was apparent other ears had been straining, too. All of Vicksburg seemed to be heading for the depot. The crowd sang out in delight each time the whistle blew.

The town charged toward the station like a rowdy crowd of partygoers. Men, women, children, horses and dogs mixed together to welcome the first train in months from Jackson.

The locomotive rolled to a stop at the depot. Surlina was shocked to see her brother-in-law lean out of the engine cab! There he was, Thayer Cabell the Great, returning at the end of the victory column! If he wasn't literally at the controls of the engine, he had at least usurped the place of glory. He swung grandly onto the platform as the train shuddered to a halt. Some thoughtful gentleman in the crowd handed him a flask. Cabell took a deep drink, then raised his hands to quiet the cheers. It was a glorious tale he shouted. Firing the supply stores at Holly Springs! Cutting the railroad north of Corinth! Van Dorn's cavalry still busy on the road to the Walnut Hills! His own idea to bring in the train from Jackson.

The crowd cheered. However, Surlina noticed a few impatient men stamp their feet and edge away from the speechmaking. In twos and threes, the eager scavengers climbed onto the steps of the railroad cars. More followed, the crowd breaking up as it pressed hungrily toward the goods inside the boxcars.

The first sliding doors rumbled apart. Men sprang into the dark opening. Again the crowd cheered, no longer paying any attention to Cabell. The first man through the doors poked his head out again. "Hides! A car full of hides!" he shouted. From the next car came the announcement, "Pickles! Pickles in vats of brine." A barrel lid flew through the air into the crowd, dripping vinegar.

The citizens of Vicksburg swarmed onto the train like ants onto the carcass of a dead ox. Surlina, anxious to rummage for medicines to stockpile for Tandy, surged forward, too. She could hear the whoops of excitement dying away. From the third car, she heard shouts, "Nothing in here! Empty!" Furher down the row of cars, she heard the reports as the doors slid open and the scavengers scrambled in. "Empty! No food here!"

The shouts were angry and hoarse now. "No ammunition! No food! How will we hold out?"

Cabell was still wallowing in his own glory of capturing the empty train. He took another great swig from the flask, waved it over his head and shouted into the air. "We'll hold out! We'll drink 'em down! We'll shout 'em down! Sing 'em down!"

Surlina cried out furiously, "Every damned thing but shoot 'em down!" She glared at him, disdaining him for what he was; a puppet politician.

She felt a nudge in her back, which quickly changed to a poke. A crotchety voice whispered, "Come on! There's salvaging to be done. These pickers tore through here so fast, they missed a few nits, I reckon."

Surlina whirled around as she identified the cranky voice of Dottie McDune. "What are you doing here?"

"Same thing as you. Looking." With that, the old woman scrambled into the opening of the boxcar and disappeared. Surlina watched the crowd toting away the last of the pickle vats, then she followed Dottie. "Nothing here!" Dottie complained.

As they made their way to the next car, Dottie asked, "Say, was that circus bear who made the speech your brother-in-law?"

Surlina was feeling with her hands into dark corners, finding only cobwebs, clumps of cotton, and empty gunny sacks. "Thayer Cabell is a charlatan . . . as well as my sister's husband."

"He's the cotton trader, right? Well, I'm back to running a few bales myself. I'll hit him up for a pass."

"He's leaving for England, thank goodness."

"Then I'll speak to him tonight."

"I've never seen a woman hotter after a dollar than you!"

Dottie chuckled, sounding pleased by what she considered a compliment. "You don't let much silver slip through your own fingers, as I remember . . . I got a load of cotton on my wagon right now, ready to be shipped from Friar's Mire. Soon as I get the proper paper, I'll be taking leave of this city!"

They crept into the next railroad car. It was apparently full of discards the crowd had ignored in their frenzy for food. Rubbish. Sticks of broken furniture. A pile of what seemed like musket covers. It was hard to tell in the dark what anything was. Surlina stepped backward, her ankle striking something hard. She tottered backward and sat down unceremoniously. Her hands shot out to break the fall, splaying against something metallic and evenly spaced. Ignoring the pain of her wrenched ankle, she groped with her hands, grasping around the hard sections of cold metal.

Carefully moving onto her hands and knees, she found the edge of a wooden crate with her fingers. She felt her way along the bars, inching to avoid falling into the spaces. She ran her hands forward as far as she could reach, finding again the sharp edge of splintered wood. Crates! Iron bars! She began to tremble. "Dottie! Bring a lantern! Quick!"

"What you onto, girlie?"

"Not sure. Hurry with that light!" She held her breath as Dottie slid out the door. Could she have literally stumbled into her silver?

She spread her arms and legs, trying to measure the size. Cautioning herself against unreasoning hope, she argued it might be another false find. She began scratching the surface with her nails, trying to claw her way through. A tiny giggle, high-pitched and eerie, escaped her lips.

Seeing a sparkle of light, she looked around, glad Dottie was back. Then her gratitude turned to panic. Silhouetted in the doorway, holding a lantern aloft and peering inquisitively into the boxcar was Thad Muller! She stifled a gasp and shifted deeper into the shadows.

"Hey, in there! What you found?" he called, giving no indication of recognition.

She drew back again, hunching down upon herself like a snail attempting to withdraw into its chamber. Disguising her voice, she called loudly, "Nothing!"

"Why you setting there, then?"

"Just resting a minute!"

He put the lantern on the rim of the car and hoisted himself up onto the floor. "Resting or *guarding* somethin'? You find loot the others missed?" His voice was subdued, full of hunger and greed. As he turned up the wick of the lantern, she caught a full glimpse of his ugly face. He rooted and slobbered like a boar, moving on his haunches, licking his fat lips.

"I twisted my ankle. But I'm all right! There's nothing here!" She kept her head down and turned sideways, acting as if she were bending over her injury.

He studied her a moment, then abruptly blew out the lantern. His whisper echoed through the darkened car. "Silver Belle!" Suddenly there was fumbling and rattling as though he was after a weapon.

Surlina scrambled to her feet, ignoring the fire in her ankle. Aiming at the spot where she'd last seen the light, she ran for the lantern.

He caught her by the arm and hair, twisting her neck savagely, bringing her down against the floor with a thud. Her face hit the lantern and she felt the burn blend with the jarring of her jaw against the railroad car. Stunned for an instant, she drew up, protecting herself instinctively.

The next sound she heard was alarmingly soft—his voice crooning with excitement and power. "All alone here, Silver Belle! I say we take up where we left off!" With a jerk, he grabbed her from behind, pulling her backward into a sitting position, his hands grabbing at her breasts.

She jabbed with both elbows, knocking his hands

304

from her body. "You keep away! Thad Muller, you killed my father!"

"Hell, no, missy! I only put the bullet in his double-crossing back! He deals with me, then leads me into ambush! No one defies the Mullermen and lives to brag about it!"

She was shocked by the admission but too numb to absorb its impact. Muller had killed her father! Again, she tried to get to her feet. The throb in her ankle tilted her off-balance. Muller's hand closed around her leg. She caught a glow of light from outside the box-car. "Dottie!" she screamed. "It's Muller!"

Instantly there was the click of a pistol as Dottie swung into view, holding her lantern high in her left hand, her right hand bringing her gun to bear. Surlina was already scrambling away. Suddenly Muller's foot raised, kicking his lantern toward Dottie. At the same time, he dived for the doorway, arms flailing for his own gun.

Dottie didn't blink as she shot point-blank. Muller's scream sounded abrupt, like a honking goose. Then he fell out the doorway, his arm dangling unnaturally. Despite the wound, he leaped up, ran behind the box-car and disappeared, squeals of pain coming from his throat. Dottie moved as if to pursue him. Surlina grabbed the old woman's coattail. "Don't go after him! He'll kill us!"

Dottie seemed uncertain. "Ought to finish the bugger off!" She stalked up and down the tracks looking for Muller but could not spot his trail. "Mebbe that arm will keep him laying low till we can git!"

Surlina was stricken with fright. Now she'd put Dottie in danger, too! If he lived, he'd pursue them—that much was certain. Surlina shivered, then remembered the gates in the boxcar.

"Let's load up," Dottie counseled, tugging Surlina to her feet. "Whatever you've found, it ain't safe here." She leaned out the door, gave a small yodel and a moment later the cotton wagon arrived, pulled by Murray and driven by Kuffy. Dottie issued orders. "Kuffy, go to Planter's Hall—that big building at the end of the block. Tell anyone you see that Thayer Cabell wants dockhands at the tracks to uncouple the cars. Don't bring nobody but slaves," she cautioned.

"Even with slave labor to load these gates, it won't do me any good," complained Surlina. "There's no place in Vicksburg to hide them! If I tell Tandy or Cabell, they'll notify the Confederacy Council! There's no way I can get them upriver to St. Louis or downstream to the ocean. I damned sure can't sit on them and wait for Muller to come back with his men."

"You need a smelter," advised Dottie. "Muller needs a surgeon and some healing time. He won't give us no bother for a few days. By then we can make ourselves scarce."

"But where's a smelter still in operation?"

Dottie slapped her hands together and laughed. "Our fortunes are tied together again, I reckon. Friar's Mire—where I'm headed with my cotton—is the shipment point for everything these days. From there, you can go on to Yazoo City."

"Why do I want to go there?"

"That's where you'll find your blast furnace and smelter and tools."

"How soon can we leave?"

Dottie peered into the darkness. "Kuffy's leading back about twenty black boys." She decided the wagon could be loaded in an hour, the cotton rearranged atop the gates, the whole shebang camouflaged by morning. "But we can't leave till after New Year's."

"That's another week! We must go now!"

"Hellfire, no! I ain't stirring me behind until after the battle. Everybody knows Sherman is fixing to wrap this town like a present. I want a front-line seat!"

30

Dottie was not alone in her enthusiasm for the coming battle. Spies roamed into the woods, filtered back with timetables and estimates of Sherman's strength. Runners went out from the courthouse square every four hours, informing the citizens of the latest rumors. On the day after Christmas, Sherman and his cavalry, accompanied by Porter and his gunboats, were reported at the head of the Yazoo in a howling rainstorm. The river was rising, and he would have to press forward toward the town. There was no way to turn back through the flooded marshland. The people on the streets shook their heads gravely and agreed: it was exactly the kind of weather they wished for Sherman.

"Holiday war fever! That's what's wrong with this town," complained Surlina on December 27, when new gossip circulated. She bawled Tandy and Cabell out at the breakfast table after returning from sleeping atop Dottie's cotton wagon. The unique arrangement kept Cabell and Surlina from going at each other tooth and claw, while allowing Surlina to guard the silver without saying more than that she was passing the time visiting with Dottie. Since Dottie's reputation was questionable Tandy was pleased the visiting was not done at her house.

"Look at this, sister," Tandy chirped, handing an embossed handwritten invitation across the table.

Surlina wondered how people could issue invitations which read: "Drop around to our open house after the battle or before New Year's, whichever comes first." Both Tandy and Cabell were consumed with fervor. They sent out little printed cards which read: "Requesting your esteemed presence on the occasion of the glorious defense of Vicksburg." The date was left blank.

Early on the morning of December 29, Sherman arrived. From behind cliffs and fences, redoubts and shutters, the citizens of Vicksburg watched the cavalry line up.

The battle was farcical and lopsided. Horses and men charged up the cliffs and were immediately repulsed. Like snakes recoiling in the poisonous smoke, the riders struck again and again. Soon dead men and animals littered the slopes. The people atop the hill laughed and screamed with delight!

Surlina sat silently on Dottie's cart, cringing.

This wasn't courage—it was carnage. As the smoke cleared, she could see piles of bodies, torn and bleeding horses, blood running down the wet hillside in rivulets. The noises of dying men filled the air. The smell of gunpowder barely masked the stench of mud and carion.

Outrage welled up in her. She climbed down from the wagon, unable to take her gaze from the terrible massacre.

How must Sherman feel now, she wondered as she watched the casualty counting. He had no dry ground on which to pitch tents for his wounded. There was no place at all to camp an army! Every square inch lay directly under Confederate guns. He had no place to even bury his dead. If he stayed, scraping up dead and wounded, his remaining men would have smallpox, malaria, measles and dysentery within a week. And if it kept raining, as it appeared it would, the river would put ten feet of water over his head.

Surlina choked on the smoke-filled air. Again she felt that the land itself had been poisoned.

"Insanity! Insanity!" she muttered, shivering by the wagon.

Her soliloquy was broken as Dottie walked up and slapped her on the back. "That takes care of that!" Dottie chortled. "Proves once and for all it'll take a large land force to capture Vicksburg. It will take awhile for them to get here, so it's on to Friar's Mire for us."

"Dottie, was this a great battle? One that will go into history books? Or just a lot of useless killing?"

"Too soon to say. Only a couple of thousand men dead." She climbed into the wagon, clucking to the mule.

As Surlina turned to get on, she saw Kuffy sitting atop the cotton bales, his eyes wide in horror, looking as if he'd flee if he had any idea where to run.

Surlina climbed to the top of the heaped wagon and reached for Kuffy's rigid body. She cradled his head, murmuring useless platitudes. "Poor baby," she crooned. To herself she thought, 'Oh, the poor children! These last dishonored heirs to what will be left of the South!'

Dottie cracked the whip across Murray's ear, making noise but not lifting a hair of his head. The wagon rolled forward inch by inch. Surlina had told Tandy and Cabell she would be gone for a few days and not to expect her at their victory open house. Now, as she saw them standing grandly under a newly embroidered banner of defiance, she thought it just as well if she never returned.

Ahead, in the pale afternoon light, Surlina made out a cluster of buildings. "Friar's Mire? Is that it, Dottie?"

Dottie urged the mule forward. "Hope so, after a week on the road."

In a few minutes, Surlina cried, "What's wrong? There's no smoke from the chimneys. No horses hitched outside. No cargo stacked in the open sheds. The weeds are overgrown by the outhouse. Dottie! If you've led me on another wild-goose chase . . ."

"Hold on! Wait till we get close up."

Surlina's heart numbed as they neared Friar's Mire. Obviously it was no longer the transshipment point for anything. The ferry house had been torched, the outbuildings gutted, the supply raft sunk and the ropes chopped. Horses' hoofprints were visible in the frozen mud. A bridle lay abandoned in the dried grass. A

jumble of bricks and charred posts marked the gate-
house where tolls had been collected. The big ferry-
boat was visible downstream about sixty feet. It was
merely a gutted hunk of twisted rafters, half-submerged.

"Who did it?" Surlina shouted in desperation as if
she expected the woods to answer.

Dottie pulled Murray to a halt at the water's edge.
The cold green bayou was forty feet across, rimmed
with low pawpaw, chinaberry and cypress trees.

"Who knows?" replied Dottie, bringing Murray to
a halt.

Surlina stifled an urge to curl up and cry. "Maybe
there are other crossings . . ." she began thinking aloud.

Dottie nodded. "I'll take Kuffy and investigate
downstream a bit. Look in the woods for something
munchable, too. You take guard duty. You'll have to
hold Murray, too."

Surlina pulled her jacket closer to her body, un-
kinked her cold fingers inside her mittens and climbed
down to steady the mule.

Dottie and Kuffy ducked out of sight behind the thick
brush. "Raccoon tracks," Dottie shouted. "We'll follow 'em!"

Surlina thought she heard a tree branch snap behind
her. She peered alertly at the direction of the sound.
A wild animal? Maybe she could provide lunch! On
guard, she moved along the slough, holding Murray's
reins in one hand, a gun in the other. A jaybird
squawked raucously.

Surlina paced up and down, stamping her feet to
keep the circulation going. Such thin boots! Hand-me-
downs to start with, patched with care and repatched
with exasperation. Not worth wearing on a day like
this. She was looking down in disgust at the raggedy
boots when she heard another branch snap. Instantly
she whirled, half-tangling the reins around her waist.

Her eyes squinted, raking each tree for inhabitants.

When she heard the footstep, loud and crunchy on
the frozen leaves, she panicked. Head darting to look
every direction, gun swinging wildly right and left, she

dropped the reins. Murray took a step farther toward the bayou, putting his head down as if getting ready to drink.

"No, get back," she ordered, unable to bend and retrieve the reins. She feared the wagon might start down the incline and there'd be no way to stop it. "Murray, get back!" She kept her voice low, attempting to get between him and the bayou while keeping her eyes on the underbrush. Another sudden snap of wood. "Dottie?" she called weakly, praying for a reassuring answer. "That you, Kuffy?" She bravely raised her voice. "Sing out loud and clear now! Dottie! Kuffy!"

Her shrill voice must have startled Murray for he lurched forward, braying. Aghast, Surlina swerved to grab the reins from the ground. At that instant, she caught sight of something moving in the woods. But she was already bent over, clutching at the ground, unable to lift the slender leather reins with her thick mitten. Quickly, she put her hand to her mouth, tugging off the glove while barricading the mule by dancing in front of him. The gun slipped from her elbow crook and hit the ground.

The moment the gun slid, there was a loud crashing in the woods. She screamed. Fear sent her reeling backward, squatting for gun and reins while only wanting to run. In an instant, she'd realized a man was running toward her. He burst from his shelter, racing full tilt, a bandage on his right arm, a knife upraised in his left hand.

At the same time she cried, "Muller" she grabbed the gun. His body shoved against her; his foot kicked the gun from her hands. It hit the ground and slid into the water. Muller's knife came up in a threatening position. As she started to run, he grabbed her around the waist. She struggled. Then the knife was against her throat, pressed against her throbbing veins.

Muller kept the knife tip to the hollow of her neck, his bandaged arm reaching up from behind to grab at the opening of her jacket. He shoved her forward toward the wagon violently, and she felt the point of the long bowie knife prick her skin.

"Don't talk, Silver Belle, or you'll be spitting blood!" Muller warned as he worked her toward the wagon. He held the knife so close to her throat that she felt she couldn't swallow or breathe. "So! Nothing in the box-car, eh? Nothing worth shooting Thad Muller about, eh? Nothing but something you took a lot of trouble to bring to Friar's Mire. Thinking to ship it upriver on the pirate express, eh?"

"No! Nothing here!" she gasped out.

He slammed her against the wagon step, bruising her legs. Now he moved in front of her, facing her directly, the blade of the knife turned sideways as if to slash her neck. The veins around his nostrils stood raised and purple, the smallpox scars on his cheeks gray and rough. His thick lips worked up and down, mashing against each other emphasizing the wild stubble of whiskers that grew over his chin. He transferred the knife to his bandaged hand, lowering the point directly at her belly. With his good hand, he scratched the fish-face tattoo on the back of his neck.

He made slashing motions with the knife. "Cat got your tongue, Silver Belle? What was in that railroad car in Vicksburg?"

When she shook her head, he raised his strong hand to slap her. She saw the blow coming, flinched, bit at his fingers—but missed. The sting sparked her cheek, making her eyes water and jaw burn.

"Now, Miss Silver Belle, I aim to *learn* you to be smart and answer me prompt. You're gonna be courteous, too. You're gonna be downright entertaining to Thad Muller!" He licked his fat lips and slanted his eyes. "Yes, sir, you're gonna be flat-out hospitable to me!"

Suddenly he held the knife to her jacket, slicing away the buttons. They popped off and bounced on the ground. "Take it off! Get rid of them boots, too! Let's see what tricks you know."

"I'll freeze!" she protested as he maneuvered to yank away her cloth jacket.

"No sass!" he ordered, tossing the jacket into the brush. "Off with them boots. Set your ass on the ground and tug 'em off, sis! I hear you like to dance. I hear you danced with a Union general on the *Radiant* and with a Confederate captain at the courthouse ball. Well, let's have a little dance for me now!"

She ducked down hastily, stripping off her boots, her teeth chattering in the cold. Muller edged around to pick up the reins. Murray snorted, apparently tired of standing. Keeping the knife upraised, Muller used the reins like a whip, striking the ground, then Surlina's feet, yelling again, "Dance!"

She lifted her feet and attempted a jig. He twitched his nose and wiggled his fat tongue. "You know, I'd strip you right here if we wasn't in such a hurry. But we got to float this wagon across the bayou before we can take our ease."

She stopped dancing in mid-step. "There's no ferry-boat! There's no way across!"

"It ain't deep. We'll ford it. Your mule looks sure-footed and them cotton bales will buoy us up. Then, we'll be off to fortune and happiness—for *me,* that is! For you I got certain things in mind." He twisted the knife in the air as if thinking of plunging it inside her. "Now get in the wagon!"

"Dottie! Kuffy!" She screamed full force.

He laughed. "Don't wear out your vocals. Your crone friend and her darky are a mile to the east there, skinning themselves a deer. Take 'em most of the day-light to finish. You and me'll be long across this bayou by then."

"We can't cross Friar's Mire!"

"And just why not?"

"The wagon will sink! It's too heavy!"

His sunken eyes narrowed further, glowing like a cat's. He held the knife between his teeth, the blade extending like a metal tongue. His hands grabbed her wool tunic, the strong one ripping at it while his weak hand pinched her arm. She felt his cold knuckles against her breastbone. "Is the silver in the wagon?" he demanded.

She shook her head 'no.'

He slapped her neck, then her shoulders, then her

313

breasts. The blows were like broadsides of sharpness, the hurt compounded by the cold. "You going to tell me where the silver is?"

"Never!"

"You spirited filly!" He grinned lewdly. "It's going to be an almighty pleasure to bridle you down." He rubbed her cheek with a calloused hand, sending pain deep through her bruised cheekbone. His face reddened and he blew a gust of foul breath at her. Then, with the knife at her breast, he brought his lips across her mouth, forcing saliva and tobacco juice onto her lips.

She squirmed in revulsion, fearing she would retch. She shoved his bad arm, causing him to yelp in pain. "Leave me alone!" She was frantic to the point of bribing him. "I have the silver!"

"That ain't news! Where the hell is it?"

"Hidden!" She sensed he wouldn't kill her until he knew . . . and she wouldn't tell him as long as she lived.

Suddenly he seemed in a hurry. "Git up on that seat. We can't stall no longer." He prodded her with the knife in her back, then looped the reins of the mule around her wrists to secure her until he climbed up in the driver's seat. He pulled her up roughly, shoving her into the seat while holding the mule steady. For a moment he smiled. "Heh, heh, heh! Imagine me and the Silver Belle finally setting out on the road to riches!" He swatted Murray across the back, but the beast didn't move. He whipped the mule again. Reluctantly Murray snorted, rippled his flanks and picked up one foot.

"Don't!" Surlina cried. "We'll sink!"

Muller ignored her, intent on moving the mule. Frowning in concentration, he kept a tight pull on the reins with one hand and a steady grip on the knife and Surlina's wrist with the other. Even bandaged, his arm was strong. Murray took two steps down the incline. The wagon lurched forward. Once started, the gates and gravity combined to push it effortlessly downhill. Surlina braced her legs against the buckboard, realizing Murray would be unable to stop now.

"Whoa! Whoa!" shouted Muller, yanking back on the reins. But the wagon rolled forward out of control. It gathered speed, swerving slightly as Murray twisted and jerked. Muller tugged the reins frantically.

When Surlina saw the green water rising up to meet them, she knew the impact was inevitable. "Ho!" yelled Muller. Now he was standing, scrambling to tighten the reins. The knife fell to the floorboard as he loosened her wrist for an instant.

That was all Surlina needed. She dived out of the seat, flinging herself toward the water at the side of the moving wagon. She heard a sharp crack as the harness catches and trace chains gave way. Murray whinnied, then splashed wildly. Cold water covered her like a heavy shroud. Fighting her way back to the top, she saw Murray floundering, the wagon skidding into the bayou and Muller flying through the air.

She kicked her arms and legs ferociously, glad for the moment to be without heavy boots and jacket. She lifted her head above water, shouting wildly for help. Murray floundered into deeper water, bucking and keeling over sideways. The wagon, loose of all restraint, toppled sideways, sending out waves of scum across the bayou. As she fought the water and the cold, she kept a frantic watch on the spot where the wagon was sinking. How could it be disappearing if Friar's Mire wasn't deep?

She put her feet down, hoping to find the bottom. Instantly she felt a sucking sensation—loose, slimy grit tugging at her cotton stockings. She kicked loose, tried again a few feet away, found no bottom at all. Quicksand! No wonder the wagon was practically gone! Panicked, she tried to establish landmarks—so many yards from the outbuildings, the angle from the cypresses, the exact look of the bank directly behind the bubbles where the wagon had disappeared.

Gone! Her silver in a bottomless pit! She flailed at the water, swimming for shore, keeping watch for Thad Muller. Perhaps he'd drowned! God, she hoped so. She flung herself toward a low-hanging moss cluster, inching forward through the slime until her feet hit solid embankment. Murray clambered back up the rutted slopes, muddy and heaving. She thought she heard noise on the opposite shore. "Thad Muller?" She clutched a tree root and hoisted herself, shivering, onto the firm ground. "I hope you drowned and went to hell!"

"No sech luck," came a hoarse answer. She spotted him crawling in the underbrush across the bayou. "I'll be back!"

"I'll see you hanged! You're a deserter, murderer and thief! I'll kill you myself if the army doesn't get you first!" She felt braver with the bayou between them, especially since both the gun and knife were beneath the quicksand.

"One of these days I'm going to take my satisfaction of you *and* the silver, mark my words!" He loped away into the woods like a wet hound.

She looked around her. At least he was gone! Murray was grazing at frozen tufts of gorse. The bubbles in the bayou had disappeared, the scum settling back on the spot where the wagon had gone under. She'd lost the gun, all Dottie's contraband cotton and the silver. But she was too cold to think of it. Hurriedly she ran to get her boots, tugging them on over the wet stockings.. Next she retrieved her jacket from the brush where he'd thrown it. Her body shook inside and out, trembling with effort and cold.

At that moment she heard Dottie and Kuffy's voices. She ran toward them, shouting, "Dottie! Come quick!"

The woman and boy rushed from the woods, huge hunks of venison over their shoulders. Dottie's face went blank with surprise. "Jesus H. Christ! What's happened?" She ran first toward Murray, then toward Surlina, apparently unsure which to look after first.

Surlina, Murray, Kuffy and Dottie used the burned tollbooth as shelter. When Surlina had finished relating the story of Muller and his attack, Dottie stood staring at the bayou. The crusty old lady neither soothed nor reprimanded Surlina.

"We got to march," announced Dottie. "There's a

tin shed about a mile back. We'll hole up there for the night. Kuffy, climb aboard." She boosted the skinny boy onto Murray's back. "Let's set our faces to the wind. Looks like a blue norther blowing in here."

Surlina started walking, full of remorse. "I dived off the *Radiant* into the Mississippi River, escaped Butler in New Orleans, ran out of Natchez without even a coat on my back, and now here I am again—wet clothes, wet boots, half-frozen and no silver! By God, it can stay at the bottom of Friar's Mire!"

"I don't believe a word," insisted Dottie. "You're just wallowing in self-pity."

They reached a tin shed before dark, cooked the venison and gathered straw from the field to help shield them from the night's coldness.

They piled everything they could find against the north side of the shed, forming a windbreak. Cow chips, hay, straw, frozen weeds, broken pine branches, loose tin from the roof all went into the shelter. Next they stationed Murray closest to the wall. Finally the three of them nestled down, their backs against Murray, Kuffy in the middle. The loose boards and roof rattled continually. The tiny flickers of the fire struggled feebly against the wind. Every few minutes, Dottie would kick another cow chip onto the smoldering blaze for fuel.

Suddenly there was pounding at the side of the shelter, a whinnying of horses and loud voices. "Open up! Who's in there?" Surlina grabbed for Dottie, afraid Muller had returned, then realized it was not his voice.

Dottie pulled her pistol. "Who wants to know?" She and Surlina both jumped to their feet, ready to fight.

"Hey! That a woman's voice I hear? You all right, ma'am? This is Lieutenant Turk from the Union outpost on the Big Black."

The two women looked at each other, Dottie frowning and Surlina smiling. "Let him in!" whispered Surlina. She called, "What do you want?"

317

"I found a horse running loose by the ferry landing. You lose one?"

"That horse belongs to a deserter!" cried Surlina, flinging open the makeshift door. "Thad Muller! He's a deserter from your army! You must capture him immediately." By the glow of the tiny fire she saw Lieutenant Turk was not alone. Another officer rode a second horse, leading the stray by the bridle.

"A deserter?" chorused the two men. "Near here?"

"Yes! Just across Friar's Mire! If you track him immediately, you can capture him tonight! It would mean great honor for you! Grant would promote you both on the spot if you catch Muller!"

The two men leaned toward each other, conferring in low voices. "Can you give us a description of the man?" asked Turk.

Surlina launched into details about Muller. The officers seemed satisfied that she had not invented the story of a deserter but they did not seem inclined to pursue him, either. "Why are you camped in this shed?"

"Lost my wagon in the mire," Dottie answered.

Surlina shot her a glance of warning. She wanted no one to know the location of that wagon! Upstanding as these soldiers looked, they might not be above a fishing expedition.

Dottie added, "You fellows need to fetch us to a place we can get a new wagon."

The men consulted each other again. Finally Turk proposed a plan. "One of us will escort the mule, the old woman and the boy to the camp at Haine's Crossing." He nodded at Surlina. "You, miss, will have to come to headquarters with me and fill out a report on the deserter. If he's in as bad shape as you say, the cavalry can find him at first light."

"Whose headquarters?" demanded Surlina. "Sherman's?"

"No, ma'am. Grant's. General Grant is newly arrived on the river to take charge. I venture to say he'll want that deserter caught and strung up!"

Surlina felt her lips crack as she smiled with wide joy.

318

31

Surlina rode Muller's horse, facing into the wind, her cloth jacket whipping around her body. Soon her ears began to ache. Then she felt dizzy and light-headed as the wind wailed and the cold crept into her bones. "I can't be sick," she moaned, but already she felt the fever seeping into her blood while her flesh crawled with chills. By the time they reached camp, she was weak and delirious from fever and exhaustion.

Lieutenant Turk caught her as she toppled from the horse. "Get this woman to the hospital tent!" she heard faintly, then a new wave of chills and darkness swept over her.

When she woke up, she realized that a lot of time had passed. The frozen journey from Friar's Mire seemed ages ago. Had they caught Muller? She rolled onto her side, feeling stiffness in her wrist and arm. She touched her face, wondering if the bruises had disappeared. Her skin felt puffy beneath the eyes and tender across her cheekbones. How long had she been here? She looked down at the cotton hopsacking gown. Long enough for someone to thaw her out, clean her up and let her sleep in a private tent. She tested her legs on the floor and found she could move without dizziness or pain. Her feet were slightly tender, per-haps from the freezing hours spent in the wet boots, but she walked steadily, lifted the tent flap and peeked out.

"My stars, woman! Get back in there!" growled a masculine voice. Suddenly a man loomed up from the dim outer room of the tent. "You're not supposed to raise your head or your voice! Get back in bed!" He moved toward her briskly.

She ran for the cot, jumping in and pulling the

covers up to her chin. "I'm well!" she protested timidly. "I want to get up! I have business with General Grant!"

"Oh, no you don't! That's precisely the man I'm supposed to keep you away from. Sherman's orders. He said the first thing you'd ask for when you came around was Grant." The man chuckled and pulled a chair to the side of the cot, planted himself across it backward, leaning over the rim and tilting toward her. "I'm your doctor—Michael Beshoar—and you are to follow doctor's orders, just as I'm to follow Sherman's."

She inspected Michael Beshoar. He had a broad forehead and intelligent hazel eyes. She liked him immediately, except for his professed duty of keeping her from Sam. "That damned Sherman!" she blurted. She was relieved to see the surgeon smile.

"Hold on," laughed Dr. Beshoar. "Sherman only said you'd wake up talking—not cussing." He checked her pulse and touched her forehead, checking for fever. "Now, I'm indecently curious as to why Sherman considered you contagious. As far as I can tell, you had only a touch of pneumonia. Tell me, are you a deadly threat in some other way to our commanding general?"

She threw back her head and laughed. "I'm a tigress! And just wait till I get my claws into that red-bearded, belly-achin' Sherman! I'll tear his central headquarters to pieces!" She stretched her arms over her head, flexing her hands, ready for battle. She cursed Sherman roundly.

Dr. Beshoar put up his hands for quiet. "Enough! I see that whatever disease laid you low has not subdued your temper. Now, you may boss *me* without mercy, but you may not sabotage my medical quarters. Since you're up and about and obviously in high spirits, I'll have to ask you to move to the laundry barracks. Sherman can post a new guard on you there. I need this private room for a serious case—a deserter with an infected arm. I may have to amputate."

"Have they caught Thad Muller? Praise be!" She stifled her outcry of joy, trying not to be so pleased

320

that a man might have to have his arm cut off. But in truth she felt little compassion. She would even forgive Sherman a bit if he'd managed to bring in Muller.

"All right," said the doctor. "Out with you! You'll find some clothes and boots which I've scavenged from the camp. Stay out of trouble until I can escort you to the laundry barracks."

She begged him insistently, "Will *you* tell General Grant I'm here?"

"And find myself horsewhipped by Sherman? Indeed no! Besides, rumor has it no one sees Grant these days."

"Busy?"

"Or drunk."

"I don't believe it!" Oh, she must redouble her efforts to get to Sam. She giggled with relief at finding herself alive and well, Thad Muller captured and ill, and Sam no farther away than across the camp. She smiled congenially at the doctor and promised perfect behavior. The moment he left, she scrambled into the boots, quartermaster's shirt and small-sized federal blue breeches he'd scrounged for her. What a considerate man! For a moment, she felt inconsiderate at what she was about to do. Then she deftly removed the mantle and wick from the tent lantern, poured the lamp oil onto the bedding, struck the flint and set the pillow ablaze. Covering the sound of breaking glass by crushing the mantle beneath the blanket, she broke a jagged section of lantern to use as a knife. Cutting quickly, she ripped straight through the back wall of the tent. By the time she heard cries of "Fire! Fire in' the surgical tents!" she had rounded the cattle pen on her way to find Sam.

She found herself in a genuine traffic jam of horses, men, wagons and carriages attempting to pass each other. The predominant movement seemed to be toward the river, so she joined the crowd going in that direction. Falling in beside two sergeants, she inquired directly, "Anyone seen Grant today?" She tried to walk and sound like a soldier.

"He's coming overland with his boat, they say!"

They ignored her and went on talking among themselves, she listening eagerly. "Imagine a boat coming overland," said one, shaking his head. "Towed by half an army! Ought to make Lake Providence by afternoon."

"Clever scheme, you have to admit. Grant hauls that steamer into the lake, then floats all the way to Vicksburg's city limits!" They moved ahead briskly, apparently anxious to watch the spectacle of a boat roaming the dry land.

So that's where everyone was heading! To see the launching of Grant's steamer! For a moment she wondered about her reception when they met. After all, she'd left Rosie Mound without saying good-bye. Then, shortly after her departure, the whole plantation had been blown apart.

Crowds were pressing across the fields. Soldiers lined the road. Sutlers had drawn up wagons, selling cakes, pies and coffee. Money from pay envelopes was changing hands in roadside poker games. The sunny day seemed a holiday with everyone taking time off to watch a parade. She saw that the local harlots knew it was payday, too. Fancy girls in wagons and barouches pranced their horses up and down the road, calling to the men and handing out little cards with directions to their tents. Far ahead Surlina could see the stern of the *Tigress* high in the air.

Then she saw Sam. He galloped by on horseback, ragged and muddy, his eyes dull, beard unkempt, wearing a dusty uniform and threadbare yellow gloves.

Startled, she called to him. He reined in, rubbed his eyes, then pulled his horse aside and walked it back to where she stood. He did not dismount. Neither did he smile. He sat in the saddle of his brown stallion, frowning, not at all happy to see her. She quivered inside, seeking courage to speak.

She assessed his appearance more closely, disturbed at his thin neck, prominent blood vessels, dirty hair and harassed eyes. "Sam, you're shaking."

"The weather."

They had covered the formalities in tones as clipped

as if they'd been reading telegrams to each other. The mutual antagonism had them both shaking.

"What are you doing here, Surlina? And in those clothes?"

"I came to report a deserter."

His eyes blazed. "From which side, madam?"

His temper was showing more than she'd ever seen. It was such a rare display of his anger, she wondered again if he were physically ill. He slapped his gloves together, knocking dust into the air. "You witch! You green-eyed harlot! You played me for the fool, then thought to abandon Rosie Mound with an act of sabotage for me to remember you by!"

"Not true!"

"Surlina, don't insult me with more lies!"

As usual, when attacked she sought to turn the assault by counterattack. She looked at him carefully, seeing he was shaking beneath his jacket. His eyes were unsteady. He had no sash, no sword, no decent gloves, no starch about him at all. Was he sick? Or drinking? She charged back at him, "So! The great general ends up drunk on his horse!"

"Not true!"

A strained silence settled between them. Suddenly he held out a quaking hand. "Come, Surlina, before we harm each other. Our words are loaded guns." He swung down from his mount. The effort to stand without falling required obvious concentration.

Was he exhausted? Overburdened with work? That would account for his tremors. Or malaria! That would explain his poor color and faded eyes. Suddenly she felt protective, terribly concerned about him. She apologized for her accusations, feeling love for him renew itself despite her better judgment.

The crowd had pushed to the water's edge now. Soldiers crowded around Grant, one asking him to break a bottle of champagne over the *Tigress*'s bow as the boat was relaunched. He declined, looking embarrassed. Sherman came racing up on his horse, displaying rare good humor. "Ah, Grant," he called gaily. "A little jollification is in order. I've surveyed the back

323

country behind the lake, and there's a fine plantation with an excellent wine cellar. Let us cross Lake Providence for the maiden cruise of your steamer! We can take along the staff—bands and ladies included.

Surlina was shocked. *Sherman* suggesting a party! Obviously he hadn't realized she was present. She turned slightly to face him, making a little crowing noise to attract his attention.

He glanced at her, apparently saw only the quartermaster's shirt, then did a double take. She smiled at him and executed a comic curtsy. "Thank you for the kind invitation to cruise the lake," she murmured, realizing she had the upper hand in this wrestling match.

Sherman blanched, looking between Grant and Surlina to see what had transpired between them. But he could not back down on his loudly proclaimed arrangements. "Of course you may come, Miss Defore. It will be a pleasure to welcome you aboard—"

"My own boat?" She loved riling up this man. "The steamer was only a gift. I'm thinking of taking it back if Sam doesn't behave."

The skirmish ended with Sherman captitulating. He acted as if he hadn't seen her at all. "All right then, a party!" he proclaimed. "Agreed, Sam?"

Grant seemed too preoccupied or ill to care. He waved away his second in command, answering offhandedly, "Whatever you want, Cump. See to it."

Sherman reined his horse and was off in a gallop.

She dreaded going aboard. She didn't want to see the grand salon full of horses and hay or the ladies' parlor stuffed with muddy boots, but late in the afternoon she stepped across the gangway.

So much rearranging had been done to her steamer, she could not find her way. Occasionally Surlina spotted something she recognized, but most of the items had suffered badly.

She staked out quarters for herself in the pilot's cubicle behind the upper wheelhouse. Determined not to wear boots and pants to supper, she prowled the ship for women's clothes. Once she'd devised a dancing dress from a shawl and chambermaid's skirt. Now, she'd fashion tablecloths together if necessary!

In the galley she found supper preparations in full swing.

A giggle, soprano and flirtatious, jolted her. She cleared her throat to warn whoever was dallying behind the cookstoves of her presence. Then she pulled back silently as she spied a pair of women's blue kid buskin slippers lying on the floor. From somewhere farther back in the galley the teasing laugh sounded again, this time accompanied by a masculine counterpoint. A brocade gown skittered across the deck, stopping by the garbage pails. In an instant she had scooped the dress and shoes into her arms and fled the kitchen, trying hard to contain her laughter.

Safe in her pilothouse cubicle, she dressed for dinner, delighted with the soft blue slippers and violet brocade gown. Just her size! Half-sleeves and full skirt for dancing! Perfect.

When Sam did not appear in the wardroom for supper, she went in search of him. She spotted him on the starboard side of the hurricane deck, staggering along with one hand in front of him.

"Sam!" She rushed to him, putting out her arms to steady him. He leaned against the railing, mopping his brow with a bandanna.

From behind them in the twilight darkness she heard a snicker. Then a snide voice called out from the shadows, "Old Gentleman Tipsy got you, General?"

Outraged, she put her arms around him. "Come to your cabin. You're ill."

"I thought the air would help. I have about outlasted these chills and shakes which have plagued me for a month. This southern climate sets my lungs to working hard as pumps to keep from filling with phlegm." He leaned against her. Softly he admitted, "I was trying to avoid you, Surlina."

She withdrew her arm as if burned. "You want me to leave?"

"No," he said quietly. "I want very much for you to stay with me." He straightened his shoulders as if a

325

final decision had been made. They moved along the deck toward his stateroom. She was dismayed that with chills racking his chest, people still besieged him. There were endless details that it seemed no one but he could attend. Where was that fussbudget aide Rawlins who should handle all these petty matters? And now here came Parsons, the supply officer, with a stack of requisitions to be signed. No wonder Sam was sick. Even if he drank too much, he had plenty of cause!

Grant finished signing the last requisition slip with a shaky hand. As he handed it to Parsons, he remarked casually, "By the way, while you are procuring that six million rounds of ammunition, those five thousand pounds of bacon and two hundred wagons, would you please find this lady a set of gates?" He smiled for the first time since they'd met. "Large metal gates."

She looked at him and laughed. Parsons stood at attention, bewildered. Grant laughed, too. He looked relaxed for the first time all day, offered her his arm and walked steadily toward his cabin.

She confessed, "Sam, I'm worried about you. The battles are taking too big a toll. Like tonight, you have no time to enjoy the pleasantries."

"Battles, battles! No way to avoid them. No chance for—" he looked at her with longing, "for pleasantries."

He had seemingly summed up his convictions. Keep the battles going. Don't back off. Don't spend years planning like the generals in the East. No, meet things headlong, like today when he'd greeted her with accusations of sabotage. He was succinct and direct, without empty gestures. She reveled in her ability to understand him, to share his innermost personality.

In the stateroom, Surlina found his things in their usual disarray. He sank into a chair and smoked his pipe instead of his normal cigars. She rummaged through his gear until she found a gray flannel dressing gown with red trim, red belt and red piping on the pocket. When she urged him to put it on, he looked uncertain again. "And you need to eat," she decided. "What sounds good?"

326

"Nothing. Simply sit with me, my dear."

"They are having steak and rabbit in the officers' mess." She tried to tempt his appetite. "Food will help your strength." She took his hand and held it.

He let his fingers curl over hers, sighing as if grateful for the touch of human companionship. He lifted his arms to encircle her neck, then let his fingers slide across her shoulders. "How far we've traveled to end up back on this steamer. How often our paths have diverged. Now we are together more as victims than lovers." He laid his head tenderly against her shoulder.

A little shiver of delight passed through her. After all these months, they still wanted each other! She could sense it in his touch, the lingering tone of his voice, in her own inner expectancy. She turned her head slightly to caress his cheek. "Sam, I think I'm good for you. Sherman doesn't think so. And Beshoar might not prescribe me for your ills, but I'm feeling more like a lover and less like a victim every moment!"

She turned her lips toward his and he sought her eagerly. Her heart fluttered as his arms clasped her, his copper beard tickled her cheeks and she felt the excited rise and fall of his chest. He lifted his mouth from hers, smiling. "Ah, Surlina! You make me strong as a stallion! Yes, bring me a supper tray. Oysters, cucumbers, vinegar, chili sauce—all my favorite dishes."

She stood by the door, uncertain for a moment if she dared tease him. "Oysters are fine this time of year . . . and quite an aphrodisiac, I understand."

Sure enough, he blushed. The pink coloring toned up his cheeks and set his pale blue eyes to dancing. She smiled. "Now see that you have recovered your wits by the time I return." She wantonly let her eyes travel downward below his belt buckle. "And see that your strength is at its peak as well!"

"God's word, Surlina! You must be the one who's had her nose in the bottle to let your tongue wag so loosely!" He seemed mildly startled, not genuinely shocked.

She laughed at him. "How can you command thousands of hell-raising soldiers and be so prim? Or is it that you don't understand women? Don't you realize females curse, sing, shout and squeal with delight just like men? Have you been alone so long that you've forgotten?"

Suddenly she saw he was no longer joking. He crossed the room in a sudden bound, seizing her wrist. "Or have you been with a man so recently as to remember in detail?"

A spark of jealousy! The first time she'd ever seen his steady, quiet reserve give way. But the subject was not one either wished to confront. She put her arms around his shoulders, lowering her head in a confessional pose. "I've never asked assurances from you, Sam. I've never asked pledges of you. There's no question of home, family or sacred honor between us. But, oh, Sam! Tonight I want you!"

She trembled in his gentle embrace, proud she'd said the word, half-afraid he might not respond. But there was no doubt in his caress which traveled over her body, seeking her throat with his lips, her breasts with his hands. He was heavier and stronger than she remembered. And his voice was softer as he whispered, "I love you. I'm not good with words—"

"Then tell me with your kisses!" Suddenly she pushed at him playfully. "Oh, I've nearly forgotten your dinner tray altogether!" She covered her warm face with her hands in mock amazement. She nipped at his earlobe and rushed from the stateroom.

For the next hour, she badgered the galley master into concocting the delicacies Sam wanted. She felt a bit uneasy in the kitchen, wondering what had become of the giggling girl who had found her dress and shoes stolen. Surlina left when the cook began to eye her suspiciously.

Carrying the tray carefully, she made her way back along the deck. Approaching the stateroom, she encountered a messenger hurrying from the opposite direction. He, too, was heading for the stateroom. She tried to prevent him from knocking, but he made it to the door first and rapped sharply. Grant opened the door. He was obviously freshly bathed, his hair still damp, beard neatly trimmed, attired in pajamas and dressing gown.

The young messenger was apparently unsure whom he was confronting. He said hesitantly, "These are for the general," and extended a sheaf of dispatches.

Sam silently put out his hand.

"No," persisted the soldier, "I mean for the general —personally."

She saw a little smile of modesty part Sam's lips, but he did not embarrass the messenger. He simply took the papers and murmured, "Yes, thank you."

As the messenger saluted and left, she held the tray toward Sam. "This, too, is for the general—personally." She tossed her head and posed provocatively. "And this, too."

He laughed, took the tray and gestured her back inside the cabin. He had obviously done some housekeeping in her absence. The books were neatly stowed, the ashtrays empty, his uniforms hung on pegs and the desk cleared of papers. To her delight, she saw Peter Defore's silver-armed rocking chair. Why, Sam must have kept it safe all these months! She ran over and sat down in the chair, murmuring happily, "I never expected to see this again!"

"To be honest, Surlina, I never expected to see you again after Rosie Mound."

She inhaled sharply. For a few quiet moments, she sat silently rocking. Sam put the supper tray on the desk and sat down, taking the sheaf of messages to read. She decided that truth was as good a commodity as any. "I asked Julien Rainbeau to steal a pair of gates from Rosie Mound. Blowing the place apart was his own idea." She waited to see how Sam would respond.

He said nothing, gave no clues by frowns or smiles, simply sat silent, eating oysters.

"I could have saved all three of us—you, me, and Captain Rainbeau—a great deal of grief. My silver gates were not there."

"So I heard."

She skipped several months of details. "But, Sam,

329

I know where they are now! After I chased them in every direction, they've ended up at the bottom of Friar's Mire!"

He consoled her gently without offering to help her. "You're not the only one to have misadventures this winter, darling. I cannot get my armies anywhere near Vicksburg! All I've discovered is innumerable routes to failure!"

She felt close to him, sharing their troubles. They talked openly, recounting their problems, their rebuffs and consolations. At least they were agreed on one point: the best thing that had happened all winter was the capture of Thad Muller. "No, the second-best thing," argued Sam. "You, Surlina. You are the *best* thing that's happened to me this long, cold season."

"You are a person worth searching for once in a lifetime," she told him. Surlina thought the joy of being near him would make her giddy if she didn't soon hold him in her arms.

His hand lightly stroked the back of her neck and then he bent down to kiss the top of her head. At that moment, there was a loud knock which echoed through the stateroom, instantly shattering the rapport. "Who is it?" questioned Sam gruffly.

"It's McIntyre, sir! Of the Missouri Volunteers."

Sam opened the door.

"General," said the messenger breathlessly, "the rebs are up to their old tricks! Scouts brought word. Crews from the packet boats have cut the levee at the far end of Lake Providence! We'll be high and dry here in forty-eight hours."

Sam snorted to himself as he dismissed the soldier. "So they learned a trick or two from our dynamiting at Yazoo Pass! That settles it! In two days this place will be too wet for men and horses, but not deep enough for steamboats!" He sat down, head in hands, then looked up, snapping his fingers. "Rainbeau again! Of course! It has his mark of genius all over it."

"Have you met him, Sam?" She couldn't help wondering how the two men would react to each other—

Sam so full of detail, certain and unassuming, and Julien so dashing, spirited and imaginative.

"I only know of him. But he's as good a man as can be found, I'll wager. Even so, men like Rainbeau cannot dissolve the Union!"

All at once Surlina believed him fully. Despite speeches of secession, despite vigorous shaking, the nation would not dissolve. Amid the terrible fighting, an underlying brotherhood remained. She touched his cheek. "Sam, you are a man of great loyalty . . . and great emotion."

The surprise on his face was genuine. His blue eyes were no longer dimmed with harassment and decision making as he answered, "The first I never questioned. As for the second, I never knew—until you, Surlina—I never knew . . ." He pressed her hands against his heart.

As she came into his arms, she felt not only his strength but his stature. He was no taller than she, but he gave a sense of the wide space his army must inhabit, the large spaces his mind must invest. She kissed him again and again, as if never to have her fill of him. Breathlessly, she insisted, "Sam, please believe I did not sabotage Rosie Mound. I am not—" She broke off. Past history was unimportant. Her arms wound around his neck. "I never thought I had a stake in this war before. And now, I have no airs of being a lady. Tonight, with you, I am only what I am."

His voice was gentle. "I have no airs either, as to being a great general or a fine gentleman." He held her close. "For this one night, then, we are simply what we are."

She felt her body crying out to touch him. She leaned against him trembling. "Oh, Sam, let me say the words! Let me tell you with every breath I draw, I long for you!" In the back of her mind she felt a hot rising of passion, then a cold pang of guilt. Hadn't she said nearly the same words—and meant them just as honestly—to Julien?

Lost in the rapture of Sam's embrace, she thought how a year ago she'd known no man. It pleased her to

331

hear Sam's rapid breathing, feel his pulsebeat, hear him whisper as he touched her breasts, "Such beauty! Such beauty!"

There was no awkwardness any longer, none of the blushing or teasing they'd shared earlier in the evening. Clothes were simply taken off, the covers spread back on the bunk, the pillow fluffed. He was tidy and considerate, hanging her stolen dress on a peg beside his wool jacket. She sensed he had no more flair for the dramatic in lovemaking than he had in battle.

However, she was misguided by her own imagination. In the darkness and security of his locked cabin, he had no need to pose for an outer world which wanted reserve and strategy. Now, he could indulge himself as a man. He moved beside her on the bed, circling her waist affectionately with one arm, then stretching full length as if delighted to have his clothing shed. "Surlina, do you know when I realized I was in love with you?"

"In Memphis, you told me—"

"No. Long before that. It was when I thought guns stopped roaring whenever you smiled. And later, at Rosie Mound, I found I forgot strategy and went off buying lockets."

She turned on her side to find how their bodies fit, to delight in the heightened sensation of smooth skin against hardened silkiness. "I still have the locket, Sam. With your sketch in it." Surlina burrowed her head to nuzzle his jaw.

He stroked her face, tracing the pattern of her lips, across her eyelids, around her ears. "You're as dazzling as the first time I saw you, when your long legs were kicking wildly at me and those emerald eyes spitting fire."

"A tigress does not always claw and fight. Sometimes she is content to lie quietly in the dark." She stretched on her back, tilting her head back and arching her throat as he kissed it gently, rubbing her neck with his beard.

Their mouths met in kisses of prolonged ecstasy, astonishing her with the way they began languidly and sweetly, then moved into deliberate probing which set her trembling. A little convulsion of delight passed through her, making her breasts heave and her mouth pull against his. They breathed heavily, harmonizing their rhythms. It all seemed so natural, strong as a sea's tidal pull, inevitable as the moon's waning.

He cushioned his hands beneath her head, the rising cadence of his thrusting tongue making her tingle and yearn for his mouth against her breast. She offered; he responded by taking the rosy tips between his lips, kneading gently, then sucking firmly. He cupped his hands wide, holding her fully, massaging the outer globe, then flicking his fingers back and forth across the darker portion. Her nipples stiffened and stood out prominently, sending flashes of sensation to her womb. When she kissed him in return, it seemed they were woven together with threads of their own substance.

"Take me, Sam."

"Yes, yes! Let me pour my soul into yours!"

Pleasure ran over her skin like scented oil, beading up in little spots of sensitivity—her spine, hips, wrists and tongue. The turmoil inside her grew, making her undulate to seek him. She wanted to make this moment of surrender last forever. When she felt the tip of his sex touch the outer lips, she stifled her desire to push against him and envelop him all at once.

His tongue flicked caressingly against her lips. Again she tried to hold back, but pleasure was making her curl upward against him. Then warmth coursed through her as he entered fully, with a moan of satisfaction and delight. Vibrant contractions shook her, making her arch and lift her hips. He slid his hands beneath her buttocks, squeezing firmly, holding her tightly. One hand moved atop her, pressing firmly on her belly, then lower, massaging circles on the soft mound, opening the lips and touching lightly. She felt urgent sparks within her, brilliant as fireworks, shooting in all directions.

She grew desperate, aching for release. He leaned over, whispering tenderly, "You are my love, my woman . . ." Then she felt his own palpitations growing frenzied. She let the fog of desire blot out everything except the peaking rhythm. How lovely this mingling wildness could be! The hot friction of his thrusts now weakened her. She couldn't breathe, couldn't moan or speak. Could no longer capture his rhythm or share his movement. Suddenly she went stiff, bright rings of painful rapture spreading from her center. A melting heat devoured her, contracted, burst. She dug her nails into his shoulders and gave a piercing cry. A second later, she felt his shuddering throb give way to a single immense wave of power.

Spent but not weary, she crooned to him, untangling his hair, rubbing his shoulders. He made no move to leave her, so she locked her arms across the small of his back as if to stay entwined forever. She shivered slightly and felt the immediate response reflected in his skin.

"We'll not sleep," he whispered. "Come, sit with me in the rocking chair. Let me hold you."

He positioned the chair so it could rock smoothly without creaking against the desk or bunk, then sat down, took her on his lap and pulled a blanket around them. She nestled against him, her legs crooked over the silver arm of the chair. The gentle to-and-fro motion wedged her head against his cheek, her breast against his chest, her hips to his sex. One hand she brought up around his neck, the other traced his features, learning intimately the contour of his lips and eyes. Slowly the rocking made her drowsy and she stopped touching him, only passively resting and letting the gentle movement blend their flesh together.

But she fought sleep. This time was too precious to spend unconscious, even securely wrapped in his arms. She tried to praise him, to tell him of the happiness she felt. "It's like starlight," she explained in hushed tones. "It starts from darkness and then moves through me, taking me completely. Oh, Sam, you were wonderful!"

He planted a feather kiss on her forehead and she saw his eyelids flutter in contentment. She sought to memorize his presence, so deep and satisfying. The

334

masculine scent of his beard combed with lemon water, the movement of his eyes when he looked at her body, the striking silhouette when he turned his head to kiss her breast.

She felt a shifting of his legs beneath her. "Am I too heavy?" she asked, maneuvering to take some of the weight off his lap. Then she realized he was aroused again, seeking her in this sitting position. A little thrill made her feel airborne, as if this combination of slippery moisture and movement would be a secret adventure. He lifted her slightly, positioning her, then pressed her downward, settling her over him.

She leaned against him while his hands sought the arms of the chair, guiding the movement so that their bodies could reflect the gliding. She felt ensnared, not having to move, as she felt him extend into her secret recesses. She held her breath, wanting to capture all the vibrations deep within and let nothing escape. Every inch of their flesh seemed magnetized together, uniting in a tender give-and-take.

The chair moved back and forth, taking them with it like a trapeze swinging through the air. At the backward apex of movement, he touched his heels to the floor, stopping the rhythm for a lingering second of deep penetration. Then the slow forward thrust would bring them upright again. Her pulse quickened until she could hear it beating in her ears. The warmth of her lips extended down through her breasts and into the curves of their mingled spirits. The love she felt seemed alive, moving and streaking like a meteor.

This time she did not cry out in climax but silently she sagged against him, holding his straining arms as if clinging to a life raft. The rumble of consummation passed through him as she felt the liquid throbs touch her womb. She loved this sensation of extreme union, like a little fountain within her. The magic of desire washed through her again.

But now she could absorb nothing more. She felt fragile and luminous, like a silken crescent moon. Even as she felt weak, Sam seemed stronger. He carried her to the bed, striding as if he owned the world. The steady confidence on his face was as solid as his step.

As he placed the pillow under her head, she put her arms around his neck. "Will you have regrets, Sam?"

He sat down on the side of the bed. "Yes, many. I'll regret loving you and then never truly making you my own. I'll regret leaving you time and time again. I'll regret—"

"That doesn't matter." She held him against her fiercely. "Only never regret tonight! Never regret our love." She felt somber, thinking of what lay ahead for them. "*Forget* tonight if you must. But Sam—dearest Sam—never regret it!"

32

Before Surlina left for Vicksburg under a medical pass from Dr. Beshoar, she made a sketch of the *Tigress,* stranded in Lake Providence, and left it pinned to Sam's pillow. She drew a tiny tigress frolicking on the deck, clambering over the rails as if to dive off. How complex were her feelings for Sam! She thought him thorough, dependable and infinitely capable, like steel armor. Why, then, did she compare him to Julien and feel deprived? When she thought of Julien, she felt charged, as if he were a force which might break loose at any moment. All she could really sense was that she loved two men, had commitments to them both, and that her night with Sam aboard the steamer would stand as a definite break in what had happened before and after in her life.

Back in Vicksburg, she took up the role of Tandy's guardian. For the rest of the winter she brooded, wondering if the army had hanged Thad Muller, wondering if Julien had finished hating her, wondering if Dottie had forgiven the loss of the cotton wagon and wondering if there might be a way to liberate the silver from

Friar's Mire. With the transportation and communication links cut between Vicksburg and the rest of the South, Surlina knew that the silver would be a greater asset than ever. If she had the money, she could hire foragers to find food, bribe pirates to bring in medicines, assure Tandy of a healthy, fat baby. She worried that Tandy wasn't getting enough to eat.

With the coming spring, Surlina felt the sunken silver sucking at her like a leech. She excused her obsession as the need to care for her sister. Occasionally she'd burst out, "Friar's Mire is only a damned ditch! There has to be a way!"

Tandy gave her strange looks until Surlina finally explained. "I can trust you, Tandy. With Cabell in England and the rest of the Confederate Council playing games in Richmond, my secret is safe with you. I'm going to outfit an expedition to Friar's Mire—even if I have to hire Mullermen!"

"I don't think you should try it," counseled Tandy timidly. "Where would you get winches and cables and anything strong enough to heave a wagon out of quicksand?"

"A boat!" cried Surlina with sudden inspiration. "Why did I always think I had to drag the gates up on shore? Of course! A boat can pull them much easier." She hardly dared admit her next idea. "I'll get Julien to bring the *Quail* up Friar's Mire!"

Tandy shook her head. "From what you've told me of Captain Rainbeau, I doubt he'll help you."

"I doubt he'd give me the time of day! But he'll probably bend over backward to do a favor for his Aunt Dottie. I'll tell him it's her cotton wagon we're trying to retrieve."

Tandy fanned her pale face. "You'd *lie?*"

"Not only that, I'll wring your neck if you breathe a word to anyone!"

Properly shocked, Tandy went back to sewing. But Surlina noticed later that her sister spent a long afternoon closeted with the maid. Then the black girl disappeared, came back an hour later, disappeared again. Was Tandy sending messages? To whom?

The answer became apparent in the evening. A knock on the front door was followed by Pat Martha's excited exclamations, "Yes, sir! Come right in, sir! Miss Surlina, a gentlemen here to see you—Master Ramsey Arnauld."

Of all the people she *didn't* want to see! Surlina shot Tandy a disdainfull look, then went into the front parlor to confront her adversary. "So you've come to prevent me from doing a good deed in Dottie's behalf!" She planted her hands belligerently on her hips, smoothing down the housedress she wore. She knew she looked tired and worn from the long winter and bad food, yet she held her head high and shoulders back to meet his handsomeness on its own terms.

He looked as well fed and rested as if he'd wintered on the Côte d'Azur. He seated himself in the Windsor chair and tapped his walking stick on the threadbare rug. "Has Julien paid you no calls this winter?"

"You know he hasn't!" She wanted to take his walking stick and beat him over the head with it. Sitting opposite him, she tried to maintain her composure. "But I intend to seek his aid in pulling Dottie's wagon out of the bayou—as I'm sure Tandy has already informed you."

"Yes, yes," he agreed hurriedly. "And he's just the man for the job. I'll send him to see you tomorrow morning bright and early."

Her shock was absolute. What was going on in Ramsey's treacherous mind to be so accommodating?

"Now, Surlina, I don't know exactly what you're up to, but cotton wagons are as good an excuse as any. My interest in sending Julien into Friar's Mire is more military. The Union gunboats are attempting to thread their way in that direction, sneaking in from Steele's Bayou and Chickasaw Creek. So, for once, our aims coincide."

'Well, perhaps Tandy had her wits about her after all', thought Surlina.

Ramsey continued. "Julien's been reluctant to leave the Mississippi. This tale of woe of Dottie's wagon and your personal invitation ought to be just the trick

338

to lure him into the backwaters." He stood up, apparently ready to leave.

She stood to escort him to the door. Suddenly he leaned toward her and captured her hand between his fingers. "Why this frigid demeanor, my dear? And this hand like ice? I had hoped to find your green eyes sparkling and your heart beating passionately for me." He pulled her against him roughly. "Since Julien is no longer in competition for your favors, I thought perhaps you'd extend me more hospitality." He nibbled her fingertips.

"Never, Ramsey!" she told him, trying to pull away. "I wouldn't feed you poison on your deathbed!"

"Then perhaps you could nurse me back to health as you did Sam Grant! Oh, that was some miraculous cure you performed on him, Surlina! I'm shocked he doesn't send for you once, twice, three times a week!"

She gasped in astonishment.

Ramsey went on crudely. "You must be quite serviceable, to keep two stallions snorting and frothing at the bit. Or do I underestimate your capacity? Are you anybody's dog that hunts?"

She reared back and slapped him hard, jarring his face and making him drop the walking stick. A huge red welt raised up instantly, like a brand. Gingerly he put a hand to his face, disbelieving. He moved to the door, then spoke quietly. "I must have hit very near the truth to have incurred such wrath. The truth is that you are a slut and a—"

She threw his walking stick like a hatchet. He caught it in mid-air, ducked out the door and ran.

As the *Quail* nosed about, searching for the poorly marked channel which led to Friar's Mire, Surlina stood on the bow, rehearsing how to admit to Julien that he was dragging more out of the bayou than Dottie's wagon. He'd been so agreeable! So polite. So distant. This morning he'd called for her, escorted her aboard, brought her chicory and never once looked directly at her.

Surlina kept her eyes on him every moment. She

339

watched his casual saunter, the way his boots creaked and his shirt hung loose over his denim pants. She noticed every detail, how the creases beneath his gray eyes were deeper, the high cheekbones more prominent. He seemed totally unconcerned, chewing on the end of a stick and whistling along with the birds in the overhead branches.

The bayou was closing in now, trees locking branches overhead. The March sun made the water look sleek. The trees at water's edge were two feet thick, hung with Spanish moss, grapevines and trumpet flowers. Bougainvillea and briars tangled and cascaded like lacy purple curtains, locking out sunlight, locking in the dank smell of swamp, mud and animal life.

She asked Haloo about the prospects of encountering Union boats.

"Excellent," he assured her.

She could see plenty of évidence that David Porter's boats had preceded the *Quail*. The Union tugs and mortars had been forced to butt their way through the winding bayou, uprooting logs, hitting driftwood and half-submerged trees.

When Julien came on deck, Surlina asked him outright, "If Porter has mortars and tugs and you have only the *Quail* . . . Oh, you don't intend to fight so many ships, do you?"

"Goddamn, yes! Can't wait!"

She looked at him in alarm. "Your impatience scares me more than Porter. This isn't Island Number Ten, Julien! This isn't a fair fight at all."

"I *want* a war of impatience! There'd be no gray-haired admirals if I had my way! Wars should be fought fast, by cowards and worthless fools like myself. I say let's roll up our sleeves and go at it. I'm thirty-four and tired of living! I'm ready to let the Rainbeau curse catch up with me right here in Friar's Mire."

My God, he was all but admitting this was a suicide raid! If she admitted it was a foray to find her silver as well, he'd probably be enraged enough to kill her.

"Surlina, it is not necessary to scowl at me. Steele's

340

Bayou will fight Porter better than I can. The farther in the Yankees go, the tighter they'll be stuck. All I have to do is be the plug in the end of the bottleneck. We'll get Dottie's wagon and head home."

She smiled, not reassured at all. Now she was more petrified than ever to tell him the truth. Clammy inside and out, she feared that the longer she waited, the more severe his reaction might be. But her courage was nonexistent as he spoke to her again.

"Surlina, I owe you many apologies for my behavior the last time we met. I let you go ashore without saying good-bye. I think more kindly of you now, helping Dottie. Today will mark a new beginning for us. I will shed my mistrust and beg you with all my heart to give me another chance." He held himself rigid, not openly looking at her but clearly making an apology which had been on his mind for a long time. Yet he hadn't the nerve to take her hand, search the depths of her eyes or bend his lips to hers.

She could hear indecision making his musical voice tremulous and see pride clouding his eyes. She must tell him! She reached for him, flinging her arms around him for one agonized second. Then she faced him openly. She felt the color draining from her face. Ducking behind her hands, unable to look him in the eyes, she blurted, "The silver gates are in Friar's Mire!" She cringed as if expecting a certain blow.

From behind her fingers she saw him look stunned. Then he exploded in laughter. "By God in heaven and the devil in hell! I should have guessed why you were so eager to go forth to battle! Only other women shrink from confrontations. You invent them!" He danced up and down, swatted her hands away from her face and kissed her full and hard.

At that moment she spotted the remains of the ferry station. "We're nearly where the wagon rolled into the water last January." She pointed out the landmarks to him, trying to judge distances and estimate currents. "Maybe here? Or downstream a little more? Do you think we'll find it? What are the odds, Julien?"

"Doesn't matter, since they are not in our favor."

He was stern but she saw the magic twinkle in his eyes which meant he liked the adventure, if not the possible outcome.

He ordered the engines cut. "Boys, we're going fishing." He studied the current, motioning her to do the same. "We'll haul out this wagon, then see if we can't make some hot work for the Yankee gunboats."

With the noise of the engines gone, the bayou seemed darker and quieter. From far off she could hear muffled shouts and the light purring of other engines. "Porter?"

Julien nodded and sent Haloo overland to ascertain the Union fleet's whereabouts. He ordered a launch prepared. "I'll have Professor Box paddle you about, Surlina. You can poke and peer to your heart's content."

"You're not coming?" Suddenly her elation was diminished by his somber voice. She lowered her eyes. "You really don't want me to find it, do you? It's still between us, isn't it?"

He nodded, looking melancholy and tired. "But I hope you find it this time, Surlina. I honestly do."

"But . . . why?"

"Because your eyes are still hungry for it. I fought against you before on the wrong grounds. Until you get that blasted money back, you'll always be after it—using up your years and passion."

At that moment, Haloo's excited cry rang out from the far shore. "Captain! Ahoy, *Quail!* Get underway! They're coming. Porter's gunboat is backing down the bayou. He's just beyond the second bend."

"Swim!" shouted Julien to the boy, motioning him to make for the boat. "Start engines!" He muttered excitedly, "Hell's going to flop now!"

Surlina ran to hold the rope ladder for Haloo to scramble aboard. Then to her shock, she realized Julien was taking the boat *forward.* It lurched for the first bend, chugging and tossing scum from shore to shore.

She was much too frightened to take cover, too excited to go below. Julien was actually careening through the bayou to do battle at terrible odds. Daring, irresponsible, suicidal madman!

The ship rounded the bend speedily, making waves ahead and behind, churning up mud. Suddenly there were shouts. She peered ahead to see the enemy, then bit her lips in surprise. A willow bed! The channel was completely choked with willow sprouts. No wonder Haloo had mentioned only one gunboat coming back to fight—the others were stuck tight in the saplings.

How marvelous! A whole fleet like sitting ducks, just waiting for Julien to capture them.

Surlina examined the bayou carefully. The limber willow shoots grew up from the bottom of the slough as densely as if they were a field of cornstalks. It was easy to see why the Union boats had chugged into the mess. The litle willows looked as if they would move aside easily. But the saplings had tangled the tugboats and mortars like tight ropes. Porter's fleet, except for the one approaching boat, was stuck—unable to fight, unable to turn around, unable to go ahead.

"The willows have evened the odds!" Julien said jubilantly.

So he was still anxious for a bloodbath! And the enemy? One thing was for certain: Porter meant to fight. His ship was backing along the bayou, shearing off trees and clay banks, sideswiping the shore and preparing for battle.

Julien did likewise, shouting orders to everyone—to fire control parties, to Haloo to prepare shot, to a carpenter to go below the waterline and be ready to plug holes.

Then the first gun sounded. The deck of the *Quail* vibrated violently. Another shot was fired, deafening Surlina and slamming her onto the deck. She put her hands up, tossing her head back and forth as she covered her ringing ears. Haloo shouted across to her, grinning as he spoke. "Tends to rap you atwixt the shoulder blades, don't it?"

Julien called to her, "When you hear the concussion, open your mouth!"

Now the *Quail* was busily answering the shots in

343

kind. The noise of charges whizzed overhead, ripping into the forest like iron hammers beating on iron barrels. Then she smelled fire. Quickly, Surlina joined the bucket brigade, putting out the small orange flames in the woodwork around the pilothouse. From somewhere below, she heard the sound of a saw, the carpenter apparently being hard at work plugging shots at waterline.

Then a noise exploded right next to her. Unprepared, she felt herself flung forward. Her head slammed the bulkhead, twisting her neck. She doubled up, sideways, doing a somersault. Speechless, she sat upright. She blinked, and got to her feet again, unhurt.

Suddenly a white flag of truce was hauled out onto the stern of the Union boat.

"Hold your fire!" Julien ordered.

The famous David Dixon Porter stepped out onto the stern, looking self-possessed and blustery. "Ahoy there, Rainbeau! What are you doing up here in this blasted bayou? Don't you know a river from a pisspot?"

Julien stepped to the bow to answer. He looked jovial; only seconds ago, he had been flinging gunpowder. As Surlina watched him eyeing Porter across the dark bayou, she again had the feeling war was ridiculous. This whole encounter was against all rules of fleet warfare.

Julien cast a sideways glance at Surlina and smiled as he answered Porter. "I heard this was a silver mine! And you, Porter? What's your business here?"

Porter gazed despondently at the willow beds. "Forestry, sir! The lumber business!"

"Come aboard, Porter. I have a bottle of Kentucky bourbon."

"Thank you kindly, but no, I have had quite enough of your Southern hospitality."

Surlina was shocked. These scoundrels were delighted to see each other.

Julien addressed him with polite formality. "Do you wish to surrender, sir?"

Porter laughed. "By God, I just might! Then *you'd* have the problem of taking these ships apart and dragging them out piece by piece!" He consulted his watch. "But no, no, I've not the time to surrender, and I'm not of the nature to do so either." His hand went to his brow in mockery of his position. "I shall be the only sea captain ever to lose a fleet in the middle of a goddamned forest!"

Julien extended his sympathy, laughing all the while. "Then I shall not force your surrender but simply sit here and keep you penned like a goose."

"Not advisable, Rainbeau! Not unless you are in a mood to contest with Sherman's army, which will be along shortly."

"I am presently in a mood to contest every inch of this land and every single drop of this bayou." Julien shook an upraised fist and slapped his sidearm holster.

Both men turned away abruptly. Surlina expected the shooting to start again. How could grown men act like such little boys! As each captain stalked his deck, conferring and casting furious black glances at his opponent, she sensed the hostilities would not resume. They were more interested in a contest of wills than ammunition.

Surlina withdrew to the pilothouse and thought about her silver. This would be her last chance to capture it. Soon Tandy's pregnancy would be too far along for Surlina to go adventuring. She had almost worked up her nerve to ask Julien to try the grappling hooks or that newfangled diver's gear when she heard the engines start. Rushing on deck, she found the crew busy waving good-bye to Porter, coiling the *Quail*'s anchor lines and shoving empty crates overboard to block the Union retreat.

The *Quail* inched backward, over the spot where she imagined the cotton wagon buried in quicksand. Surlina stood at the rail and murmured, "That's the end of it. No one will get the treasure."

Suddenly she felt Julien's presence beside her. "Do you think I won the battle today, Surlina?"

It had all been so silly! Did he want praise for hurling insults and witticisms? "It struck me as inconclusive."

345

"Yes. And it remains inconclusive whether you've given up that silver. Your heart is still as divided as the nation's. Our countrymen kill each other over the proposition 'a house divided cannot stand.' "

"And a heart divided?"

"Cannot love."

33

During April and May 1863, Surlina watched her sister grow large with child and the city grow large with earthworks. The fortifications were brilliantly planned and brilliantly executed by an inventive twenty-five-year-old West Point engineer who served as chief Confederate architect. Brilliant, yes, but useless with the noose of hunger drawing ever tighter around starving Vicksburg.

"Tandy," declared Surlina on a mild Sunday afternoon, "I believe you should walk more. Get your parasol." She worried about her sister's wan cheeks and thin arms.

Tandy was scandalized at the idea of appearing on city streets while pregnant but Surlina insisted. Tandy decked herself out in a full-length spring coat, a hat with veil, and parasol. Once she was outdoors, her curiosity got the best of her. "Let's walk along the forts and see the wonderful progress," she chirped.

Surlina did not bother with coats, hats or shoes anymore. The weather was warm and clothes were scarce. She wore cast-off remnants of Tandy's outgrown wardrobe. For this outing, she chose a shapeless black skirt and one of Cabell's red silk shirts which bloused loosely over her breasts and had to be tied up at the sleeves.

They started their inspection trip at Jackson Road, where the Great Redoubt completely crossed the highway. Earth, timbers, wire, grass, thatch and cane were woven like a tapestry. "It's a wonderful trap!" cried Tandy proudly. "Marvelous! Not even a bird will be able to get into Vicksburg!"

As brilliant as the layout was, it would trap the people inside as well as attackers. The citizens of Vicksburg with their faces to the forts and their backs to the river would have nowhere to go except down in defeat. Surlina kept these pessimistic views to herself as Tandy went on drawling about how she hoped the attack would be soon and all those damned Yankees would be killed in the ditches.

"Tandy, I think we'd better contract for a cave." Surlina broached the subject she had been thinking about but had feared to bring up. "Almost everyone is fixing a cave in the hillside now. It's simple to tunnel back in the soft loess. I believe if we can scrape thirty dollars together, we should hire one dug."

"If we had thirty dollars, we could buy food!"

Thirty dollars now amounted to a fortune for them. Surlina chided herself for not having the foresight to make Thayer Cabell leave money for Tandy. He'd talked grandly of certificates of deposit, then left for England. Now with siege about to seal the city, the two women lacked both food and shelter. "I am sick of turnips and mulberries," she said, summarizing their recent diet. It was not safe to venture away from town to the bogs where blackberries and wild pigs and sweet potatoes could be found. Federal forces were there in numbers now, courtesy of Grant's steady conquest of rivers, marshes and swamps. Any place the Union troops didn't occupy, looting and plundering was going on. Mullermen operated in broad daylight, stronger than ever.

Tandy remained cheerfully brave. "We'll substitute. Make do!"

"We've done that." Surlina thought of the strange substitutions they'd made already. Ashes and lime to cure meat, coffee boiled from parched corn, tea from leaves, soda from sour milk, vinegar from bark, ink from berries.

Despite her admonitions to herself not to think of

the silver, Surlina said, "But there's no substitute for money!"

She must not desert Tandy. But, on the other hand, they'd both starve unless Vicksburg fell rapidly. From the looks of the breastworks all around them, the siege would be long. She phrased her words carefully, hoping not to alarm her sister. "It is still possible to get out of the city and back in. We must find a way to protect your health and provide nourishment for the baby. We need a stockpile of food and medicine."

For once Tandy didn't object. "I'll go with you, Surlina." She clutched her veil and looked serious.

Surlina shook her head. No, one did not take pregnant sisters on foraging raids in the terrain between opposing armies. She began listing the things she'd need. "A wagon. A gun. And a companion—someone who can talk fast and shoot straight. I need somebody not adverse to stealing."

"That sounds quite unrefined, Surlina."

"That sounds like Dottie McDune!" Surlina laughed with relief, knowing that the crotchety old lady with the raccoon-colored hair and itchy trigger finger would be glad to sign on for adventure.

Tandy sniffed again. "I've heard of that woman. Why, she makes rice wine and sells it to our own brave soldiers. I've heard a cupful makes them drunk as lords! You'd better watch your step. Dottie McDune is no lady."

"Thank God, and she'll help me get us a cave, too."

Surlina knew that Dottie was working at the *Daily Citizen,* but until she found the woman deep in the basement of the brick newspaper building, she hadn't realized that Dottie's business was counterfeiting Confederate bills of large denominations!

Dottie wiped the ink from her hands and said sadly, "It's a dying occupation. Both me and the newspaper are running out of material to print on." She inspected the galleys of the day's edition, then turned back to Surlina. "But the worst thing about this paper is the news of the day. Your enemy, Muller, done busted out of the brig at Young's Point."

"What! You mean the army didn't hang him months ago?"

"Apparently not. All that fancy rigamarole about court martial slowed 'em up, I reckon. Now they done law and ordered themselves right out of a prisoner!"

"Dottie, do you think he'd come back *here?* After *us?*"

"The thought's crossed my mind." She looked at Surlina brightly. "That's why you're here? Want to head upcountry for a spell? Or are you fixing to say the magic words 'Sam Grant' again and kiss me goodbye?"

"Neither. I can't leave Tandy. But I do need help. Yours."

Surlina proposed her foraging plan. She realized it sounded doubly foolhardy with Muller loose, but she had to go.

Dottie was agreeable. "I'd be proud to ride shotgun while you scare up some eatables! If we see Muller, we'll get him good."

Surlina gave her a hug. "What's a Dottie McDune for if not to help out a friend in a jam?"

"Stand aside, Muller," declared Dottie. "We're coming through! We'll take the newspaper delivery wagon for transportation! Fresh air will set well with me after this basement."

They left town on the back streets, via Baldwin's Ferry Road, taking interest in every section of farmland. Most of the fields were completely shorn of livestock, poultry, dairy animals and pigs.

At the top of a small rise, Surlina took out Cabell's mother-of-pearl opera glasses and swept the countryside. She saw nothing to indicate which way they should go. She handed the glasses to Dottie, who promptly took a look, swung the binoculars back to the spot where the trees and river met and began to whistle. "Surlina, your constitution strong enough to take a view of naked men?"

The unseasonable heat had wilted Surlina's hair into a mat on her brow. She pushed back the curls and grabbed for the glasses, quickly focusing on the scene.

349

In the river, she spied six men bathing. Their army wagon was neatly parked uphill on the bank, the horses tethered loosely so they could graze. Six muskets were stacked upright, leaning against a live-oak tree.

Dottie clucked like a schoolteacher. "Why, imagine that! Shedding their clothes and going swimming instead of doing their soldiering! Ought to take me a stick and whale the whole bunch of 'em." Her voice went smooth and conniving as she took the field glasses away again. She nudged Surlina with an elbow. "And I ain't opposed to finding out what's in that wagon, neither."

They moved quietly, putting their own team and newspaper wagon behind a privet hedge which bordered the trace. "Watch for lookouts," Surlina cautioned. Dottie nodded, patting her holster. "We'll sneak up the back way," continued Surlina, "put their guns in the back of their wagon and then——"

"Then the sooner our git turns to gone, the better."

Exhilaration replaced fear as Surlina glided into the tree break. They approached the rear of the wagon, Dottie watching for lookouts and Surlina scooping up guns and clothing. She tucked the muskets and clothes into the back of the wagon.

They climbed onto the wagon, and Surlina took the reins. With a Rebel yell from Dottie, they made their spectacular getaway.

Surlina drove the horses into a lathered frenzy, arriving in Tandy's front yard by way of a backwoods cutoff. She pulled the team to a halt, laughing with crazy relief, still wondering what they had stolen. Except for the muskets and Yankee uniforms, she had no idea what was in the wagon.

"Tandy!" she yelled, then piled down from the driver's seat. Dottie was already tearing into the mysterious bundles. The first parcel broke, paper flying, to reveal army hats. "Caps!" Surlina cried, alarmed they might have made off with a wagon full of uniforms.

Tandy came onto the porch, wide-eyed and embarrassed as other people began arriving as if they'd been sent for. But the urge for food was greater than her urge to be ladylike and stay inside for appearances.

350

Surlina was pleased when Tandy trudged out into the yard and foolishly stuck a Yankee cap atop her chignon. "The latest fashion, I hear!" She giggled modestly, then threw the hated cap to the ground and stamped on it daintily.

Dottie was the one who found the treasure, prying up a loose board with her knife to reveal a false bottom in the wagon. Surlina tugged at the flimsy board, yanking it away with her bare hands. She stepped back in awe at what she saw—obviously booty from a raid on a local plantation. "Hams! Dozens of them! The *real* kind —where you scrape the mold and cut it thin with a razor blade! They'll keep forever! Biscuits—twelve dozen tins! And oh, here's a box of fruitcakes! Marmalade! A whole root cellar—potatoes, onions, rutabagas, carrots! Oh my God! Here's *coffee!*"

The people in the yard, strangers, neighbors and mere acquaintances, reached up frantic hands for the provisions. Tandy gave things away almost as fast as Surlina could unload them. The cries of the crowd sounded like geese squawking. "Thanky, Mrs. Cabell! Thanky, thanky! Much obliged!"

Surlina tried to intervene. She'd brought these things for her sister, not to provide a picnic! But Tandy's nature was generous and she smiled and nodded as she handed food to whomever wanted it. Frantically, Surlina scooped apples, onions, one ham, two tins of biscuits and a jar of coffee into her arms and ran into the house to hide them. Tandy would be their undoing yet.

People followed her inside, opening the food parcels and sitting down to eat. Tandy welcomed everyone, apologized there was no wine, then made Surlina bring back the last ham and share it. Discouraged, Surlina gave up the fight. She sliced huge hunks from the pork and gobbled, stuffing her cheeks so full she couldn't swallow. Then she abandoned the party to keep company with Dottie, who was sitting on the doorstep. "That entire wagon of food won't last the night. How can they be such pigs! Don't they realize no one's going in or out of this city anymore?" She felt tears of frustration welling up. There had been enough food to last a month with careful rationing. Now it was gone in one evening of bloated, careless feasting.

Surlina wanted to put her head down in Dottie's lap and cry. "Maybe you should take this team and wagon and escape Vicksburg permanently. If you can make it back to Whispers, it might be best."

"No one tells Dottie McDune where to go!"

Surlina walked back in and motioned people to go home. They left willingly, taking every scrap of food with them. Tandy went to bed without eating even an apple. Dottie came in and fell asleep on the living room floor. Surlina walked around the yard littered with Union caps, kicking the hats while cursing the Confederacy. Out there in the night, armies were pinching Vicksburg in a vise of death. Siege was coming. She had Sam's word for it. She had Julien's word for it.

She stared at the stars, blinking along with the twinkles of cold light. Would she ever see either one of her loves again?

34

The siege of Vicksburg began at daybreak. Guns shook the earth like thunder, the echoes piercing the houses, making dishes rattle.

"*Now,* Tandy," insisted Surlina. "Time to go." She gathered a handful of candles and hardtack, convinced the guns would let up at intervals and she'd be able to go back to the house on Harrison Street for supplies.

Tandy loaded a little handwagon with her "necessities"—a Staffordshire pitcher, wash bowl, Bible concordance and the unfinished crewel banner emblazoned "Victory or Death!"

In the streets people greeted each other as if heading to a ball. They trooped along, trying to look casual, pulling wagons, baby carriages and chairs. Men had picnic baskets on their arms. Women took sewing baskets. Several older men carried card tables. One elegant family consisted of a father in a white suit, mother with an extra hat, girls in ruffled pinafores and a slave carrying a fully loaded tea tray.

At the entrance to the small cave, Tandy did not hesitate. She piled right in, declaring, "We'll be so happy in our little burrow!"

Surlina was not so eager. She lingered at the entrance, glancing backward at the daylight, a feeling of claustrophobia swarming her senses.

However, the cave was not as bad as she feared. Stuffy, yes, the sandstone holding the heat of the earth like a clay cooking pot. Yet there was room for Tandy to rest on a quilted mat. Surlina preferred to stay near the front, poking her head out between rounds of the Parrott guns.

"What can you see?" asked Tandy.

"Smoke in the sky. Gunpowder odor." Surlina did not report that she could hear occasional screams. Downtown she could see fires burning uncontained. The big guns boomed again, answered by the monstrous Southern cannon. She ducked back inside, worrying how long she could stand being buried alive. She needed to be out and around. There were clothes to wash, work to do in the garden, bartering and bargaining for Tandy's medicines. She worried incessantly that there would be no food for the baby when it arrived. Crouching on the floor of the cave, Surlina did some arithmetic. Four thousand people in the caves. Thirty thousand troops in the garrison. No supply trains.

As the echoes died away again, she heard laughter from the next cave. The rattling of coins and loud male voices indicated a poker game in full swing. The guns struck anew with sounds like earthquakes.

After a week of living in caves with only snatches of respite, the early partygoing atmosphere gave way to a mad scramble. Women shrieked at the first sound of bombardment. Children whimpered at the echoes. All eyes turned toward the forts—wide, panic-stricken eyes.

Tandy developed a terrible affinity for the cave. On the nights they spent at home, she would awaken before dawn and insist on "getting a head start on the morning rush." Surlina was unsure whether the cave gave Tandy security or whether Tandy was merely embarrassed to go about the streets now that her baby was nearly due.

Tandy spent more and more time cooped in the back of the smelly, hot cave. She'd lie in the darkness, not moving, or sew by candlelight. In the evening, when Surlina plunged into the open air with relief, Tandy balked. "Can't we stay here? It's so cozy!"

"It's poison in there, Tandy! You must come out!"

"I don't feel well. I want to rest here."

"No wonder you run fevers and get nauseated! It's this foul air we breathe!" She grabbed her sister's arm and pulled her along.

In the next week, the screams turned to morose silence. Now the faces of the children were blank. The morning procession to the caves became a funeral cortege. Quiet, dignified, no other place to go, the townfolks traipsed along dully. Routine set in, even for a siege.

Surlina now pulled Tandy in the little wagon. Food was almost nonexistent, and Tandy's face had yellowed with jaundice. She still loved the cave, peevishly resenting the time she had to spend on Harrison Street.

At the end of a month of cave life, Surlina had limited their food intake to one meal a day. Cooking this small portion proved to be a gamble. Surlina learned to gauge the lull of the guns around noontime. She crept to the door of the cave, frying pan in hand, determined to make the most of the short interval. Hurriedly she built a fire, threw tripe into the skillet and dumped in a handful of weevil-infested cornmeal.

The guns renewed their slaughter. Surlina dived for the cave entrance, grease flying. When she peered out again, little luncheon fires were burning merrily along the cliffside, but not a soul was in sight. She wiped the cornmeal from her fingers, licking them ravenously. "Tandy, lunch!"

She looked at Tandy deftly stitching by the light of a candle stub. The air was stagnant, the inside of the cave sizzling with June heat. Tandy's brown hair had lost its shine and hung straight down, tied in a knot at the end. Her face was sickly yellow, with sunken eyes which blinked dryly in dark sockets.

Sweating and frustrated, Surlina ran her hands over her grimy face. Her lungs were begging for air. Her throat was dry, nostrils filled with sandstone dust, eyes gritty with debris. "I can't stand it!" she cried, raised up, hit her head and burst outside.

"Where are you going?" cried Tandy, alarmed.

"Home! I am going to Harrison Street and cook you a decent meal!" The guns were still booming, but she ignored them. Overhead the gray smoke held a pall over the town. She strode briskly, preferring death by cannonball to death by suffocation and starvation.

Tandy's condition weighed heavily on her mind. Damn Thayer Cabell for not taking his wife to England where it was safe! Damn him for not providing adequate food, shelter and money!

As she walked along, quite alone, Surlina took in the devastation.

Harrison Street was littered with iron. All the glass in the city had long since been shattered. Windows hung with curtains, newspapers, wallpaper and boards. Storefronts were a thing of the past, as were chandeliers, dishes and vases. Houses which had not taken actual hits had been fairly well demolished by the continual concussions.

Tandy's house was still standing, with the front porch leaning and the back bedroom ripped away. Surlina went in, wondering what she could prepare for supper. Boiled potato skins, dandelion greens from the yard, and a small hunk of dried orange rind. As she started back to take the food to Tandy, she felt bitter. They were eating garbage. She chided herself. They were lucky to have it.

Suddenly she spotted a familiar shape scurrying along the business street. "Dottie! What brings you out? How's your cave?"

355

"Bad. How are you?"

Surlina simply nodded in agreement.

Dottie glanced about furtively, eyes scooting along the storefronts as if to make sure no one was watching. Then she reached inside her dirty plaid shirt and pulled out a stained brown paper-wrapped package. Silently she proffered it to Surlina.

"What is it, Dottie?"

"Meat."

Surlina grabbed at the parcel, falling onto it with both hands. "Meat! How wonderful!" She felt her mouth begin to salivate and her stomach kink with anticipation. Her mind raced ahead. She must hurry to the cave, cook it and force Tandy to eat some! "Thank you! Thank you! This isn't the first time you've saved my life! Oh, Dottie! Where in the world did you find meat?"

There was a crackling noise in Dottie's throat and despair in her faded eyes. Then her shoulders bristled and she turned away. "Slaughtered my mule." She rushed down the street.

Surlina stood stunned, realizing what a sacrifice Dottie had made—not just in killing the animal, but in sharing the meat. She was doubly appreciative, tightening her grip on the parcel. She held it close to her body, making sure by frantic glances that no one was on the streets to fight her for it. Then she ran for the cave.

"Tandy! Tandy!" She burst through the cave opening, tears of hunger mixed with happiness. "This will put roses in your cheeks. Meat!"

"I'm not hungry." Tandy's weak whisper barely whimpered.

"You *are* hungry! That's mostly what's wrong with you! Get up! Eat!"

"I'm too tired." She lay curled on the straw mat, the quilted pad over her legs despite the heat. "Too tired."

Surlina knelt, wiped her sister's perspiring forehead, felt the weak, fluttery pulse and held her bony hand. "You *must* eat."

"Surlina, please. I don't want to eat and I don't

356

want to go back to Harrison Street anymore." She attempted a brittle smile. "Why, this is home now!" She lay back, her eyes closed, looking like an effigy of wax and ashes. The flickering candlelight sent ghostly shadows across her pallid features. "It's nearly night for me anyway, Surlina. Night is coming fast now."

Surlina recoiled from the terrible words, but there was no point in blurting 'Nonsense!' There was no point in talking about how delicious mule meat would taste, no point in chatting about the need to deliver a healthy child and raise it for the glory of the South. There was no point in talking at all! The only way to deal with Tandy was by force.

Surlina scooped her sister into her arms, horrified to find she could lift her easily. "You're going home and sleep in a real bed. I'm going to the battlefield surgeon and find you some medicine!" She put Tandy into the wagon and pulled her out of the cave. Outside, in the smoky afternoon, Tandy shivered and cried. Surlina paid no attention. She pulled her all the way back to Harrison Street, settled her in bed with root tea and a comforter over her cold feet. "Now—I'm going to the hospital. I'll be back in an hour. Then you're going to eat a real supper!"

Tandy had little strength left, but she had plenty of moral conviction. In a frail voice which quivered with outrage, she protested. "It's improper for a lady to go traipsing in the trenches! Only common camp girls do that!"

"Oh, Tandy, you are hopeless! Since when do ladies live in caves and eat mules?" she asked, looking in the last shard of mirror at her own sallow complexion and dirty hair. Her blouse had streaks of loess and grease patterned on it, the black skirt was dusty and she had no shoes. 'I'll not be mistaken for a tart in this getup,' she thought. Their cheeks are rosy and their dresses have patches! She tucked three fingers into the waistband of her skirt, feeling the gap where she'd lost weight.

Then she left the house, whistling to calm her nerves. The smoke hung in the treetops like a gray flannel cloth. Behind the smoke she could see thunder-clouds building up, promising welcome rain.

She approached the battlefield from the town side. She felt hesitant and squeamish despite her bravado. But the guns had quit early, due to the impending thunderstorm. Electricity charged the air in the flashes of lightning which lit the summer sky to the east. From the downtown streets she was able to go directly to the protected headquarters building. There she asked to see the first doctor whose name she read on a door —Dr. Lockett. She was told to wait.

When he came out of a conference, she put her request to him briefly. "My sister is pregnant and is suffering from fever, nausea, and a weak pulse. Her ribs stick out and her cheeks are sunken."

"Cave symptoms," diagnosed Lockett, "and famine. Unbearable for a normal woman, deadly for a pregnant one."

"What medicines do you have?"

"None." A hint of sympathy strained his clipped reply.

"Give me *something* for her!"

He touched Surlina's arm. "There is nothing that would help." He steered her down the corridor, walking briskly. "I am going to the dispensary now. You can see for yourself. There is really nothing." He walked stooped and old, though he appeared to be about thirty, thin to the point of emaciation and humble to the point of numbness.

"But surely you have battlefield supplies! Let me have laudanum and bandages. I may have to deliver a baby next week!"

He turned the key in a heavy oak door. She peered into a dimly lit storeroom. Gauze bandages were piled higher than her head. All around she saw stacks of brown paper and empty medicine bottles.

"Help yourself," he said bitterly.

Lockett sat down on the window sill, musing aloud. "Where Grant's surgeons have opium and morphia, I have only homemade remedies. I have calomel and horsehair sutures to deal with lead bullets which shatter

358

bone. My surgeons are making poultices of flaxseed and bread to stanch hemorrhages."

"Oh my God, Doctor. How can you carry on?"

"We will make do."

She thought how often she'd heard those words. And still the South was carrying on while losing everything.

Lockett appeared past caring. He spoke again. "Where Grant has medical commissaries and sanitary commissions following his army, I have fleas, lice, typhoid and dysentery. Maybe . . ." he said, "maybe I could go across the lines and see General Grant. I'd ask for a medical truce. He might consider it. We're both West Pointers. I wonder if he would see me—"

"I doubt it," she interrupted. "I understand Sam Grant does not see emissaries under any circumstances." She thought of Sam's steady blue eyes, gentle touch against her lips, and absolute power over her body. She remembered his fairness, judgment and humanity. Carefully she lifted her skirt around her ankles and took a step forward. "But I think he might see me."

At sunset, accompanied by a flag of truce and one other messenger, Surlina started across the lines. She tried to walk straight ahead, eyes above the battlefield, but the ground was slippery and she had to look down to find footing around twisted corpses piled around their guns. Crews shoveled away bodies like garbage, making space for tomorrow's victims.

She tried not to see, not to hear, not to smell, but death was all around her.

Oh, to see Sam again! Even under these terrible circumstances, Surlina's heart felt lighter. It would be reassuring just to see his smile, hear his steady voice, be near his commanding presence for a few minutes.

She was grateful to be safely across the lines.

Beneath the torn federal flag, in the shade of the tree, sitting in a collapsible chair and writing hurriedly at a propped table was Sam Grant. He did not look up as she approached. Indeed, he did not glance from his writing until nudged. "General, the truce messenger is here," an aide pointed out.

As he spied her, his eyes narrowed. His hand went to his beard in surprise. But he did not move from behind his table. He stood, cold and reserved. "State your business."

"General, I have come to ask for a truce to bury the dead and resupply the medical corps."

"No." He did not change expression.

She looked at him bewildered. How could he dismiss the idea in one word?

He came around the table, motioning to go inside the tent. As they moved beyond the canvas flaps and out of range of others' hearing, he took her arm. "There are tears in my heart, Surlina. But my train of thought tonight is short—only unconditional surrender."

She rephrased his stiff words. "No truce." She felt it useless to argue, yet was driven to persist. "The city is hungry, General."

"They have only to surrender, and rations will be available." Suddenly, as if her thin cheeks had only now become visible to him, Sam ducked out, summoned an aide and asked that refreshments be sent immediately.

Surlina remained standing, thinking how like him it was to accommodate her courteously while yielding nothing on a wider scale. She felt pride in his mastery of the situation and humiliation at her own requests. "Please, Sam—a truce for burials. Your army needs it more than—"

"No."

"Then your goal is not victory, it's annihilation!"

"My goal is moving south." He sat on his cot, knees spread, manners swept away in tiredness. "Moving south until I can head home permanently." He stifled a yawn. It was not discourtesy but nights of sleeplessness.

She felt a strange elasticity between them then, he the soldier who wanted to go home, she the woman who had sought to avoid the war by staying neutral. Now they faced each other not as adversaries, but almost as strangers.

"I cannot dawdle, not even for your most humane

request. I am here to take this city, and *I must not stop.*"

Surlina felt herself shaking uncontrollably and put her hands to her ears to blot out his words. He was right, so goddamned right *militarily,* but she couldn't bear to hear it. "The city will fall soon enough anyway, Sam. A little food and medicine now won't deprive you of your ultimate victory."

"Nothing."

"You're going to have so many starving prisoners of war when this town surrenders that you'll have no room to put them! You're going to have women and children on your hands, and babies with haunted eyes and old men with starved bodies. I *beg* you to resupply the city!"

"I cannot." She heard the iron in his voice, but clearly saw the pain in his eyes. Sam's fist was clenched, but more to prevent tremors than to indicate anger. "I cannot stop." He bowed his head, admitting the suffering which racked him with such a decision.

She moved to sit beside him, not to ask for anything more, but to comfort him. He raised his arm and let it fall around her shoulders, an acknowledgement of the sincerity and force between them. Silently, hunched like two mourners, they sat on the cot, staring at the ground.

A voice outside the flap announced, "Refreshments for the lady, sir!"

She smiled weakly as a tray was set before her. She pushed it away, unable to eat. "May I take the food back to my sister? Tandy is so sick, I fear for her life! She must have food and a doctor or something terrible will happen!"

"I will give you a pass for her," Sam said thoughtfully. "The instant the city surrenders, have her brought to the hospital." He pulled paper from the desk and began writing. "Pray God these misguided people of Vicksburg do not hold out until it is too late for her."

"It is very bad in the caves, Sam. No food, water, sanitation."

"I promise you, my first act upon surrender will be

361

to reprovision the entire town." He slammed down his notebook. "My God, I'd reprovision the whole South if I could!"

She wrapped the dinner in the corner of her truce flag. Sam draped a heavy arm across her back, accepting the burdens they both bore. "Surlina, it will be over soon, and these conditions that break our hearts will ease." He hesitated, soft blue eyes gazing at her thin cheeks. "When it's over, will you come to me again, Surlina?"

For an instant she wanted to say, "Yes, I'll come to you, love you, stay with you." Deep in her heart Surlina felt the union between them was undamaged. But on the surface, there were too many rips to conceal. She stood, erect and formal, hardly daring to meet his eyes. "Give the city a few days' grace, Sam. They are out of everything."

He took her hands and kissed her cheeks, correcting her gently. "They are out of everything except courage like yours." He lifted the tent flap for her.

35

After giving Dr. Lockett the bad news, Surlina trudged back to Tandy's home without thought of her bare feet crusted with dried blood or the smell of gangrene clinging to her hair. As she turned into Harrison Street, she began to run, seeing a carriage in front of the house.

She rushed inside, flinging open the door. "Tandy! Has something happened?"

Tandy rushed into the living room. "Cabell is home! He is back, Surlina! They managed to slip upriver and onto the cliffs! I'm so thrilled!" Suddenly she put a hand to her mouth. "What has happened to you?"

Surlina shook her head, dismissing her appearance. "I have been to see General Grant."

Tandy was even more aghast. "Oh! How could you? Where is your patriotism?"

"For freedom—very deep. But for North or South—none!" She headed for the kitchen to wash. "Think about it, Tandy. Don't you remember when we were children? We lived on the frontier, not part of *any* nation. We worked as equals to Father. Where in hell you found this modest, clinging female habit I'll never know! But I can never adopt it. And I refuse absolutely to adopt your fervent political style."

Tandy looked healthier than she had in weeks, her cheeks excitedly pink and her eyes brimming with passionate tears. Raising her voice to a rare shout, she yelled, "You *must* see the right of the Cause!"

Surlina hugged her, thinking she'd crack her ribs and mash the baby if she wasn't careful. "Oh, Tandy, there's no right! Only horror."

Tandy pulled back in distaste from her filthy sister, apparently as much offended by the words as by her griminess. "Trudging the forts like a whore! Surlina, I'm appalled!"

Hopeless Tandy! Surlina soaked her hands in a pan of water, trying to tell of the actualities of the battlefield. "It's not filled with stalwart warriors in dapper gray and glistening buttons, Sister. Probably never was. Both sides are dirty and tired. They hold lice races for diversion. When they get half a chance, they desert. They play poker and craps and read dime novels and trade calotypes of French nudes. They eat corn dodgers soaked with spit and *they kill each other!*"

Tandy shied away, hurriedly clattering pans and hot water and proffering the household's last sliver of soap. She darted away entirely as Thayer Cabell returned to the house, back from a round of greeting the townsfolk.

Surlina watched them from the kitchen, greeting each other surreptitiously, shaking hands like formal acquaintances instead of man and wife. He kissed Tandy lightly, handling her like French crystal, presenting her a sprig of freshly picked violets. Cabell looked meanfaced as ever, a little less florid but still composed of

363

shades of tan, beige, greengage and scarlet. Those abominable stork legs and porkpie belly. Those owl eyes in that moon face. That elegant suit of clothes, no doubt the latest from London, with a bobtail coat, pocket flaps outlined in braid, brown plaid shirt with spotted collar and a wide, flat hat. He'd acquired a cane with a horn handle and more girth in his waistline.

Surlina made a conscious effort not to hate Cabell. She wanted to get his cooperation in sending Tandy to the Union hospital to have the baby. She'd have to handle them *both* like infants!

Finished washing, she then put on a demure outfit of leftover clothing. No shoes. But she found a pair of hose and made the ladylike motions of covering her feet.

As she joined Tandy and Cabell in the living room, she heard Tandy reporting on the visit across the lines. "Surlina went to see Grant. She thinks the South will fall very soon."

Cabell made a retching sound, then stared at both women—at Surlina for having expressed such unthinkable filth, and at Tandy for having dirtied her ears hearing it. "Ah, my beloved South—"

"Cabell!" interrupted Surlina. "Listen and leave off those beloved abstractions!" She rolled up her sleeves as if intending to knock sense into his head with fisticuffs. "Consider this, even if Tandy is incapable. Your wife is going to have your child very soon, possibly next week. Do you want her to endure childbirth in this house with cannons shaking the bed? Or in a cave with no ventilation? We don't have medicines for either place."

Tandy stammered bravely, "It doesn't matter."

"Shut up, Tandy! Cabell, listen to me! Don't you see there's a chance both mother and child could die?"

Indignant to the point of blowing through his lips, he squealed, "Watch your tongue!"

Surlina pulled the pass from her waistband. "I have asked a favor of General Grant. He has given permission for Tandy to go to the Union hospital . . . as soon as Vicksburg surrenders. Cabell, you must use your influence. This town is doomed anyway. Tell them to surrender! Tonight. This minute."

Cabell repeated the words in a wondering hush. "The *Union* hospital?"

Both Tandy and Cabell sucked in their breath. Tandy looked befuddled, glancing first at the floor, then at her husband, then out the open window. Apparently the idea of the federal hospital scared her, but her husband scared her more.

"Never!" he cried. "I would wrap myself in the Stars and Bars and put a pistol to my head before I'd hand over my dear, sainted wife to Yankee doctors!"

Surlina gave up. There was no way to make Tandy believe or Cabell behave. She put on a front of practical courtesy. "How was your journey, Cabell?"

"Ah perilous, indeed! I had to travel upriver with that riffraff, Rainbeau. He was up to his daredevil tricks at Grand Gulf. Bishop Polk and I traveled overland from there. By the way, Polk says he will preach here Sunday. He sent you a special invitation to hear him, and Julien Rainbeau asked to be remembered to you as well."

The mention of Julien's name jarred Surlina. How long since she'd thought lovingly of him. She almost began to blurt questions. Was he well? Did his gray eyes twinkle and his golden hair shine as she remembered? Did he have the special way of saying her name?

She heard Cabell's voice breaking her reverie. "Rainbeau's well, but bound for a bad end. His plans for Grand Gulf are nothing less than inflammatory."

Why were all these people intent on sacrificing themselves? Tandy! Cabell! Julien! What flaw ran through them? Almost in a trance of fury and longing, she took the silly bouquet of violets, stuck them in a cracked teacup, poured water around them and watched it dribble out. Julien's flair and authority were as misdirected as Tandy's nobility and loyalty. The South was a bouquet of cut flowers—cut at the roots and dying rapidly.

The Episcopal Church of Vicksburg consisted of part brick, part frame, and part open air. A shell had shorn off the vestry. Pews were dumped over as if kneeling. The steps, however, were intact, and it was on the steps that the Sunday-morning parishioners conducted their visiting. Cabell was preening like an ostrich in his fine attire, posturing and shaking hands, telling of his trip to England.

When Bishop Polk arrived, he seemed disturbed, hurrying to the front of the altar, offhandedly smoothing his garments, reaching for a hymnal, then slamming it shut. Finally, his eyes roaming the congregation and meeting Surlina's for a single instant, he rumbled, "Let us pray." She was strangely disturbed. There had been a warning in the way his eyes pierced her.

The bishop began a long prayer for the battle to end in the Confederacy's favor. She began to drift away in her own meditations. The past months had seemed so difficult. Caves in the ground, silver in the quicksand, castles in the air. She had forgotten her silver for weeks at a time, nearly forgotten Thad Muller. But never had she forgotten Sam Grant and Julien Rainbeau. Never had she abandoned hope for getting out of Vicksburg alive!

She was jolted back to the service as halfway through a choir solo, the guns began their loud litany. It was a queer combination of sound, the shriek of firearms blending with the groans of the organ.

Bishop Polk cut his sermon short, realizing the guns were sounding the call to the caves. After dismissal, people lingered on the steps—almost defiant—shaking the bishop's hand, forcing jolly benedictions on each other, issuing invitations. With false bravado, they called to Cabell, "Haven't seen you in a coon's age! Drop around to our cave next shelling and catch us up on the news!"

Surlina waited patiently to speak to Bishop Polk. He looked thinner now, his reedy voice deepened to the tones of an alto recorder. She saw his fretful eyes trail her urgently. Quickly she moved apart from the crowd, signaling him with a nod of her head.

He clasped her in an embrace. Instantly, she went cold, fearing his words. "What has happened, bishop?"

366

She forced low, calm words when screams were hiding right behind them.

Polk's hesitation, the rapid blink of his sad eyes and slight, diffident turn of his head alerted her to unbearable tension. "The *Quail* is lost."

"Lost! Julien . . . ?"

"The *Quail* has sunk. A few survivors are coming ashore at the longboat wharf here." He lifted his hand to point down the hundreds of steps. But by then she was already running.

She jumped the last steps, heart pounding and feet flying. Already on the creaky pier she could see rows of bodies beneath tarpaulins. Ten, twenty, oh God, there must be thirty men! A brisk breeze scoured the river, blending fish, summer dankness and death odors. Surlina felt faint, but surges of blood pounded at her temples. She tried to call for Julien but only a windblown croak came forth. His familiar image filled her mind, his wicked grin and laughing eyes, the hair which would never lie sleekly, the tawny body. Then her mind overlaid a picture of him stretched still beneath the canvas, blackened and cold.

"Julien, where are you? Not lost. You can't be!" She was at the pier now, heart choked with fear, panting from exertion. She wished tears would dim this scene, but her eyes stayed clear, letting her see the vivid shapes beneath the tarps. Could she find the courage to lift the edge and look?

Then she spotted him, standing with his back turned in the corner of a loading shed. She moaned, rushing to him. "Oh, my dearest Julien!" As he turned, face immobile, a half-drowned Squeebob in his arms, she stopped as if dealt a blow, staggered by the haunted look in his eyes. Lifeless. No vitality. She touched his hand gently, as if not to frighten a wild animal. Cold as alabaster. She raised one finger to his cheek. His unfocused eyes did not seem to follow. "Oh, Julien, my dearest Julien," she whispered again.

He spoke from a voice of ashes. "I have lost my men. I have lost the *Quail*."

Surlina hardly dared speak. "All? Haloo? Professor Boxt? Proctor O'Keefe?"

He nodded, indicating the tarpaulins. "And Kuffy. Ramsey had sent him aboard for safekeeping."

Her tears sprang up for the child who had seen more warfare than most men.

"I have lost everyone except the three in the pilothouse." Suddenly he sagged, crumpling to the floor of the shed, kneeling in agony with his head in his arms.

Quickly Surlina knelt beside him, her hand barely touching the back of his neck. "What happened? Can you tell me?"

He recounted the story without looking up. Staying behind the other ships at Grand Gulf. Waging a last fight at Warrenton. A storm. The *Quail* chased upriver, grounded in the shallows. "Then I made the fatal error. Rather than surrender, I tried to blow the *Quail* out of the water. The charges were set. They went off prematurely, killing everyone at waterline or below." He sat cross-legged, hands folded, his voice sounding as if it came from a cellar. "I put my ship in danger when I did not need to. I killed my men by my own lack of judgment!" He indicted himself fiercely, moaning in disgust. "The dipper is empty now, Surlina. I owe my defeat not to bad weather or bad fuses, but ultimately to my own pride." He shook his head and rose to his feet, starting toward the steps. "I must report to Pemberton."

She ran after him. "What will you do now? Where will you go?"

"I'll go into the trenches of Vicksburg as a common foot soldier. Who cares if one more man dies?"

"You must not! You can't!" Suddenly Surlina was overwhelmed with a desire to protect him. He looked fragile, unable to defend himself. Horror knotted inside her as she thought of him as one of the bodies she had seen on the battlefield.

"How will I forget the deaths I am responsible for . . . How will I *forget?*" He turned his back and rushed away, apparently unable to choke out more.

Surlina darted around him, facing him again, needing

to give him something to cling to. He did not dodge, but he did not reach out to her either. She grabbed at him fiercely. "Your hopelessness will destroy you! Julien! You won't last two minutes under Grant's guns! Don't go, Julien! I love you! I love you."

He held her. But the sounds of the great cannons cut off speech. Dreadful and distinctive, the Parrott guns shook the ground. The earth heaved around them as if it would crack and swallow them. She closed her eyes, head against his shoulder, and remembered how they'd loved, how they'd held each other, how when they'd danced, other people had leaned near to see what magic words they spoke. She remembered exactly where his thumb had pressed against her spine, how they'd lain on the blanket on the sandbar, the time he'd said, "You make me feel a god!"

Now they stood reduced to quaking. They were helpless, and she was so certain of the outcome if she could not find the single strand of life that would bind her to him.

"Julien, by all that's blessed, you're the only man for me! We need each other! Love each other!"

"That part is true. I love you as much as it is possible for a man to love a woman." With tears streaming down his cheeks, he took her in his arms. His eyes were full, pleading with her to believe.

Surlina held him tenderly, stroking his back as if holding a baby bird who couldn't fly. *"Nothing* will hurt you! You are my love! Now and forever, you are my one and only love."

36

Surlina and Tandy put up a united front. Cabell shouted them both down. "Nonsense," he bellowed. "We've been invited to the finest cave on the cliffs! Of course we'll go!"

369

"No, please no," declared Tandy, her hands across her extended belly. "What if I should—" The mortification on her face was clear. She was terrified at the lack of privacy should she go into labor.

Surlina came to her defense. "She is right, Cabell. We have no business in the big cave with half of Vicksburg."

"Why, there's rooms and rooms and rooms in it, they tell me! Holds twenty people comfortably."

Surlina was not impressed. "That means it was dug to hold fifteen and will have forty crammed in!"

"Now, now, girls, come along quietly," he protested and picked up the picnic basket which held the layette. "Perhaps we'll take this along. Rumor says the guns won't let up tonight at all."

Surlina pulled together her makeshift midwife kit. Tandy put on the new hat Cabell had brought her from London. All the things the woman needed—and he brought her an elegant hat! Surlina looked at her sister, all ragbag and tatters except for the marvelous blue velvet bonnet with the big grosgrain bow and the layers of tulle which swathed her face. Tandy's face, however, bore the telltale traces of deprivation. It was swollen beneath the eyes, fevered on the too-rosy cheeks, parched around the lips.

The cave into which Cabell had bullied his invitation was already crowded when they arrived. Surlina went in unwillingly, more afraid of suffocation than being shelled.

Forty people stuck in a sandbox! The heat was pervasive, filled with body odors and uncirculated air. Two dogs romped through the cave rooms, knocking over poker tables.

Would this be the final day of being stuck with their heads in the sand like ostriches? Surlina half-expected it to be; people were utterly exhausted. At dusk, the guns did not let up; instead, the bombardment increased. Surlina remembered the axiom: after forty-five days, any fort will surrender. This was day number forty-two.

370

At a lull, she pleaded with Tandy to go outside for a moment.

"But it's all smoky outside," argued Tandy.

"But not as foul as in this cave."

Tandy lay perspiring on her mat, refusing to rouse. "I can't, Surlina. Really, I shan't go out again. I'm very . . . very happy here."

She had said the words lightly, but Surlina saw the doomed look in her sister's eyes—a woman half smothered, bombed out of her house, held prisoner under the earth. She'd seen the same terrifying look in Julien's eyes before he'd gone into the trenches with Pemberton.

Tandy must take some responsibility for her own welfare. "Tandy, which would be best? To have you near the front of the cave, where you can get air, or at the back, where it's safer?"

"In the back. I'm certain the baby will come tonight."

Surlina felt fear and panic at Tandy's pronouncement. "You'll be fine," she said quickly, silently cursing Cabell for bringing them to this overcrowded gathering of gossiping women and card-playing men. "You'll be fine, just fine." Her inane words rang hollow in her throat.

She settled Tandy again on the mat, then rushed to find Cabell. He was playing brag. Surlina drew him aside, despite his objections, and said, "There are too many people in here tonight. Ask some of them to leave—or let us."

But he wanted only to play games, have drinking companions and gather an audience to hear of his travels to England.

The night dragged on. The smell in the cave changed from dank to sour. The loud sounds of labored breathing began to cut off conversations. At the back, Surlina sat holding Tandy's hand and mopping her sister's brow. The dogs lay on their sides, whining. And the shells continued to fall, coming closer and closer. "Aye, that was a flapdoozy! A jiz-banger!" Then the cries would die down and the card games would continue.

371

Surlina felt strangled. She *must* move Tandy toward the front. Then, in a burst of noise, the problem no longer existed. A sharp crack echoed, then a rain of gravel from the roof of the cave peppered her face. The shellburst must have landed directly on them. The cave shuddered. The soft ground which made tunneling so easy began to collapse in sections.

The shouting began. "Cave-in! Hold still! Don't move! We'll dig out in a minute!"

Surlina, shielding Tandy's face from the choking sand, heard the ominous creak of the support timbers. "Hurry, Tandy, turn over! Lie on your side! You can cover your face better—conserve air and keep debris off your nose and mouth."

"I can't."

"Why not?" She tried rolling her sister, but Tandy shuddered in sections, stiffening and fighting. Labor? The squeeze of Tandy's hand seemed to indicate that. Surlina felt for her basket of supplies. What good would they be in the dark? How could they breathe?

The men were digging now, making muffled sounds at the front of the cave. Women were mostly silent. The dogs growled low in their throats. Children cried out in terror as one after the other of the candles extinguished. But Surlina noticed no sudden thuds of bodies toppling. People weren't fainting. Perhaps enough air filtered through the sandstone to sustain them for a few hours.

"Dig in shifts, men!" came the command. "Take shallow breaths and hold them! Save what air we have. Don't move about."

Tandy shifted, drawing up her knees. She whispered, "The baby is going to come fast."

"No! Hold on!" whispered back Surlina, moving her sister's skirts, tugging down the drawers, loosening the tie around the midriff. "Cabell! Come here!" Cabell did not appear but several women did respond. One muttered only "Oh, you poor thing, oh, you poor thing," when told what was happening. The other, with practicality born of the situation, didn't panic but began fanning Tandy and washing her face.

Surlina had no way of gauging how much time had passed. The digging continued, faint and frantic. Cabell did not appear at the back of the cave though she sent word to him three times.

The lack of air acted as anesthesia. Tandy moaned softly, snorted like a pony and took noisy shallow breaths. But she didn't whimper, complain or scream.

Surlina could tell almost nothing of the way things were progressing. She felt her sister's head, hands, abdomen and pelvis without being of any real use. Tandy would hold in a long breath, her hands would go limp and she'd faint away. Surlina felt faint, too, groping in blackness, feeling wetness, bulges, ripples of muscular contractions, clammy skin.

"Get Cabell back here!" she ordered again.

But now no one in the cave could move. People began fainting from lack of ventilation. Only those nearest the air supply in the roof could suck in enough oxygen to work. Even so, some frantic women were pressing against them, begging to be held up to breathe.

Battling fear and faintness, Surlina struggled with Tandy. The one woman who would help knew little. Together they forced Tandy back when she struggled to sit up, spread her legs against the involuntary seizures. Other people were falling against them now. "Get away! You'll suffocate her!"

Surlina's hands felt the baby's head. "Hang on, Tandy! You've nearly done it." She attempted to slide the infant along. "Help me, Tandy!" But there was no help, no outcry, no strength in Tandy. Surlina put a hand on her stomach. Nothing was contracting.

Then she felt the sudden draft of air! There was a rushing of coolness and a burst of damp earth smells. A flickering candle pushed into the utter blackness. "Quick! Bring me the light!" She breathed deeply of the air laden with the odor of gunpowder.

She looked down as the candle was brought near. In the pulsing yellow light, she could see blood on her hands. The baby was dangling, slipping out of the tunnel. But, there was no movement in the child! Expelled, but lifeless. Now she could see the child was a

373

little girl, whole, perfect . . . stillborn. The umbilical cord was wrapped tightly around the neck. Surlina and the woman looked at the child and shook their heads, knowing full well that the baby would never make a cry, never take a gasp of the foul vapors in the cave.

Surlina rubbed the baby but could not send the blue pallor from the tiny features. She wrapped it in the blanket from the picnic basket and tended to Tandy who, reviving now, was sobbing softly.

When Surlina was able to go in search of Cabell, she found him at the entrance of the cave, bellowing drunk.

"Your baby was a daughter, Cabell."

"Name the child Dixie! Dixie Victoria! Dixie Victoria Cabell, rocking in the cradle of rebellion!" He splashed brandy into a tin cup, soaking his linen shirt in the process.

Her hand drew back, delivering a bloody forceful slap to the mouth of her bellowing brother-in-law. "Hear me! The child is dead!"

The newspaper printed its last edition on wallpaper, defiant to the end: "Grant thinks he'll have Fourth of July dinner in Vicksburg? Ha! He must find a way into the city before he can dine here!" The date on the paper was July 2, 1863.

On July 3 the Confederates sent their terms for peace. Grant sent a two-word reply: unconditional surrender.

Then, at noon on the Fourth of July, it was all over. Despite the posturing, speechmaking, tears, humiliation and harangues, unconditional surrender was a fact. The key to the Mississippi was finally in Sam Grant's pocket.

Surlina was too busy to hear speeches or think of the future. Tandy was still in the cave, too weak and feverish to be moved. The dead baby was buried at the back of the cave in a feed-sack christening gown.

On the evening of the Fourth, Surlina left the cave with only one thought in mind. Food! Perhaps a soldier would give her some cheese from his haversack. Her eyes fluttered with dizziness.

She was uncertain which way to turn in the dim streets. A few hungry men stood in line at a hastily reopened bakery, though there was no evidence of bread. Pickets stood guard over empty storefronts. At the street corner she heard sentries accounting the day's surrender. "Vicksburg gave up thirty thousand men and sixty thousand muskets! Gave up nearly two hundred artillery pieces. But she didn't have a single damned ration left to surrender!"

Surlina knew she would faint if she didn't find a crust of something. Where was Sam Grant's famous promise to resupply the city the moment it surrendered? Why, of course, the breadlines would be where the army was! She turned toward the fort, jogging erratically, her feet willing but her strength wobbly.

At the fort she found the block-long queues for hardtack. She slipped to the end, shaking and light-headed from the exertion of getting there. Over the remains of the Great Redoubt the Stars and Stripes now flew, lit by the flames of torches.

Suddenly she saw the ragged lines of prisoners marching by. She strained to look for Julien but all the men looked alike, gray, grimy, exhausted.

All at once a rider on a horse reined in near her. Glancing up, she was shocked to see Sherman, red beard sticking out stiffly, his reins taut and his shoulders reared back. He pointed at her. "Come with me! I've had the devil's own time finding you!" Before she could answer, he leaned down and swooped her up in front of him. He gritted his teeth as if searching for her had cost him personal honor. "Two million things on Grant's mind, and he asks for *you!*" He spurred the horse and away they went in a gallop, up the hill, past the breadline, straight to the headquarters tent at the crest of the divide.

Sherman dropped her from the horse like a sack of potatoes. "You can find your way in, I presume."

She was too weak to fight him. Sam had sent for her, and she was grateful to be here.

Inside the tents, she found victory celebration mixed with the monumental task of straightening out a city in chaos. She spied Rawlins lecturing subordinates with an uplifted finger. He recognized her, left off in mid-sentence and steered her to a chair. Staring at her dirty hair, ragged clothes and pallid face, he blurted, "We can't send you to see Sam looking like this!"

"I'm hungry" was all she could manage.

Suddenly Rawlins was clucking over Surlina like a fluttery mother hen. "Get her into the inner tent. Quick, bring supper—oyster stew with plenty of cream, corn-cakes, beef pie, some brandy. Find a washbasin and comb. Sergeant! Bring a clean set of blues!"

For the next two hours, Surlina was tended and shown every courtesy. She ate greedily, then lay down to avoid the cramps and churning the rich food caused. Through the walls of the private room she could hear the celebration continuing. There was no sign of Sam. She dozed off, warmed by the food and lulled by the noises of peace.

When she woke, the supper tray was gone, the candle lit, a little array of soap, hairbrush and washcloth by the basin. Much stronger now, she tried to make herself presentable. The siege had taken care of beauty, rob-bing her hair of its shine, her eyes of their luster, her body of its curves. To her delight, she heard Sam's voice mingling with the others beyond the tent wall.

She could hear reporters attempting to interview the reluctant Sherman. When asked about casualties, he did not falter. His voice boomed, "To clear the Missis-sippi for navigation, I would slay millions!"

From Sam she heard only a modest "thank you" now and then when congratulated again. He uttered spare remarks, even now directing matters to be set in motion for the next day. One of the requests he made concerned a complete list of prisoners. She wondered what he would think when he read the name Julien Rainbeau. What compassion would he have for a man who had caused him such grief at Rosie Mound and Lake Providence?

It was nearly midnight by the time he excused himself and came into the inner apartment. Surlina stood up, no longer ravenous or dizzy, but giddily expectant. He

376

took a step forward. She surged into his arms and he held her close, their hearts beating against each other. It was an embrace of release, not passion, as if this moment was a reward for the horrors they'd both shared.

She raised her head from his shoulder. "It was a great Fourth for you, Sam."

He threw his cap on the cot and sank onto the metal chair. He appeared as drained as the long line of prisoners she'd seen shuffling by in the twilight.

"Did you hear my speech today?" he asked.

"No." It surprised her how much pride she took in his humble attitude. Had he thought of her today, beyond seeing she didn't go hungry? Surlina felt her attraction to him renewing itself, lingering like a long-unplayed melody suddenly remembered.

He told of his speech. "Who can call circumstance a victory? Who can call pride a defeat?"

"Oh, Sam," she breathed. "You've found a way with words!"

She felt tears welling up in her eyes. The weeks of starvation had left her coiled; now emotions were unwinding unbidden. She was so proud of him! No longer was he unsure of himself or tongue-tied as he'd been eighteen months ago aboard the *Radiant*. Now he had the self-possession of long command. "How much you've grown in stature during this war, Sam!"

He agreed urgently, his voice almost ardent. "More changes are coming, and we shall both be borne along on their tide. For now I must stay at the center of this war's whirlpool. But eventually—"

"What *do* you see for the future?" she broke in. "Can you sense peace? Brotherhood? Union? So many men have died."

"I don't know . . ." He looked at her steadily, as if seeing the effects of the siege embodied anew in her. "War leaves suffering, like your hunger tonight. I don't know. Victory will not bring peace unless citizens return to the Union willingly." He repeated her words. "And so many men have died."

"So many men have died who had no need to die!"

Her head began to throb. It dawned on her to ask for an ambulance to take Tandy to the federal hospital.

She made her request. Almost before she'd finished, he'd dispatched Rawlins to tend to the matter. Suddenly she felt wrung out, putting her face forward into her hands. She cried, spilling forth the tears she had held for six weeks.

She felt his hands, small and strong, against her bowed neck. He rubbed gently across her spine. For long minutes, she could not quit crying. It was as if she must sob herself dry, emptying herself for a time obliterated, a city demolished. She steadied herself to ask for his mercy concerning Julien.

"Sam, what happens now?"

"For the South—a twilight." He cleared brandy glasses and cigars from his desk, then emptied the trash can and stacked his papers as if clearing some space between the two of them. "It is a twilight now between war and whatever will succeed it—not exactly peace. Fighting will continue." He sighed as if, for tonight, he could not handle the idea of more battle. "I dread heeding the call of more fighting and dying, but there can be no backing off now."

He moved against her slightly, pressing her hand to his lips, then holding her fingers spread at his cheek. "There can be no backing off from what must be done. Do you understand that? Do you realize that's why I sent Rawlins and Sherman to find you?"

"I thought it was because—" She broke off, sensing reticence on his part. Something was wrong. His blue eyes were anguished, not passionate. "*Why* did you send for me?"

"There was a time when we thought we cared for each other, wasn't there?"

"*Thought* we cared?" She jerked her hand away. He did not meet her angry gaze. How could he phrase their relationship so casually? "Those weren't exactly passing thoughts, Sam." She laughed at him sarcastically. "Can't you admit it? Can't you say we *loved?* From the moment we set eyes on each other aboard the *Radiant?*"

378

"No. I cannot." He turned away, the familiar rounded shoulders painfully erect. "From now on, the distance between us will widen." Sam sank to his knees, the starchy exterior disappearing like ripping away tissue paper. "Surlina, my wife and children are to join me here. From Vicksburg, I'm to go on to the East. From there—"

"Maybe to greater things? More stars on your lapel? National political office?" She pushed him away. Now she realized he'd sent for her in order to send her away permanently! She fought down the urge to cry out in dismay. "Get up this instant! Don't put on this act of groveling on your knees when you are actually kicking me out!" She stamped up and down in the tent, flinging her hands out, biting her lips. "Now I understand why Rawlins and Sherman were so pleasant tonight. Why, they went all-out to make sure I saw you! Ha! The joke was certainly on me!" She tried to act chipper.

Suddenly she remembered the locket she wore, the one he'd brought her at Rosie Mound. She snatched it from her neck, breaking the golden chain. "I have something of yours," she said coldly, extending it toward him in her palm.

"Surlina! Don't mock me!" He ran his hands through his hair. "The center of power is a lonely place. Don't mock me by dismissing my longing for you." He swept her to him in an embrace which squeezed her ribs painfully. The grip on her arms made her cry out. He cut off her hurt wail with a kiss which was more anger than desire.

She stepped back, lips stinging, cheeks burning.

He seemed to have regained some of his self-composure. "Do you hate me, Surlina?"

She felt the conflict of hurt, humiliation and hate. But simultaneously she sensed regret, tenderness and the power that had been between them. "Hate you? At the moment, my mind passes judgment opposite my body. I'd cheerfully string you up by the neck, then fall weeping on your corpse!"

He flinched from her bitter words, then nodded. She sensed he wanted to embrace her again, to kiss her more gently, but lacked the courage. She said honestly, "I understand. Men far less honorable, far less loving, have found themselves away from home and lonely." She kept her voice light. "I hereby give you back your honor as a soldier and a man! Tell your wife and the world you're back in harness, Sam." She tossed the locket over her shoulder, making sure it hit the floor.

His voice cracked with gratitude. Now his arms drew her against him firmly, as if he were no longer afraid of a stab in the back. A sensual tremor shook him as he pressed his lips across hers. Surlina did not protest. He seemed stirred by this lack of resistance and probed her mouth, separating her lips, pressing her breasts tightly against his chest, distending his thighs to rub against her legs. How easy it would be to lie back and let him fit himself to her. How simple to yield her flesh by merely withering. And how guilty that would make them both!

The tension was cut by a voice outside the canvas. "The prisoner lists, sir, as you ordered."

With a sigh, Sam turned her loose. He straightened his jacket and tossed his hair into place. Without a word he moved to the tent flap and took the list.

Surlina spoke before she could assail herself with logic and politics. "Sam, look for one particular name. Julien Rainbeau. If you have any justice and mercy in your heart—"

"I wondered how long before you'd ask me."

Surlina stood before him like a vanquished warrior. 'Oh God,' she prayed, 'let his determination, resolve and fairness overrule his manhood.' "What will you do with Julien?"

He sat down at the desk. "I would like to hang Captain Rainbeau from a sour apple tree, then spread a picnic beneath it."

"Will you send him to the Ohio federal prison? Will you put him on trial?" She wanted to explain how the loss of the *Quail* had defeated Julien already.

Sam walked back and forth in a narrow path, head furrowed in thought. He stooped, picked up the locket she'd thrown, carried it in his fist. Finally he stepped to the doorway. "Mr. Rawlins! Have Captain Julien Rainbeau of the Confederate River Defense Force brought to my tent immediately!"

Weakness prickled the hair on the back of Surlina's neck. Watch Sam and Julien react to each other face to face? No thanks! "May I be excused? This is not a confrontation I wish to see."

"Sit down, Surlina. You've been a thorn in both our sides for a year. You can exist in the same room with us both for five minutes."

As she slumped into the chair, she begged him outright. "Don't, Sam! Don't give way to jealousy. All the things I loved in you—don't throw them away in a fit of rage at me!" She began to sob, but without tears forming. "Don't harm Julien! You don't want me. You said so tonight—"

"Oh, Surlina, you didn't hear my words at all! I want you far more than I ever wanted anything. God forgive me, I wanted you even more than to win this—"

They were cut off by the sound of boots, a rustle in the outer tent and Rawlins' head poking into the gap in the canvas. He surveyed them, gave a snide little smile of satisfaction and ushered in Julien.

Her heart stopped when she saw him. Julien looked ready to kill! He had the stance of a fighting-mad rebel and the look of a man bent on conquest. He'd do himself more harm than good with such an attitude. A hush of expectation settled into the tiny canvas room. The shadows of lantern light flickered on the walls, casting patterns across both men's faces. Surlina sat between them as they boldly examined each other, much as she'd stood between them for a year and a half.

Slowly Julien raised his hand and saluted. Sam briskly returned the gesture. Now, maybe they could conduct this situation with some grace.

Sam sat down, while Julien stood at attention, head back, hands locked behind his spine, eyes centered. He acted as if he didn't care if Surlina were present. His arrogance baited her. Oh, men!

Exactly as she feared, Sam led off with the statement,

"Older wine and younger women rank high on the list of this world's virtues—don't you agree, Rainbeau?"

"Yes, sir! Indeed I do, sir! Couldn't agree more, sir!" Julien snapped his boot heels together for emphasis.

She looked at him in amazement. His gray eyes were steady and proud—a man who knew exactly what he wanted. Suddenly Surlina remembered how he smelled of ships and salt, how he tasted of ocean and musk, how he laughed in tones like a summer shower, trailing off softer than dewdrops. 'Oh, Julien, don't let him sully what was between us!' She was terrified into utter silence as Sam spoke again.

"And how do you feel about the adage, 'Victors rule but losers remember,' Captain?"

"Exactly right, sir! Well put, sir!" He looked cocky and mean as the devil.

'You'd better stop,' she warned Julien mentally. 'Sam is not a man to play games. I can't protect you if you persist in acting cute.' She shrugged; she wasn't much protection as it was! Oh, who needed protection! They were ignoring her! It made her feel cheap. Suddenly she was incensed. By God, she was no prisoner of war *or* love! No one could hold her in a six-by-eight-foot canvas room in the middle of the night! Not Julien Rainbeau! Not Sam Grant! Especially not while they engaged in verbally running swords through her body!

Abruptly she jumped to her feet. "Good night, gentlemen! You shall have to conduct whatever inquiries you have in mind without me." Before they could answer, she executed snappy salutes in both directions, whirled and ran.

"Innovative bitch, isn't—" she heard before she was totally out of earshot, but couldn't tell whose voice had damned her.

A longing overwhelmed her that she had not experienced in months. The silver! Greed came back to her with the force of an unexpected hailstorm. Her treasure was the one thing that wouldn't betray her!

It was no sin to think of money! Especially not her

own. I've lost a father to this war. A steamboat. Two men. But I'll be goddamned if I'll leave that silver in Friar's Mire! Victors rule, but losers remember? Thad Muller would remember well enough. She'd go partners with him, if necessary. Leave Sam and Julien to their masculine pastime of comparing notes.

She walked across the parade ground and seated herself on the damp grass beneath a hawthorn tree. All along the hillside she could see the outlines of parapets. The night was filled with firecrackers and good-natured shouting. The sorrow came creeping back. So many men had died who had no need to die! The grass beneath her was matted and rubbly, but tomorrow a green shoot would stand tall again. The pickets to her left had probably shot at each other day before yesterday; tonight they shared a canteen, smoked, laughed.

Her bones ached with weariness as she walked across the mangled remains of the Great Redoubt. She must go back to Harrison Street, make sure Tandy had been sent to the hospital, pack for a journey to Friar's Mire. The river spread out wide and serpentine below the hundreds of steps, boat lights twinkling. Only yesterday the river had lain naked.

As she climbed down the hill toward home, she heard horse's hooves pounding behind her. As she turned, it appeared that the animal would gallop straight into her. Ducking and dodging, she jumped aside. The stallion reared, the rider swinging down fully.

In the darkness, it took a second to recognize him. "Sam!" A million thoughts jumbled her mind as to why he'd followed her but they dwindled to one as he swooped her into his arms. "Oh, Sam!"

His voice was rough. "I must tell you!"

"What?"

"Your silver gates were pulled out of the mire two weeks ago."

"How could you!" She accused him of betraying the confidence she'd given him at Lake Providence. And now he had the gall to taunt her. Her lips puckered with revulsion.

"*I* didn't find the silver, Surlina, though I knew where it was and might have looked for it after Vicksburg. No, Grierson's Cavalry was chasing Muller again after his escape. He led them there—"

"And was recaptured? Don't waste time again on military justice. Hang him tonight, Sam, from any gallows you have handy!"

He was shaking his head vigorously. "Muller's loose in the countryside, damn it! Slipped off while Grierson was retrieving the gates."

"You can't do a damned thing right, Sam Grant! And that includes capturing deserters and stealing gates and making love!" She bent her head as if to butt him out of her way.

He held her shoulders brusquely. "The gates are not my affair any longer. Grierson turned them over to the Department of the Gulf at Baton Rouge. From there on, Ben Butler is back in charge. He intends to use them at his new headquarters in the bayou country west of New Orleans at some plantation he'd once envisioned as headquarters and been denied."

"Whispers! Whispers on the Rainbeau." Her elation was suddenly smothered. "Why are you telling me this? When did you find it out? Tonight?"

He hesitated—one of the few times she'd seen him waver. "No. I've known."

So he'd known all along! When he was kissing her and when he was shaming her in front of Julien and when he had booted her out of his life. Now he was buying her off! "You coward!" she whispered, too furious to shout. "You bastard! Buying me with my own silver."

His apology was simple and horrifying. "I should not have." He leaped into the saddle, struck his horse with his crop and galloped away.

She shouted a final question after him. "And what botched fate did you impose on Captain Rainbeau? I suppose you'll hang him!" She glared into the darkness, hands on hips.

Sam pulled up short on the adjoining hill. In silhouette, atop the stallion, he seemed very dark and powerful, but his voice carried softly. "I paroled him. He is free, provided he does not take up arms again. There are no ghosts between Captain Rainbeau and me. The rest is up to you, Surlina."

She started down the hill without answering. Her emotions were much too complex—elation, thanksgiving, suspicion, fascination and fury. She glanced back twice. Each time, Sam was sitting silent astride the stallion. Once he called across the darkness, "Safekeeping, Surlina. Safekeeping, my darling."

The last time she looked behind her, he was still there, silhouetted above the river loop, unmoving—but, as she knew, not unmoved.

37

"Tandy," said Surlina, tidying her sister's hospital room, "since you are so much improved, it is time for me to go. You are feeling much better today, aren't you?"

Tandy tried to lift her head to nod agreement. Surlina ignored the obvious weakness. She went on fluffing the pillow, tucking in the sheet, rearranging the roses Cabell had sent.

"I tried," whispered Tandy. "I tried to get well."

"You are much better!" shouted Surlina, instantly embarrassed by her angry outburst. Tandy must improve! The silver was at Whispers and waiting. No one else knew its whereabouts—unless Muller has somehow caught the scent again. Surlina stood at the window, trying to make pleasantries. "Lots going on in the wide world, now. Boats filling the wharves. Carriages in the streets. Houses being repaired."

Tandy managed to turn her head and look. "Why, I don't see anything different."

Surlina pulled the shade down. True enough, nothing was happening for Tandy, probably never would. She'd live on as an invalid, propped on pillows, embroidering banners. A new world had formed at the instant of Vicksburg's surrender, but Tandy hadn't noticed.

Tandy sighed. "It's a pretty day with nothing happening. Like the old times."

Surlina kissed her sister's cheek. "That's right." She gathered her shawl and adjusted her bonnet. "Goodbye, Tandy. I'll write you when I can." For a moment she felt guilty leaving, but Tandy didn't really need her.

Surlina hurried back to the house on Harrison Street, a plan already in mind. As she was packing her few belongings, Thayer Cabell paced up and down the hall. Finally he stuck his head into the room and asked point-blank, "Miss Surlina, have you had word of your silver of late?"

"Do you think I'd tell *you?*"

He was full of remonstrations, supposedly concerning her safety. "It is not wise for you to go careening about in occupied territory. Let me purchase you a steamer ticket north to St. Louis now that the river is open once again."

"Yes, do that," she agreed. "Go immediately. Can you?" She didn't like his interest in the treasure. Perhaps rumors of its existence had resurfaced. It was best to lead him astray. "You're very generous, Cabell. Please see to the ticket at once!"

For once their aims seemed to coincide. He rushed to the piers and returned with a ticket on the *Imperial*, the first steamer to ply the open river. Surlina thanked him, put the ticket in her handbag and wondered how late the office would be open. She would cash in the ticket and use the funds to travel in the opposite direction.

She looked up from folding clothes to find Cabell still in the doorway, watching her intently, as if he knew what she had on her mind. "When you finish," he said politely, "would you join me in the study?"

She finished within an hour. When she entered, his back was to her. He was attired in his new white suit, the polka-dot silk handkerchief nearby on the desk. A sprig of fresh greenery lay atop the handkerchief, his beige straw hat nearby. She studied the back of Cabell's swarthy head where the sweaty curls rippled, turning under across his fat neck.

He did not rise as she circled the room and sat opposite him at the writing desk. An open bottle of bourbon was half-empty. He poured two fingers into his glass, one into hers. Around and around he swished the brown liquid, continuing to stare down into the glass moodily.

"Still searching for some quintessential spirit of the South, Cabell?"

He was deep in melancholy mire. "It takes many generations and many barrels of whiskey and many docile wives to build a true aristocracy."

"And one good war to end it." Surlina never tired of puncturing his balloons. It was the one activity she enjoyed in his company.

"We don't have to actually win. We can win, ultimately, simply by not losing."

"That's not the same thing."

"As long as there are units in the field, as long as the slaves are loyal, as long as my people assert their independence—"

"Your people and your South are flat out sitting on their naked bottoms with rifle butts up their noses! And you march about the streets of surrendered Vicksburg, shaking hands and making speeches! That's *not* winning."

"How can the battle be over when we fought with such hope and such gallantry and such ferocity and—"

"And such futility. It's over. Accept it."

"The troops are low, it's true. But the slaves are still loyal!"

"Emancipation is inevitable, Cabell. Not only inevitable—but right!"

He lit a cigar. Surlina blew out the match, wondering why the fire of his illusions should not have gone out long ago. "It's finished, God help you!"

"No! The rocket of revolution, once launched, shoots far beyond its original takeoff point." Cabell puffed fiercely on the cigar, emitting sparks and flicking ashes.

They both had to stand to avoid the rain of fire. "I am one of the men who ignited this Southern rocket. And I am not dead!"

She grabbed his cigar and stubbed it out. "Think of the men in the trenches who have done all your fighting for you. You sent them to their death with exactly that kind of talk!"

He staggered slightly as he moved around the table to refill his bourbon glass. He raised it in solemn pledge. "I shall be their spokesman. I shall be their prophet. I shall redeem their pledges. When they call me, I shall—"

"Cabell, no one is calling for you!" She moved away to the window, paying attention finally to the urgency in his voice. So that was it—beneath all the finery and the faking, beneath the smiles and politics and drinking, beneath it all, Thayer Cabell had the enormous self-love to see himself as a Southern Redeemer.

She took his whiskey bottle and poured a tiny amount into her mouth, swished it around and spat it into his ashtray. "The taste of the South is already bitter, Cabell. It will last long in the throats of those who have suffered. Don't add to it."

He snatched his riding crop from the couch. Brandishing the whip overhead, he stormed, "I shall stir the Southern heart! Fire the Southern intellect! Instruct the Southern mind! And at the proper moment, I shall be ready, when called, to lead!"

Surlina knew the only thing he'd be capable of calling forth would be the hottest heads in Mississippi. Yet, in his way, he was dangerous. With men like him at the helm of the Confederacy, the war could go on for years.

She tried to calm him by appealing on Tandy's behalf. "Cabell, think of your wife. Abandon some of your dreams of glory and think of the practical things you can do to help Tandy get well."

"Tandy?" He seemed startled to hear her name.

"Surely you remember you have a wife!"

"Oh, yes, of course, dearest Tandy. Ah, so young,

388

so fragile, my darling bride. She was a worthy woman in her way." His smile seemed to be one of mourning.

Perhaps she had misjudged him. For a moment Surlina felt compassion. In an impulsive act, she patted his shoulder.

Instantly he captured her hand, retaining it between his own, not in a grief-stricken pose but in an avaricious, calculating way. "My dearest Tandy will not be a strong wife in the new aristocracy, however. You see that, don't you, Surlina?"

Confused, Surlina attempted to withdraw her fingers from his greedy clasp. He restrained her, taking her other hand and pulling her close. "But you—ah, you! Yes, the time is now! Carry the banner at my side! Come, Surlina, the hour strikes, calling us forth!"

She broke away. Fearful of him now, she flung open the front door, admitting the July heat and river smell. She decided to ignore his insinuation that she replace Tandy. "I hear only the wind tonight. Certainly I hear no one calling you forth."

"The man is ready, even as the times call." He posed with his hand against his heart. "We must fight on."

"With what? With whom?"

"As Paris is France, as the sun is our universe, I *am* the South. We must go beyond Confederation. Republic, perhaps—or in place of President Davis, we must have a titled—"

"A *King?*" She blurted the interruption in amazement. Yes, of course! That was what he saw! A southern kingdom with himself ruling. The idea was certainly not alien to his European background. Long ago her father had called him a "revolutionary in exile."

"You are mad, Cabell! The mad king of Mississippi!" She began to laugh.

In two quick strides, he crossed the room. His hand flung out, delivering a slap which hit her hard across the mouth, breaking the skin on her lower lip. She felt the taste of salty blood. But she stood, head high, looking at him, fully aware that in another time and place, he would have had her guillotined.

"I leave tomorrow for Europe," he announced.

389

Her practical instincts overruled her desire to remain quiet. "You can't do that. There's Tandy to think of!"

"She need not concern us!" Thayer began to pace. "France remains watchful as a bulldog set hard by the master's gate. Semmes and the *Alabama* fight on." Again he whirled toward her, catching both hands around her waist. "Come with me, Surlina! With your youth and beauty and silver and hard determination—come with me! Sit with me in the seat of power. Wear the crown of prestige."

"There will be no crown." She pulled back from his liquor breath and kneading hands.

She saw fury in his eyes, but he transferred his vengeance to the room. He tore at the furnishings, wrecking the desk by swiping it bare with the back of his hand. The bottle and glasses crashed to the floor, breaking on the worn woolen carpet. He shouted wild plans, incoherently. The Surlina Silver must finance the South! Again he chanted his chorus. "You must come with me, Surlina! I will dress you in silks! We'll use the Spotswood Hotel in Richmond for headquarters, temporarily. Do you think the Spotswood suitable?"

"The Spotswood? Richmond has been torn down in rioting for bread! It's just like Vicksburg. Women and children fight in the streets for moldy crusts."

Suddenly he slumped in the chair, legs sprawled, complexion turning from splotchy to vibrant purple. Both fists beat his brow. "If the war will only go on long enough!"

"Go on long enough . . . ?" Aghast, she understood his plan. Prolong the war. Perpetuate his own chances of coming to power.

"There are ways to make it last," he asserted, a superior hint of intrigue in his voice. "There are rumors Jefferson Davis could be deposed—by assassination."

"You wicked man!"

"I demand that you come with me to Europe!"

"You've lost touch with reality, Cabell. I'm not your mistress, I'm your sister-in-law! Never would I consider myself as your empress . . . and certainly not your whore!"

"The Southern Council has met. Ramsey and I are agreed you must join—"

"Ramsey Arnauld! This sounds like one of his rutting schemes!" She mentally damned Ramsey and Cabell as a pair of idiots. They weren't the ones who had served under fire in Vicksburg's trenches. Cabell had worn a white suit and straw hat and made speeches! Ramsey had probably fended off the enemy at Whispers by playing the accordion! Now they sniffed silver around her again like a couple of jackals. She reaffirmed her decision to find the gates. More than ever, she'd need the money to care for Tandy if Cabell should flee to Europe. "I'm leaving this house tonight. I cannot bear to be in the same room with you, you evil jackass."

There were only two things she loved more than a good fight. One was the silver. The other was Julien. She left the house determined to have both, and never, never again to sit in the same room as Thayer Cabell.

The next morning, Surlina scanned the lines of tattered Confederates waiting to be paroled. Tramping up and down the row in the hot July sunshine, she feared Julien might already have been dispatched. Surely he wouldn't leave without seeing her!

Suddenly she spotted a tall man, his back to her, a lump of mottled fur peering over his shoulder. Silly Squeebob! She rushed forward, thinking Julien gorgeous even in a cast-off uniform which left his ankles showing and wrists dangling. For shoes, he had merely leather soles tied to his feet with laces. But his golden hair was blowing in the breeze, ruffled as a halo. And when she called his name, he turned, eyes laughing, and threw back his head, smiling. His small knapsack dropped to the ground.

She was so ecstatic she blurted out her news. "Julien! I know where the gates are! I'm on my way to get them!" She tossed his cat on the ground so she could hug him.

He drew back, studying her, but his eyes were sparkling happiness. "So! You are all set to desert me again for those gates." Idly he leaned down and patted the cat. "And then?"

"And then?" She hadn't plotted past finding the silver. "Why, and then we'll go wherever we want! Do as we please!"

He sat down near a small peach tree, moving his legs in front of him stiffly. "I'm too tired to even contemplate any more options."

She knelt beside him. "Nonsense, darling. You're just tired. Hungry, hot, weary—I don't blame you. Please hurry with this business of the parole. Then we can decide our next move. There are so many possible—"

"I don't think so." Julien was quiet, no laughter on his lips or in his eyes. "I am going away."

"Away? Where? You'll come with me to Whispers and we'll get the silver, then we'll go wherever you want!"

"No! I must hurry to Shreveport. That is where the Rainbeau-Arnauld aunts have gone with little Laurel. I have a telegram from them, saying to come as quickly as possible. After that, I am simply going away. I shall never go back to Whispers!" He stopped her fingers from drumming the side of her purse, then held her hand to his lips. "Come with me."

"Of course! As soon as I retrieve the silver."

Suddenly he seemed shy, dipping his head and studying the grass. "I can't wait. Come with me *now*." An aura of defeat crossed his face, a taint of fear coupled with complex guilts, desires and hopes.

Slowly she began to realize the depths of the cowering man in front of her. His eyes were clouded, his fingernails dirty, his clothing makeshift. But worse, his spirit was desperate. Far from being sympathetic to Julien, she was blunt and scornful. "You'd just walk away from here with nothing?"

"You're right. I'm walking. Surlina, that's the only thing I *can* do. The only choice left to me that is both an act of courage and volition is to walk away. The only thing I can ask is that you walk away with me."

392

The recent months of privation filled her mind. "We wouldn't have a thing!"

"Nothing? I'd have myself. Laurel. You. The world. All I need." He scrambled to his feet. "The terms of my parole are clear. I'm not to fight again. And I cannot fight with you either. I leave today for Shreveport. Will you come with me?"

The old riddle crossed her mind. Should she opt for Shreveport and Julien today, or gamble she could travel to Whispers, retrieve the silver and then catch up with him? She stalled for time to make up her mind. "Where will you go, ultimately? Back to sea?"

He was amused. "Sea captains who lose ships rarely get second chances." For a moment his fatigue dropped away and his eyes flashed their gray mischief. "So I didn't win the war! But maybe I can get the Northern frogleg franchise." He leaned against the tree, making the green peaches sway. "Actually, I hope to march from the ranks of the Confederate River Defense Force into total obscurity."

Surlina could abide his attitude of defeat no more. It horrified her that this man who once had such a vivid imagination had simply given up. "The great Captain Rainbeau tosses in the towel!"

"I'm not bitter, Surlina. Don't you be. I'm not vengeful either. But my mind is made up. I served in a navy with little physical fact and no heritage. So when it died, I didn't lose much. When I lost the *Quail,* I lost something more. In a strange way, Grant gave me back courage the night he wiped the slate clean between us. But I've lost—"

"You lost your will to fight! Well, I have not lost mine! I still ache to find my silver! I still crave to win my battle!"

"You will always want something more than I can give you." He picked up Squeebob and tucked him under his arm. "I cannot make you turn loose of the silver. And if we walk away from here together, it will be empty-handed." He put the cat in the peach tree, opening his arms to her. "But, darling, we'd have a clean slate for the future—to fill with each other."

393

"Julien, you're such a dreamer."

He took her face in his hands, pushing the dark hair away from her forehead. "Well, since I'm rolling out promises, let me offer you a few more naïve dreams. I believed all along that some of us would survive this war. And I believe now, with a little luck and wit, some of us are even going to live happily again. If I didn't believe that, I'd never ask you to come with me. And I *am* asking—begging, Surlina."

This was no time to cry. She buried her head in his shoulder to hide her face.

His voice went on, strong and confident. "We've both seen death, tragedy, defeat. But we're young and strong. Who's to say we won't have joy and striving and triumph? All I'm asking, darling, is for you to be a little less worldly. Oh, Surlina, you kept me alive that day in the shed when we brought in the bodies from the *Quail*. Let me kill this need in you for the silver with the same words. '*You* are my love! Only you! Always and forever!' Love me, darling, but be less greedy. Thou shalt not covet."

She raised her face, laughing. "Julien, when were you ordained to preach?"

"When did you begin to believe with the devil's own fervor that money was your salvation?"

She was silent, thinking he wanted too much. If the silver was hopelessly gone, it would be different. But now she knew where it was. On his home ground! He *must* help her. She resorted to teasing. "A real Southern gentleman would have the chivalry to give me some time to make up my mind."

"Our world has run out of time and gentility."

"If only I could see the future! Despite your promises—your dreams—we might desperately need that treasure! Surely you don't think I can instantly forget the lessons of hunger and hurt I've learned?"

"I don't remember you in those ways. I remember you only as daring and wonderful, a woman with the courage to leap from a burning steamboat into a frozen river, a girl who loved me without feigning reserve.

394

My love, my beautiful, compassionate partner who cried with me over the *Quail*."

"If only I could read the future, then—"

"You still want prophecy? Then let me be your prophet. Suppose you go to Whispers. Suppose by some strange luck the silver is there. You claim it. Ensconce it behind bars in vaults. The war ends. What have you gained? What have you done but put yourself up for bid?"

Suddenly he was bold, slashing at the slender tree with his fist, knocking the cat and green fruit to the ground.

"I want you, Julien! I love *you!*" she yelled, trying to make him understand.

"Then come with me now."

Surlina threw her arms around him, clinging like a fragile bubble at a waterfall's edge. "I'll come to you soon. The moment I can!"

"Surlina, you are absolutely foreign to me!" He shoved her away. "I forgive you your lust for power —which is what I imagine you saw in Grant. I forgive you the adultery and treason that accompanied him—"

"That's not fair! There was nothing between us that concerns you! Can't you see I love you for your own sake?"

"No, it's compulsion for the silver which kept you near me all that time—brought you to Whispers, took you to Natchez, Vicksburg, Rosie Mound. It breaks my pride to admit it was the silver, not me."

He picked up his small knapsack. "Those gates are ones you'll have to pass through alone. You've jilted me twice for them. Not again, Surlina."

"Please! Please let me try this one last—"

"I'm tired of decisions that never quite get made." He settled a cap over his golden hair. A tuft of cottonwood fuzz stuck out from the brim. "Good-bye, Surlina." He tipped the cap and took his place back in line to be paroled.

She watched the line move slowly downhill. No tears or shouts. No forgiveness or embraces or tearing at each other. He'd simply said good-bye and walked away. Now his figure was a dark dot at the bottom of the valley, heading north to Shreveport and Laurel.

A voice close at hand inquired, "Going to run after him? Or run away from him? Or stand there planted till you take root?"

Surlina collapsed into Dottie's outstretched arms. Dottie patted her comfortingly. "Shake, shiver and fall apart. What is it about my nephew that sends you into chills and fevers? You're damned near panting with your tongue hung out while your fingers is curled up in snowballs."

"I've done terrible things to Julien," blurted Surlina. I've harmed him with my pride."

"You do look plumb discombobulated, girlie. Hair frizzed and cheeks red, eyes wavering like waterspouts. What happened? He tell you good-bye?"

"He walked off." The tears were threatening now, but the pain was more of jealousy than longing. Why would he be so stubborn when she was so obviously right? She folded her arms across her chest, trying not to break down.

Dottie surveyed her with a cross-eyed grin. "Better come down off that throne, Surlina. Seems to me everything you and Julien gave each other—including hell and what for—was done of your own free wills."

"He wanted me to go with him without a penny in our pockets."

"Don't doubt it. Probably had an old-fashioned wedding in his mind as well. Julien takes to legal churchings and christenings." She aimed a mouthful of tobacco juice at the grass, wiped her mouth with the back of her hand and asked shyly, "You want to tag along with me to Whispers?"

"Oh, Dottie! Is that where you're heading? Do you have a wagon or team?"

"Horse and buggy." She pointed to the hitching posts where a grand surrey rig was held by a smart-looking black racehorse. He was pawing the ground, impatient at being restrained.

"Where in the world did you find such a getup?" asked Surlina, impressed. She refrained from praising

396

the trim horse for fear of hurting Dottie's feelings about her old mule.

"Won the surrey playing poker with the quartermaster's boys. Real guttersnipes they were. As for the horse—there is such a thing as horse races." She looped her arm through Surlina's and gave a little swat to her backside. "In the buggy, girlie!"

The wind in her hair perked Surlina's spirits. Why, with Dottie's determination and this horse's speed, they'd be at Whispers in two days' time! "Dottie, I have a little money, courtesy of my brother-in-law. I want a gun."

"Seems sporting enough. You a fair shot?"

"I will be when you teach me." Surlina laughed, refusing to think of Julien walking north on the road to Shreveport. In the darkest recess of her mind, she continued to feel there might be a way to have both the silver and Julien.

Apparently Dottie was thinking about Julien, too. "Why couldn't you and that hardheaded nephew of mine patch things up?" When there was no answer, she slipped a long, curved knife from her leather breeches. "Use this."

"For what?"

"To cut that Gordian knot tying you, Julien and the silver together."

"If it isn't at Whispers, I'll give it up forever!" Surlina's voice rang with clear conviction.

"Three cheers and a tiger for you, dearie," cackled Dottie sarcastically. "Bet you wouldn't swear that on a stack of worn-out King James's, though. Oh, hellfire, Surlina! You don't believe that. I don't believe it. Can you blame Julien for not believing either?" She wadded a corner of her bandanna into her mouth, chewing it as well as her plug of tobacco.

Surlina began to drown in tears of self-pity.

"No sniffling," ordered Dottie. "Nobody likes the salt of rebuke poured in the wounds of truth. But the fact of the matter is, you ain't even recognized the basic truth of this situation. You never were no Silver Belle!"

Surlina batted her eyes at such a farfetched notion.

"Nope, you weren't. When I met you, you was down and out in a navy blanket, and you been penniless ever since Julien fell in love with you. Now, a real set-back-on-her-haunches heiress wouldn't have hung around after her steamer got shanghaied. She'd have hightailed it back to St. Louis, sent out telegrams and Pinkerton men." The old woman urged the horse to gallop. "But you didn't run for home. Had any number of excuses as I recall—your pa, your sis, your stay in the New Orleans jail, Sam, Julien. You name it, and you used it as a reason not to go back."

"I couldn't lose the trail of the silver," Surlina defended herself.

"Aha!" cried Dottie, standing in the surrey and slapping the horse with the whip. "That's it! The trail! Your love isn't that money, Surlina! It's the pursuit."

Surlina was shocked at Dottie's perceptiveness. She'd explained things Surlina had only half understood, feared, recognized and kept buried.

38

On the third day into the bayou country, rain set in like a monsoon. Steady, straight down, undramatic dripping. Soggy weather with the sky low enough to blend with the brackish waters of the sloughs and the moss in the gray-green live oaks. The racehorse's trim ankles mired in mud. Surlina lamented the foul weather, cursing it for slowing their descent into the lowlands and Whispers. She had new fears, too, as each mile farther south brought discoveries of wreckage in the countryside. Here a shack was burned, there a whole plantation gutted. In the oak alley a gallows stood, by the bayou a heap of burned furniture, in the fields nothing but straggly blackberries.

"Butler's troops?" she quizzed Dottie. "Or Southerners so hotheaded they'd burn their own homes rather than surrender them? Or Muller?"

A new gust of rain swooped down, drenching the landscape. The wind blew stronger, whipping the surrey fringe against Surlina's face. She searched the soggy terrain for signs of marauders, imagining Thad Muller hiding in the rain-soaked woods. She asked Dottie the same question she'd asked every hour: "Do you think it will be there?"

"Whispers? Why, sure! Pillars on its privies and statues on its porches. This storm will have the hinges flapping on both."

"I mean the silver."

"Who cares?"

Rain sluiced like a water pump, blocking vision ahead. The racehorse faltered, spooked by the noise of thunder. The wind shook the trees, sounding like high-pitched screech owls, cutting off conversation. The road was a quagmire. At this rate of inching along, it would take weeks to reach Whispers! For a moment, Surlina longed for sturdy Murray. He'd wallow right through this sinkhole. "How much farther?" she shouted.

"Depends on whether we try the back way through the cutoff or go in proper through the West Wind Gates."

"Dottie, you ever seen it rain this way before?"

"Sure. Lots of times. The hurricanes of '53 and '48 and '39 and—"

"My God! Is this a hurricane?"

"Not yet, but it's aiming its snotty nose in that direction!"

"Will we be able to get to Whispers at all? Take the shortcut through the bayou! We must hurry!"

"Not hell *or* high water gonna keep you from that silver, hunh?"

Dottie pulled her wet felt hat lower across the brim of her forehead, clucking hopelessly to the stranded horse. "Have to walk a spell, Surlina. This racer has done tuckered out. We can make it by evening. Forget your traveling kit, too. We'll have our hands full with just our pistols and hominy." She laughed as she unloaded into the mud. "Reminds me of your first visit to this neck of the woods, when you came bobbling out of the bayou."

Surlina realized that Dottie was right. Walk or abandon the plan. She tucked her pistol into her belt, patting the cold metal of the 1860 model Colt '44. It had taken double-talk and double dollars to buy the gun. She wasn't about to let it rust in this downpour. She hadn't quite settled on a scenario for making Butler deliver the gates into her hands, but she envisioned the pistol entering into it somehow. Arranging her oilskin hat to shelter her face, she climbed down into the orange slime, sinking ankle-deep around her boots. When she stepped, the ground sucked loudly and puckered as if boiling.

They trudged forward, bent low against the wind which roared from the southeast like a fury. Dottie cut a path through cane, willows, sawgrass and knee-deep ooze, making use of fallen logs, grapevines and hickory bark as handholds. Surlina felt inept, slipping and catching up, falling and staggering upright again. But single-mindedly she followed Dottie through the swamps.

Her excitement revived when Dottie suddenly stopped and pointed ahead. "Big as life and twice as pretty!" shouted the old lady, forging toward the mansion which glowed through the dense rain. "Upright as a preacher on Sunday morning!"

Surlina grabbed Dottie to keep her from bursting into the clearing. "Wait! We've got to see who's there!"

"Don't wet your drawers. Looks to me there's *nobody* home. But we'll sneak up like a couple of old tomcats out for a prowl." She ducked behind a live oak.

They approached by skirting the croquet court and the sundial garden. The poplars bent low in the wind, thrashing like acrobats. The great house rose out of the haze, its onion dome shining blue in the gray rain. Long tails of Spanish moss flapped like ties from cypresses. No sign of life. Everything was apparently intact; porches, hollow statues, the swing, the cook-house, the brick walkway to the sawmill. But no horses, army wagons, gates with B. B. carved on them to indicate Ben Butler. Surlina remained suspicious and guarded, clutching her pistol with her right hand, wiping the rain from her eyes with her left.

They crept to the portico; the back door was unlocked. They looked at each other, steadied their guns and slowly pushed it open.

The inside of the house was dark. Silent except for rain hissing at the windows. Locking her hand around the pistol grip, Surlina moved through the darkened breezeway toward the main hall. Whispers seemed intact and uninhabited. How strange!

Circling into the grand foyer, Dottie fumbled in her myriad pockets for a dry lucifer. Behind them a screen hinge creaked, then the sound was blown away in the wind. The yellow blaze of the oil lamp sprang up, cheerless and wan. Dottie held the light aloft.

The shadows widened out. Surlina gasped, failing in her intent to stay quiet. Despite its perfect exterior, Whispers had obviously been the scene of internal violence. The women looked at each other, stunned, too shaken to even move at first.

The battlefield at Vicksburg had been no grimmer than the scene inside the beautiful house. The wallpaper now peeled down the walls, streaks of lye eating away the plaster beneath. The floor ran dark and sticky with molasses, an ax in a barrel testifying how the mess had gotten there.

Dottie led the way with the lamp, not speaking but motioning with her pistol barrel to scenes of destruction. In the music room, the top of the piano was propped open with a sword, the strings poured full of flour and kerosene. The fumes from the gummy mixture penetrated the hallway.

'It's good all the Rainbeaus and Arnaulds went away,' Surlina thought. 'Julien was right in his determination to make a new life.' She thought for a moment of Grandmere's imperial design to hold the fortress against all comers. Now, all was litter—the

401

portraits ripped from the gilt frames, the canvas, curtains and rugs used for campfire fuel. Remnants of dishes and mirrors dotted the grand staircase. Dried flowers hung in the chandeliers and over the curtain rods as if they'd been tossed, vases and all. Syrup coated the stair banister, and imprints of horse's hooves marked the pine steps. Manure blocked the landing.

"Foul as he is, Butler would not have done this," Surlina whispered. "If he was here, he's long gone."

Dottie held up her pistol, pointing to a smoldering pile of coals, the remains of a campfire built directly on the tile of the hearth. "Mullermen, ten to one. Recent, too."

Surlina's heart began to quake. The pistol in her hand began to tremble despite her frantic grip. Her face twisted with the effort of attempting to see into every shaded nook. Upstairs, the armoires had been ransacked, piles of clothing and curtains strewn on the floors. The big pinewood bed had been axed for kindling; frying pans stained white eyelet pillow covers with grease. Crude drawings in charcoal defaced the gallery wall. She ran to the window, remembering how she'd watched the patient slave sift the earth. Now rain blockaded her view.

Finally they entered the narrow staircase which wound to Grandmere's third-story sanctuary. The door to the tiny alcove near the copper dome was standing open, wind and rain gusting through. Surlina instinctively started for the window to close it. Halfway across the room, she glimpsed something outside and pulled back. Pistol raised, other hand pointing, she watched for the movement again. Only a shadow? A tree branch broken by the wind? 'Be calm,' she told herself. 'No outlyers are flying around the third story.'

Then the dark shape swung past the window again. A human shape. Hanging lifeless, blown by the wind, turning round slowly in the rain, battered and dead. Dangling as if caught by the hair. A scream caught deep in her throat. All she could do was point and clutch Dottie's sleeve.

Dottie bounded across the room, shielding the lamp

while peering out into the storm. "Ramsey!" she croaked as the form drifted into view again. "They've hung him!"

Surlina felt nausea and blackness gallop across the back of her brain, then slide into the pit of her stomach. A sudden gust of wind whirled the corpse, bringing Ramsey's face close to the open window—the broken neck, the flapping arms, the open eyes. She shielded her face by raising her arm. The rain pelted the body, sounding like fingers tapping on wood.

Dottie had the curved knife. "Take this, Surlina. Cut him down when I call to you. I'll trench a pit in the mud. Pour in some charcoal. It's the best we can do." Her practicality seemed a mask for emotions which would rip her apart.

"Do we have to? I mean, can't we just leave? This was a mistake! We shouldn't have come." Her objections tumbled out one after the other as she put the gun back into her belt and reluctantly took the knife handle.

The loud slam of the door behind them sent both women whirling. Too late. In the doorway, guns in both hands, stood Thad Muller. Surlina gasped and willed her hand to grab her pistol and fire, but she was transfixed by the evil on his face.

What happened next occurred in an instant, yet Surlina saw it in detail. Muller's command to drop the weapons. Her hand tightening on the knife till it seemed an extension of her fist. Dottie balancing the lamp in one hand, gun in the other, then leaning slightly backward as if to hurl the lantern. The corpse at the window riding the wind like a hobbyhorse. Rain lashing through the open room. The odors of wet hemp and Ramsey's body mixed with the stagnant past of Grandmere's alcove.

Muller's gun traced a circle in the air. Surlina followed his movement as if hypnotized. Then Dottie's hand flew upward, tossing the lantern toward the ceiling at the same moment that she twisted her pistol toward Muller's belly.

The shot. Muller's hand twitched; his gun roared.

403

Dottie flew backward, lifted from her feet and flung against the wall. The bandanna around her neck covered her chin and mouth. A hole, round and perfect like a five-dollar gold piece, opened in the right side of her neck. The vein shuddered, then spurted, spitting blood jaggedly. Her hands raised toward her face as if surprised, then fell lifeless as she toppled to the floor.

Now Surlina found her voice in a scream which echoed above the banshee wind. "Dottie!" She ran toward the old woman. Muller's arm intervened, catching her across the back of the neck, knocking the gun from her belt and the knife from her hand, sending her splaying against Dottie's boots.

"Lie still, Silver Belle, or you'll kiss those boots as your coffin lid." She shuddered, trying to spot the knife or gun, feeling the wetness which was pouring from Dottie's neck and trickling over the floor. She kept her face down, expecting a blade in her back or the instant stinging death of a bullet.

"There's nothing here, Muller," she pleaded. "Don't kill me for nothing."

"That's right. Nothing here but you and me." She felt a loop of rope whiz through the air above her. 'He's going to hang me!' she thought. Dry retching buckled her midriff. Then her arms were yanked from beneath her, caught tight in the cord and bound behind her back. 'I'm done for,' she thought again, and laid her cheek against Dottie's boot in a gesture of farewell and mourning.

She heard his pistols swat leather as he stuffed them into his holsters. Next, she felt his hands check the knot of rope at her wrists, heard his grunt of satisfaction. 'Kill me now,' she prayed fervently. Then he yanked her upright by the hair and neck. "On your feet, Silver Belle. The time has come for you to let your screams ring loud and clear." He kicked at her buttocks, pushing her toward the door. Blind with fear and grief, she lunged forward, thinking she could throw herself from the third-story portico landing.

He broke her lunge by yanking back on the rope at her wrists. "No, no! Don't cheat me! I made a mistake in not killing you long ago. But it's a mistake I want to correct." He guided her down the stairs, tugging the rope tight to keep her from stumbling in the darkness.

Halfway down the last flight, he stopped her abruptly. "Far enough! Now scoot your tail over that banister." She pulled back, uncertain what he meant, suspecting he now intended to murder her. She was breathless with fear, oozing sweat which had the stench of panic in it. She felt him loosening the rope knot. Then he pushed her arms above her head without releasing them. He latched the knot between stair posts, tying it twice around the sturdy oak banister. Then he lifted her in his arms, leaned over the railing and dropped her.

She screamed as the intense strain on her arm sockets gave way to burning pain. A dizziness swept through her, then her eyes wavered. The house seemed to undulate, then settle back into its place. She whimpered against the unbearable tug on her wrists, elbows and shoulder joints. But she was held fast, dangling two feet above the floor, pinned and torn by the rope fastened to the banister.

Surlina heard his boots clomping down the stairs, heard his throaty laughter as he cursed her pain. Rounding the bottom step, he swung her to and fro like a punching bag. "Strung up like a side of beef, Silver Belle! Now we'll see how brave you are!" She kicked at him, but each time she moved her legs, the strain on her arms became unbearable. "That's right: Settle down like a good filly." He stood on a small stool, grabbing her face, his eyes shining with savage delight like a wild dog's. Thick saliva beaded up on his lips. She let her head go slack against her chest, hoping she'd faint from the pain in her arms.

Suddenly she felt a fierce pull. He ripped away her wet shirt, exposing her cotton chemise. She let her head hang down, unable to bring her knees up as protection. Any moment she felt her arms would pop from their sockets. Slowly, he withdrew his knife, honed the blade against her breeches, then slashed the air. "I want to leave my mark on you, Silver Belle. Just like carving initials on a tree. And I want a souvenir, too—sort of like cutting a sow's ears off at butchering time."

The knife point came near her chest, probing the damp chemise. The tip of steel was cold against her breastbone. She could feel blood pounding beneath the blade, lifting the knife as she gasped for breath.

She tried to force contractions from her stomach upward through her throat to make screams. But only gurgles of fear came forth, sounding as if she was choking. "Blow me some kisses," he advised, "or save your breath. We got a long night ahead of us. This storm's making me cold. You're going to have to provide me a fire for my poker!" He sliced away the chemise, held the knife point against her nipples, then squeezed her breasts with calloused hands.

She used all her strength to buck her knees, drawing up violently, kicking him in the chin, tossing him off-balance from the stool. As he fell backward, she drew a scream from her depths which rang through the house like a gunshot.

As Muller scrambled from the floor, he flailed his hand to his heart, as if she'd knocked the breath from him. Behind him, she saw the door open. Not rapidly, as if blown by the wind, but stealthily as if moving by its own volition. A hand reached around, stifling the latch from making a sound. Too terrified to cry out, she caught the movement, while still intent on protecting herself from Mullers' knife.

"You bloody fool!" he roared, raising the knife and slashing away the last of the cotton undergarment. "You want the taste of blood in my mouth? Then, I'll drink yours!" He caught her to him, mounting the stool and capturing her right breast to his mouth. He bit down hard on the nipple, gripping it in his front teeth and shaking his head like a dog worrying a bone.

She felt the obscene pain blossoming in layers. The burning gave way to a sting which gave way to a bright stabbing. She felt the warm glow of blood bubbling its way to the surface. Then she let the noise of hurt drown her ears, howling wildly with her head thrown back and legs twitching.

406

Suddenly she heard running footsteps, a sound like wood hitting bone. Then, she felt Muller sag against her heavily, his arms going around her waist, then her hips, then brushing against her legs as he fell away. He made no sound, only a little exhalation like a dog makes when unexpectedly kicked. Through her blurred eyes, she could make out a man shoving Muller's form away, a rifle butt upraised, the heavy stock crashing against Muller's skull, the body skidding on the sticky floor, the stool rolling away.

Dangling in the darkness, the pain eating away all feeling, she willed her eyes to focus. The man was bent over Muller now, a bayonet in hand. The metal glinted upraised, then slammed down with the force of a hammer. She heard the impact, the gasp of hatred from the man, the final chuff of breath from Muller.

The man raised up, knife in hand, and for a horrible instant she thought she was to receive the next blow. Then, out of her whirling sensations, she moaned, "Julien!" An instant later, she felt the ropes slacken as he bounded up the stairs and cut through the hemp with the bayonet point. She dropped to the floor, hitting her legs, doubling over, the jolt blotting all feeling from her flesh. The blackness rose up to blind her, taking away her breath. "Julien," she gasped before fainting.

She came around slowly, feeling first the splat of rain against her face, then the smell of wind fighting her nostrils. Finally she jerked as the pain in her arms renewed, the fire in her nipple pulsated and her memory of the ordeal came rushing back. "Julien! Where are you?" She staggered to her feet, finding she was outdoors among the porch columns, a jacket covering her naked shoulders. Upright, she felt dizzy. She put her arms around the statue column, head down against its whiteness, summoning her strength. "Julien!"

Suddenly a tiny cry answered her call. A mewing like a cat close by. Startled, she alerted her senses to pinpoint the sound. Images of Julien lying wounded in the bushes made her bend down toward the tangled ivy. She called his name softly again.

This time the tiny voice answered, "Grandmere?" The questioning twitter was barely audible, right by Surlina's ear. But when she whirled around, seeking the person who'd whimpered, she found nothing.

She raced along the porch, calling, "Who is it? Who's here?" The wind shifted. She heard a small snuffling sound. Bushes rustling? Porch creaking? This was a human sound! A child's sound! "Where are you? Tell me!"

At that moment, Julien staggered from the front door, Dottie's body in his arms. She ran to help him, overwhelmed anew by the tragedy. She blurted, "Muller killed her."

"And Ramsey. I saw." He lowered the body to the back of his wagon in the front circle. "That's not the worst of it! I would kill Muller three times over for what's he's done to my child!"

"Your child? Laurel?" She drew back in horror. "But you went to Shreveport—"

"She wasn't there. When the soldiers came here, she was frightened. Ran away and hid. No one could find her. That's why I came back. Oh, God, my Laurel! Muller must have—"

She cut him off by pulling him along the porch with both hands. "She's here! I heard her. I'm certain it was a child."

He looked at her in bewilderment, as if afraid to believe her. "Where is she?" He roared again, over the whine of the wind. "Where is she?"

Helpless, she pointed down the row of statue columns. "I heard her! She answered my voice." She panicked now that she had only imagined the sounds. She cried, "Laurel! Where are you?"

"Grandmere?" The little voice sounded faintly, almost blown away by the wind. Clearly the child was responding to another feminine voice, but wanted assurance of identity. After a moment, the chirp came again. "Aunt Dottie?"

Julien raced along the porch like a madman, tearing apart the bushes, pawing at the windows, upsetting greenery pots, his boots echoing dully as he leaped and

408

pawed. "Laurel! Laurel!" He looked at Surlina in utter desperation. "Night and water are both coming fast. We must get out the West Wind Gates before we're cut off!" He called the child again, but there was no answer. Frantic, he grabbed Surlina's shoulders. *"You* call her! She only answers you!"

"Laurel Rainbeau! Come out right this minute! Mind me!" Tears of anxiety stood on her lashes. She ran down the steps, trying to peer into the darkness beneath. Julien grabbed the storm cellar door, calling into the pit. The rain beat and the wind gusted in whirls of blackness. By a flash of lightning Surlina saw the tree limbs flailing, the creep of bayou out of its banks in the sundial court. Her arms ached, her head throbbed and the fear of losing the child after nearly finding her made her heart beat wildly. "Laurel!" She heard the terror in her own voice.

No. She must attempt to sound calm. Give the child some reassurance. In total desperation, she attempted a game. "Oh, where is Laurel hiding? Surlina is looking for her! What fun this hide-and-seek game is! But I can't find her. Where, oh where, did she find such a good hiding place? Behind the porch swing? No. I give up, Laurel!"

Suddenly, right in front of her, the child popped from behind of Faith. She grabbed at the little girl as the hollow, hinged *back* of the statue column swung back into place.

Despite Laurel's squirming, Surlina held her like a prize. The child was pale, trembling with wetness, her clothes stained, obviously weak and hungry. "My God! How long have you been in there? How did you get in there?"

"I hid." She looked down, the guilt of doing something wrong transparent on her five-year-old face. "When the soldiers put the aunties and Grandmere in the wagon, I ran away. I didn't want to go. I hid." With the sudden triumph of childhood, she blurted, "Nobody could find me! They thought I fell in the bayou!"

Julien rounded the other end of the porch, his syllables piling on top of each other like drum rolls. "Laurel! Laurel!"

The child tensed as she recognized the voice. Then she reached up to Surlina, flinging her arms around her neck as if fearing a spanking. "It's Papa!" she whispered.

Surlina held the child tight. "Here, Julien! We're here!"

Julien gathered them into his embrace, like capturing something wild and elusive, then bowed his head in silent gratitude. He raised his head, shouting, "We must get out quickly! The water's over the croquet court! Hurry! The road through the West Wind Gates is barely visible."

He herded them toward the wagon, grabbing for the horse's reins, lifting Laurel across the mire as Surlina scrambled forward to the seat. He cracked the reins and the horses trembled, whinnied and surged ahead into the hurricane's teeth.

The ruts were submerged now, the only landmarks the whipping cypresses of the alleyway and the massive West Wind Gates. The huge gates were closed, hinges rattling against each other, the rain streaming through the bars. Julien jumped down, sinking above his knees in mud, shoving with his whole torso to push the latch apart. Surlina held the horse's reins with one hand, Laurel with the other. Suddenly she saw Julien pull his knife, dig at the bars, and look toward her.

"Hurry!" she cried.

He went on scraping for another moment, then slogged back through the mud, calling up to her, "The gates! See their outline? They're not the old West Wind Gates at all!"

The discovery took her breath away. "Are you sure?"

He held up the black flecks of paint on his knife. "These are your silver gates, Surlina."

"But this is a hurricane!"

He hesitated, looking at the rising water, the gates, then back at her.

"Oh, for God's sake, Julien! Get in the wagon!

410

What are you going to do? Unbolt them in the middle of a tropical storm and sink the wagon with their weight?"

He held his stance doggedly. "If you want them, I'll get them!"

She shouted the words she'd never believed herself capable of saying. "I don't want them!" Crazy laughter boiled up from deep within her. "Julien, Julien, my love! You haven't an ounce of sense in your head! What a dreamer you are! I don't want them! *I never have!*"

Clearly he couldn't believe her. He squinted against the rain, leaned closer to hear her.

She looked him straight in the face. "Can't you *ever* be practical?" she shouted. "For once, help me! Leave well enough alone!"

Three days later, the flood had subsided enough so that they could leave the way station. At noon of the fourth day, they sat in the wagon, atop the last rise visible above the floodwaters. They sat quietly, looking at Whispers with its back to the sea and its balconies on the bayou.

"It's still standing," Surlina said sadly, thinking it was worse to see it now than to find it gone altogether.

"Do you remember how I once told you that after the war, even if it was left standing, it would be gone?"

She nodded, watching the brown flood swirl through the lower floor, cresting in waves at the necks of the Fates and Seasons. The small island with the moat and the West Wind Gates were gone entirely, the ground beneath them sawed away by the hurricane and towed out to sea. Or buried in the swamp. It did not interest her so much now.

He asked her gently, "Why were you able to give them up, once you found them?"

She thought for a moment. "My interest in them ran out. Like the hurricane's power spending itself. Like water pouring from a dipper." She tried to smile, wondering if, by her wits, she could find more treasure if she needed it. But that didn't seem likely. In the

411

end, she'd captured the quick, refreshing dipper of adventure and gained the lasting sureness of a well of love, too. "The time for being the Silver Belle simply ran out."

"My luck ran out like the *Quail*'s anchor line. Then you saved me, as you saved Laurel. You defeated the Rainbeau curse."

"But Dottie's life line ran out."

"And Ramsey's." He swept his hand across the scene in silent benediction for the curses, causes and contradictions they'd shared. Unexpectedly, he chuckled and pulled her close. "Farewell, Silver Belle?"

She rejoiced that he could laugh, fling back his golden hair and let his wonderful gray-flecked eyes look fully at her. She felt no sense of loss, only the freedom to start a new, complete love. "We have no business here, Julien. Let's go."

He turned the wagon around toward higher ground. "Where would you like to try our luck now?"

"Could we go to California?"

"Californy? Sure! We'll take the boat."

"Boat? Steamboat? *Whose* boat?"

He laughed in his musical canter. "Surlina," he said sternly. "Precisely how many boats do we own or command between the two of us?"

"None, thank God almighty!"

He slapped the horses lightly, obviously anxious to be on their way. "Know what I heard about the West?"

"What?"

The sun glinted on his gray eyes, causing opalescent sparks of mischief while his sideburns caught the gilt reflection of his hair. "I almost hate to tell you," he nodded. "But, out west, I've heard there's *golden* gates."